THE SECRET CHILD

Lynne Francis

PIATKUS

PIATKUS

First published in Great Britain in 2021 by Piatkus

This edition published in 2021 by Piatkus.

1 3 5 7 9 10 8 6 4 2

A CIP catalogue record for this book is
available from the British Library.

PB ISBN 978-0-349-42462-0

Typeset in Caslon by Hewer Text UK Ltd, Edinburgh
Printed and bound in Great Britain by Clays Ltd, Elcograf S.p.A.

Papers used by Piatkus are from well-managed
forests and other responsible sources.

MIX
Paper from
responsible sources
FSC® C104740

Piatkus
An imprint of
Little, Brown Book Group
Carmelite House
50 Victoria Embankment
London EC4Y 0DZ

An Hachette UK Company
www.hachette.co.uk

www.littlebrown.co.uk

THE SECRET CHILD

PART ONE

1805

CHAPTER ONE

Molly looked at her three daughters, each bent over their needlework, and bit her lip to suppress a smile. She felt quite sure that Catherine, the youngest and possessor of wild chestnut curls, would be the first to fling aside her embroidery with a wail. She would undoubtedly have pricked her finger, knotted her thread or discovered that she had run out of space to complete the word she was stitching.

Sally, the eldest and named after Molly's mother, had inherited her father Charlie's height and dark eyes and was guaranteed to carry on methodically until she was told to stop. If she was given a task, she liked to complete it, and it went without saying that the work would be neat, the stitches precise.

Agnes, aged almost ten, exactly fifteen months older than Catherine and fifteen months younger than Sally, had stopped to gaze out of the window. Molly guessed that she was wondering what creative touch she could add to her sampler. She'd already included an oak tree at the side of the grand building that represented Woodchurch Manor – just visible across the fields from the window of the kitchen where they were sitting. Sally had been shocked by this flight of fancy, while Catherine had been envious. Sparrows were squabbling in the cherry tree outside their own window as they stitched, and Molly had a feeling their likeness would appear in her middle daughter's work. Indeed, Molly noticed that Agnes had chosen some brown thread from the selection on the table and had bent over her work once more. The thread was almost the exact shade of Agnes's hair.

'Thank goodness there are only five of us, Ma,' Sally said. 'I've added your name, and Pa's, and there's just room enough for the three of us across the bottom.'

She held out her work for Molly to see. Under the neatly stitched mansion she had included 'Molly Dawson' and 'Charles Dawson' in tiny cross-stitches, either side of the year of their marriage, 1792. Below this, she was stitching the names of herself and her sisters, leaving just enough room next to her own name to add the current year, 1805.

Molly smiled to see the unusual formality of the name 'Charles' used for her husband, instead of Charlie. Then her lips began to tremble and her eyes filled with tears.

Sally's own smile faded and she looked down at her work, then back at her mother. 'Have I done something wrong?' she asked. She looked rather as though she might cry, too.

Agnes and Catherine had both laid down their samplers and were watching, worry creasing their brows.

'No, no, it's beautiful,' Molly was at pains to reassure her eldest daughter. 'You've put so much work into it. Why, you've all but finished.'

She glanced quickly at Agnes and Catherine. 'You've all worked really hard today. Just another half-hour and then we can put them away.'

Molly put down her own sewing and moved to the window to gaze out over the fields. She had been living in this cottage, one of a terrace tied to the Woodchurch Manor estate, for

4

thirteen years now. Charlie was the head gardener and would be hard at work somewhere in the grounds, or perhaps in a meeting with Mr Powell, the owner of Woodchurch Manor, going over the latest plans.

Despite the passage of time she was still, every so often, floored by the terrible memory of the child who wasn't there, whose name wouldn't be stitched into the family sampler. Her darling boy, whom she had left at the Foundling Hospital in London, two years before her marriage. Left behind when he was but a few weeks old.

She had never told Charlie of his existence, although when she had given up her baby she had been determined to reclaim him at the first possible opportunity. Indeed, for the first two years she had scrimped and saved, hoping to find enough money to make reparation for his care. But she hadn't been able to make a respectable home for him, and when her savings were stolen, she had fallen into despair. As time passed she had tried to convince herself that, with a new name and undoubtedly no memory of her, he was better off without her. A small part of her knew, though, that this was no excuse.

How could she explain him to Charlie, to her own family and now, of course, to his half-sisters? She still had her portion of the tokens she had left behind with him at the Foundling Hospital, her unique mementoes that would allow her to reclaim him. She knew that Charlie would have given her the money needed to repay the hospital for her boy's care, but she had never asked for it. And she had never visited London in all the years since she had left it, although Charlie went frequently on Mr Powell's business. Molly rarely strayed far from the environs of Woodchurch Manor.

Now, in any case, it was too late. Her son was of an age at which he would have left the school at the Foundling Hospital. He would be apprenticed somewhere, or perhaps he had gone into the Navy. England was at war with France, which lay just a few miles distant over the sea from where they were sitting. Molly knew that many young men had volunteered for the Navy, and many of those who hadn't had been 'persuaded' that it was in their best interests. Would her son be among them? Would his life be at risk?

She had berated herself many times for leaving it too long to reclaim him. Now she feared that she would never know what had become of him. Sally's rejoicing that there were only five family names to stitch into her sampler had struck Molly hard. Her son's name – whatever it was now – would be missing for ever from this family record.

Molly gazed out of the window, gripping the edge of the sill as she fought to hold back the sobs that would frighten her daughters if she gave vent to them. It seemed impossible that so many years had passed. So many years since her girls' first tottering steps, first teeth, first words. And with every new milestone she'd been pierced through the heart that her son would have had these milestones, too, and she'd missed them all. Someone else had mopped his infant tears, held his hand and sung him to sleep. She hoped they had been kind.

Her heart turned over at the thought of him sent back to the Foundling Hospital at the age of five by his foster mother. His life would have changed again: he would have found himself sleeping in a dormitory, going to lessons in the Foundling School in that brown-and-white uniform she'd seen all the children wearing. He'd have had no one to comfort him if he fell over, to soothe him when he had a fever, to tell him that whatever ailed him would pass.

6

Why hadn't she gone to reclaim him? It puzzled her, even now. She'd tortured herself with memories, so faded that she couldn't even remember his face – just the horror of being parted from him. She hadn't fetched him, she thought, because once she was wed and with children of her own to care for they had been her priority. How would they manage with an older, bigger boy to feed?

But she knew that was nonsense: they would have managed perfectly well. She wondered now whether she had been frightened. Frightened that he would hate her for what she had done by leaving him for others to bring up. And then it had been too late. She'd persuaded herself that it was better they never met, never knew: that the past was buried.

Each year on his birthday, 7 January, she remembered how it had felt to have his small head nestled into her shoulder in those first weeks, his snuffling noises as he stirred, and she wept a few tears, alone. Then she went on and faced the day, and every day after that, but she didn't forget.

Behind her, Catherine flung down her sampler. 'Half an hour has gone by. Can we go and see Pa?'

Molly was ready to reprimand her youngest daughter for her impatience, but when she looked at the clock she saw that Catherine was right. 'It's a beautiful afternoon,' she said, moving away from the window. 'Tidy up your sewing and we'll walk along the lane. It's too early to disturb your pa at work but we can see what the spring sunshine has brought to the hedgerows.'

Catherine hastily rolled up her sampler and stuffed it into the workbox, then hurried in search of her shawl and bonnet before her mother changed her mind. Agnes had spread hers on the table to gaze at the effect, and Molly saw that birds were indeed fluttering from the tree, ready to land on the roof of Woodchurch Manor. Sally was reluctant to be dragged away – she had been intent on finishing her sampler that day.

'We must make the most of the weather,' Molly told her. 'It may be raining again by tomorrow. It's only April, although it looks more like summer out there today.'

She joined Catherine in the doorway, where she was ready and waiting with Molly's bonnet and shawl in her hands. As Catherine unlatched the door and opened it, a cool, fresh scent wafted in. Molly bent to tie the laces of her boots. It would be good to be outside in the fresh air, away from the memories crowding in on her. She told Catherine – already in the lane – to wait, and turned back to Sally and Agnes to chivvy them along. Then, picking their way around puddles left by the morning's rain, they set off for their walk. Molly, with the grim determination that had worked for her many times before, attempted to banish all thoughts of her lost son from her mind.

CHAPTER TWO

There had been many happy days for Molly since her arrival at Woodchurch Manor thirteen years earlier. Yet the happy memories were mingled with sad ones. Molly remembered when Charlie, made clumsy by anxiety and nerves, had first tried to ask her to be his sweetheart. She was sixteen years old and he was barely seventeen but had recently become an under-gardener on the estate. She had laughed and rejected him. It was only much later she realised how cruelly she had spurned his offer. Her head had been full of nonsense about marrying her handsome cousin, Nicholas Goodchild, and becoming a captain's wife. Even now, as she walked along with her daughters in the spring sunshine, the thought of it made her shudder.

She was glad she hadn't told Charlie of her foolish notion. Nicholas had taken his pleasure, then thrown her over without a thought when the chance of an advantageous marriage had come his way. Molly hated to admit it but she had been culpable, too. She had thought his flattering attentions meant he loved her, that she would be raised from her station as the poor relation helping in her aunt and uncle's household. She had naively believed that she and Nicholas would be married and would live happily ever after.

Disabused of this notion, she'd fled to London and there she had given birth to her son. With barely a penny to her name and too ashamed to come home, she'd been forced to make what she considered the second greatest error of her life: to give up her boy. She'd barely escaped falling into degradation in London, and if Charlie hadn't stumbled upon her where she'd taken refuge in the Apothecaries' Garden on the banks of the Thames, she didn't know what would have become of her.

Molly's heart swelled with pride as she looked at her daughters, running on ahead of her along the lane, laughing at some shared nonsense. Catherine, the youngest, was fast outstripping Agnes in height and would soon be as tall as Sally. Agnes looked as though she would be petite and fine-boned, like her mother, but surely her creativity must come from Charlie. Molly smiled as she considered how her own looks and attributes had blended with those of Charlie in each of their daughters, along with their own unique personality. Then she frowned: their boots and the hems of their pinafores were smeared with mud already.

She was lucky, she knew, to have help at home in the form of Ellen, their maid-of-all-work. In times past, before she was married, this was a role that Molly had fulfilled. She might not have achieved the status of a captain's wife but she was very fortunate to be in the position she was in. When sadness afflicted her, she reminded herself of this.

Their walk had brought them to the little church on the estate, which lay midway between their house and Woodchurch Manor. Although the leaves were still sparse on the trees and the flowers in the hedgerows were the fresh yellows and whites of spring, rather than the pinks and blues of summer, Molly's thoughts took her back to that June day when she and Charlie were wed there.

She came to a halt, oblivious to the girls running on ahead, and felt as if she was enveloped by the warmth of the summer sunshine once more. The trees then had been in full leaf, making a bridal archway of the lane. Molly remembered how, as she'd walked up the little pathway to the church, she'd turned to Charlie and gripped his hand, and the smile he gave her in response had melted any remaining doubts that she was doing the right thing. She had been twenty years old, fresh-faced and seemingly untouched by all that had gone before, but that was due solely to Charlie and his devotion to her.

He'd brought her back from London and looked after her while she recovered her wits after what she supposed was a nervous collapse. He'd put no pressure on her to repay her debt of gratitude by marrying him. It had taken a good few weeks before she had come around to that way of thinking, but his care for her, and the devotion with which he tended the garden, had convinced her. She smiled as she remembered how the conviction that they should marry had grown after he had shown her the pomegranate tree, newly planted in the walled garden at Woodchurch Manor. He'd brought it back with him from London on the same trip that had thrown him together with Molly once more. He'd been so proud of how well it had overwintered and she'd known then that his nurturing, loving nature made him a far worthier man than her vain and selfish cousin. In any case, Nicholas had already proved his unworthiness by abandoning his wife and his ship and exiling himself in the West Indies, bringing disgrace on his family.

On the day of their wedding, Molly and Charlie had walked up the path and entered the church hand in hand. There were hardly any guests in attendance, just a few of the Woodchurch Manor workers who could be spared from their posts on a Saturday morning. Charlie had no living family, and while Molly had intended to visit her own, only five miles distant in Margate, to tell them of her return and make peace with them over her abrupt departure, she had delayed, putting off the moment until finally it was too late. She'd told herself that she would visit after the wedding, that it would be easier to smooth things over if she appeared before them as a respectable married woman, rather than the foolish girl who had fled without a word.

Molly had looked down at the bunch of flowers in her hand and smiled with happiness. Charlie had presented it to her that morning. He'd gone early to the gardens and picked them for her – a simple posy of pale pink rosebuds and blue cornflowers.

It was an unconventional gesture, Molly thought, but then their relationship after Charlie had borne her back from London had been unusual. They had shared a house, but not a bed, and Molly had observed how Charlie trod his own path at Woodchurch Manor and was respected for it by workers and Mr Powell alike.

Indeed, as they'd stood before the vicar, Molly trembling a little in anticipation of the vows she was about to make, the oak door of the church had creaked open and the vicar had paused in the proceedings. Everyone, including Molly and Charlie, had turned to look at the latecomer, and when they saw it was Mr Powell, a little flutter of excitement passed through the small congregation.

Mr Powell gestured to the vicar to continue as he slipped into the family pew at the front of the church. Molly noticed the smile he exchanged with Charlie and felt a burst of pride that carried her through the ceremony, so that she found herself outside in the sunshine again with barely any memory of the words she had uttered.

Mr Powell had pressed some coins into Charlie's hand before taking Molly by the shoulders and declaring her to be a very lucky young woman. She'd blushed and nodded but before she could speak he was striding away down the church path.

The newlywed pair had walked up to Woodchurch Manor with the vicar and the wedding party. Cook had prepared a wedding breakfast for them, which she insisted was simple but seemed luxurious to Molly. They ate freshly baked rolls, ham and eggs and, when this was cleared away, Cook brought out a wedding cake: a rich fruit cake that she'd iced. They drank wine out of crystal glasses and, as the sun shone in through the windows, Molly felt quite giddy with delight.

Not once in the years since her marriage had she regretted her choice. If she'd agreed to be Charlie's sweetheart when he had first asked her, would their lives have turned out so happily? She wasn't sure. She had a feeling she would have been restless, wondering what else life might have to offer. She was glad she'd found out, although she would always have to live with the fact that this knowledge had come at a price.

'Ma! We've been calling you! Whatever is the matter?'

Sally had walked back to stand in front of her, her sisters dancing impatiently from foot to foot further up the lane.

'I was daydreaming.' Molly shook her head to clear her thoughts. 'I was just thinking back to when your pa and I got married here.' She took Sally's arm and they hastened to join the others. She felt cold and wondered just how long she had been there, lost in thought. She must be more careful: she didn't want her daughters, and certainly not Charlie, to have any suspicion of her hidden burden of unhappiness.

CHAPTER THREE

The girls persuaded Molly that their father would be delighted to see them and she knew they were right. She was always more reserved when they visited Woodchurch Manor: when Charlie had first brought her back with him from London, she had worked as a maid in the house. She still felt a little in awe of the place, and of Mr Powell and his family, but he was never other than welcoming to them if they met him around the grounds.

Mr Powell had sons, somewhat older than her girls, and all of them away at school. In his boys' absence, he was inclined to treat the girls as the daughters he had never had, but Molly was cautious. She didn't want their heads to be turned as they got older, as hers had been by Nicholas Goodchild, and she feared them getting ideas above their station.

The girls didn't view the situation in the same way. To them, the Powells were just their neighbours, albeit very well-to-do ones who lived in a house rather bigger than their own. Indeed, Catherine had been puzzled as to why they were stitching Woodchurch Manor into their samplers, rather than their own house. Molly had to hide a smile as Sally had solemnly explained that it was traditional to include a grand landmark from the area.

'It looks more refined,' she had said, startling Molly with her choice of words.

Now, as they approached the walled garden at the back of Woodchurch Manor, Molly noticed Mr Powell and Charlie deep in conversation on the sweeping back lawn.

'Girls, let Mr Powell finish his conversation with your father,' Molly said, but her words were lost in the whoops and cries as Charlie's daughters sought to attract his attention, then made off across the lawn towards him.

Molly flushed as she followed them at a more sedate pace. Whatever would Mr Powell think of her daughters' behaviour?

'Heavens, anyone would think we had been parted for weeks instead of sitting across from each other at the breakfast table this morning,' Charlie exclaimed, as he disengaged himself from Catherine's embrace. He turned to smile at Molly as she approached.

Molly relaxed a little at the sight of her husband's familiar, open face – weather-beaten now by daily exposure to the elements so that his brown eyes were set among deep crinkles as he smiled. His untamed curls, still brown and glossy, caught the sun. It was a face that was very dear to her, all the more so for belonging to a man whose goodness she still marvelled at. Out of loyalty to his employer but also to his family, he had chosen to turn down all offers of work far away from Woodchurch Manor at salaries that might have tempted a lesser man.

'What need do I have of anything other than I have here?' he'd said to Molly, when she'd wondered at his refusal of the latest offer from a landowner in Scotland.

'But this must be the fifth or sixth attempt to lure you away from Mr Powell,' Molly said. 'Are you sure you wouldn't relish the challenge of taking on some new estate?'

'There's enough here to keep me busy until the day I die,' Charlie stated. 'And this area is home to us all. Let no more be said on the subject.' It was the closest they had ever come to a quarrel, but neither of their hearts was in it.

Molly became aware that Mr Powell was addressing her. 'I beg your pardon, sir,' she said. 'I was distracted and didn't catch your words.'

'I was just saying what a credit your girls are to you,' Mr Powell said, raising his voice over the excited chatter. 'They are always so delighted to see their father and always so interested in his work.'

Molly and Mr Powell watched as the girls pulled Charlie in the direction of the gate leading to the walled garden. 'I do apologise, sir. I hope they haven't interrupted you in the middle of important business.'

'It was nothing that I haven't already said to your long-suffering husband,' Mr Powell replied. 'He is always most polite and accommodating with regard to my schemes.'

They watched in silence until Charlie was out of sight, then Molly made to excuse herself and follow.

Mr Powell stopped her, saying, 'Ah, I almost forgot. We are to receive a visit from someone of your acquaintance: the artist William Turner. I do believe you knew him as a young boy in Margate.'

Molly half stifled a gasp. Will Turner! She hadn't seen him for fifteen years. The memory of her situation when she had last seen him, in Covent Garden, caused her to cast an involuntary glance towards the walled garden. She wouldn't like Charlie to know any details of that time. She caught Mr Powell's quizzical look and quickly tried to disguise her alarm.

'What brings him to these parts, sir?' she asked, praying her heightened colour wasn't obvious.

'I purchased a painting from his studio on a recent visit to London,' Mr Powell answered. 'We fell into conversation about where I lived and I mentioned I had some of his early works – watercolour sketches done at a very young age. He became quite animated when I described them to him. He told me of the circumstances in which he had made them and said that he had been guided to particular sketching points by a local girl, Molly Goodchild. It took me barely a moment before I realised that, of course, she must have been you, Mrs Dawson.'

Molly still found it odd that Mr Powell, who had known her as Molly when she was a maid in the house, now gave her the courtesy of her married name. She could only hope that Will Turner hadn't mentioned their subsequent meetings in London to Mr Powell. When she had arrived in Covent Garden, she had been quite unaware of the reputation of the area and of the nature of the house in which she had taken a room. She wanted to laugh now at her naivety, but at the time the place had suited her. Mrs Dobbs, the landlady, had kept her busy with errands for her girls in the market, which was where she had chanced upon Will. It had transpired that he lived locally, around the corner in Maiden Lane with his father, a barber, and was studying at the Royal Academy. She had been happy to see him again: he was a link – but not a close one – with her past in Margate. She was reminded, all at once, of the little painting he had given her that Christmas, which she had been forced to leave behind when she fled. Uneasily, she also remembered telling the Foundling Hospital that Will Turner, the artist, could vouch for her good name. Had they written to him? she wondered.

That two-year period spent in London was one she didn't care to dwell on. She had hidden the details from everyone, passing it off to her father, aunt and uncle as a time spent mainly working in low-paid jobs, which wasn't so far from the truth. She didn't think that admitting to living in a brothel, or working behind the bar of an inn that offered additional services to its customers, would be well received by the good folk of Margate.

Oh, heavens – could Will Turner be relied upon for discretion? Molly had been expecting a baby when she'd last seen him, and they hadn't met since. Would he enquire after her child?

Molly's attention was caught by her husband emerging from the walled garden with their daughters in tow. Charlie also knew nothing of her London history, other than that she had been in some distress when he came across her, and he had never pressed her to enlighten him.

Mr Powell was speaking again: 'You will join us, I hope, when Mr Turner visits? I'm sure he will be delighted to see you again. Such a coincidence that you should be living here.' Mr Powell's expression suggested pride, as though he himself had engineered this.

'A coincidence indeed,' Molly said. 'It would be delightful to be reacquainted. I am, though, expected to visit my aunt shortly. I do hope the visits won't coincide.' She thought she'd done well to prepare the ground for excusing herself. She saw no need to share the fact that the aunt she referred to lived just a few miles away and wasn't expecting a visit from her niece in the immediate future.

Mr Powell looked disappointed and Molly felt contrite. She would dearly have loved to see Will but feared she couldn't risk it. She was glad that the timely reappearance of Charlie and the girls now put paid to any further discussion of the visit. They could make their farewells and head for home.

Molly tried not to let her preoccupation show but the glances Charlie cast her way told her that her silence on the walk back hadn't gone unnoticed. To ease any suspicions, once they were home she made a show of taking a powder, saying she had fallen prey to a headache. Later that night, as Charlie slept peacefully beside her, Molly found that her thoughts, which were going around in circles, threatened to induce a real headache. Was the carefully preserved history of her time in London about to be exposed as a lie?

CHAPTER FOUR

As it turned out, Charlie was away on Mr Powell's business in London when Will Turner was due at Woodchurch Manor. Molly dithered over what she should do. She had had to abandon the pretence of going to visit her aunt Jane, for she could hardly leave the girls behind alone and would have had to take them with her, turning the pretence into a reality. In any case, she would like to see Will again and catch up on the events of the last fifteen years. There was still a danger, though, that he would make some reference to the last time he had seen her, when she had been expecting the baby. If he mentioned it in front of the Powells, Molly wasn't sure how she would be able to pass it off.

She was still unused to her new station in life – far below the Powells in social standing, of course, but more respectable now than she might have seemed when Will knew her. She had been a milkmaid, a dairymaid and then a servant, although he had been just a schoolboy and then a student, albeit a very talented one. She could not afford her newly acquired respectability, which was entirely due to Charlie's talents and hard work, to be damaged in any way, if not for her own sake then for the future of her girls. Molly was determined that they would never be reduced to taking on the type of work that she had been forced into, or to endure any of her past privations.

She decided, on going to bed the night before Will's visit, that she would still have to find an excuse not to appear in the early evening, as the Powells had requested. They had invited her to dine with them, but Molly had already evaded that ordeal by pleading the need to look after her daughters. She knew she would be overwhelmed by the number of courses and the range of knives and forks required, even though she was not unfamiliar with such things. As a servant in her early years at Woodchurch Manor, she had helped to lay the table for many similar events. To be a guest at that table was quite different, though.

She would have been happy enough to stand with the Powells in the drawing room for an hour beforehand, hoping for a few minutes of private conversation with Will. She knew, though, that conversations at such events were public affairs and any attempt at a private one would be looked at askance. Molly went to bed that night, convinced the best thing to do was to stay away – only to wake up the next morning with quite a different view.

Almost as soon as she opened her eyes, it came to her that Mr Powell might ask his guest more about his acquaintance with the wife of his head gardener. Will would be unlikely to grasp the need for discretion. It was more than likely that he had called in on Mrs Dobbs in Covent Garden to enquire whether Molly's baby had been born. Mrs Dobbs would undoubtedly have given him short shrift, telling him that Molly had left without a word and he would have gone away, perhaps believing her disappearance had meant she had returned home to her family with her baby son.

Molly threw back the covers, overwhelmed by rising panic. She would have to go to the Powells that evening and try to have a quiet word with Will. She told herself that she was worrying over nothing but, time and again, she imagined Will asking about the whereabouts of her son in front of all the other guests. As time ticked by that morning her anxiety rose and only the need to keep her daughters occupied drove her on.

Molly's own schooling had been non-existent, although with Charlie's help she had learnt to read and write since she had been at Woodchurch Manor. She did her best to fill the girls' days with tasks beyond sewing, including reading and writing, as well as household duties. They would need to understand domestic management, she reasoned, even if they married as well as she hoped they would.

The girls were busy practising their handwriting when a knock at the door startled Molly. Visitors to the house were few and far between, especially when Charlie was away. She stood up, removed her apron and glanced in the looking-glass before she opened the door.

She didn't recognise the man on the doorstep. He was a little younger than she was, with light brown hair, and he was wearing a coat in a style that was unfamiliar to her. She noticed he had ruined his boots by walking through muddy fields to reach her door.

'Can I help you?' she asked.

'Molly!' the man said, and when he smiled, ducking his head slightly to look up at her from under the hair falling across his brow, she recognised him at once.

'Will!' she said, then remembered he was a famous gentleman now. 'I mean, Mr Turner.'

'I hope I will always be Will to you,' he said, laughing. Then, as Molly seemed struck dumb, 'May I come in?'

'Of course! You must excuse me. I wasn't expecting to see you here.' Flustered, Molly stepped aside and ushered him in, thankful that the morning had involved putting the house in order, although she didn't think Will would be one for noticing such a thing.

'And these are your daughters?' Will asked. Sally, Agnes and Catherine looked up from their books at the table and regarded him solemnly.

'They are,' Molly said, suddenly anxious that little ears might hear something they shouldn't. 'Can I offer you refreshment? Some coffee, perhaps?'

'Lord – when did we become so grown-up and formal?' Will asked, laughing again. 'I've escaped from Woodchurch Manor. They think I'm looking for a setting for a landscape painting and Mr Powell would have accompanied me, but I insisted I needed to walk alone if I was to find the right spot. I was determined to seek you out and discover your news before this evening's reception. What chance would we have there to talk properly?' He made a wry face.

Molly set the kettle on the range, then told the girls to tidy away their books and put on their bonnets and shawls.

'Go out into the lane, but don't go any further than the church, and bring back some flowers for our drawing class.'

She turned to Will. 'Let me show you through to the parlour,' she said, but Will was already settling himself in a chair by the range. He stretched out his legs and ruefully regarded his muddy boots.

'I'm more than happy here, and you won't thank me for traipsing mud through your house.'

He waited, smiling politely, until Molly's daughters, delighted to be reprieved from their books, had made their escape. 'Now, tell me,' he said, as the door closed behind them, 'how are you? The last time I saw you was in Half Moon Street. When I went to seek you out, wondering about your baby, Mrs Dobbs made it known in no uncertain terms that you'd left the place or "scarpered, and after all I've done for her", as she said.' Will looked amused, before quickly becoming serious again. 'And then I received a letter from the Foundling Hospital, telling me you had left a male infant there and asking me to vouchsafe for your good character. What happened, Molly?'

Molly bit her lip and turned away as she poured the hot water onto the coffee grounds. 'I didn't really think they would contact you. I'm sorry. I had no idea who else to suggest.'

Her hands shook as she set the coffee cups and saucers on the table.

'It was of no concern to me, Molly,' Will said. 'I sent a short reply, telling them what they wanted to know. But the infant in question – what of him? Is he away at school?' Will glanced around, as if half expecting the room to supply evidence of his whereabouts.

'No,' Molly said, setting the coffee pot on the table. 'I had to leave him with the Foundling Hospital. And when I married Charlie I . . . I didn't tell him what had happened.'

Molly thought she'd shocked Will, but he recovered himself. 'He's still there, your son? At the Foundling School?'

'No.' Molly shook her head, unable to meet his eyes. 'He will be well grown now – fifteen years old and an apprentice, or in the Navy, perhaps. I lost touch with him.' She had to hold the lid of the pot to stop it rattling as she poured the coffee: her hands were still shaking.

She looked up at Will as she passed him his cup. 'I beg you, please say nothing of this to Charlie, or the Powells, or in front of my daughters.'

Will seemed about to say something, and indeed he made a tentative start, then settled on, 'If you wish it to be a secret, my lips are sealed.' There was an awkward pause before he said, 'Let us talk of something else.'

And so, until the girls returned with their flowers, they spoke mainly about Will, for Molly very determinedly turned the conversation away from herself. She learnt that he had travelled to Switzerland and then France, studying in Paris. He told her he was working on a painting that showed a shipwreck in a great storm, and he hoped a study of the seas in Margate during the high spring tide might help him capture the ferocity of the waves. It was only as the girls returned, and Molly made proper introductions, that he mentioned he had a daughter himself, although much younger even than Catherine.

It was Molly's turn to be surprised, but no more information was forthcoming, and since Will seemed disposed to help the girls with their drawing, she was glad to sit back and watch. It was soon apparent, though, that he was unused to working with students quite so young and unskilled, and when Molly observed Catherine's quivering lip, she declared that it was time for the girls to take a break and have something to eat.

'Won't you join us?' she asked Will. 'It will be simple – just bread and ham and pickles – but you would be most welcome.'

'I would like nothing more,' Will said, getting to his feet, 'but I fear my hosts will be wondering where I have got to. I must return to them, full of praise for the fine landscapes I have observed on my walk.' He winked at the girls and turned to Molly again. 'I will see you this evening, of course, and look forward to continuing our conversation.'

As Molly stood on the doorstep, preparing to wave him off, he turned back to her. 'Your daughter, Agnes. She shows promise, Molly. You must encourage her in her art.' Then he was away, with a wave but no backward glance, and Molly smiled as she saw him strike out over the fields, ignoring the lane to take the shortest route back to Woodchurch Manor.

CHAPTER FIVE

Molly was able to go to the Powells' at four o'clock with a light heart, knowing that there was no danger of anything awkward being said in front of the guests. She was wearing her newest dress, a high-waisted sprigged muslin recently acquired from a dressmaker in Canterbury, and she had reason to be glad of it when she entered the panelled drawing room at Woodchurch Manor. Her first impression was of a room already full of people, a good many of them very smartly dressed indeed. Most of the younger women sported high-waisted dresses in a similar style, but in sheer, pale fabrics with braid edgings and sleeves much shorter than Molly had felt comfortable wearing. The young men were soberly dressed, in dark tailcoats and breeches, their colourful cravats the only flourish accepted by the fashionable. Among those already assembled, she spotted Aunt Jane and Uncle William, both resolutely eschewing the current fashions. No doubt they had been invited because William's business interest in Margate had made him a wealthy man, while his position as a trustee of the Prospect House poorhouse gave him an additional social standing. Molly remembered, with some alarm, that she had planned to use the excuse of needing to visit Aunt Jane as a way of evading this very gathering. It was lucky she had changed her mind: she would have offended her hosts if she'd been found out in a falsehood.

Before she made her way to her aunt and uncle, she let her gaze roam around the room, decorated in the past year at Mrs Powell's insistence. The oak panelling had been painted in a pale shade that filled the room with reflected light. It was rather flattering to the guests, Molly decided, which perhaps had been the intention. Her eyes alighted on two women of about her own age talking to an older woman, whose dress and bearing suggested someone of importance. She was not familiar to Molly but the two younger women caused her to pause and frown. Why did she think she must know them? In the moment that they linked arms affection-ately and laughed in response to something the older lady said, she had it. They were surely the two young ladies – girls at the time – who had inspired one of Will's early paintings, now on the walls of the picture gallery in this very house. They had been in the milliner's shop in Margate all those years ago, when Molly had been delivering hat decorations her stepmother, Ann, had made. She struggled to remember their names – a Miss Bridges and a family visitor . . . Jane, perhaps? She sought out Will, wanting to tell him at once of the coincidence, but he was barely visible for the crowd around him. The news would have to wait.

A large painting was displayed on an easel in front of the double doors that opened into the garden. Molly assumed that this must be Mr Powell's latest purchase from Will, the one he had used to persuade the artist to come to Woodchurch Manor. She began to move across the room towards it, side-stepping little knots of guests engaged in conversation as she did so. As she drew closer, she noticed a tall fair-haired man, standing to one side of the easel, studying the painting. There

29

was something about his stance that caused Molly to hesitate, while she tried to work out where she had seen him before.

Realisation dawned at the same moment that her aunt and uncle bore down upon her.

'Molly!' Aunt Jane exclaimed. 'How delightful to see you here. I was saying to your uncle in the carriage, "I wonder whether we shall see Molly and Charlie." And is Charlie here?' Her aunt looked around the room and Molly shifted her own position slightly, as if to allow other guests free passage, but really to place her back towards Will's painting.

'No, Charlie is in London, Aunt. And even if he was at home, it's unlikely that he would join us here. He would find a task in urgent need of his attention in the gardens. He has little liking for standing around making small-talk, as he describes it.'

Molly smiled as she spoke, imagining how uncomfortable Charlie would have been had he been there that evening.

She accepted a glass of punch from the tray proffered by one of the servants, a young girl of around fifteen years, who looked terrified at being expected to perform the task in such important company. Molly's own hand shook slightly as she held the glass, so she clasped it firmly and chanced a glance over her shoulder. There was now a small group in front of the painting, but no sign of the blond-haired man.

'Have you looked at the painting yet, Aunt?' she asked, noting that her uncle was already scanning the crowd, hoping to make the acquaintance of someone who might prove useful to him: the Mayor of Margate, perhaps, or a visiting dignitary from Canterbury.

'Not yet – shall we?' Aunt Jane put her arm through Molly's and drew her over to the easel.

They gazed it, Molly only half taking in what she saw. It was a boat in a heavy sea, its pale sail billowing as it fought against the rolling waves, the storm clouds on the horizon suggesting more bad weather was on the way.

'Powerful depiction,' a man to Molly's left said, as his neighbour nodded sagely.

'I hear he's much talked of in London. Quite the honour to have him down here,' the first man went on.

Aunt Jane, who had been listening in too, nudged Molly. 'Your uncle should have heard that,' she whispered. 'He'll love his cow painting even more now.'

Molly smiled. She rather preferred the painting of her uncle's cows, done by Will years ago, to the piece displayed before her. But Mr Powell loved naval scenes – the walls of his picture gallery contained many such pieces.

The heat in the room had become oppressive from the number of bodies and one of the servants opened all the doors to the garden to allow in some air. Molly could see that it would be almost impossible to speak to Will, such a throng had gathered around him, hoping for a few words with the famous man. She smiled at her earlier folly in imagining he might say something untoward in front of the guests. She had assumed that the reception would be much smaller than it was.

Her aunt was claimed by an acquaintance from Margate and Molly decided it was time to make her escape and return to her girls, left at home under Ellen's watchful eye. There was still another hour of the party before the family would move through for dinner, but she was sure that her early departure would go unnoticed.

She returned her empty glass to the young servant girl's tray and gave her an encouraging smile before she stepped through the doors into the garden. The cool of the May evening struck her after the warmth of the room and she caught a delicate floral scent carried on the light breeze. Molly stopped to see whether she could identify where it might be coming from in the border along the house wall. She would have to ask Charlie: it was something she would like for their own small garden.

Someone else was out there, walking back along the path that crossed the lawn from the walled garden and making for the house. For a moment, Molly thought it might be Charlie, home unexpectedly early, but it was the blond-haired man she had seen earlier. She put her head down and turned along the path that ran beside the house, intending to skirt the building and go home by a different route.

'Excuse me!' The voice that rang out was clear and carrying, and Molly could hardly pretend not to have heard. Reluctantly, she stopped and waited as the man strode the last few yards, until he was standing in front of her.

'I thought it was you!' He looked pleased with himself. 'I do believe we've met before. At the Waterman's Arms, in London.'

Face to face with the man she had last seen as a youth, whose workmates were keen to purchase a tryst for him in Love Lane with the prettiest barmaid at the inn, Molly held her breath. Joshua from Margate. She had hoped their paths would never cross again.

CHAPTER SIX

The man who stood before Molly was not the shy, blushing youth she'd last seen fifteen years earlier. He had a confident air and his clothes – a navy wool frock coat and plain breeches – marked him out as prosperous. Her first inclination was to deny ever having seen him before, turn and walk away. But something made her hesitate and, even as she did so, she felt sure her guilt – such as it was – must be written all over her face.

She sighed. 'Yes, we have met. But it was a long time ago and my circumstances are different now.' She made a point of looking him up and down before she said, 'And it would seem that your life has changed for the better, too.'

'Indeed, it has.' Joshua smiled. 'I have my own business, a brick works on the outskirts of Margate. I will be supplying Mr Powell with the bricks and stone for the constructions he has planned in the gardens.' He turned to look out over the lawn. 'I was hoping I might find the head gardener here today, but I'm told he is on business in London.'

Molly's heart sank. It looked as though this was not to be a chance meeting with Joshua, but one that had every prospect of being repeated. Should she throw herself on his mercy and beg him to say nothing about their previous encounter? She was weighing up her options when he turned back towards her.

'The head gardener, Charlie, is my husband,' Molly said. She looked Joshua in the eye. 'Are you married, Mr . . . ? I'm afraid I don't know your surname.'

'Symonds,' Joshua said. 'Joshua Symonds. I am married, yes, and I have two children now, both boys.'

'And I have three girls,' Molly said quietly. 'I feel it's not in either of our interests for our past acquaintance, such as it was, to be made known.' She tried to gauge Joshua's reaction.

He seemed momentarily taken aback. 'Perhaps you are right. I didn't intend to cause you any distress.'

Molly was about to move on, but paused. 'You do know that during my employment at the Waterman's Arms I never worked as anything other than a barmaid?' She gave him a frank look, remembering how Joshua's companions had been thwarted in their wish to procure Molly for him, but that another of the girls – Sophy – had been happy to oblige.

Joshua couldn't meet her gaze. He blushed and stared at his feet, reminding Molly in an instant of his youthful self.

'I'll tell my husband you were looking for him,' she said briskly, and turned for home.

Once away from the uncomfortable situation, she felt her colour rise. Could Joshua's discretion be relied upon? She closed her eyes briefly and tried hard to dispel a sense of panic. She had feared that Will might say something untoward and reveal unpalatable truths about the time she had spent in London, but she had never thought that exposure might come from another quarter. Were there other dangers she hadn't foreseen?

* * *

That evening, with the girls tucked up in bed asleep, she sat by the kitchen range and thought back over the history she had created for herself. Only two people had known she was with child when she left Margate – her father and her aunt's cook, Hannah – and that her cousin Nicholas was the father.

On her return from London, she had delayed telling her family she was back in the area. It was only Charlie's gentle coaxing, after they were married, that had persuaded her. A week after the wedding, when they were walking together in the walled garden, Charlie pointing out all the new growth that summer had brought into bloom, he had spoken gently to her. 'Molly, it can only be a matter of time before your father discovers that you have not only returned, but are married now. He'll be upset,' he added, not unreasonably.

Molly had stared unseeing into the heart of the rose he had picked for her. She was reluctant to make the visit, even though she knew she must. Part of her reluctance was her anxiety at seeing her aunt Jane, who lived next door to her father and in whose home she had been living when she had fled. It had seemed obvious to Molly that her leaving had coincided with the announcement of Nicholas's imminent marriage to Sarah. Surely her aunt had guessed her reason for leaving. And if she hadn't, had Hannah told her?

'I could come with you?' Charlie's words had broken into her reverie. She looked into his brown eyes and marvelled once more at what a good man he was. It was the last time that Molly remembered being fearful that the truth about her London years and her lost son might come out. She had decided there and then to go to Margate and face her family.

It had been August, though, before she summoned the courage to visit, taking a ride with a carrier who had made a

35

delivery to Woodchurch Manor and was returning to Margate. She would walk back, she decided, once her visits had been made. It would help to clear her head and, in any case, she had a fancy to take the path through Margate Brooks, last trodden in the company of Will Turner.

She had arrived in Margate late morning and decided to make her way to her father's stable-yard in Church Street, in the hope of catching him there after his return from his rounds with the milk churns. As she approached, it became clear that the horse and cart were not in the yard and her steps faltered, as she wondered whether she would have to visit her aunt first, after all.

Then a clatter and a clang from the yard, carried on the warm, still air, told her that someone was there. She hurried onwards to see a figure in a print gown bent over a milk churn set in the shade at the side of the yard. Molly pushed open the gate and the young woman at the churn straightened up.

'You're out of luck, I'm afraid,' she called, shading her eyes against the sun. 'I've just sold the last drop.' Then she said uncertainly, 'Molly?'

Molly hardly recognised her sister Lizzie who, at seventeen, was now the same age as Molly had been when she worked in the yard. She had grown tall and slender and now outstripped Molly, as she discovered when Lizzie hurried across the yard, wiping her hands on her apron, to fling her arms around her sister.

'Oh, Molly,' Lizzie said, and burst into tears.

Molly was dismayed, and also close to tears. 'Whatever is the matter?' she asked, stroking Lizzie's back as she sobbed.

Lizzie pulled free and, half crying, half laughing, glared at her. 'The matter? Why, you vanish without a word three years ago and turn up out of nowhere, looking so well. And all this time I feared you dead.'

Lizzie burst into fresh sobs and Molly, chastened, was forced to recollect how her actions must have seemed to her family. She had been so caught up in her own problems that she'd barely given a moment's thought to how worried they must all have been.

'I couldn't write, Lizzie. I didn't know how,' she said, knowing it to be a lame excuse. She could have employed a scribe to do the job for her, but in truth she had wanted to be lost.

Lizzie shook her head. 'Well, you're here now. Pa will be so happy. And Mary, too.'

'How are they both? And little John and Harriet? And Ann?' Molly began to feel overwhelmed by how much catching up she would need to do.

'You'll find Pa looking much older,' Lizzie warned. 'He took your disappearance hard. Mary is well grown. She has a sweetheart now.' Lizzie smiled. 'The boy from the bakery where she works.'

'She's too young! She's barely fifteen!' Molly exclaimed. She thought back to herself at that age. 'And you?' she asked.

Lizzie blushed. 'Nobody special,' she said hastily. 'Little John isn't so little any more – he's ten now, but still naughty. Harriet has a sweeter nature. Not like her mother at all. I wonder whether she will remember you.'

'Ann?' Molly was startled. Surely her stepmother would remember her.

'No, silly, Harriet.' Lizzie moved about the yard as she spoke, tidying everything away to be ready for the next day. 'Ann is as sour as ever but Harriet is delightful. She was three when you left so likely as not she'll have forgotten you.'

The casual remark wounded Molly, even though she knew it to be true. Now that she was starting to catch up with family news, the full impact of what she had done was beginning to hit home. Three years was a long time to be away.

'Come back to the house,' Lizzie said, as she took a last look around the stable-yard. 'I'd love to say that Ann will be pleased to see you, but we both know it isn't true.'

CHAPTER SEVEN

Lizzie and Molly had linked arms and set off to walk the short distance to Princes Crescent when the clip-clop of Nelly's hoofs and the jangling of her harness announced the return of John Goodchild to the stable-yard.

As he drew nearer, Molly could see how grey his hair had become, how lined his face, and her heart turned over. She grasped now how much pain her disappearance must have caused him. At the time, she could think only about how angry he was with her when he learnt she was with child; she hadn't stopped to consider how he must have felt when she vanished. And once she was in London, it had felt such a great distance away that Margate, and her family, had begun to seem quite unreal. She supposed she had been too caught up in her own plight to spare a thought for anyone else, and she saw now how wrong that had been.

Her father reined in Nelly and stared down at Molly and Lizzie. For several moments he didn't speak and Molly's anxiety rose. Was he still angry with her? Would he disown her? At last, her father managed to force out some words, in a voice that quivered with emotion.

'Why, I thought my eyes were deceiving me. I never expected to see you again, Molly.' He shook his head in wonder. 'I thought you must be Mary, left off early from her shift at the bakery.'

'No, Pa, it really is me.' Molly tried to laugh but her throat was constricted and she feared she might cry instead. 'Am I so much changed?'

'No, no, it's just that we all thought you lost.' John Goodchild shook his head again, as if to clear his mind. 'Where have you been all this time, Molly? You vanished, without a word.'

Molly sought to divert the direction of the conversation. 'I'm married now, Pa, and living not so very far away. On the estate at Woodchurch Manor.'

'Married!' Lizzie turned to Molly. 'Why, you never said a word!'

'I didn't want to mention it until I'd seen Pa,' Molly said.

Her father was still sitting on the cart, holding the reins loosely, an expression of stunned surprise on his face.

'I married Charlie, Pa. Remember, he worked in the stable-yard for a short while? He was an under-gardener at Prospect House.'

'A Prospect House boy.' Her father spoke flatly.

'Yes, but he's done very well for himself. He's head gardener at Woodchurch Manor and he could have the pick of any great house and garden in the country if he wished.' Molly was filled with pride, and determined to make her father understand that Charlie had moved up in the world. 'And he's been very good to me,' she added.

'Charlie is lovely.' Lizzie gave Molly's arm a little squeeze. 'I remember how kind he was to us when we used to visit the Prospect House gardens.' She turned to her father. 'Pa, put Nelly and the cart away and come and join us at the house. You can catch up on the rest of Molly's news there.'

Molly allowed an impatient Lizzie to pull her in the direction of her old home, but turned back as they rounded the corner to see her father climb down from the cart to open the stable-yard gate. He looked stooped and worn. Molly knew she needed to have a private moment with him before he asked an awkward question. She had already decided that she would tell him she had lost the baby shortly after leaving home. She hated the thought of denying her son in this way but it was easier and would make an end to any conversation on the topic.

She had little time to think more on the subject for they had arrived at the cottage, home to her father and stepmother. Molly glanced at the much grander house next door, where her uncle and aunt lived. She must visit there, too, and make her presence known, but first she must face her stepmother, never an easy task.

'Here I am, Ann,' Lizzie called, as she pushed open the cottage door. 'And I have a surprise for you.'

'A welcome one, I hope?' Ann, busy chopping vegetables, had her back to them when they entered but she turned, wiping her hands on her apron, as they stepped into the kitchen. Molly caught the aroma of pastry baking and instantly felt a pang of hunger. She hoped Ann would invite her to stay and eat.

'Goodness!' Ann stared. 'Molly Goodchild. I never expected to see you again.'

'Molly Dawson now,' Molly said. She thought Ann looked well: much better, in fact, than when Molly had left. She looked around the room. 'Is Harriet here? Or little John?'

'They're playing next door. With Constance.'

Molly wondered who Constance could be. Had her cousin Clara – or even Louisa – married and had a child in the three years she had been away? Before she could enquire, the door opened and her father came in, a little out of breath from hurrying.

'Sit down, sit down,' he said to Molly and Lizzie. 'Ann, have you offered our guests anything?'

'Guests?' Ann's lips were pinched. 'John, have you lost your wits? They're both your daughters and one of them lives with us.'

'Of course, of course. I think the shock of seeing Molly has—' John, lost for words, sat down suddenly at the kitchen table. 'Sit, sit,' he said, gesturing to Molly and Lizzie.

'I'll help Ann,' Lizzie said hastily. 'Go and sit in the parlour with Molly and you can catch up with her news while I lay the table.'

She helped her father to rise, pulled back his chair, then shooed both Molly and John out of the room. Molly thought once more how her father had aged in the three years since she had last seen him. He seemed drained of strength and energy, while Ann seemed replenished.

'Are you quite well, Pa?' Molly asked, with some concern, as she closed the parlour door.

'Aye, well enough,' John replied. 'A touch of rheumatism and a bit of old age. But better for seeing you.' He reached over to her and patted her hand. 'You must tell me what has happened to you over the last three years. When did you marry?'

'Just two months ago, Pa.'

John's brows knitted into a frown. 'So how long have you been back in the area?'

'Since late last autumn,' Molly said. 'I'm sorry I didn't come to visit before now. I wasn't – I wasn't well.'

Her father looked as though he was about to speak but she rushed on, only too aware that Lizzie might call them through at any moment and she needed to tell her father about the baby.

'Pa, I lost the baby.' Haste made her blunt. 'Soon after I left. I stayed in London and worked. I was fearful of coming back, frightened of being in trouble for running off. I worked as a servant, then in an inn. I'd fallen ill when Charlie discovered me and brought me back to Kent with him.'

She had covered three long years in a few sparse words but she hoped it would suffice. She didn't want to have to answer any questions about how she had spent her time away.

'I'm glad,' her father said. 'About the baby,' he added, registering Molly's puzzled expression. 'It was better that way.' He was silent for a moment or two, then added, 'Nicholas turned out to be a bad lot, you know. Abandoned his ship in the West Indies and refused to come home. Left his wife and child to be cared for by his parents.'

'Constance,' Molly said faintly. 'Constance must be Sarah's daughter.' It all fell into place.

'Yes.' Her father nodded. 'A bad business. Her own parents wouldn't have her back once the baby was born – said the marriage had brought shame on their good name. William was equally ashamed of Nicholas, yet still insisted that they take in Sarah. They both dote on Constance.'

Molly tried to absorb the news. Nicholas had fathered two children in a matter of weeks and abandoned them both. Her son had a half-sister and neither would ever know the other.

CHAPTER EIGHT

Lizzie put her head around the door. 'Dinner will be on the table very soon. Come and sit down. I'm just going next door to fetch John and Harriet. Molly, shall I tell Aunt Jane that you're here?'

Molly had intended to visit her aunt later that day, but the knowledge that Sarah would be there, and the existence of Constance, made her unsure. Could she face seeing a little girl who was, in many respects, almost the twin of her own son?

Lizzie, in a hurry to be gone, said, 'I'm sure she'd love to see you,' and had left the room before Molly could beg for more time to consider.

Their meal was a surprisingly jolly affair. Ann seemed determined to be polite; Molly put this down to her relief at discovering that her errant stepdaughter was now married with a home of her own and wouldn't require anything of them. Harriet, at six, was as delightful as Molly remembered her, while little John remained strong-willed. Molly noticed that her father seemed unable to keep him in check and that he wasn't disposed to listen to his mother. He would be trouble in the future, she thought. Mainly, though, Molly was preoccupied with worrying about what awaited her next door, later that afternoon. When Lizzie had returned with

Harriet and John, she told Molly how astonished Aunt Jane had been at the news of her reappearance and how much she looked forward to seeing her when their meal was over.

The rabbit pie was rich with gravy and tasted delicious but Molly, despite her earlier hunger, struggled with each forkful, dreading the encounter to come. She tried hard to engage with Lizzie's questions about her time in London but caught one or two of the sharp glances that Ann cast her way and she wondered whether her stepmother suspected her of evasion. Her father also ate little, but glanced up from his plate to gaze at Molly as though scarcely able to believe his eyes.

Once the plates were cleared and Molly felt that a decent interval had elapsed, during which she had made an effort to catch up on the family news, she rose to her feet. 'I'd better go and visit Aunt Jane, then make my way home,' she said.

'Can we come?' little John and Harriet chorused.

'No, you can't,' Lizzie said firmly. 'You've already spent a good deal of time there today and, in any case, Constance and her mother are going out this afternoon.'

Molly was startled. 'You mean . . . it will just be Aunt Jane?'

'I think so.' Lizzie frowned. 'I suppose Uncle William might be there, but he doesn't usually come home for dinner until four or five o'clock.'

Molly felt the knot in her stomach ease. If only she had known this earlier, she wouldn't have had to worry her way through the meal. Her smiles as she made her farewells were warm and genuine, and she thanked Ann for a delicious dinner, promising to return soon.

'You must come and visit me at my new home,' she added, although she noticed that Ann's response lacked enthusiasm.

Then Molly was back out in the sunshine, at the foot of the steep steps leading up to the front door of her aunt and uncle's house. As she hesitated, the basement door flew open and her aunt's cook, Hannah, stepped out.

'Molly!' she exclaimed. 'Did you think to pass me by without saying hello?'

Molly couldn't suppress her delight at seeing Hannah: she'd worked alongside her for many months in her aunt's kitchen. 'Oh, Hannah, it's so lovely to see you. And, no, I wouldn't have dreamt of leaving without a word, but I haven't seen Aunt Jane yet.' Molly didn't want to risk offending her aunt by giving her cook precedence.

'Your aunt is taking her afternoon rest,' Hannah said. 'We can have twenty minutes together before I take a cup of tea up to her. Come.' She held the basement door open wide.

Molly needed no second bidding. She hurried down the familiar steps and into the kitchen. She was comforted to see that there had been no changes in the last three years and Hannah, too, looked the same: grey-haired, a smile crinkling the corners of her eyes, and a dusting of flour across her ample bosom, above her apron. A rolling pin lay on the table, beside some pastry that was ready to go into the pie dish that sat beside it.

'I'm disturbing your work,' Molly said.

Hannah pulled out a chair for her to sit at the table. 'I can work and talk, as you well know,' she said.

While Hannah put together an apple tart she told Molly the family news: how Clara had married a distant cousin and gone to live in London, how Louisa was well grown and considered quite the catch in town, 'despite the shame that her brother has brought on the house'. Hannah frowned. How Aunt Jane had taken on a new lease of life now that she had a granddaughter to dote on, although Constance's mother, Sarah, had looked fit to pine away for several months after her daughter was born.

'Her father's not seen her even once,' the cook said, banging the rolling pin down on the pastry trimmings. 'I don't know what manner of devil has got into that man since he decided to live out his life in the West Indies.' Hannah, pink with indignation, gave the pastry another thwack, as if delivering a blow to Nicholas's head. Then her hand flew to her mouth.

'Oh, Molly, I'm so sorry. What with all the distress Nicholas caused Sarah, I'd clean forgot the state you were in when you left here. Whatever happened about . . .?'

Her voice trailed away and her eyes flew to Molly's waist, as though she expected to see evidence of the baby Molly had told her about three years earlier. Nicholas's baby.

'I lost it,' Molly said. When she had sat down at Hannah's kitchen table her resolve over her story had weakened. Hannah had been her friend and confidante when she'd worked for her aunt and seeing her again made her want to confess all, just as she had three years before. But hearing Hannah's anger over Nicholas's behaviour made her realise that it was safer to stay with her pretence. It wasn't fair to burden her with Molly's own sorrow over her son.

'I lost the baby,' she repeated firmly. 'In London. I stayed there and worked because I didn't think I would be welcome here, after disappearing without a word. But I'm married now. To Charlie.'

Hannah's expression, troubled throughout Molly's brief explanation, cleared at her last words and she smiled. 'Charlie! Such a lovely boy.' She had known him when she was the cook at Prospect House.

It was Molly's turn to smile. 'He's a man now. And head gardener at Woodchurch Manor, which is where I live, on the estate.'

'It's for the best,' Hannah said. 'About the baby,' she added. 'That Nicholas is no good. It's bad enough that there is one child in the world he fathered, let alone had there been two.'

Molly felt her colour rise and she was on the verge of admitting the truth when she heard footsteps on the internal stairs leading down from the hallway.

'Is that voices I hear?' Aunt Jane said, stooping to peer into the kitchen as she descended. 'Molly, is that you?'

'It is, Aunt,' Molly said, scrambling to her feet. 'I didn't want to disturb your rest.'

'I'm wide awake now,' Aunt Jane said. 'And I'm looking forward to hearing all about what you've been up to these last three years. I could hardly believe my ears when Lizzie told me you'd turned up.'

Molly thought her aunt's expression was a little stern and she was reminded vividly of how she had fled this very house, disguised in a stolen bonnet, without a word to anyone.

Aunt Jane turned to Hannah. 'Would you bring my tea up to the drawing room now? Molly, come upstairs and tell me all.'

CHAPTER NINE

Molly dutifully followed her aunt, but with some trepidation. Her father and Hannah were the only two people who knew the real reason for her abrupt departure from the house – or thought they did. No one knew of her pursuit of Nicholas to Chatham, where he had made it very plain that he wished to have nothing more to do with her. Her aunt had no inkling of a baby or even of her son's liaison with Molly, whose disappearance, in the midst of the excitement over Nicholas's forthcoming marriage to Sarah, must have been irksome and troubling. As Molly followed her aunt's ample skirts up the stairs, she realised she hadn't thought to prepare a story that would satisfy her.

Could she say Charlie had proposed to her and she had taken flight? It wasn't so far from the truth – but would it colour the way her aunt might feel about her new husband?

Could she say her head had been turned by a man she had met, with the promise of work and riches in London for a hard-working girl? The disadvantage of that was that she laid herself open to an accusation of foolishness, and also close questioning as to what kind of work he'd had in mind.

She was no nearer knowing what she should say by the time she was seated in the drawing room, feeling more awkward than she ever had before in her aunt's presence.

There was a short silence, during which Molly looked around the room, remembering how she used to dust the ornaments and the framed samplers on the wall, stitched by her cousins. Will's painting of her uncle's cows still held a prominent position next to the door and she smiled at the memory of its creation.

Her aunt spoke suddenly, making Molly start. 'Before Hannah brings in the tea things, I just wanted to say I know why you left.'

Molly gazed at her, wide-eyed, not daring to speak.

'Nicholas told me.'

Molly looked down at her hands in her lap. She was anxiously twisting her wedding ring. Had Nicholas really told his mother how Molly had pursued him to Chatham, telling him that she was expecting his child and begging him to give up his forthcoming marriage to Sarah? And that he had turned her away with a bag of coins, in an attempt to pay her off?

Aunt Jane spoke again. 'He told me how he had led you on, made you believe you were special to him, when all the time he was courting Sarah. He said he thought that might be why you had run away and he was sorry for it.'

'When was that?' Molly asked faintly.

Aunt Jane frowned. 'Why, after his marriage, I believe, when I told him how worried I was that you had vanished without a word.'

Did she suspect that Nicholas 'leading her on' had led to him sharing her bed? Molly wondered. She rather thought not. Aunt Jane was always disposed to think the best of her son. And she probably wouldn't have imagined such behaviour taking place under her roof, either, Molly thought ruefully. Her cheeks flamed at the memory and she wished that Hannah would hurry with the tea.

Just as she heard the faint rattle of cups, signifying that Hannah was climbing the stairs with the tray, her aunt spoke again. 'I can only apologise on his behalf, Molly. But you must have known that you could never have made a match with Nicholas. William would never have allowed it.' Her aunt sighed. 'If only I'd followed my own advice and found you a suitable young man to walk out with.'

By the time Hannah opened the door, Molly was quite cross. She sprang up, partly to help Hannah set the tray on a side table and partly to hide her feelings. Her aunt and uncle considered Molly's father, and his children, to be their inferiors in every way.

It gave Molly some pleasure to deliver a cup of tea to her aunt at the same time as she said, 'Well, Aunt Jane, you will be pleased to hear that I have found a suitable young man and I have married him.'

Her aunt gasped and Molly had to steady the recently delivered cup as it rattled against the saucer, threatening to slop the tea.

'Molly! Lizzie didn't mention any of this when she told me you had come back. Who is this young man? And where are you living?'

Molly told her aunt about Charlie, and how he was a Prospect House boy made good.

'Your uncle will be so pleased!' Aunt Jane exclaimed. Molly thought wryly that Uncle William would no doubt find a way to take credit for how well Charlie had turned out.

'A gardener, you say?' Aunt Jane mused.

'Head gardener,' Molly corrected her. She thought that Charlie having a good, solid trade was pleasing to her aunt, although she wasn't sure the older woman fully understood the nature of his work. 'Like Mr Fleming at Prospect House

– I'm sure you remember him, Aunt. Charlie was recommended for the job by Mr Fleming and he is most highly thought of by Mr Powell, the owner of Woodchurch Manor.'

'Well, that's very good news,' Aunt Jane declared. 'I hope William and I will have the pleasure of paying you a visit there before too long.'

Molly made encouraging noises, glad she had escaped being asked how she had passed the last three years since she had left Margate. Aunt Jane, she felt, was too busy calculating how the news of her marriage might benefit her husband: he was always keen to make the acquaintance of those who might prove useful in his own advancement. The Powells of Woodchurch Manor probably sounded as though they could be a fortuitous connection.

Molly finished her tea and stood up, returning her cup and saucer to the tray. 'Aunt Jane, I'm pleased I found you at home today. But now it's time for me to return home, or Charlie will start to worry about me.'

That wasn't strictly true: in the summer months Charlie was absorbed in the garden until the deepening dusk made it too hard for him to see what he was doing. Molly was keen to be on her way, though, her duty calls all made. She would be glad of the walk home to give her time to mull over the day. There was plenty to consider: her own family's reaction to her reappearance as well as her aunt's revelation of Nicholas's surprising confession. Molly had never expected him to admit that he might be, in some way, responsible for her departure.

It was this last thought that prompted her to say, 'Aunt, I hear that you have a granddaughter.'

Her aunt's face lit up. 'Why, yes. Little Constance. What a shame she isn't here so that you could meet her. Her mother has taken her out visiting this afternoon. I expect they will return at any moment if you can wait a little longer.'

'I'm afraid I really must go, Aunt,' Molly said, now even more eager to be on her way in case Sarah and Constance should suddenly appear.

'Next time you come, then,' her aunt said. 'Constance is very fond of Harriet and even little John, although I declare that boy is the naughtiest I have ever met.'

Her aunt shook her head indulgently at little John's bois-terous ways and Molly, keen to take her leave, planted a kiss on her cheek. 'Goodbye, Aunt. Don't get up. I hope to see you again soon, and Uncle, too.'

Then Molly slipped out of the room and made her way to the front door. She was sorry not to say goodbye to Hannah but she didn't want to risk still being there when Nicholas's wife and child returned. She ran down the front steps and hurried along Princes Crescent, breathing more easily as she turned towards St John's Church and the edge of town.

It was late afternoon and the lingering warmth of the day would make for a pleasant walk through the Brooks, in the direction of the Dent-de-Lion, where she could pick up the track to Woodchurch Manor. She smiled at the memory of Will sketching the medieval gate that she, and all the locals, knew as the Dandelion. Their encounter there with a visitor bound for Woodchurch Manor was the first time she had heard of the place and now, six years later, she was living in its grounds.

Charlie would be pleased that she had made today's family visits, Molly thought, as she walked home. In distant fields, the hay was being piled into stooks but all was tranquil by the Brooks, the only activity the flit of a dragonfly and the swooping flight of the swifts and swallows as they feasted on the insects over the water. As she drew closer to Woodchurch Manor, a flash of russet crossed the path ahead of her. A big dog fox stood his ground and turned his eyes on her, as though she was trespassing on his territory. She smiled at his impudence, even as she wondered whether he was responsible for the loss of one of the plumpest hens from the run in the kitchen garden.

*   *   *

Now, as Molly sat by the kitchen range, she realised that it had grown completely dark while she had been lost in her memories. She got to her feet, a little stiff from sitting motionless for so long, and was about to light her candle to take up to bed when she heard footsteps outside.

The door opened, making her heart leap in her throat, until she recognised the figure of her husband silhouetted on the threshold. 'Charlie! You startled me. What are you doing back so early?'

'And what are you doing sitting without a candle lit?' Charlie asked in return. 'I feared, seeing the house in darkness, that you must still be at the party but I'm glad to find you home. I couldn't bear to stay away from you and the girls for another night.' And he enveloped her in a hug so tight that she could scarcely breathe and had to struggle to free her face, which was pressed into the cloth of his jacket.

'Would you smother me?' she protested, laughing, then offered him something to drink after his journey, and a selection of whatever she could find in the larder.

He shook his head, and took her hand in his warm one, drawing her upstairs in the darkness to their bedroom.

CHAPTER TEN

Sally, Agnes and Catherine were delighted to find their father at the breakfast table the next morning.

'Pa, you're home early,' Agnes said. 'Did you miss us?'

'Did you bring us something?' Catherine asked hopefully.

'Sssh!' Sally said, glaring at Catherine. 'It's rude to ask for presents.'

Catherine looked down at her plate and Molly saw her lower lip wobble. Tears spilt from below her lashes onto her cheeks. Molly sighed, but before she could attempt to sort things out, Charlie spoke up.

'I did miss you all, and your mother, too. You know I can't bear to be away from you. But I had to work extra hard so I could leave early to come home to you. There wasn't time to buy presents, I'm afraid.'

Sally looked a little smug, while Catherine sniffed and bit her lip.

Agnes got up and flung her arms around her father's neck. 'We just want you, Pa. We have everything we need.'

Charlie smiled and fished in the pocket of his work jacket. 'Wait – I did pass a stall selling hair ribbons, though. Will these do?'

He held out the coils on the palm of his hand: one pink, one blue, one lilac. Catherine's eyes lit up and she reached out her hand, then clearly thought better of it. Molly could see that her gaze was fixed on the pink ribbon but she was trying hard to be selfless.

'Which one would you like?' Charlie asked, addressing no one in particular. There was a short silence and Molly held her breath, wondering whether his good intentions were about to go awry.

'Pa, you choose,' Sally said, exhibiting sense beyond her years.

Charlie looked at his daughters, then back at the ribbons in his hand. 'Then I say pink for Sally, blue for Agnes and lilac for Catherine. I thought of my favourite flowers and my favourite girls when I chose them.'

Molly exhaled a sigh of relief. Catherine's disappointment was alleviated by her father's words and she climbed onto his lap to hug him until, laughing, he lifted her off, removed Agnes's arms from around his neck and stood up.

'I must go into the garden and check how it has fared in my absence. They're not expecting me back until tomorrow so it's the perfect time to catch them slacking.'

Charlie was smiling as he spoke – the team of gardeners at Woodchurch Manor loved their jobs and he had every confidence in them.

'You be good to your mother today.' Charlie bent down to lace up his boots. 'Why don't you bring a picnic to the gardens later this afternoon and we can eat it by the lake?'

He went out with a wave, leaving Molly to deal with their daughters' excitement.

'Come, girls, you haven't even had breakfast yet. We can think about the picnic later,' Molly cajoled them. But their father's suggestion had put them in a holiday mood and Molly saw that it would be hard to get them to concentrate on household tasks or lessons. So, once the breakfast things were cleared away and the girls had helped to brush each other's hair – Catherine protesting, as always, that hers was being pulled – and the new ribbons were tied in place, Molly said they could each take whatever they would most like to work on out into the garden. It was a beautiful day – sunny but not too hot – one of the first glorious days of the year and she didn't see why they shouldn't all make the most of it.

Sally had no hesitation in declaring that she wanted to finish her sampler, while Agnes went off clutching paper, paints and brushes, as well as trying to balance a jar of water.

Catherine looked anguished – she couldn't decide what she wanted to do until Molly suggested she might like to improve her darning, at which point she settled on cutting paper scraps for her album.

They were all busy in the garden, Molly having decided that the beautiful weather would have to be her compensation for the basket of mending that she must tackle, since she had sent Ellen to the farm to buy eggs for the picnic. They had been there barely fifteen minutes when she was startled by a voice calling, 'Hello there! Anyone home?'

Will strode into view, rather overdressed for the weather, Molly thought, in a tweed hat and jacket with thick woollen socks over his breeches and the same muddy boots as the day before.

'Will, I wasn't expecting to see you,' Molly said, putting down her work and standing up. In truth, with Charlie's return home she was fully absorbed once more in family life and had forgotten all about the previous evening's party.

'I knocked at the door,' Will said, 'but no one answered. And just as I was about to go back the way I had come I spied you all here in the garden, working away very quietly.'

Molly's daughters had their heads bent to their work. She rather suspected they were wishing fiercely that the intruder would go away. Agnes might have warmed to him the previous day, but they were probably thinking they would be expected to sit quietly and endure a good deal of boring grown-up conversation.

'Let me fetch you a chair,' Molly said. 'And a cold drink, perhaps.' Will had taken off his hat and was now mopping his brow with a handkerchief.

'That would be very welcome,' he said. 'I hadn't expected it to be quite so warm at this time of year.' He sat down on the chair that Molly had vacated while she went to the kitchen, wondering all the while at the purpose of his visit.

When she returned with another chair and a glass of small beer, Will launched straight into the reason for his appearance. 'At breakfast this morning, Mr Powell told me that there was quite a to-do, down in Margate harbour, with three ships waiting to take troops and horses on board. I thought I might make a trip there to do some sketches. Perhaps you would like to join me.'

Agnes looked up at the reference to sketches, but Sally and Catherine worked on.

'Remember how we used to go to the harbour when I wasn't much older than Sally here?' Will said.

'I do,' Molly replied, thinking back to her attempts to find somewhere that Will would find pleasing enough to sketch. It had been hard to guess the sort of places that would appeal to him. 'But this afternoon we are going to have a picnic in the gardens, I'm afraid.'

Will looked disconsolate and scuffed at the ground with the toe of his boot.

'Perhaps tomorrow?' Molly ventured, feeling sure that

Will would either have set off back to London, or the ships would have gone.

He brightened up at once. 'Perfect. Mr Powell assured me that the ships would be there for a day or two longer and I'm sure you will all find it interesting.' He addressed the girls as he spoke and Molly was surprised. She had assumed he had meant them to stay behind.

Will stood up and went over to see what Agnes was doing, then complimented Sally on her stitching and Catherine on her paper cutting, so that Molly felt guilty for wishing him on his way.

In a moment of generosity she said, 'Would you care to join us this afternoon, for the picnic? Down by the lake, with Charlie?'

Will, who had been crouched alongside Agnes, suggesting something about her painting, stood up, clearly pleased. 'Indeed I would. I have to be away from here the day after tomorrow and I've yet to find the view that Mr Powell would have me paint. I'll take myself off over the fields now, for another look around, and I will see you all later this afternoon.'

He made a deep bow, encompassing the girls and Molly, then set off down the lane. They could hear him whistling for quite some time.

'Ma, who is he?' Sally asked, after a short while.

Molly had given them no explanation of their visitor on his first appearance, the day before. 'Goodness, I first met him when he was just a bit older than you, Sally. I found him sketching in a churchyard in Margate, near the stable-yard where I sold the milk. I could tell his work was very good – he was three years younger but he didn't draw like a child. He was visiting the area while he studied, staying with his aunt who lived close by. I used to help him find good places to sketch, but after a while he went home to London. I didn't see much of him after that.'

Molly didn't mention her chance meeting with Will later, in Covent Garden, when her life had taken a very different turn. 'He's a famous artist now. Very famous, by all accounts.'

Agnes looked interested but Sally shrugged and returned to her stitching.

'Well, I think he's odd,' she said, with an air of finality. Perhaps Molly should have scolded her for being impolite but it was hard to disagree. He was a little impetuous, perhaps, and in the years since she had last seen him in London he had evidently become used to getting his own way.

CHAPTER ELEVEN

The girls were as excited about their afternoon picnic as they would have been about a trip to Canterbury, Molly thought, opening the larder door and trying to decide what they should take.

A hesitant knock at the kitchen door disturbed her ruminations. Not another visit from Will, she thought, although surely his knock would have been bolder. She opened the door to find the shy young maid from the party the evening before standing there.

'Please, ma'am, the mistress said she will provide the picnic and you're not to worry and she hopes you won't mind her and the master and Mr Turner joining you.' The maid looked triumphant at having remembered the whole message.

Molly was taken aback. This would not be the relaxed picnic, sitting on the grass with Charlie and the girls, that she had imagined. She feared it might be rather formal, with tables and chairs and staff serving tea. But since their planned destination, the lake, was part of the grounds of Woodchurch Manor she could hardly complain.

Molly looked at the girl on the doorstep. 'I'm afraid I don't know your name.'

'Betsy, ma'am.'

'Thank you, Betsy. Please tell Mrs Powell that she is most kind and we are very much looking forward to it. Can you remember the message?'

Betsy nodded vigorously and set off back down the garden path, then onwards in the direction of the big house. Molly watched her go, smiling. Betsy would be repeating that simple sentence all the way back.

They set off for the lake at three o'clock, Catherine grumbling because she had already decided what the picnic should consist of – pork pie followed by any kind of cake – and distrusted what might be on offer instead.

'It will be lovely,' Molly said firmly, trying to alleviate the girls' disappointment at having to share their planned picnic with the Powells and Will. 'I feel quite sure there will be something special and perhaps there will be games, too.'

When pressed, though, she struggled to think what they might be offered to eat. Her days as a servant at Woodchurch Manor had taught her that their picnic would be much fancier than the fare in Molly and Charlie's house, but she was hard-pressed to describe any of it to the girls. 'Tartlets, I expect, and maybe a pigeon pie. And jellies and junkets,' she said vaguely.

As they drew closer to the lake, Molly saw that her premonition was correct. There were tables and chairs, and the servants were opening a hamper and setting dishes on the table. Mr and Mrs Powell and Will were standing by the lake, glasses in hand, talking to Charlie, who appeared to be doing a lot of nodding but little talking. He looked visibly relieved at the approach of his family.

Mrs Powell, elegant in a pale green gown that Molly couldn't help but notice toned beautifully with the setting, turned to her and said, 'I do hope you don't mind us joining you. When Mr Turner mentioned what you had planned, it seemed too good an opportunity to miss.'

Molly could feel her own smile become a little fixed as Charlie glanced at her, no doubt blaming her for spoiling the happy relaxed hour or two he had envisaged. But what could she do? This was the Powells' property and Charlie their employee. They were entitled to join in with his picnic on their land.

Mrs Powell was gazing over the lake. 'I must say, everything in the garden is looking delightful already. We were just telling Mr Dawson how pleased we are with all his hard work.' She turned to Molly. 'This picnic is such a good idea. We have vowed to make more use of the gardens for entertaining, starting this summer with a garden party, which we hope will become an annual event.'

Molly nodded and smiled some more, only too aware that this would mean Charlie having to work even harder. But Mrs Powell was clapping her hands and calling to Betsy, who was standing by the hamper. 'Find the girls some lemonade to drink,' she said. She turned to Sally, Agnes and Catherine. 'Go and have a peep in the hampers. I think there are one or two things in there that you might enjoy.'

Molly, who would have preferred lemonade, too, found a glass of fruit punch pressed into her hand by Will. Charlie held a glass of ale, which he sipped politely while listening to Mr Powell, who was likely holding forth about his garden-party plans.

Molly's fears that the picnic was to be an entirely formal event were dispelled when a manservant arrived bearing a long wooden box. He proceeded to hammer a low iron hoop into the ground at either end of a suitable flat area by the lake, while the girls watched him curiously. Will declared this to be a game of pall-mall and, seizing a wooden mallet from the box, began to demonstrate what they must do before the hoops were even in place.

The afternoon flew by, and almost before Molly knew it, the sun was setting and a sudden chill, caused by their proximity to the lake, made her shiver.

'Girls, girls,' she called. 'It's time to go home now.'

The blanket that had been spread on the grass for her daughters held three plates, empty of all but crumbs, and the whole party had been happily employed in playing pall-mall ever since the hoops had been set up. Just enough food remained on the table to make Mrs Powell feel her guests hadn't gone hungry. They had feasted on a selection of raised pies – chicken, pigeon and pork – along with chutneys and salad fresh from the kitchen garden. Three different kinds of cake had kept Catherine happy.

The presence of the Powells and Will prevented the girls from complaining about having to go home to bed. Charlie hoisted Catherine onto his shoulders and Molly tucked Sally and Agnes's hands into hers as she thanked their hosts. 'We've had a lovely afternoon,' she added.

'Don't forget our outing tomorrow. We ought to leave no later than half past ten,' Will said.

Molly had forgotten all about the excursion to Margate harbour and, after such a busy afternoon, she wondered at the wisdom of it. The girls would be tired. But Will, full of boyish enthusiasm, was impossible to disappoint. If they were to be up and ready in time it was even more important to get everyone home, Molly thought, as – farewells made – they hurried through the gathering dusk back to the cottage.

Once the girls were tucked up in bed – after bitter protests that they weren't even tired, although flushed cheeks and overexcited chatter suggested otherwise – Molly settled by the kitchen range with Charlie. There was laundry and mending still to be done, she thought, but it would have to wait until the next day. Then she remembered the planned outing and a sigh escaped her lips. She had grown used to the routine of their quiet life here on the Woodchurch Manor estate. Her younger self would have welcomed and enjoyed the disruption Will's visit had caused but now she was content with her lot. She was looking forward to order being restored.

'Why the sigh?' Charlie asked.

Molly noticed that he was frowning, his expression hard to read, which was most unlike him. 'I was thinking about what I needed to get on with here, when I remembered about tomorrow's outing. I'm half hoping that the weather will change and make it impossible,' Molly said, suppressing a yawn.

'You're having quite a time of it with your friend, Will. Does he remind you of your London days?' Charlie's tone was uncharacteristically hard and Molly looked at him in surprise.

'Why, I barely saw Will above twice when I was in London and he was just a boy then, studying at the Royal Academy of Art,' she replied.

'Well, he's older now, famous and prosperous with it. He seems very taken with you, Molly.'

Molly stared at her husband, wondering why he was speaking to her in this way. They had never discussed her time in London, Charlie seemingly content to accept that she had suffered there and to throw all his efforts into ensuring that she felt safe and secure in her new life at Woodchurch Manor.

'Taken with me? Whatever do you mean?' It was Molly's turn to frown. 'He's just a bit odd, Charlie. Even Sally noticed that when he visited earlier today. He lives by his own rules. He's an artist.' Molly shrugged, not knowing quite what else to say.

'He came visiting earlier?' Charlie asked.

'Yes. And yesterday. Before the Powells' party.' Molly saw no reason to lie but realised – too late – that her answer had made Charlie less than happy.

'Molly, I saw how his eyes followed you while you were playing pall-mall today. And how he watched you as you sat at the tea table with Mrs Powell.' Charlie's lips were set in a thin line.

'Oh, Charlie, that's nonsense.' Molly spoke without thinking, then said hastily, 'I mean, I wasn't aware of it, but if he was watching me, it's just because he's an artist. He looks at people, situations and settings all the time. He's storing images away in his head for future paintings.' Molly was grateful that Will had explained this to her a long time ago, when she first knew him in Margate.

'And, in any case, he has a child.' It was an irrelevance, but Molly hoped this might help Charlie to understand that she was nothing to Will.

'And no evidence of any wife,' Charlie said. 'I think it would be better if you didn't see him again.'

Molly could hardly believe her ears. What had brought them to this? 'But there's a trip arranged tomorrow. With the Powells,' she protested. 'I couldn't care less about it. But it will appear rude if I have to make excuses for us all in the morning.'

Charlie got to his feet. 'I'm going up to bed. It's been a long day and I'm still tired from yesterday's journey home. You must suit yourself.'

Molly sat on, listening to his footsteps on the stairs and the creak of the floorboards above as he moved around in the bedroom. She could imagine him sitting on the side of the bed to remove his boots, piling his clothes on the chair ready for morning, then heard the mattress settling with the shift of his weight and all fell silent above. She wondered whether he had fallen straight to sleep or whether he was lying there, thinking about what had passed between them.

She was deeply unsettled. In their thirteen years together, Charlie had never exhibited such behaviour. She could only put it down to one thing, jealousy. It was misplaced: Will was nothing to her but a friend and a connection with her childhood. But Molly *did* have secrets that she had assumed she would take with her to the grave. As she sat in her kitchen in the dark, she shivered at the thought of just how Charlie might react if he ever had an inkling of her past. Resolutely, she lit her candle and prepared to go up to bed. She could see little choice over their proposed trip the next day. Charlie must surely know it would be unwise to cause offence to the Powells by denying Will their company on the excursion, although Molly feared pride wouldn't let him acknowledge it. It was with a heavy heart that she, too, climbed the stairs to bed.

CHAPTER TWELVE

When Molly woke the next morning she discovered Charlie had got up and left the house without disturbing her. This wasn't unusual in the spring and summer – he was always keen to be out in the garden at first light, his head already full of what needed to be achieved that day. But it saddened her that morning, for she knew he had done it on purpose because he was still upset with her.

She roused the girls from their beds and made sure they all had a good breakfast – she wasn't sure what the arrangements might be for their outing. She suspected, though, that Mr and Mrs Powell would be keen to take refreshments somewhere in Margate during the course of the day, not least so they could show off Will, their famous guest.

With that in mind, Molly paid extra care to the girls' appearances, making sure that they put on clean dresses, not the ones they had worn to the picnic. In any case, she saw that these had suffered grass stains and sticky smears and Ellen would not be pleased at the extra effort needed to launder them.

She brushed their hair and observed with some delight that the girls generously agreed to swap their new ribbons around, so Sally now had the blue one to match her dress, Agnes wore lilac, while Catherine could lay claim to the coveted pink. Luckily, this was just the right shade to suit her chestnut hair.

Molly paid extra attention to how she looked, although she had to wear her third-best dress and felt it hardly warranted the term 'best' any longer. The cornflower-blue fabric was more than a little faded, either from washing or being dried in the sun. She took comfort from the dress-maker's words, that white and pale colours were very fashionable for ladies at present. White was best suited to the well-to-do who could afford to travel everywhere by carriage, Molly decided. It would never do for someone who lived in the countryside with household duties to attend to, and muddy paths all around.

She rounded up the girls, made sure that they all had sun bonnets and that their hands and faces were still clean, then took her light shawl and a bonnet.

'We mustn't be late,' she said, chivvying everyone out of the door. 'We don't want to keep the Powells and Will – I mean Mr Turner – waiting.'

In view of Charlie's remarks last night, she had decided that it would be better to put her acquaintance with Will on a more formal footing in front of the girls. When she noticed Agnes clutching her sketchbook, though, she smiled. She hoped Will wouldn't be too caught up with his own sketching to give her some encouragement.

Molly and her daughters took the path to Woodchurch Manor, cutting through a small stand of trees to approach the front entrance, where carriages were already waiting for them. Mr Powell liked to put on a display when he went to Margate and he had ordered the phaeton for himself and Mrs Powell, complete with his liveliest pair of horses. Molly, Will and the girls were to travel in a more sedate fashion, in the two rows of seats facing each other in the barouche.

Will lifted the girls in, then gallantly handed Molly up. She was scarlet with embarrassment and made clumsy by it, tripping on her skirt and almost landing in an inelegant heap. She was far more accustomed to travelling on a wagon beside the driver or sitting in the back with the load. Now she found herself seated next to Will, facing the girls. She hoped fervently that Charlie was busy in the walled garden and wouldn't witness this travelling arrangement. After last night's discussion she knew he most certainly wouldn't approve.

As the barouche moved off, pulled by four horses, Molly had to suppress a shriek. It felt less stable than a wagon pulled by great carthorses and it bowled along at what seemed like a dangerous speed, although she could see that the Powells' phaeton was already a long way ahead, kicking up a cloud of dust.

Will chuckled. 'Powell has been itching to be out in that phaeton of his since before breakfast. I caught him in the stable-yard this morning, practically stroking it. He said the roads close to home aren't good enough to put it to the test but he's going to give the horses their head when we're nearer to Margate.'

Molly felt alarmed for Mrs Powell. Did she know of Mr Powell's intentions? she wondered. Will had a wistful expression on his face and indeed his next words were 'I wonder whether Mrs Powell would change places with me on the return journey? I've a mind to see what it's like.'

Molly noticed that her daughters, who were travelling backwards, didn't seem to share any of her fear at the speed they were travelling, so she did her best to relax and smile and point out anything of note on their journey. Still, she was delighted to recognise the buildings at the western edge of Margate, and to find that the coachman slowed the pace of the horses to suit the sudden increase in carriage traffic. It seemed that word had spread about the spectacle to be seen in the harbour and, as it was the last chance to see the ships, it had become quite the day out for those at leisure.

The barouche had to stop to let its passengers down a little way from the harbour, the coachman assuring them that arrangements to collect them later had been made with Mr Powell. Molly, taken aback by the crowds, bent down and instructed the girls to hold each other's hands.

'Catherine, hold onto Agnes. Agnes, take Sally's hand, and I will take Sally's, so. Don't let go,' she warned. 'Otherwise I fear you will be swept away.'

But Molly's plan proved impractical – they simply couldn't walk four abreast. Will solved it by taking Agnes's hand while Sally and Catherine walked on either side of their mother. In this fashion they were carried along by the crowd towards the pier. Molly noticed that the smaller and lighter phaeton had succeeded in getting much closer, and Mr Powell had left it in the care of a small boy, who was looking self-important, if not a little nervous of the highly strung horses.

Molly spotted a good many ladies of fashion, wearing the draped white muslin gowns that her dressmaker had spoken of. They were strolling arm in arm with gentlemen in splendid uniforms, mostly dark blue jackets with a good deal of gold braid, worn with cream breeches, but some also wore scarlet jackets, crossed with gold sashes.

Piles of baggage waited to be loaded from the quayside onto tall-masted ships, which were moored side by side all along the sea edge of the pier. Young sailors on errands, dressed in baggy trousers and short jackets, pushed through the crowds, uttering 'S'cuse me,' every few seconds. Molly was overwhelmed by the level of noise and activity and struggled to take in everything that was going on around her. She glanced back frequently to make sure Will had tight hold of Agnes's hand.

'Look, look, Ma.' Catherine was tugging at her mother's skirt and pointing. Molly gasped as a horse, a broad hessian strap girdling its middle, was hoisted over the heads of the crowd, whinnying in fear as two men hauled on a rope-and-pulley system to winch it aboard one of the ships.

'Is the horse going to sea, Ma?' Catherine asked.

'I suppose it must be,' Molly said, as surprised as her daughter. What use would the Navy have with a horse at sea? She looked around for Will, to see whether he might be able to answer that question, but he and Agnes had stopped a little way back to watch a young sailor shinning up the rigging of one of the ships.

The boy looked to be little older than Sally and Molly was all at once struck by the thought that her son could be among this crowd. She had wondered before whether he might have joined the Navy after he left the Foundling Hospital. She began to look at the youngest sailors with new eyes. Was there a young lad here who looked like her daughters? Before she could pursue the thought, she came upon Mr and Mrs Powell standing to one side a little further on.

'There you are,' Mrs Powell said. 'We feared we would never find you in this crowd.'

'Mr Turner is back there, with Agnes,' Molly said, clutching Sally and Catherine, and side-stepping as an overloaded handcart bore down on them, pushed by a young sailor who could barely see over the top of it.

'Such a noise!' Mrs Powell exclaimed, as oaths broke out to their right, where more horses were being loaded. She eyed a group of local men loafing at the side of the quay with some distaste. They were drinking from a stone flagon, passing it between them as they watched the mêlée in front of them. Mrs Powell turned her back on them and clutched her husband's arm even more firmly.

Molly had just lost sight of Agnes in the crowd, handicapped by both her own petite stature and that of Agnes, when a smartly dressed naval officer, walking alone, approached them. He addressed Mr Powell, who exclaimed, 'Captain Austen!' and clapped him on the back.

They exchanged a few words, then Captain Austen turned to Mrs Powell and Molly. 'I wonder whether I may suggest that you join my sister and my wife, who are waiting at the Kings Head? I think you will be more comfortable there, away from all this noise and confusion.'

Molly nodded in gratitude. Although fascinated at first by the unusual spectacle, she had begun to feel uneasy as they had progressed along the pier. The few women here were mainly wives of officers taking a last walk with their husbands before they embarked. There was just one other group of women, made conspicuous by their brightly coloured clothes and gaudy jewellery. They called out to unaccompanied officers and sailors alike with suggestions Molly was anxious that Sally and Catherine shouldn't hear.

It was clear Mrs Powell was as keen to be away from them as Molly, for she turned at once and took her husband's arm to walk back towards the town, leaving Molly – who was thankful to have caught sight of Agnes, still with Will – to walk beside Captain Austen.

'Who are all these men?' Molly asked, as they passed yet more men in uniform. She was a little overawed by her companion but couldn't pass up the opportunity to have answers to her questions.

'It's quite a mixture,' Captain Austen replied. 'You are witnessing an unusual event. The high spring tide has brought in several ships that would normally be lying at anchor outside the harbour. They are all taking the opportunity to load up at once. It's a little chaotic,' he said, skilfully guiding Molly and the girls out of the path of yet another handcart. 'They have only a short time left before they must sail, hence the rush.

'These are naval officers and ratings,' he said, pointing at a group standing ready to board one of the ships, the men in the familiar blue-and-gold naval uniforms and the boys wearing the wide-legged trousers and short jackets that Molly had noticed earlier.

'And the red jackets?' Molly asked. 'And the horses – why are horses being loaded onto ships?'

'The red jackets belong to Army men, cavalry mainly, who are boarding the same ships as their horses, ready for duty overseas. Bound for France,' her companion added.

The final ship they passed as they neared the entrance to the pier was surrounded by men hard at work loading cargo – wooden barrels, sacks and bales of cloth – but with not a uniform in sight.

Captain Austen was bent on continuing Molly's education. 'This is a merchant vessel, bound for Africa, most likely, with rum and other goods on board.' They stood for a moment, watching the flurry of activity, and Molly spotted

Will and Agnes standing nearby. Will was sketching furiously while Agnes looked on, half hidden behind his legs.

Molly, concerned by their proximity to the work going on, left Captain Austen's side to take Agnes's hand, instructing her to hold tight to Sally.

'Just look,' Will said. 'Magnificent!'

He held out his sketchbook and Molly saw that the page was covered with drawings of men at work. Stripped to the waist because of the increasing warmth of the day, their muscles bulged and rippled as they tossed the cargo from the quayside to their fellows on the boat, maintaining a rhythmic chanting as they did so. Will had sketched disembodied arms and hands clutching boxes, backs straining under their load, faces grimacing in concentration. He had drawn only one man in full – a dark-skinned fellow, taller and broader than all the others. Molly, made awkward and uneasy by these men, was still able to marvel at how Will had captured their strength.

Captain Austen was by her side again. 'May I suggest we walk on?' he said politely. 'I think we are obstructing their work by standing here.'

'Of course,' Molly said, making hasty introductions as she drew her girls away. 'Captain Austen, this is William Turner, the artist. Mr Turner, Captain Austen.'

She left the two men to walk together and hurried on ahead, feeling for all the world like a mother hen herding her chicks. Once they had gained the roadside, she breathed a sigh of relief. The pavement was busy but calmer than the pier. She glanced at the girls, who were quiet and wide-eyed. She hoped they hadn't been frightened by their outing. She didn't like to think of them telling their father about it before she had had a chance to describe it to him.

Captain Austen caught them up. 'Shall we go and join my sister, Jane, and my wife, Mary? They will be delighted to meet you all.'

He led the way to the inn and Molly followed him across the road with the girls. Here was another worry: how would she pay for the four of them to dine?

CHAPTER THIRTEEN

In the event, Molly's worries were needless. Mr Powell had procured a large circular table in the window and, once the flurry of introductions to Captain Austen's sister and wife was over, he announced that he had taken it upon himself to order a selection of food to suit the whole party. Soon the table was laden: oysters, veal cutlets, a large pork pie, a dish of potatoes, a selection of cheeses and bread rolls along with a jug of ale for the gentlemen and another of lemonade for the ladies and children.

Molly was thirsty. The day was warm and the streets dusty from the hustle and bustle outside. She accepted a glass of lemonade with gratitude and tried not to gulp it down, although she observed the girls had no such reservations. Since Mr Powell had ordered, he was most likely to pay the bill so she felt she could relax. Her girls had already loaded their plates, Catherine taking an extra-large slice of pork pie.

Molly was content to sit back, attend to her daughters and listen to the conversation swirling around her. Will was describing a painting in great detail to Miss Austen, who managed to maintain an expression of determined interest in spite of her sister-in-law's unsuccessful attempts to hide her amusement. On the other side of the table, Captain Austen was telling the Powells about his role in training the local boatmen to defend the coastline in case the French attacked.

The dining-room window afforded a splendid view of the harbour and Molly ceased to listen to the conversation around her as she watched the passers-by. She half expected to catch sight of her aunt and uncle or her sisters, but she didn't see a single familiar face. Her attention was caught by Agnes, who had left her seat to gaze out, too.

'Look, Ma!' she said, and pointed.

The sails of the ships were being unfurled and Molly observed how the canvas immediately filled with the breeze and started to billow. The activity on the pier had slowed – now just one or two sailors were making last-minute dashes back and forth to load the remaining items.

Captain Austen spoke up, attracting the attention of all the company. 'It looks as though the tide is on the turn and the wind is just right. The ships will be away shortly.'

He went to stand by the window and Sally and Catherine slipped from their chairs to join Agnes. Molly noticed that the rest of the company seemed to have lost interest in the goings-on at sea and returned to their conversations until, shortly afterwards, Mr Powell declared it time for home.

The barouche was ready and waiting outside for Molly and the girls. Molly marvelled at the ease with which Mr Powell had ordered food, settled the bill and arranged their transport home; it was a novelty to not have to think of everything herself. Once farewells had been made to the rest of the party, she climbed into the barouche with the girls and Will, who had clearly forgotten about his earlier wish to drive home in the phaeton.

The white sails of the ships, already a little way out to sea, caught the sunlight as they left the harbour behind. Molly sat back and watched her girls, smiling as they all fell into a doze. Lulled half asleep herself, she listened to Will enthuse about their outing.

'I've been working on a piece for a while now and I just couldn't get it as I want it. That fellow I sketched, the one loading the ship, is perfect. I know he will be just right, a focal point for the whole painting.' Will continued to talk on, now clearly impatient to be back in London so that he could get on with his work. It was only as the carriage turned up the drive to Woodchurch Manor that he thought to ask Molly about her impressions of their day out.

Caught unawares, she could only say, 'Quite different from what I was expecting.'

What that was, she couldn't say and, luckily, Will didn't seem curious. He handed her down from the carriage and she expressed her grateful thanks to the Powells, who had arrived ahead of them in the phaeton, for their generosity in including her family in their day out. Molly then lined the girls up in front of Will and bade them say goodbye, before she made her own farewell.

'I hope to see you again before too long, Will.' Molly smiled. 'Let's not leave it another thirteen years. I suspect you will be back here before I visit London, though.'

Pleasantries observed, Molly and the girls took the path home. The girls were busy chattering about what they had eaten and the sight of the ships sailing away and she felt relieved. She had feared they might have been overwhelmed by the strangeness of the scene on the pier, but the novelty of dining at the Kings Head seemed to have overshadowed everything else.

She longed to see Charlie and to tell him about their day, and she hoped he had forgotten their argument of the previous evening. As it happened, Charlie was late home from the gardens and the girls, worn out by their adventures, were fast asleep in bed before Molly heard the kitchen door open. She had been fretting that he had stayed away because he was still angry, and she had cried more than a few tears as she prepared the stew for his supper.

Unable to eat more than a mouthful or two of her own meal, she had pushed her plate aside and left the table to sit by the range. The evening had grown cooler as the light faded and she'd fallen into a troubled doze, waking with a start at the sound of the back door opening.

She didn't know what to say at first and Charlie was also hesitant, loitering on the threshold. The silence stretched before Molly broke it by getting up and saying, 'You must be hungry. You've had a long day.'

She set Charlie's stew to heat on the range then, as he was still standing, silent, in the doorway, she said, 'Come in before you let out all the warmth.'

Molly felt awkward, something she had not felt with Charlie for a very long time. She moved away from the range to slice some bread for him, setting the plate on the table. The door closed and Molly, with heightened senses, became aware of Charlie's every move.

'Sit down,' she said, preparing to ladle stew into a bowl for him. She dropped the ladle back into the pot with a clang as suddenly, Charlie's arms were around her waist and he was pulling her close to him.

'I'm sorry,' he murmured into her ear. 'I don't know what got into me last night. I was still angry this morning but a day in the garden has made me see sense. I was almost too afraid to come back this evening. You have every right to think me a foolish, thoughtless man.'

'Oh, Charlie.' Molly felt a rush of relief. 'I was so worried when you didn't come home. I could never think you foolish or thoughtless.' She turned in his arms to look up at him. 'Let's agree not to quarrel like this again.'

Charlie kissed the top of her head, then pushed her gently from him. 'Can I eat now? It smells so good.'

They both laughed and Molly dished up his stew, then reheated her own, relief having given her an appetite. She glanced occasionally at her husband as he ate, and wondered. Had they damaged their relationship with that foolish quarrel? Was it truly resolved? Then she pushed away the thought and told Charlie about their outing, emphasising the crowds, which she knew he would have hated, and talking more of the Powells and Captain Austen than she did of Will. She promised him that when the girls awoke the next day they would give him full details of everything they had eaten at the Kings Head. She kept her fingers crossed that they would remember only the exciting elements of their day out.

CHAPTER FOURTEEN

As Molly had expected, the girls couldn't wait to give their father the highlights of their trip. She could have predicted some of it – Catherine's memories revolved around the pork pie. The horses that were hauled into the air to be loaded onto the ship were all that Agnes could talk about and she promised to draw the scene for Charlie, who had looked sceptical at her description. Sally's contribution was 'The uniforms,' which earned her a sharp look from Molly. Had her head been turned by the glamour of gold braid and brass buttons? Then, as her daughter talked of the splendid stitching and the frogged fastenings and the design of the deep cuffs, she realised that Sally was viewing them with the eyes of a seamstress.

True to her word, Agnes drew one of the poor horses, dangling helplessly in its sling over the quayside. Molly praised her work and her admiration was entirely genuine. How could Agnes capture an image so precisely with simple strokes of her pencil? She wondered again whether to speak to Charlie about the possibility of arranging tuition for her, then discounted the thought. It would only make Agnes feel there might be some future for her as an artist and Molly couldn't see how that might be. There was no point in raising false hopes. If Agnes had been a child of the Powells, engaging a drawing master would have been perfectly normal, but her future would more likely lie in marrying into one of the genteel families of Margate and the surrounding areas. She would do better to improve her sewing skills, Molly thought, and with that in mind declared that the afternoon would be devoted to stitching their samplers, which pleased only Sally.

After the busy days of Will's visit, Molly had been looking forward to a return to their normal routine. Yet now that he had gone, she was strangely unsettled, the feeling exacerbated by a change from the sunny spring weather they had been enjoying to a much wetter spell. Charlie was delighted, saying that rain was much needed in the garden, but Molly and the girls – confined to the house – grew restless. The paths were too muddy to make local walking a pleasure, even when there was a brief respite from the rain. Molly, then, was delighted to receive a letter from Aunt Jane, inviting her to bring the girls for a visit on the Friday of that week. She would send their uncle's carriage for them at nine o'clock and they were to spend the day.

Molly thought the 'carriage' was more likely to be the wagon of a carrier he used for his business, but as long as it was covered and they could remain dry, she would be happy. And, if the weather was kind during their visit, they could walk into Margate to buy sewing threads and hair ribbons, the two things that the household seemed to have more need of than Molly thought possible.

She felt sure that the invitation had been inspired by seeing her aunt and uncle at Will's reception at Woodchurch Manor and Molly felt a pang of guilt. Since Molly's father had died, not six months after her visit to see him on returning to the area, she knew she had not been a dutiful niece. The presence of Nicholas's wife, Sarah, and their daughter, Constance, in the house was, of course, off-putting, but she had been forced to face them at the funeral.

Molly's father had collapsed one day while loading the milk churns onto his cart, and all Lizzie's efforts to revive him had failed. Molly's grief had only been intensified by her feeling of having disappointed him.

After she'd seen how frail he had become during the years she'd been away, Molly had vowed to visit more frequently to make amends. Her good intentions had barely been tested before she discovered that she was expecting a baby. Charlie's delight knew no bounds but Molly struggled to share his joy. She was reminded only too vividly that this would not be her first child, and with the memory came the sorrow of her secret lost boy. This time, though, she was not as energetic as she had been before when she was with child. She felt lethargic, drained, and no sooner had this started to improve than she began to feel sick. After one or two journeys to see her family in Margate had left her exhausted, nauseous and craving her bed, Charlie had dissuaded her from further visits.

'I don't like the idea of you being jolted about on the road there and back,' he said, surveying her grey face after she had returned. 'And winter is approaching. It's cold on the open road and the days are short. I think it would be better to postpone further trips until the spring.'

Molly, though relieved, had demurred a little, then given in with good grace. So when Charlie came to her, white-faced, to tell her that he had received bad news from her family, she had found it difficult to stop crying. She did not know whether the tears were prompted by grief, guilt or self-pity but it hurt her deeply that she hadn't been able to say goodbye. She hadn't even been able to visit her father at Christmas, for the snow had lain too deeply on the ground.

She stood in St John's Church on a bitter January day, wrapped up as well as possible against the cold, and nothing that Lizzie could say would console her.

'I should have been there,' she said, as they waited for the church to fill with those wishing to pay their last respects

'It would have made no difference,' Lizzie said. She sounded offended. 'I did the best I could. His body just gave up. He'd been tired for so long.'

'I didn't mean on that day.' Molly's voice shook as fresh tears came. 'I should have visited more often.'

'Oh, Molly, you weren't well and the weather has been so bad this winter. No one expected you to make the journey in your condition.'

After the service, Molly stood back and let Ann receive the condolences on the family's behalf, but several people sought her out to tell her what a lovely man her father had been. She was listening politely to the words of one of their milk-round customers when she saw Aunt Jane bearing down on her, with Sarah in tow.

'Molly, you look fit to freeze standing here by the church door in this bitter wind. Come back to the house. We've invited some of the others, too.'

Molly began to protest but Lizzie took one of her arms and Mary the other.

'Charlie won't mind. Come, Molly, we've spoken to everyone we need to.'

The small crowd was already dispersing, the flakes of snow borne on the wind convincing them that it was time to go home to their firesides. The sexton had apologised, saying that their father's grave would have to be dug later, the ground too hard for a spade to penetrate. Molly's tears froze on her cheeks as they made the short walk back to Princes Crescent.

As they climbed the steps to her aunt and uncle's house, she could see a few people already gathered in the drawing room. Hannah met them as they came through the front door and gave Molly a hug.

'Goodness, I can barely get my arms around you,' she exclaimed, looking down at Molly's belly. 'Now go through and take a glass of something to warm you up. Your father – such a lovely man – wouldn't want you catching cold on his account.'

Hannah, a little flustered by the numbers who had come to the house, hurried back to the kitchen while Molly was propelled into the drawing room by Lizzie and Mary. She endured a repeat of conversations she had already had with many of the people there, before she came face to face with Sarah, Nicholas's wife.

'Molly, it's such a long time since I've seen you. I'm sorry that we meet under such sad circumstances.' Sarah's face was solemn. 'And your baby is nearly due.' Her eyes were on Molly's belly. 'Your first – you must be so excited. Constance has brought such joy to your aunt and uncle. I don't think you've met her yet.' She cast around as though imagining she would find her daughter close by, although she was surely in the care of the housemaid, somewhere out of sight.

Molly survived this encounter with Sarah, barely uttering a word. Her attention was quickly claimed by Mary, who said that Lizzie needed to speak to her. Molly nodded politely to Sarah as she moved away. She wondered what Sarah would think if she knew that this wasn't her first baby: that Nicholas, Sarah's husband, was the father of her first child.

She had no time to consider this further because Lizzie had some news, which wiped everything else from Molly's mind.

'Molly, Ann is planning to return to live with her father.' Lizzie wasted no time, speaking plainly.

Molly frowned. 'What – out at Eastlands Farm?' It struck her that Lizzie and Mary could soon be lost to her, too. 'Are you planning to go with her? Do you want to live all the way out there?'

Lizzie laughed. 'I do not. And neither does Mary. But, in any case, we're not invited. Ann will take little John and Harriet, and Mary and I will stay here.'

Molly tried to marshal her thoughts. 'But where will you live? How will you manage?' At the back of her mind was a worry as to how Harriet and little John would cope, away from their relatives, but her first loyalty lay with her sisters.

'I'm to be married,' Lizzie said. 'Uncle William has said we can stay next door and pay rent, and Mary will live with us, too.'

Molly could only stare, unable to find words. Who was Lizzie planning to marry? How long had she known him? Did she know what she was doing?

Lizzie laughed at Molly's expression. 'I'm eighteen now. I've known Paul for over a year and he's asked me to marry him more than once. It makes sense. Mary is working at the bakery and can help towards the rent. I think we'll be a very happy household.'

Molly didn't doubt it. Lizzie was aglow with happiness, despite the sadness of the occasion, and Mary was trying unsuccessfully to hide her smiles.

'I should meet this young man of yours. Is he here?' Molly peered around the room, searching for an unfamiliar face in the knot of men gathered by the fireplace. 'And you are sure that this is acceptable to Aunt Jane and Uncle William?'

'I'm delighted for them.' Aunt Jane had arrived at her side in time to hear her words. 'Molly, Charlie says it's time for you to go, so you must make ready. Come back very soon to catch up on the news.'

Molly was loath to leave but she was persuaded to hurry out to join Charlie, who was waiting for her in the carriage lent to them by Mr Powell. Snow was falling more heavily now and Charlie was keen to be away before the roads became treacherous.

Molly's distress over her father's death was replaced by worry over her sisters' futures. She had been determined to return to Margate at the first opportunity to see them settled but her intention was thwarted by the weather. Snow fell heavily that night and lay on the ground throughout February. By March, Molly felt that she was too close to her confinement to risk the journey, which turned out to be well founded. On 5 March, she gave birth to a daughter, Sally.

CHAPTER FIFTEEN

Sally's birth had been bittersweet for Molly. She was delighted with her baby daughter, but the early weeks fuelled memories of her firstborn, and she was prone to bouts of weeping. Charlie was anxious and insisted on a doctor attending. To Molly's relief, the doctor said he had seen such a thing with his own wife and it was often a natural consequence of childbirth. He recommended beef tea to build up Molly's strength and, if possible, that a girl should be engaged to help.

Molly had imagined the doctor would recognise that this was not her first child and denounce her, a foolish notion, she realised later. She thought the midwife suspected something but she said nothing, no doubt unwilling to risk the sizeable fee that Charlie had paid her. The Powells sent one of their young maids, Ellen, to assist. She endeared herself to Molly by being very good at soothing Sally, a colicky baby, confiding that she was the eldest of five siblings.

'Your mother must miss you,' Molly exclaimed, on hearing this.

'I dare say, but the wages I send home are what keeps the family together,' Ellen said, wise beyond her years. She became so indispensable that her loan from Woodchurch Manor soon became a permanent arrangement. Molly wondered how she had managed alone the first time, before remembering all the girls at Mrs Dobbs's household in London, who were only too delighted to come and look after her darling boy whenever they could.

Agnes and Catherine had joined Sally over the three years that followed and now here they all were, driving to Margate in a carriage, not a wagon, that Uncle William must surely have either borrowed or hired. It had been decided that they should stay the night, so they could spend more time with their cousins, for now Mary as well as Lizzie had married, Mary to her long-time sweetheart, Michael, from the bakery. Lizzie's two children, Susan and Helena, along with Mary's son Lewis, were only a little younger than Molly's three girls.

At their mother's suggestion, Sally, Agnes and Catherine had made small gifts for their cousins. Sally had used her sewing skills to embroider the initials of each of her cousins onto three white handkerchiefs. Agnes had painted three small pictures for the children to put on the wall by their beds. She had painted the birds that sang outside the kitchen window, the bluebells that had filled the woods on the estate that spring and, for Lewis, the farm cat that liked to come and lie on the warm flagstones in the walled garden at Woodchurch Manor.

Molly had been careful to offer praise as even-handedly as possible, but it was hard not to enthuse over Agnes's skill. Mr Powell had chanced upon her painting the cat as he visited Charlie in the walled garden and declared that he would have taken the artwork off her hands if she hadn't already had a home for it. Agnes had been puzzled by his words, and unaffected by them, but when Charlie reported them to Molly she wondered yet again whether Agnes should have some proper tuition.

Catherine had been determined to create paper filigree pictures for her cousins but, alas, her ambition proved to be beyond her capabilities. Molly cut the paper into narrow strips for her but while Catherine's fingers were small, they were not nimble, and by the time she had rolled and re-rolled the strips into coils to represent the petals of a flower, they had become grubby and misshapen. Tears flowed, until Sally saved the day by suggesting Catherine should cut a chain of paper dolls for each of her cousins. Agnes drew the outline for her and Catherine produced three passable chains of hand-holding dolls, two of girls recognised by their dresses and one of a boy wearing short trousers. A suggestion that she might colour them in had kept her happily occupied for as long as it had taken her sisters to complete their work.

Now, their offerings neatly wrapped, the sisters were impatient to get to their destination. Molly was looking forward to spending time with her own sisters and, when she had learnt that Sarah would be away, taking Constance with her, a weight had lifted from her shoulders. Despite the passage of time, she still found it difficult to be with the pair because of the memories they raised.

In the end, the overnight visit stretched to two nights, for the girls were having such fun. Molly sat with Lizzie and Mary and they looked on as the six children – the girls quite evenly matched in age, Lewis the youngest by two years – played beautifully together. There were none of the quarrels that would have broken out over the course of a day at home with just the three of them, Molly reflected. When it was decided that fresh air was desirable, Molly and her sisters shepherded their brood towards the sea, stopping in the high street to buy the much-needed thread and ribbons. Molly was surprised to find Mrs Hughes, the milliner, still running her shop – now extended into the empty one next door to give her even bigger premises.

'I still rue the day that we lost your stepmother, Ann, to the countryside. A great shame – her nimble fingers created such clever decorations for my bonnets,' Mrs Hughes lamented.

Sally pricked up her ears and Molly saw her looking speculatively at the ribbon rosettes adorning many of the hats. Mrs Hughes indulged the sisters, young and old, by letting them try on her stock while the shop was quiet. Molly finally persuaded her daughters that they must get on for the sake of Lewis, waiting patiently at the side for them to be done.

'Do come back, my dear,' Mrs Hughes said to her. 'The bonnets that are fashionable today make the perfect frame for your face. Quite charming.'

Molly looked longingly at one in particular, with the brim all to the front and blue silk ribbon decorating the sides. An additional length of ribbon, tied into a bow beneath the chin, kept the bonnet securely in place. She wondered, though, whether it was more suited to a younger woman, rather than a matron with three daughters. And when would she have occasion to wear such a thing? She thanked Mrs Hughes and promised to return next time she was in town, only half intending to do so, then followed her sisters as they set off towards the pier.

Her enjoyment of spending time with them was all the greater for its novelty. Bringing up her own three children had prevented her visiting Margate as often as she would have liked over the years. She had continued to miss important events after her father's death – Lizzie's marriage to Paul had taken place within a month of Sally's birth and Molly had felt unequal to the journey. Lizzie had assured her by letter that it would be a quiet affair, but Molly was bereft nonetheless. Then Catherine's birth had coincided with Mary's marriage to Michael so Molly had missed that, too.

As she watched her sisters' easy interaction with each other, Molly suffered a pang of jealousy. She knew, though, that their closeness had begun when she had first moved away from them – at first only to her aunt's house next door, it was true. After that, though, she had left them entirely alone, in the care of their stepmother, while she had fled to London, remaining there for three years while they believed her lost for ever. Their closeness then had protected them from Ann's uncertain temper and turned them into the lovely young women they were today.

Molly's thoughts moved her to the point of tears and she was forced to claim that the wind off the sea was making her eyes water when Sally noticed and asked, with some concern, 'Ma, are you crying?'

Molly diverted her attention to Agnes, who was in the middle of describing their previous visit to the pier to an open-mouthed audience of her cousins.

'And then the poor horse, which was hanging in this sling up in the air ...' Agnes paused to add drama '... did his business all over the heads of the people watching him.'

'That's quite enough, Agnes,' Molly said, as the cousins dissolved into fits of giggles and Lewis, eyes like saucers, started retelling the story to them, creating more laughter. 'You know it didn't happen like that.'

She was wasting her breath, though. She turned to find Lizzie and Mary laughing at her.

'Agnes is quite a character, isn't she?' Lizzie said.

Molly sighed. 'She is. Talented and creative and strong-willed with it.'

93

'I wonder who she could take after,' Mary teased, taking her sister's arm.

Molly protested that she didn't possess an ounce of creativity then stopped short. If headstrong Agnes took after her, might she also run off one day after some unsuitable man? The idea was immediately upsetting.

She had no time to dwell on this for the dark clouds gathering out at sea suggested the onset of a summer storm. They all turned for home, skirts flapping in the sudden stiff breeze and bonnets clutched to heads. Lewis's little legs struggled to keep up with their pace and Mary swept him into her arms, carrying him as far as she could before a stitch in her side forced her to stop. Lizzie took over, then Molly, and so they arrived at Aunt Jane's, the whole party filling the front steps and the children squealing as heavy drops of rain began to fall.

Chapter Sixteen

Hannah opened the door to Lizzie's insistent knocking and everyone tumbled through it into the hallway, laughing and shrieking as a wave of squally rain swept across town.

'Heavens above!' Aunt Jane was in the hallway, too, hands over her ears but smiling at the same time. 'You got back just in time. I've been watching the dark clouds gather and hoped you wouldn't be caught out. I really thought we'd seen the last of the rain.'

Hannah struggled to shut the heavy door against the force of the wind as Molly, Lizzie and Mary jostled for position in front of the looking-glass on the wall, taking off their bonnets and attempting to tame their windblown hair.

'Hannah, take the little ones downstairs and see whether you can find some treats for them after their walk. Molly, Lizzie and Mary, come in here and tell me about your adventures.' Aunt Jane opened the drawing-room door and ushered them through. 'Hannah will bring us refreshments once the children are settled.'

Aunt Jane was no longer as spry on her feet as she had once been. She relied on others now for news from the outside world and, with Sarah away, she was missing younger company. Molly had already spent one night under her roof, dining with her aunt and uncle while Lizzie and Mary looked after her daughters next door. She had spent much of the evening trying not to look at a small portrait of Nicholas that still hung in the dining room, in defiance of the disgrace he had brought on the family. She had studiously avoided all mention of him during the evening, although her uncle had in any case dominated the conversation, always delighted to have a fresh audience.

Now, sitting in the drawing room, watching the rain beat against the window, Molly felt a pang of regret for the life she had left behind. If she hadn't left Margate for London, this might have been an everyday occurrence, taking tea with her aunt while her sisters and family lived happily next door. Then she scolded herself. If she had lived her life differently, would she have married such a loving, kind man as Charlie or had three delightful daughters?

Molly came back to the conversation just in time to hear 'Nicholas'. She hoped her face was inscrutable as she listened to what her aunt had to say but she had to still her shaking hands so that they didn't rattle her teacup against its saucer.

'We hear very little from him, as I'm sure you know,' Aunt Jane said. 'But we had heard nothing at all for such a long time that your uncle was moved to ask Captain Austen whether he had any naval acquaintances who might be passing through the West Indies and could make enquiries on our behalf. It has taken some time but we had news today.'

Aunt Jane drew in her breath and her lip quivered. 'It seems he was gravely ill when the captain's acquaintance came upon him. He refused all entreaties to return to England so the good man arranged for him to be moved to more comfortable quarters and left money with the natives there for his care.'

Aunt Jane pulled out a handkerchief and dabbed at her eyes. 'That was, of course, many weeks ago. We have no idea of his condition now. I don't know how to break the news to poor Sarah.'

Molly was surprised by how detached she felt. Nicholas was a stranger to her now, and even sitting in this room, she found it hard to remember the effect he had had on her sixteen years earlier. She was sure, though, that Aunt Jane must be distraught. Nicholas was her first born, her only son. Her aunt was disguising her grief as concern for Sarah, a façade she no doubt adopted to avoid provoking Uncle William, who judged his son more harshly for the disgrace he had brought on the family.

That night, alone in her bedroom in her aunt's house, her thoughts turned to her own son. He had never known his father, and it seemed unlikely that he would ever meet him now. Neither would he ever know his mother, although she supposed there was still a chance that their paths might cross in the future. Would she know him if they did? It seemed most unlikely, since she'd parted with him when he was just a few weeks old. It was on that uneasy thought that Molly drifted into a restless sleep.

The next day saw the end of their stay in Margate. Molly foresaw tears from the girls at being parted from their cousins and she delayed her departure from her aunt's breakfast table a little longer than she might have done. She made a point of going downstairs to say a proper goodbye to Hannah, promising to return before long.

'You'll have heard about Master Nicholas?' Hannah asked, her eyes on Molly's face.

'I have,' she said. 'You must take good care of Aunt Jane. She's trying to put a brave face on things but I know she must be very upset.'

She didn't want to be drawn into any further discussions about her cousin, and Hannah took the hint.

'Sarah will be back later today and she will be a comfort to your aunt,' she said.

Molly glanced sharply at Hannah but she appeared to intend no malice with her words so she nodded her agreement, gave her a hug and went back upstairs to make her farewells.

The arrival of the girls, their cousins and Molly's sisters put paid to any protracted goodbyes. The girls managed to be overexcited and tearful at the same time, and Molly noticed Aunt Jane wincing at the noise. To Molly's relief, the carriage drew up outside and she told her daughters to take their seats while she said her own farewells.

With everyone else now outside in the roadway, Molly turned to her aunt. 'I hope we haven't been too much for you, Aunt Jane. Thank you so much for having us here, and please pass on my thanks to Uncle William for arranging such a comfortable journey for us.' Molly wondered whether to bring up the subject of Nicholas, then decided against it. 'Hannah tells me that Sarah and Constance will be returning later. You will be glad of the company.'

'Indeed I will,' Aunt Jane said, embracing Molly. 'The house will be quiet without you all.'

Molly kissed her cheek, then hastened down the steps to the carriage, promising to return before too long.

She, too, began to feel tearful, bidding her sisters goodbye in turn. 'We live just a few miles apart. We have no excuse not to visit each other more often,' she said. She climbed into the carriage, then leant out through the window. 'I had almost forgotten – there's to be a garden party at Woodchurch Manor before the summer is out. You must come and join us there.'

Then she settled back into her seat and the coachman set off, guiding the horses through the Margate streets, encouraging them into a brisk trot once they were on the open road. Molly, who had enjoyed her stay away, now found her thoughts turning to home. She was looking forward to stepping back through her own front door, and to seeing Charlie. She listened to the girls' excited chatter as they discussed what they had seen and done. Her sisters' children were growing up fast. She must make the effort to bring the families together more often.

CHAPTER SEVENTEEN

Molly was a little put out that Charlie didn't appear to have missed them as much as she had expected. In fact, he seemed surprised to see them when he returned that evening.

'Back already?' he said.

Molly, about to chastise him for being so late home on their first evening back, saw how exhausted he was beneath the deep tan he developed every summer.

In any case, Charlie was already apologising. 'I'm sorry,' he said. 'I'd lost track of time. Since you left I've been working all hours to make sure we have the grounds ready for the garden party. Mr Powell has decided to hold it in two weeks' time.'

'So soon?' Molly was surprised.

'Well, August will be upon us and the date coincides with his sons returning home, as well as the arrival of some important guests. I daresay Mr Powell will be intent on impressing them.'

'The gardens always look lovely, Charlie,' Molly reassured him. 'Surely they won't need too much more work.'

She set about placing some food before her husband who, after giving her a hug, had seated himself at the table. He winced and sighed as he eased muscles that had been pushed hard all day.

'You must remember what it was like to get the gardens at Prospect House ready for an open day,' he said, dipping bread into his soup. Then he smiled wryly. 'But why would you? You only saw the results of our labours. We worked solidly for a month to get the gardens into perfect condition.'

'And then it rained and destroyed all your hard work.' Molly shook her head at the memory of flowers flattened by the rain, paths running with water, rose petals beaten from their blooms. 'But at least everyone had seen it by then.'

'We have just a fortnight left and there's a lot to be done,' Charlie said. 'All the flowerbeds need to be edged, the woodland walk cut back and cleared of any loose and overhanging branches, the fountain spruced up, the panes of the glasshouse cleaned – and that's before I even think about getting the flowers looking their best on the day.'

He laid down his spoon and a frown furrowed his brow. Molly had the feeling he was about to head straight back to the garden to tackle one of the jobs on the list, even though it was dark.

'Well, if you overtire yourself now it won't help anyone,' she soothed. 'Since Mr Powell wants everything made ready at short notice, can you ask him to hire some extra help?'

Molly knew her husband well and his expression told her all she needed to know. 'You prefer to work with your trusted team, of course,' she said hastily, 'but perhaps you could use extra labour on the woodland walk.'

Charlie grunted, but he picked up his spoon and began to eat again. Molly foresaw that there would be many more evenings like this before the weekend of the garden party.

Molly loved the gardens at Woodchurch Manor, but there were times when she felt stifled by their formality and then she would escape. She took off across the sweep of the fields surrounding the estate, her heart lifted by the flash of yellow tail feathers as the yellowhammers swooped along the hedgerows, calling to entice her away from the last broods in their nests. In tangled brambles below the hedges, rabbits scrambled for cover, flashing their white scuts at her approach.

With Charlie gone before breakfast and back after their bedtime, preoccupied by the gardens, Molly took the girls out nearly every day over the next fortnight to make the most of the spell of fair and settled weather. They picked woundwort and betony, mixing the red and pink flower spikes with the lilac pincushion heads of field scabious, still in flower at the edge of one meadow. The white froth of hedge parsley, found along the lane, made the perfect addition to take home to fill the jug on the kitchen windowsill.

While the girls chattered, stopping only to watch the rabbits bound along the path ahead of them, sometimes followed by the dash of a weasel in pursuit, Molly stood and looked up at the open skies and smiled, watching the swoop of the swallows. She loved the countryside and she wanted her girls to feel the same way about it. She hoped they would never want to leave it behind.

Agnes saw something to fascinate her wherever she looked. She was no painter of landscapes: for her, the detail of the brown and yellow whorls of an empty snail shell, the broken blue speckled eggshell of a robin or the detail of each individual floret on the flat panicles of hedge parsley was enough to absorb her. She was constantly being left behind by the others as they walked. Molly encouraged her to bring a basket and to collect her finds so that she could take them home and study them more closely. Soon, Sally and Catherine were copying her, Sally so that she could embroider the blooms and Catherine to make a picture from the pressed flower heads, first laying them between sheets of white blotting paper before piling books on top. Molly had been startled, then impressed, when she had arrived home with the blotting paper, struggling under the weight of some leather-bound volumes from the library at Woodchurch Manor. She declared them to be a loan, achieved by persuading Francis, the youngest son of the Powells, to procure them for her.

Francis and his brothers, Robert and Edward, were now at home for the holidays. Molly and her girls came across them early in the fortnight before the garden party, cutting switches of willow in the woodland bordering the estate. Robert and Edward smiled politely and moved on, but Francis had lingered to talk to Catherine. They had known each other throughout their childhood and had been friends until Francis was sent away to join his brothers at school nearly three years previously. They could meet only in the holidays now but Molly was pleased to see they took up their friendship again as though they had seen each other only days previously, rather than weeks.

On this particular day, Mr Powell was out too, walking a little way behind his sons. He greeted Molly and the girls cheerfully, telling Catherine to be sure to come up to the house to visit now that Francis was at home. As the girls and Francis walked on ahead, Mr Powell turned to Molly. 'I fear I've made your husband a stranger to you, with all the work he has to do to accommodate my whims for the garden party.'

Molly made polite noises, to signify that it was of no consequence, all the time wondering whether Charlie would be annoyed if she broached the subject of some extra help.

Mr Powell continued, 'I've invited your aunt and uncle, of course, but I believe you have sisters in Margate, Molly.

Would they care to come on the day, with their families, of course?'

Molly coloured, only too aware that she had invited them already, without considering that a formal invitation would be necessary. 'Thank you, sir. I will send to Margate to ask them. I'm sure they will be delighted.'

All thoughts of petitioning for extra help for Charlie were pushed from her mind by a sudden vision of the bonnet she had tried on in Mrs Hughes's shop. Surely nothing but a straw bonnet adorned with blue ribbons would do for such an important occasion as the garden party.

Molly's mind was made up and she determined to make the trip to Margate the very next day, using the excuse of needing to tell her sisters the date of the garden party. She could ride there with one of the carriers who came regularly to Woodchurch Manor – even more regularly now with so much work under way on the gardens. Ellen would look after the girls: Agnes and Catherine were more than happy to stay at home – Agnes so that she could get on with her drawing undisturbed and Catherine so that she could spend time with Francis. Sally, however, sighed and pouted when she heard of Molly's intentions.

'Why can't I come with you? I can spend some time with Susan and Helena while you visit Aunt Lizzie.'

'I'll be there such a short time,' Molly protested. 'It barely seems worth undertaking the journey.'

Sally's dark brows knitted in a frown. 'Then why don't you send them a letter to tell them of the garden party date?' she asked.

Molly was silenced. Sally was right: a letter would suffice. She would have to confess the true reason for her visit: to buy the bonnet. She still suffered pangs of guilt over spending money, thrift being second nature from her early years. Charlie, who cared nothing for his own appearance, regularly encouraged Molly to buy a new gown. 'We are comfortably off now,' he said, 'and you should spend accordingly.'

But the occasions when Molly felt the need to dress up were few and far between. It had dawned on her that the garden party might be one of those occasions. Indeed, if all went well and Mr Powell was pleased, he would undoubtedly praise Charlie in public. It would be no bad thing for him to have a new linen shirt and a silk cravat for the occasion.

That night, she broached the subject with Charlie. 'I plan to go to Margate tomorrow, to tell Lizzie and Mary of Mr Powell's kind invitation to the garden party.' She noticed Charlie's raised eyebrows and added, 'I came across him when I was out walking with the girls. I thought the trip would be a good opportunity to buy a bonnet that I saw on my last visit there. It will be useful should the sun be hot that day.' She noticed Charlie's expression change to one of amusement and she hastened to add, 'I thought you should have a new shirt and cravat. You will be on show that day, Charlie, and must look your best.'

The conversation was being conducted in the bedroom, where Charlie was seated on the edge of the bed. He'd removed his boots and began to pull his shirt over his head, barely able to keep his eyes open.

'Whatever you think best,' he said, trying to suppress a yawn. Then he climbed into bed, turning onto his side and pulling the sheet over himself.

Molly was quite taken aback. Charlie usually rejected any such efforts to smarten up his appearance.

'And Sally would like to come with me. I said no, but on reflection I think it would be a good idea. She's twelve now and growing fast – I should start to spend a little time with her on her own away from the other two.'

'Buy her something, too,' Charlie said sleepily.

Molly knew she couldn't buy something for Sally and return empty-handed to their other two daughters but she held her counsel. Perhaps Sally could help her choose something.

Charlie surprised her by speaking again as she slowly undid the buttons on her cuffs. She had been pondering her purchases and thought him asleep.

'Joshua Symonds has a wagon arriving here tomorrow from Margate with stone for the garden. Once it's unloaded it can carry you to Margate on its return journey,' he said.

Before Molly could respond, her husband's regular, deep breathing told her he was already fast asleep.

CHAPTER EIGHTEEN

Molly was awake early the following morning although not as early as Charlie, the cold space in the bed beside her a sign that he must have been up and gone before dawn. She breakfasted hastily and broke the news to her sleepy daughters that Sally would now be coming with her to Margate. This delighted Sally, who ran from the breakfast table in search of her smartest frock to wear for the trip, and raised a not-very-convincing grumble from Catherine. Molly knew she would have been cross if she had been separated from her playmate, Francis, to go to Margate.

By nine o'clock, Sally and Molly were waiting in the lane leading up to Woodchurch Manor. Molly considered that a good time for any deliveries from Margate to be arriving on the estate and, indeed, they had been standing there for just ten minutes, glad of the shade cast by the trees, for the sun was already strong, when they heard the sound of a horse's hoofs.

'A wagon?' Sally sounded hopeful.

The next moment a pair of carthorses came into view, pulling a wagon loaded with stone destined for the garden. Molly stepped forward while the wagon was still a little way off and waved it down. The driver slowed the horses to a walk as they came alongside Molly and Sally, and the young man in the seat beside him called down, 'What is it?'

'We'd be glad of a ride into Margate when you are done,' Molly called back up to him, keeping pace with the wagon. Her heart sank at the sight of the large load, though. They would have a long wait to make their trip.

The young man jumped down to stand beside them, signalling to the driver to continue on his way. Molly noticed that he was even younger than she had first thought, barely above Sally's age.

'There's another wagon behind this one,' the boy said. 'It carries the balance of the delivery and the load is smaller. We'll unload that one first and then you won't have so long to wait.'

Molly was impressed by his thoughtfulness. 'Thank you,' she said, turning her head at the sound of more horses in the lane.

The boy tipped his cap to her, nodded to Sally and set off in the direction of Woodchurch Manor, where the first wagon was already churning up clouds of dust as it went around the house to the courtyard.

'We might as well make ourselves comfortable while we wait,' Molly said to Sally, drawing her back towards the hedge as the second wagon trundled by. As the boy had promised, it was not as heavily laden, with bulging sacks rather than blocks of stone.

Mother and daughter perched on top of the five-barred gate that led from the lane into the field. Now that both wagons had passed, birdsong and the bleating of the sheep were the only sounds to disturb the peace. Sally jumped down from the gate after a while to pick flowers, even though Molly warned her that they would die before they reached

Margate from the heat of the sun and lack of any water to put them in.

True to the boy's word, the second wagon was back within the half-hour and this time he was with it. He jumped down on seeing them and the wagon drew to a halt.

'If you would like to sit up beside the driver,' he looked at Molly as he spoke, 'then I can sit in the back with . . .' He looked enquiringly at Sally. 'I'm Luke – Luke Symonds.'

'Molly Dawson,' Molly said. She was amused by the boy's confidence but a little put out at having to deal with the son of Joshua Symonds, a man she would have preferred no further contact with. 'And this is my daughter, Sally.'

Luke had already hopped up onto the wagon and shaken out some empty sacks to provide seating for himself and Sally.

'I hope you won't find it too dusty,' he said, reaching a hand down to Sally, who grasped it and climbed up.

Molly scrambled into the seat beside the driver, who nodded to her and shook the reins to encourage the horses to move on. They were still quite fresh, having travelled a short way that morning with only a light load, so they tossed their heads and took off down the lane at a smart pace.

As they turned onto the road leading to Margate, Molly glanced over her shoulder to make sure that Sally was all right. She expected to find her normally shy daughter sitting quietly, looking out over the fields. Instead, Luke was talking to her and she was nodding and smiling. The noise of the wagon as it rolled along and the clop of the horses' hoofs made it impossible for Molly to make out their conversation but she noted that Sally's cheeks were flushed and her eyes sparkling. She was more animated than her mother had ever seen before.

Molly cast anxious glances back over her shoulder as the journey continued, smiling reassuringly at Sally when she caught her eye. Sally smiled briefly in return, before turning back to Luke and grasping his sleeve to point out something in the meadow as they passed.

Molly began to wish that she hadn't conceived of the idea to bring Sally along for the outing. She had thought it would do her good to accompany her mother, but she hadn't anticipated this turn of events. She was thankful that the horses covered the road to Margate at quite a pace so Sally spent barely half an hour in Luke's company. Even so, Molly was ruffled by the time they arrived at Joshua Symonds's works, on the Westbrook side of Margate.

She was disposed to think of this as an inconvenience, being still a little way from the centre of town, even though in the past she had walked between Margate and Woodchurch Manor with barely a thought for the distance. Molly climbed off and shook out her skirts, then watched as Luke handed Sally down from the wagon as though it was the finest coach in town. To her annoyance, Molly could not fault the politeness of his farewell.

'It was a pleasure to make the acquaintance of you both,' he said. 'I hope we can be of service again when we deliver goods to Woodchurch Manor. I'm only sorry that we couldn't take you a little closer to town.'

He stood and watched them walk away, smiling, and Molly couldn't shake off the unpleasant reminder of how similar he looked to his father when his friends had tried to buy her for him at the Waterman's Inn in London. Molly couldn't suppress a shudder at the thought that he might be interested in Sally or – even worse – her daughter in him.

'Are you cold, Ma?' Sally asked, with some concern. 'If so, I fear you must have taken a chill for the sun could hardly be warmer.' She had taken off her bonnet and was using it to fan herself.

'No, I was just caught by the breeze off the sea,' Molly replied, which seemed to satisfy Sally. They continued on their way along the coast, dropping down to sea level as they approached Margate. Molly noticed that Sally was all but skipping along beside her, and she was unusually talkative. One or two young gentlemen cast admiring glances in her daughter's direction as they passed.

The visit to the milliner was first on Molly's list for the day. The bonnet she wanted was still there and she purchased it, but with less joy than she had imagined. She was preoccupied by the unwelcome discovery that her daughter had grown up overnight – even, perhaps, in the course of the short wagon journey. She bought a bonnet for Sally, too, and was forced to allow her to have one that made her look quite the young lady.

Mrs Hughes nodded approvingly. 'It suits you well, my dear,' she said, addressing Sally. 'The one you have is on the small side now – you must pass it down to one of your sisters. The gown, too,' she said, casting a meaningful glance at Molly.

Molly looked at her daughter with fresh eyes, as though she was a stranger to her, and registered at once that her dress was not only too short in the sleeves and the length, but that the bodice now fitted a little too snugly. In fact, the seams were showing signs of strain.

'Yes, yes, we intend to visit the dressmaker while we are here. Girls grow so quickly, these days.'

Molly was flustered: she had failed to register that her daughter was on the verge of womanhood and had been forced into a lie about plans to visit the dressmaker. This had not been on her list for the day, but now it must be addressed.

She was keen to get away from the shop but first Sally wished to choose decorations for Agnes and Catherine to pin to their bonnets. 'They must have something nice for the garden party, too,' she said.

Mrs Hughes pricked up her ears. 'Ah, that'll be the one at Woodchurch Manor, I expect. It's quite the social event of the summer. We've had several ladies in here in search of something new to wear. Lady Bridges and her daughter – even your aunt.'

She was smiling with satisfaction as she wrapped their purchases in tissue, while Molly tried not to let her impatience to be gone show on her face.

She was glad to close the door of the milliner's shop and turn in the direction of Thomas Broome, the tailor's further along the high street.

'We have purchases to make for your father, but first we must discover whether the dressmaker will see us without an appointment.' Molly shook her head. 'I don't know how I failed to notice that you were in such need. We must order at least two new dresses.' She looked at Sally as they walked along and felt her cheeks burn with shame. Surely everyone must be staring at them and wondering why she had allowed her daughter to appear in public in a dress so unsuitable.

CHAPTER NINETEEN

The dressmaker, Mrs Rowe, worked in her husband's drapery next door to Thomas Broome's. With a sense of relief Molly received the news that she could see them within half an hour, one of her customers having cancelled her appointment that morning.

That gave them time to buy a shirt and a cravat for Charlie. Men were far easier to shop for, Molly reflected. A shirt could be bought off the peg, without having to be tailor-made, as could a cravat, with no dithering over which fabric to choose. There were five cravats in stock and both Molly and Sally pointed out the same one, patterned in blue, knowing how well it would suit Charlie.

With another package added to their purchases, they went back to the dressmaker, where Mr Rowe gave them glasses of his wife's homemade lemonade – most welcome in the day's heat – while they waited. Molly had formed the habit of going to Canterbury to see a dressmaker there, but she had used Mrs Rowe – a favourite of her aunt and sisters – to make dresses for her daughters before.

Molly encouraged Sally to look through the bolts of fabric on display in preparation for their appointment. The choice wasn't as wide as it was at some of the other drapers on the high street but Molly still needed to see her sisters before they could return home. A limited choice of fabric would be a blessing today, Molly thought.

Sally deliberated only a short while before picking out two bolts of cloth – one a block-printed cotton, patterned in pink on a white background, which Molly could see at once would be a good choice for the garden party. The other was more formal in feel, in brown printed on cream, a choice that surprised Molly. But when Sally held the bolt up under her chin and let the fabric fall away, she could see at once how well it suited her colouring.

Mrs Rowe had come out from her little room at the back of the shop. 'You have a good eye,' she said, nodding approvingly at Sally. 'Now I see we must take a new set of measurements. You have grown since we last saw you here.'

Molly followed her daughter and the dressmaker through into the back room, where Sally was directed to a curtained alcove and told to remove her outer garments. Molly heard the dressmaker exclaim as she wielded her tape measure.

'Goodness me – you've added a full three inches to your height and well over an inch to your sleeves. And it won't be long before you'll be needing a corset.'

There was much giggling from behind the curtain before they were done, and then, while Sally dressed again, Mrs Rowe laid out her pattern books.

'I think there are only four or five designs suitable for a young lady such as you,' she said, when Sally emerged, flushed and ruffled from dressing in haste.

Molly joined them at the table, where Sally was pointing to a design with a neckline that her mother immediately felt to be too low.

'This one for the floral,' Sally said, 'and this one,' indicating a design with a higher neckline, 'for the other. It will do well for church.'

'A good choice.' Mrs Rowe looked pleased and made to pack away her books but Molly demurred.

'The neckline on this one is a little too low,' she said, pointing at Sally's first choice. 'My husband will not be pleased.' Charlie had never been known to comment on the design of any dress, but it seemed to carry more weight if she used him as an excuse.

'Oh, Ma,' Sally said, making a face, but Molly held firm.

'Well, that is easily solved,' the dressmaker said, always keen to keep her customers happy. 'A little drape of muslin at the neckline will maintain the style of the gown while modesty is preserved.' She demonstrated by gathering a length of fabric, looping it over Sally's shoulders and draping it so that the two halves met in the centre of her bodice.

Sally's brow relaxed from its knotted frown and a smile returned to her face. Molly was relieved that an argument had been deflected. 'Thank you,' she said. 'We would like the flowered dress sent over as quickly as possible but the other can follow.'

She paid quickly, trying to suppress her alarm at how quickly the money Charlie had given her that morning was vanishing. Then she and Sally went back out on to the high street, turning in the direction of Princes Crescent, as Molly realised how hungry she felt. Breakfast had been a long time ago.

'Now we'll go to Aunt Lizzie's, to see if she will feed us,' Molly said.

'My feet hurt,' Sally said. 'I think they must have grown, too.'

They both looked down, Molly in consternation, Sally wincing. Margate didn't lack for shoemakers – there were at least four on the high street, and several others in Cranbourn Alley close by, including the one Molly usually frequented. She thought about the depleted contents of her pocket and wondered whether all the walking on hard surfaces in hot weather might have caused Sally's boots to pinch her toes.

'We may have to save the shoemaker for another visit,' Molly said. 'Do you think you can walk as far as Princes Crescent?'

Sally sighed and nodded so they set off, at a much slower pace than Molly would have liked. Her daughter hobbled and grimaced, and Molly clutched all the packages in an attempt to ease the journey for her, while the sun beat down mercilessly without a breath of wind to freshen the air.

'Goodness me! You both look quite done in,' Lizzie exclaimed, as she opened the door to their knock some twenty minutes later. 'Why didn't you let me know you were coming?'

Molly fell gratefully through the door into the cool interior of the kitchen and collapsed onto the nearest chair. The string handles of the packages had dug into the soft flesh of her palms and sweat ran in rivulets down her back. She looked at Sally, who was quite scarlet in the face, and supposed she must feel much the same.

Sally sat down on the doorstep to unlace her boots, unable to walk a step further. Molly flinched when she saw how her daughter's stockings had rubbed away around the toes and heels, exposing the bright red, sore flesh beneath.

'Oh, Sally, it's worse than I thought. The heat must have made your feet swell. But however are you going to get your boots back on to go home?'

Molly made to get up to assist her daughter but Lizzie spoke firmly.

'No, you stay there. I'll see to this. Sally, I'm going to fetch some water in a bowl and you're to sit and soak your feet. Now go and sit on a chair, there's a good girl.'

Lizzie went out to the pump in the yard with a shallow enamel bowl, while Sally limped painfully to a chair.

Was there ever a worse mother? Molly wondered. How could she have failed to notice how quickly her daughter had grown? Then Lizzie was back, setting the bowl at Sally's feet. Sally gasped as she lowered her feet into the water and Lizzie, kneeling beside her, looked up at her.

'Keep them there as long as you can. I know it's cold but it will help to ease the pain. I do declare you've grown since I last saw you, just a few weeks ago. You're quite the young lady now.'

Sally looked pleased to be referred to so, but Molly sighed.

'I'm glad you think it's sudden – I was worrying over how I could have missed it.'

Lizzie got to her feet and laughed. 'Well, I expect you could both do with some refreshment. You've been busy in Margate this morning.' She nodded towards the pile of packages. 'I'll see whether I have a pair of boots that Sally can borrow. In any case, I'm sure Aunt Jane will let you use the carriage to go home. She's always complaining what a waste of money it is to keep it, since it gets used so rarely.'

Lizzie had been to the market that morning and had smoked fish and an array of shellfish to offer them, as well as the usual bread and cheese. Molly thought food had never tasted so delicious, or lemonade so refreshing, and she and Sally made short work of what Lizzie laid out for them.

'I need to fetch Susan and Helena from next door,' Lizzie said, taking off her apron. 'They've spent the morning with

117

Constance. I'll ask Aunt Jane about the carriage while I'm there.'

Molly pushed aside her plate. 'I nearly forgot – I didn't come to Margate just to shop and then to eat all the food in your larder,' she said to her sister. 'I wanted to tell you that the garden party is on Saturday week and you're all invited by Mr Powell – Mary, Michael, Paul and the children, too.'

'That's just a few days away,' Lizzie exclaimed. She looked at the packages and smiled. 'It explains all the purchases.'

Then she went to fetch the children and the sisters passed a happy half-hour together until a knock at the door announced the arrival of the coachman with Uncle William's carriage, now kept at the Church Street stable-yard.

'What about your boots?' Molly said to Sally, getting to her feet to gather the packages together.

'I can go home without them!' Sally said, making for the door in stockinged feet, her boots held by their laces.

'That won't help you when you get home,' Lizzie said. 'Wait here a minute,' and she ran upstairs. She returned half a minute later clutching a pair of scuffed boots. 'I'm sure these are bigger than the pair you have and they're of no use to me. My feet grew a little, I swear, when I had Helena.' She laughed and ruffled her daughter's hair. 'They need a good polish but there's plenty of wear left in them and they'll never fit me again.'

Molly and Sally departed, with a promise from Lizzie that the families wouldn't miss the garden party for all the world. The return journey was conducted at a smart pace, the horses glad of the exercise. Molly and Sarah were at home well within the hour, greeted by Agnes and Catherine clamouring to see what they had bought.

CHAPTER TWENTY

Charlie came home very late that night, and Molly was dozing in her chair, his dinner keeping warm on the range, when she heard the back door open. She recounted the events of their day in Margate to him as he ate his pie, pausing to admonish him to eat more slowly or he'd have belly-ache later.

'And you'll never guess what happened on the journey there.' Molly, preoccupied with confessing to Charlie that she had failed to notice how their eldest daughter had grown, suddenly remembered the first event of the day.

'Joshua Symonds's son Luke was sitting in the back of the wagon with Sally and I declare he was paying attention to her, or she to him. Either way, there appeared to be a good deal more to the conversation than the weather.' Molly grew indignant just thinking about it.

Charlie chuckled. 'Is that such a bad thing?'

'Charlie!' Molly was shocked. 'Why, yes, she's not long turned twelve.' She glared at him, although the light was so dim in the kitchen that Charlie was oblivious. She got up to light a candle.

'She could do a lot worse,' Charlie remarked.

Molly stared at him, the lit taper halfway to the candle's wick. 'Whatever do you mean?'

'A good family with a solid business. From what I've seen of him, he's a respectful and respectable young man. It would be a good match.'

'For goodness' sake, Charlie. She's far too young.'

Charlie pushed away his plate and clasped his hands in front of him on the table. 'Molly, it won't be long before she starts looking for a young man, or a young man comes looking for her. We're a little out of the way here at Woodchurch Manor and that's both a good thing and a bad thing. We can't expect our daughters to be considered a suitable match for the Powell boys, but we should start to think towards the future. I for one would be very happy to see a link between our family and that of Joshua Symonds.'

Molly tried to suppress a shudder and hoped that Charlie hadn't noticed. She would do anything to avoid putting their family on a friendly footing with Joshua Symonds. And Charlie's flat statement of the truth about the Powells had caused her a pang, too. Catherine was very close to Francis. They were just children, it was true, but surely heartbreak lay ahead when she realised their paths must diverge, and for ever?

Charlie stood up and cleared away his plate. 'I must go to my bed. Just a few more days and it will all be over. Then our life can return to normal and I'll be fit company for you again.' He kissed Molly, then turned and wearily mounted the stairs. She noticed how his clothes were hanging off his frame – the hard work and the long hours in the garden had taken their toll.

Molly sat on, staring unseeing at the glow cast by the candlelight on the surface of the table. Nothing stayed the same, it seemed. Just as she had felt their lives were settled and they could reap the benefits of Charlie's hard work on the estate, she was forced to contemplate the potential dangers and disappointments that lay ahead for her girls. She must do all she could to protect them. She remembered her own thoughtless, naive journey into womanhood. Not for the first time, she resolved that this would not be the path her daughters followed. For them, the future should be bright, their prospects good. Overcome with weariness, she took up the candle and slowly mounted the stairs to bed.

Molly filled the remaining days before the party by taking the girls outdoors whenever the weather permitted. Charlie was still out of the house more than he was in it and he was delighted when they had a day of rain, but Molly's heart sank at the thought of being confined to the house all day. Since the Powell boys had come home for the holidays her daughters had become rebellious, declaring they deserved a holiday, too, and needed a break from their lessons.

Thankfully, the wet day brought an invitation from Woodchurch Manor for the girls to spend the afternoon there. They returned full of tales of hide-and-seek played up and down the great panelled stairway and along the landings. They also had plenty to report about the lavish entertainments that Mr Powell had planned for the garden party. Molly protested that surely it was a simple open day, a chance for locals and invited guests to stroll and admire the lake and the flowers, and to take tea in the garden. She had in mind the kind of garden party that used to take place each year at Prospect House in Margate.

Yet as she listened to tales of the peafowl Mr Powell had had sent over from India, and of the famous musicians from London, who had been invited to play on the terrace, she began to have doubts. 'There will be a strolling magician,' Catherine assured her, eyes shining with excitement. 'And jugglers. And someone eating fire.'

Did Mr Powell plan to try to recreate one of the London pleasure gardens at Woodchurch Manor? Molly resolved to ask Charlie more about it that night, expecting him to laugh and declare it all nonsense. Instead, he sighed. 'Mr Powell has got carried away with the idea. He's bringing all sorts of entertainment down from London. I'm not sure what the folk around here will make of it. The party is to continue after dark now. We're to string lanterns in the trees on the woodland walk and he's talking about digging roasting pits at the back of the stables so he can feed his guests into the evening.'

Molly was temporarily lost for words. Then she felt a surge of indignation on Charlie's behalf. 'Is there any point in you taking such pains over preparing the grounds? What attention will anyone pay to them if they have peacocks and jugglers and who-knows-what to distract them?'

Charlie laughed at her cross face and got up from the table – where he had eaten his dinner but barely tasted a mouthful, being so preoccupied – to give her a hug. 'I feel much the same, but Mr Powell wants the grounds to be perfect so I must do my best.' He sighed. 'Only two more days and it will all be over. I can barely remember what life was like before this began.'

'Mr Powell must allow you time off when it is done with,' Molly said to Charlie's back, as he wearily mounted the stairs to bed. He showed no sign of having heard her but Molly resolved to speak up on his behalf. If the garden party was a success, no doubt Mr Powell would wish to repeat it every year. She wasn't sure how the family would weather the toll that it took on Charlie.

CHAPTER TWENTY-ONE

The day of the garden party dawned fair. Molly looked out at clouds when she awoke but they were high and white, not grey. She felt sure the omens were good, although she'd suffered a nightmare in which the heavens opened, sending torrents of rain onto the guests whom Mr Powell had directed to shelter in Charlie and Molly's house. When she found herself sharing a kitchen with a bedraggled peafowl while she searched the larder to find food to feed the refugees from the storm, she'd woken in a panic. It had quickly receded, leaving a sense of relief. It had still been dark but Charlie was no longer beside her in the bed and Molly wondered just how many hours he had slept that night.

She took his linen shirt from the press and laid it with the silk cravat on the bed alongside the dress she had chosen. It was a plain blue one, to match the ribbons on her bonnet. It was important that she, but more particularly Charlie, looked well that day. The challenge would lie in making sure he returned home in time to change. Resolving that Agnes and Catherine should be given the job of persuading him, she went downstairs to make sure that everyone breakfasted well.

This proved to be harder than she had expected. The girls were now thoroughly overexcited by what lay ahead and were already determined to get into their frocks and set off for Woodchurch Manor.

'It's too early,' Molly said firmly. 'You're not to put them on until just before the gates open at three o'clock, or Heaven knows what state you'll be in. Agnes and Catherine, I will need you to go and fetch your father an hour before then so he can wash and change and look presentable. He will argue with you, but don't take no for an answer.'

She had imagined it would be a struggle to keep them occupied until it was time to leave but no sooner had the girls eaten a sketchy breakfast than they were off, hair roughly brushed and, Molly feared, faces barely clean, to see who or what was arriving at Woodchurch Manor.

She discovered later that they had spent the time sitting atop the five-barred gate that had served as a seat when she and Sally waited for their wagon ride to Margate. It had been the perfect vantage point to watch all the comings and goings – deliveries of provisions to the kitchen, the arrival of chairs and tables piled higgledy-piggledy on the backs of several wagons, musicians crammed into carriages, their instrument cases strapped to the roofs. It was only when more carriages began to arrive, bearing guests who were planning to stay at Woodchurch Manor, bringing a great number of trunks and boxes with them, that Sally suggested they should return home to get ready.

'We don't want to miss the start of the party,' she said. 'Agnes and Catherine, go and fetch Pa now.'

Her sisters set off obediently and Sally hurried home across the fields, to find Molly looking anxiously at the clock.

'There you are! I was beginning to worry that nobody would be ready on time.' Molly had already changed her gown, partly to keep occupied as her anxiety grew and partly to make sure she could devote herself to Charlie and the girls once they arrived home.

She sent Sally upstairs, preceded by Ellen with a jug of warm water for washing, then looked anxiously out of the window for signs of Agnes and Catherine bringing Charlie home. Sally's need for help with the buttons of her new gown drew her away from the window and upstairs where, with a sense of relief, she finally heard voices in the kitchen as she brushed Sally's hair.

'Is that you? Is your father with you?' she called down.

'Yes, we're back. Pa's following.' Catherine was clattering up the stairs and arrived in the bedroom as she finished speaking. 'Oh,' she said, on seeing Sally, who had just stood up from the end of the bed. 'How lovely you look!'

Molly turned her distracted gaze on her eldest daughter. Her cheeks were pink, whether from that morning's sun or the sudden attention, Molly wasn't sure. The dress made her look somehow taller, Molly thought, and certainly older. It fitted beautifully, which only made it more obvious that her other clothes did not.

Molly suppressed a sigh, giving Sally a beaming smile. 'You do look lovely. Pa will be proud of you.'

'Who will I be proud of?' She hadn't heard Charlie come in and up the stairs and now he was peering enquiringly around the door of the girls' bedroom.

'We're going to be late if you don't hurry and get changed,' she scolded, pushing past him to call to Ellen to bring up more water.

She went into her own bedroom, to give Charlie a moment or two with Sally but also to gather herself. The sight of Sally, so grown-up all at once, had moved Molly to tears. The door swung open and Molly turned, a bright smile fixed to her face, only to find Ellen backing through it with a heavy china jug in each hand.

'I'll take one of those. Please go and help Agnes and Catherine to wash and change and send Charlie here,' Molly said.

She was now focused on getting everyone clean and presentable and over to the gardens as soon as possible. They made more than one false start on the way, Catherine forgetting her bonnet and having to run back and Agnes standing stock still and announcing that she was faint with hunger, which earned her short shrift from her mother.

'You should have eaten your breakfast,' she said. 'You'll have to wait now. There'll be plenty to eat at the garden party, I'm sure.'

Although Molly had thought they were in good time – it was barely ten minutes past the hour when they arrived at the back of the house – they found the grounds already busy. Sally had been in favour of going to the front of the house, 'The proper way,' as she said, but Charlie was having none of it.

'Why would I do that?' he said, and led them there via his usual route so that they entered close to the walled garden. Molly thought how handsome he looked in his new linen shirt and Sunday-best jacket, the blue cravat loosely knotted at his throat. His tanned skin could barely hide his fatigue, though, or the gauntness of his cheeks. And she was sure that a thread or two of silver had appeared in his hair, caught by the sun as he turned his head. She reached out to take his hand, wanting to tell him how proud she was of him and the girls. He looked down at her and everything around her fell away as she gazed into his eyes. She opened her mouth to speak – but Sally's exclamation distracted him.

'Oh, Pa – just look!'

The family stopped in surprise at the sight of so many people already in the grounds. Couples were already strolling across the lawns and along the paths, stooping to sniff the flowers in the borders. Molly hoped Charlie had noticed and that it would make all his hard work seem worthwhile. The warmth of the sun brought a heady waft of perfume across the gardens and she turned to Charlie to ask him what it might be, only to have her attention caught by the sight of Mr Powell bearing down on them with a couple of gentlemen in tow. She was about to lose her husband once more to his employer.

'I beg your pardon, Mrs Dawson. I hope you'll excuse us for a moment. Charlie, could you tell these good friends of mine how it is that you have coaxed such a profusion of blooms from the roses?' Mr Powell drew Charlie away to explain how he had worked his magic.

Molly turned to her daughters and was about to suggest that they went in search of something for Agnes to eat but it seemed that all hunger was forgotten in the excitement promised by the afternoon. With barely an apology, her daughters excused themselves from her company and took off over the lawn, hardly able to restrain themselves from breaking into a run.

'Girls – behave yourselves. I'll be watching,' Molly called after them, but her warning fell on deaf ears.

She set off in the direction of the main throng. She must resign herself to being without her own family for the afternoon, Molly thought, but at least she wouldn't be alone. She spotted Uncle William and Aunt Jane almost immediately, then her sisters and their families, and made her way towards them with a glad heart.

If Molly had imagined a relaxing afternoon lay ahead, she was mistaken. Her Margate visitors demanded a full tour of the grounds, during which she caught glimpses of her own family: Charlie with Mr Powell and a different set of his acquaintances, now discussing the pineapples in the walled garden; Catherine and Agnes playing hide-and-seek in and out of the woodland garden with the Powell boys; Sally deep in conversation by the lake with Luke Symonds. The latter caused her footsteps to falter as she was leading the party back towards the house in search of tea, resulting in Mary bumping into her.

'What is it? Have you spotted the peacock I hear has been got especially for today?' Mary, shielding her eyes against the sun, followed the direction of Molly's gaze. 'Why, is that Sally? How she has grown! And who is the handsome young man she is talking to?' Mary nudged Molly and laughed, then registered her expression. 'Whatever is wrong?'

'She's too young,' Molly said. 'And I'm not sure that he *is* a suitable young man.'

She turned abruptly away, leaving Mary puzzled, only to come face to face with Joshua Symonds, arm in arm with a lady she supposed must be his wife.

'Ah, Mrs Dawson,' Joshua said. 'May I present my wife, Lucy? And my younger son, Jacob.' His gaze was drawn in the same direction as Molly's had been earlier. 'My elder son, Luke, seems already to have made the acquaintance of one of the loveliest young ladies here.'

Molly acknowledged Lucy with a nod but failed to force a smile. 'Luke is talking to my eldest daughter, Mr Symonds. And she is indeed young. Not yet thirteen.'

Joshua appeared oblivious to Molly's frostiness. 'I would be honoured to make her acquaintance,' he said. 'But it appears the pair of them have become aware of our attention and made their escape.'

When Molly turned, there was indeed no sign of Luke and Sally. Her aunt and sisters were, however, loitering close behind her so she was duty bound to make the introductions.

After the required few minutes of conversation she felt able to suggest that her party moved away in search of tea, leading to polite farewells all round.

'What a charming man,' Lizzie exclaimed, as soon as they were out of earshot.

'I really don't see why you object to his son's friendship with Sally,' Mary said. 'I know them to be a prosperous family and, I would have thought, good acquaintances to have.'

Molly, unable to explain the real cause of her aversion to Joshua Symonds, was forced to maintain a cross silence as they progressed through the crowds in search of tea. Aunt Jane persuaded Uncle William to procure two tables to push together to accommodate their party. It was harder to find enough chairs to seat them all although luckily Lizzie and Mary's children were happy enough on the grass and the men declared they would prefer to stand. First, however, they were despatched to fetch tea and returned shortly afterwards bearing teacups, and plates piled high with sweet pastries.

Molly realised how thirsty she was, and hungry, too, after their tour of the grounds. She was restored to a better humour after drinking two cups of tea and eating a quantity of pastries when she saw Betsy, the young maid, picking her way through the tea tables in their direction.

'If you please, ma'am,' she said, addressing Molly as she arrived at her side, 'Mr Powell said could you make your way at once to the bandstand.' She pointed out the circular platform that Mr Powell had had installed on the lawn, to accommodate his hired musicians.

'Do you know why?' Molly asked, reluctant to stir now that the party was settled.

'I couldn't say, miss—I mean ma'am.' Betsy looked flustered, glancing back over her shoulder to where her presence was required, ferrying cakes and fancies from the kitchens to the main tea table.

'Thank you, Betsy.' Molly let her go, then sat on for a minute or two, staring across the crowded lawn. It was a kaleidoscope of colour from the summery outfits and hats of the ladies. Mrs Hughes had been right in saying that it was the event of the summer, Molly thought. Then her eye was caught by the figure of Mr Powell, Charlie at his side, progressing through the crowds in the direction of the bandstand.

She sighed and turned to her companions. 'It looks as though my presence is required. But do stay here. At least I will know where to find you afterwards.'

She stood, smoothed her gown, checked the ribbons on her bonnet and began to make her way towards the bandstand. She hoped Mr Powell was about to heap a great deal of praise on Charlie.

CHAPTER TWENTY-TWO

Molly was not disappointed. Mr Powell had procured a military drum and he took great delight in performing a drumroll with quite a flourish. It certainly attracted the attention of his visitors, many of whom began to move towards the bandstand.

Mr Powell had a confident, carrying voice and, with his wife at his side, he welcomed all the guests to the garden party.

'This is the first time we have opened the grounds in this way and I hope it won't be the last,' he said. 'It wouldn't have been possible without the dedication of our head gardener, Mr Charles Dawson, who has worked tirelessly to ensure that the garden is at its peak. He has paid attention to the tiniest detail and indulged my every whim, creating a whole new rock garden especially for today, which I hope you will find the time to visit.'

He beckoned Charlie to join him on the raised bandstand. Molly could see her husband's cheeks were already flushed from the unwanted attention and he ducked his head in embarrassment as clapping and cheering greeted his arrival.

Molly, smiling at hearing him referred to as Charles, was clapping enthusiastically when Mr Powell held up his hand for silence. 'We must also thank his lady wife, who has barely seen her husband in the last month and has probably had to put up with no end of complaints about the unreasonable behaviour of his employer.' Polite laughter greeted this remark. 'In addition, she has had to bring up her three delightful daughters during this period without the guiding hand of her husband. Mrs Dawson, I ask you to join us, too.'

It was Molly's turn to flush scarlet. She wondered for a moment whether she could flee but Mr Powell was beckoning to her and Mrs Powell was smiling and nodding to encourage her. So, on legs made suddenly shaky, she pushed her way through to the steps and mounted the bandstand.

Standing beside Charlie she gazed out over the sea of faces without recognising a soul, while Mr Powell was saying something she didn't take in but caused the onlookers to laugh and clap. She tried to raise a smile but felt her lips tremble so she grasped Charlie's hand and squeezed it, hoping it might bring her courage.

Then Mrs Powell presented her with a posy of flowers and she dropped a half-curtsy, unsure of what to do, while Mr Powell shook Charlie's hand with vigour. A moment later, she and Charlie were going down the steps again, side by side. Strangers in the crowd clapped Charlie on the back and the ladies on their arm smiled at Molly. She tried to smile back, all the while fearing her face was contorted into some awful grimace as she attempted to steer Charlie in the direction of the tea tables. Here she hoped they could be anonymous once more.

Aunt Jane and Uncle William were much inclined to make a fuss, though, standing up to offer their congratulations to Charlie, while the occupants of the surrounding tables watched with interest.

'My dear Molly, you must be so proud of Charlie,' Aunt Jane exclaimed. 'And for Mr Powell to have mentioned you in such a way . . .' Aunt Jane clasped Molly's hand in hers, narrowly avoiding crushing the posy. 'Such an honour!'

'You heard it all up here?' Molly asked faintly.

'Indeed.' Uncle William spoke up. 'Mr Powell has a fine voice.'

Molly was quite ready to sink back into her chair and, she hoped, obscurity, but her aunt and uncle had yet more to say.

'You have made a very fortunate marriage, my dear,' Aunt Jane said, supposedly into Molly's ear but loud enough so that Lizzie and Mary could hear. Molly saw them roll their eyes and had to stifle a sudden urge to giggle. 'It is clear that Mr Powell thinks very well of your husband. Very well indeed. It will benefit your girls in the future, I'm sure. But you must take them in hand, my dear. They should be sitting here with us, not running half wild around the gardens.'

Molly was instantly serious again. In that respect, she feared her aunt was right. She ought to find the girls and make them sit with their cousins and behave like ladies. Heaven only knew what they were up to. She looked around to see whether she could spot them and was all for setting off in search but Charlie wanted to eat something and Uncle William was solicitously fetching more food, then ale for the gentlemen since they had done their duty by the tea. Molly was reluctant to part from Charlie, having only so recently had him delivered back into her company. She moved her chair to sit a little closer to him and snatched a moment, when the conversation swirled around them but didn't involve them, to tell him what she'd tried to say before: how proud she was of him, and not only for what he had achieved that day. He squeezed her hand in response and was about to reply, when Lizzie came around the table and stood between them, declaring that she had been trying to attract Molly's attention for a good ten minutes. The moment was lost, swept away by the social chatter that took up the rest of the afternoon.

It was early evening before Molly finally stirred to seek out her daughters. Mr Powell had invited his guests to stay on as dusk fell to appreciate the grounds lit up, or so Lizzie said. Molly had been too embarrassed by the ordeal of her public thanks to have paid any attention to his subsequent words. Aunt Jane suggested a final turn around the grounds before they returned to their carriages. Charlie said that the lanterns would be lit in the woodland walk by now so the party set off, Molly noting that the earlier crowds had thinned considerably. She took Charlie's arm, enjoying the sensation of walking at his side – it had been all too rare a pleasure these past weeks. Yet even as she breathed in the scent of roses as they set off in the direction of the lake and the woodland walk, she was aware that Charlie's attention was elsewhere. He was on the lookout as they walked, head turning from side to side. She thought he was making a mental note of the areas that would need tending once the visitors had departed. Even she could see how the lawns had suffered under so many feet and where the flowers in the borders had been damaged as people brushed past. Even worse, Molly noticed that some visitors had felt it acceptable to help themselves to blooms and she would have glared at them if she hadn't also been carrying a posy.

The landscape was more natural around the wooded area, where the lanterns had indeed been lit. The reflections sparkling in the dark waters of the lake caused the party to stop and admire the effect.

'What a splendid idea,' Aunt Jane exclaimed. 'Mr Powell has such imagination. I would never have thought of doing such a thing and it must have been a lot of work. But how lovely it is.'

Molly only just managed to prevent herself saying that this was far from unusual in London, where the many pleasure gardens had been lighting their grounds at night for some years now. It might have led to awkward questions about how she knew of such things. Then Charlie stopped suddenly, his head turned away from the lake that they were all admiring. Molly followed the direction of his gaze, which was quite fixed.

In the gathering gloom along the edge of the woodland, Molly caught sight of Sally arm in arm with the unmistakable figure of Luke Symonds. They were briefly silhouetted by the lanterns at the entrance to the woodland walk before they vanished into the darkness beyond.

'Would you excuse me?' Charlie said, disengaging himself from Molly. He nodded to her aunt and uncle, then strode off towards the woodland walk. Molly would have followed him but her aunt exclaimed, 'Isn't that Agnes? And Catherine?'

Molly followed her pointing finger and there, on the lake, were her daughters – in a boat being rowed by one of the Powell boys. She couldn't tell who was at the oars but as she watched one of the other boys stood up and the boat began to rock alarmingly. She could hear her daughters' cries as they carried across the water, but they were of laughter rather than alarm so she bit her lip and hoped that the culprit would sit down quickly.

'Good heavens,' Uncle William said. 'They'll have the boat over if they're not careful. Who's that in there with them?'

'The Powell boys,' Molly said. 'They're very used to the boat. I'm sure all will be well.' She tried to sound more convinced than she felt.

The party watched, all thoughts of the woodland walk gone from their minds. The gathering dusk made it hard to keep track of the boat's progress but there had been no loud splash or further cries from over the water so Molly reasoned they must be safe. It was, however, definitely time to collect the girls and take them home.

Unsure of what to do first, she half turned towards the woodland walk, just in time to see Charlie emerge with Sally.

'Ah, here is Sally at last,' she said brightly, as they approached, only too aware that her family had barely seen her daughter all afternoon. Even in the dusk, Sally's heightened colour was obvious to Molly and she caught the glint of tears in her eyes. She glanced at Charlie, who was unusually grim-faced, but before she could say anything, Uncle William addressed him.

'I think you'd better fetch your other daughters, too. They're out on the lake in a rowing boat.'

Molly experienced a flash of anger: her uncle clearly enjoyed being the bearer of bad news. Had he been envious of Charlie's success that day, honoured in a speech of thanks by Mr Powell? Was this his way of bringing Charlie, a former poorhouse boy, down a peg or two?

If that was the intention, it was wasted on Charlie who barely acknowledged his words before striding off around the lake in search of Agnes and Catherine. Meanwhile, Lizzie and Mary were exclaiming over Sally's new dress and telling her how well she looked. Her tears seemed to have subsided and very soon Sally was absorbed into the family, her cousins hanging off her skirts and demanding to know where she'd been all afternoon.

Aunt Jane observed the scene for a moment, then turned to Molly. 'She's growing up fast. You'd do well to keep an eye on her,' she said. She kept her voice low, for which Molly was grateful. 'You can't keep her at home for ever. Have you decided what's to be done with her?'

Molly felt the implied criticism. She hadn't thought too far into the future – she had supposed her daughters would stay at home with her until they married. On today's evidence, though, it must look to her aunt and uncle as though she was allowing them to run wild. 'She's going to be apprenticed to a seamstress,' she said. 'She's a good needlewoman. I plan to make enquiries in Margate.' Molly had had no such thoughts until that very moment, but it was an inspired move.

'Good.' Aunt Jane nodded approvingly. 'Without your mother to guide you, it falls to me to make sure that all is done for the best. She must lodge with us, of course. Lizzie and Mary have no room, but they will be there for her, too, just next door.'

And with that, Molly realised the next chapter in her eldest daughter's life was decided. She thought it would be wise to remove Sally before her aunt spoke out in front of her.

'Please excuse us, everyone,' she said, taking Sally's arm. 'We must go and find Agnes and Catherine so I'm afraid it's time to say goodbye. I hope you enjoy the woodland walk. Tell me about it when I'm next in Margate. Which will be very soon, I'm sure,' she added hastily, with a glance in her aunt's direction. Then she drew Sally away at some speed across the lawns.

Molly's head was pounding. She loosened the ribbons of her bonnet and let it fall to her shoulders, then turned to look at Sally. 'Where is *your* bonnet?' she demanded.

'Oh!' Sally's hand flew to her mouth. 'I must have lost it. I think I put it down somewhere.' She wouldn't meet Molly's eye.

Molly closed her eyes briefly, then took Sally's arm again without a word and marched her around the edge of the lake. They found Charlie by the landing stage, surrounded by five figures with down-cast heads. Sally and Molly arrived in time to hear the end of their scolding.

'This could have ended with something much worse than wet feet. I'll be speaking to your father about this, boys. Agnes, Catherine, your mother is here. It's time to go home.'

Agnes and Catherine raised their heads to protest but, catching sight of their mother's stern face, thought better of it.

The three girls trailed behind Molly and Charlie as they went back through the gardens, towards home.

'I don't imagine Mr Powell will say anything to his sons,' Charlie said, speaking quietly. 'No doubt he'll be inclined to put it down to high spirits. But the girls could have drowned if the boat had capsized.' He shuddered. 'I dare say the boys can swim.'

They walked on in silence, each wrapped in their thoughts, until Molly rallied to say, 'Don't let it spoil a wonderful day. The garden party was a success, Charlie. You should be very proud of yourself.' She reached for his hand and squeezed it. 'Although I hope it isn't so successful that Mr Powell decides to hold one every year . . .'

CHAPTER TWENTY-THREE

The garden party was a talking point in the area for quite some time, not least because Mr Powell had caught a few local boys – farm hands and, it was rumoured, his eldest son Robert – 'up to no good' in the woodland walk, as Ellen, Molly's maid, had described it.

He'd gone down there late in the evening, intending to take some house guests for a final walk before the lanterns were extinguished, only to be alerted to what was going on by the discovery of empty ale flagons by the path and the sound of scuffling and laughter from the nearby glade.

'Some of the young servants were there, too,' Ellen said.

Molly didn't want to be drawn into the conversation beyond venturing, 'Betsy?'

'I really couldn't say,' Ellen said, although she looked as though she was keen to continue.

'Well, I daresay Mr or Mrs Powell will deal with it,' Molly said. Would Sally have been among their number, she wondered, if Charlie hadn't spotted her earlier in the evening? Not for the first time, Molly feared history repeating itself. None of her daughters could be allowed to make the mistakes she had made.

After a restless night, filled with worries about how best to punish her daughters for their behaviour at the garden party, it had fallen to Molly to deal with it. Charlie had slipped away at first light, keen to begin the work of restoring the gardens after the wear and tear of so many visitors. She called the girls into the parlour after a subdued breakfast, having resolved to give them a stern lecture.

'Your behaviour yesterday reflected very badly on this family. It was a special day for your father, who had worked so hard to make sure that everything was perfect for Mr Powell. My own family had come from Margate and wished to see you but they caught barely a glimpse. You were all too busy behaving as though you lack any sense. Sally,' Molly focused her attention on her eldest daughter, 'you should have been setting an example to your sisters. Instead you were flaunting yourself in an unseemly manner with a young man who should have known better. I'm ashamed of you all.'

Molly was quite pink in the face as she remembered the expression on her aunt and uncle's faces. Far from looking contrite, though, she could see that her daughters were sullen and Catherine was actually glaring at her.

'But, Ma,' Catherine burst out, 'we were with Mr Powell's sons. How can you accuse us of bad behaviour when we were only doing what they were doing?'

'I dare say Mr Powell will have something to say to them, too,' Molly said, hoping this was true. 'In any case, you need to remember that you can't run around behaving in the same fashion as boys.'

Seeing her daughters' lack of comprehension, Molly sighed. 'I confess I am guilty, too. I have not brought you up well. I have allowed you to run wild and failed to see that you, Sally, are almost a young woman now.' She turned to her younger daughters. 'I cannot make the same mistake with you, Agnes and Catherine.'

If Molly had hoped that admitting to feelings of guilt would appeal to her daughters' better nature, she was mistaken. They stood before her, truculent, scuffing their feet on the floorboards.

'I can see my words are having no effect,' Molly said, feeling even crosser. 'Today, you will each think about your actions and write me a piece that I can give to your father, to apologise for your behaviour and for spoiling his day.'

'But I was going to meet Francis this afternoon,' Catherine wailed.

Molly glared at her. 'You won't see him at all for the rest of the week, young lady.' Her gaze swept over her daughters. 'You can think about what I have said while you launder your dresses from yesterday and repair any damage. We will start lessons again tomorrow, once you have written your letters to your father. You have plenty to keep you busy here – you are all behind with your reading books. Now, go and fetch your dresses and I will ask Ellen to heat the water.'

The girls trailed from the room, refusing to look at her. Molly sat down on the nearest chair, feeling shaken. She couldn't remember ever having cause to tell them off in this way before. Was that why they had run wild?

As the days passed slowly, Molly had cause to reflect ruefully that it wasn't just the girls being punished. Restricting their activities was also a burden for her, since she had to bear the brunt of their ill-humour and keep them occupied at home. Francis had appeared on the doorstep that first afternoon and seemed bemused that Catherine wasn't allowed to join him as planned. When Molly, in sending him away, had asked whether his father had spoken to him about taking out the boat with the girls in it he had shaken his head, puzzled.

Charlie had been right, Molly thought. The boys had escaped without even a lecture.

However, it looked as though the late-evening escapades in the woodland walk were sufficient to persuade Mr Powell that, while the garden party had undoubtedly been a success and much enjoyed by all, he wouldn't be making it an annual event. He said as much to Charlie on the day after the party, as they surveyed the trampled lawns and mangled flowerbeds.

Within the week, he had changed his mind. A report on the event in the local newspaper had referred to the 'beneficence of our local distinguished landowner, Mr Powell', which had caused him to swell visibly with pride, Charlie reported. His employer kept the paper to hand all week, eager to read the passage to anyone who strayed into his path.

Molly was just getting used again to Charlie's presence around the house, and she could hardly bear to think of the disruption to their lives that lay ahead next summer. But disruption was to come even earlier. On the fifth day after the garden party, when Charlie was starting to look less gaunt and exhausted, he broached the subject of Luke Symonds as he and Molly prepared for bed.

'You were right not to trust him,' Charlie said. 'Although, to be fair to him, he's behaved no differently from any other young lad. But Sally's not old enough to have young men pay attention to her in that way. I've seen how she sulks and sighs around the house since I parted the two of them and I cannot see how that will change unless we find something to fill her days. If you can manage without her, I think she should be apprenticed to a trade. I would hope that she'll marry well enough in the future, but it won't hurt her to learn some skills meanwhile.'

Molly, who had had to endure far more of Sally's ill-humour than Charlie, was inclined to agree with him. 'She's a good needlewoman, Charlie. She enjoys it and she has an eye for what suits in terms of fabric and design for gowns. I've been thinking of asking Mrs Rowe, the dressmaker on Margate high street, if she would take her on. Although I would be very sorry to lose her company.'

'She could stay with your aunt and return to us each Sunday,' Charlie said. And with that, what had already been half decided between Molly and Aunt Jane was agreed, as though the idea had been Charlie's all along.

CHAPTER TWENTY-FOUR

By the time the garden party came around the following year, much had changed in the Dawson household while much had stayed the same. Sally had taken to her apprenticeship with great enthusiasm and Molly's initial fears that she might view herself as exiled in punishment had quickly been dispelled. Mrs Rowe had nothing but praise for her work and her ever-increasing skills, while Aunt Jane spoke highly of her behaviour in her household.

She's like a sister for Constance, she wrote to Molly, in a letter that accompanied Sally on one of her regular Sunday visits home. Molly was taken aback, then comforted herself that it was only natural, Sally being used to having her sisters and cousins around her. She and Constance were not blood relatives after all; that distinction applied only to Molly's lost son.

Molly was unhappy, though, when she discovered that in sending Sally to Margate, far from relieving her of the distraction provided by Luke Symonds, she had instead delivered her daughter into his presence. Even though Sally was supervised at Aunt Jane's and Mrs Rowe's, no one had thought it necessary to chaperone her on her walks between Princes Crescent and the dressmaker's, or when she was sent out on errands. At some point, quite early in her apprenticeship, Luke Symonds had chanced upon her in Margate and

144

they had contrived to meet until Aunt Jane had discovered, some months in, what was afoot. She had shared the news in another letter, which an unsuspecting Sally carried to her mother:

I am sorry that this has come about while Sally was under my roof, for I know your intention was to keep her well occupied with work and away from such foolishness. However, I have interviewed the pair of them and found them to be genuinely fond of each other. Sally, of course, is too young to consider forming an attachment. Yet, regardless, this is what she has done and I have to say, in the short time that she has been with me, she has impressed me with her maturity. Luke is also a very sensible young man and quite set on Sally, even though I have made it clear to the pair of them that you would undoubtedly have them wait a few years before considering the possibility of marriage. Sally's response was that it would give her time to establish her own business, while Luke simply said that he would wait as long as it took.

Hand trembling, Molly set aside the letter. Why hadn't she foreseen that such a thing might happen? She had intended to part Sally from Luke Symonds and instead she had delivered her to him. She had to bite her lip to stop herself speaking out. She knew that first she must discuss the contents of the letter with Charlie, so she tried to behave normally and ask Sally about her week, when all the time she wanted nothing more than to probe her about her meetings with Luke. The visit, normally a joy, was a torture. She managed to send a short note to Aunt Jane, carried by Sally on her return journey, thanking her for writing and promising a fuller response once she had been able to discuss it with Charlie.

To her disappointment, Charlie didn't view it in the same way. He had shaken his head and laughed, saying, 'Well I never,' before suggesting that, since the couple were so determined, perhaps they were to be congratulated, rather than forbidden to meet.

'I'd rather she was settled, with one young man courting her, than prey to the attentions of every young man in Margate,' he said.

Molly was silenced. Sally had grown into a beautiful young woman. Now that she didn't see her every day, Molly was better able to register this fact. Whenever Sally came to visit, her dark hair always looked glossy and well cared for, her brown eyes were open and frank and her lips wide and full. Her figure suggested she was older than she was, which Molly had first become aware of in Margate, when men passing by had openly appraised her daughter.

Charlie's words made sense, Molly knew. If only Luke wasn't the son of Joshua Symonds – resembling him, too – so that she was reminded every time they met of her sojourn in London, which she had tried so hard to forget. If she was to agree to Sally and Luke continuing to see each other, their families would be brought even closer.

Molly realised Charlie was regarding her with curiosity.

'What is it about Luke Symonds that you dislike so much?' He frowned. 'She is unlikely to make a better match in the area, you know. And if we don't give our blessing to them continuing to see each other, they will undoubtedly do so anyway, but in secret. Unless you prefer to bring Sally home?'

'No,' she protested. Sally loved her work with Mrs Rowe and she undoubtedly had talent. Her intention to run her own business wasn't news to Molly – it was a decision her daughter had reached within weeks of starting work. She couldn't bear to disappoint her in this. And her heart failed her at the thought of making Luke and Sally wait until they were able to marry without permission, when they were twenty-one. That was seven years away. She knew she would lose Sally's affection if she did.

So, Molly wrote to her aunt to say that, provided the pair of them behaved with the utmost propriety, she and Charlie consented to Luke and Sally continuing to see each other. And when Sally paid her next visit home, Molly listened to Charlie telling her that they would agree to her marrying Luke when she was eighteen, but not before. Molly tried hard to smile at her daughter's delight but, try as she might, she struggled to reconcile herself to the idea. She took comfort in the thought that since more than four years must pass before the wedding could take place, she would surely have grown used to the idea by then. Deep down, though, she hoped that in the meantime something would drive the pair apart.

By the time of the second Woodchurch Manor garden party, in 1806, all concerned had learnt from their experience of the first. Mr Powell set a firm time limit on the event, inviting guests for four hours only. Lanterns were still lit in the woodland walk, but only for house guests to walk there. The peafowl had stayed, their eerie cries ringing out across the estate, but Mr Powell decided that fire-eaters and magicians were unnecessary. To discourage visitors from helping themselves to flowers, posies were picked and arranged for sale. Charlie had gained permission from Mr Powell to increase the size of his team of gardeners so that the month leading up to the day wasn't as arduous as it had been the first year. And Molly was prepared this time when she was asked to join Charlie on the bandstand to receive Mr Powell's thanks.

Sally arrived with Aunt Jane and Uncle William, and spent much of the afternoon walking on the arm of her young man. Molly did her best to be gracious to Joshua and his wife Lucy but was forced to take a calming walk alone after speaking to them. Agnes and Catherine, who had received a lecture from Molly about the standard of behaviour she expected from them, were once more spotted playing hide-and-seek with Francis, but spent the majority of the afternoon with their cousins. Molly couldn't help but notice Catherine's wistful glances around the grounds, no doubt in the hope of spotting her favourite Powell brother.

The following year, Mr Powell decided that the party needed to be livelier. He opened the field at the side of the house for children's pony rides and had a carthorse pull a roller over an area of grass to create a skittle alley. The game appeared to go hand in hand with the consumption of a good deal of ale and the players strayed into the path of the ponies, causing a small stampede that unseated several children.

Neither skittles nor ponies were in evidence the following year. In fact, whether the garden party could take place at all was still in question until very close to the actual day. A great storm had battered Margate in January of that year, demolishing the wooden pier and causing vessels moored in the harbour to break free, only to be dashed against shops and houses along the seafront. Water inundated the lower part of the town and there was so much destruction that the harbour area was no longer recognisable.

Do you remember the Kings Head inn, where we had dinner in the window overlooking the harbour? Sally wrote to her mother, unable to make the weekly journey home after the storm: the road was impassable except on horseback. *That room is now washed away and half the building stands open for all to see.*

The storm had continued its path of destruction along the coast, taking a shortcut inland to lay waste to the trees alongside the road between Margate and Woodchurch Manor. It swept across the estate, causing Charlie to leap from his bed, straining to see out of the window into the darkness. The creaking and groaning of the roof timbers and the crashing of branches all around caused Molly to cower in bed before she wondered whether they might all be safer downstairs. The family sat huddled in the kitchen as the wind growled and churned around the house while Charlie paced the floor, waiting for dawn to break so that he could see what havoc had been wrought. He would have gone out among it but Molly refused to let him.

'You'd never see the branches flying at you in the dark, or the tree about to crash on your head. You wouldn't stand a chance. You must just wait for it to blow itself out.'

Charlie had to acknowledge the sense of her words but Molly could see the torment on his face with every crash outside. At first light he was out of the door to check on the damage. The storm had sliced a swathe across the estate, uprooting the oldest and weakest trees, one of which had narrowly missed falling on Woodchurch Manor. The woodland walk was impassable, the paths blocked by fallen branches and a tangle of toppled trees.

Molly had never seen Charlie so despondent as he was the night after the storm.

'I don't see how we are ever to clear the estate, let alone go about replanting,' he said. He barely touched his food, and even though he'd already suffered one broken night, he hardly slept. He was out of the door again with the dawn, leaving Molly to shiver in the chill of the morning and worry over Charlie's state of mind.

Slowly, though, the estate was restored – at least to a satisfactory state, if not to its former glory. Heavy horses, brought in from the farms, lifted fallen timbers away from paths and tracks. Where there was no access for horses, men were busy throughout the daylight hours, endlessly sawing to reduce hefty tree trunks to manageable piles of wood.

It was May before Charlie finally felt able to laugh about any aspect of what had happened, finding amusement in Mr Powell's behaviour. 'He's hovering about us and I know he wants to ask about the garden party but he can see how hard we're working so he doesn't. He gives us a hand with moving some logs or cheering on the horse teams, loiters some more and then he's gone. We're taking bets over how long it takes him to broach the subject.' Charlie laughed, but grimly, and Molly longed for the day that her husband would be restored to his normal good humour.

In fact, the garden party went ahead, as an act of defiance to the elements, Molly thought. Mr Powell made no attempt to insist on perfection. Instead, he advertised the event as 'a chance to see how the gardens are being restored after the destruction of the Great Storm'.

He was always one to seize the advantage, even in adversity, Molly thought, with grudging admiration, as Mr Powell unveiled plans that he had had drawn up. Where old trees had fallen at the edge of the estate, there was now to be a tower, so tall you could see the sea from the top, provided you could climb up the several hundred steps. Mr Powell took the opportunity to widen the lane leading to the house and to instigate a programme of tree planting for the areas that had been laid waste. With Charlie's help, chestnut, oak, beech and ash had been chosen for different areas, and there was to be a new orchard beyond the walled garden, which had, miraculously, survived the storm with all four walls intact.

Chapter Twenty-Five

Molly began to mark the passage of time by the Woodchurch Manor garden parties. By 1809, she felt able to take tea at the same table as Joshua and Lucy Symonds, which was fortunate because by the time of the party in 1810 Luke and Sally were married. Charlie had persuaded Molly to reward their devotion to each other by letting them marry a year early, once Sally had reached the age of seventeen.

With each year that passed, the scars wrought by the storm were gradually erased as the new planting took hold, although it would be many years before the saplings that had replaced the old trees reached their full height.

Long after I'm gone, thought Molly.

By 1812 there was an addition to the family, a grandchild – a little girl, Grace. Charlie doted on her, even though he teasingly professed disappointment and said he'd been hoping for a boy to train in the skills of gardening since none of his girls showed any aptitude for it.

Agnes and Catherine were now fine young ladies of eighteen and seventeen. They no longer played hide-and-seek with the Powell boys, Robert and Edward being in the Navy and rarely at home at the same time. Catherine still had a steadfast friendship with Francis, which had reawakened worries in her mother's mind.

'I see the same single-minded determination in her that I saw in Sally with regard to Luke.' Molly sighed. 'I'm convinced that she imagines she will marry Francis one day.'

'Have you asked her?' Charlie said, not unreasonably.

'Why no . . . If there is even the faintest chance that she doesn't think of him in that way, I don't want to put the idea into her head,' Molly said.

Charlie laughed, then took the first opportunity, when he was alone with Catherine, to quiz her.

'You are right,' he reported back. 'She imagines them married by the time she is eighteen or, since that doesn't seem far away, twenty at the latest. I pointed out to her that Mr Powell may have something else in mind for Francis and she said that since Robert, the eldest, would inherit the estate, with Edward held in reserve, what possible use could there be for Francis?'

'That doesn't mean Mr Powell would approve of his marriage to someone such as Catherine,' Molly retorted. 'Even though he holds his head gardener in high esteem, of course,' she added swiftly. 'And since these French wars show no sign of ending, who knows how it will go for those poor Powell boys?'

She was no stranger to news of losses in the Navy – rumours that the government had failed to suppress told of more men carried off by disease, which spread quickly in the confined space aboard ship, than in battle. Many a night when sleep eluded her Molly wondered whether her own boy might have been lost to war.

As time passed, though, she ceased to worry about Catherine. She had grown up to be sunny-natured and even-tempered, always helpful to her mother and father. Francis was away at school, and if the pair of them found time to meet up when he was home for the holidays, Molly failed to notice. Her days were occupied in helping Sally, who had now added a little boy – Simon – to their extended family. Although Sally hadn't yet managed to fulfil her ambition of running her own business, Mrs Rowe had stepped back to spend time with her own grandchildren. The two managed an amicable arrangement whereby they shared the work between them, each having their own clients. At first, Molly spent a part of each week in Westbrook, looking after Grace and Simon. When they were a little older, the children passed a good deal of time at Molly's house, with Catherine, Agnes and Ellen on hand to help.

After a while, it made more sense for Ellen to move to Westbrook to help Sally, since the Dawson girls were so well grown. Although the passage of time had helped Molly to come to terms with their connection to the Symonds family, she had been relieved when she no longer had to stay for part of each week under Sally and Luke's roof. They lived next door to Luke's parents and, try as she might to overcome it, Molly found closeness to Joshua uncomfortable.

* * *

As Molly dressed for the garden party one August morning in 1814, she considered how much had changed since that first exhausting event. Now the day was still tiring but the weeks beforehand ran like a well-oiled machine. Provided that Mr Powell didn't come up with any new ideas for entertainments, everyone, whether in the kitchens or the gardens, knew the roles they must play and when preparations should start.

This year's party would be extra special, though. Robert and Edward Powell were at home, the long-drawn-out French wars seemingly over now that Napoleon had been exiled to Elba. Mr Powell was beside himself with excitement to have his sons home at last but the news had come too late for him to make extravagant plans. And, in any case, the higher land taxes needed to pay for the war had left his own coffers much reduced.

'It will be enough that they are home,' Mrs Powell had soothed him. 'And, in any case, it would be wise not to make too great a fuss. You must remember that many of our friends and neighbours have lost their sons to this wretched war.'

Although talk of the French wars had dominated the men's conversation at the garden parties of more recent years, and Mr Powell might have felt the pinch on his purse, the town of Margate had profited from smuggling. The Navy had kept the British coastline safe from incursion by the French, but it had apparently failed to notice the comings and goings of small fishing vessels at dead of night. Profits from the smuggled goods had been spent in the town and brought it prosperity.

There would be many young ladies paying extra attention to how they looked today, Molly thought, as she brushed her hair. Robert and Edward Powell would not be the only ones discharged or at home on leave. She expected to see several young men looking dashing in uniform that day. Would any of them catch Agnes's eye? Agnes, now a petite and attractive young woman, was as quiet and thoughtful as she had been as a child. She made no particular efforts to distinguish herself in company, other than with an unfortunate habit of plain speaking, which, Molly felt, went a long way to explaining why she remained unattached.

'I'm a spinster,' Agnes had said proudly, although she was still only twenty years old. 'I have no particular reason to believe I will ever marry. In any case, someone will need to stay at home to look after you, Ma and Pa.' She appeared unconcerned by the idea and Molly wondered whether, perhaps, she welcomed it. Her art was still the only thing that inspired her and, since Mr Powell had seen fit to buy a few of her paintings, she had gained some local success.

'Perhaps one year I will have an exhibition at the garden party,' she had teased her mother, and Molly was hardly surprised that today, less than a year later, this was about to take place. Agnes had firm ideas as to where it should be held and Mr Powell had indulged her, loaning her one of the young servant boys to whitewash an unused section of the stable block. She had spent the day before supervising the hanging of her paintings.

Molly had only recently discovered, in a chance conversation with Mr Powell, that each year Will Turner had been invited to the garden party.

'He's always too busy,' Mr Powell had said. 'Each summer seems to find him somewhere different – Sussex, Wales, Scotland, Italy. I never a knew a man to travel so much. I should have liked to have him here.' He looked a little wistful, Molly thought. Will's presence would have added prestige, at least to the yearly newspaper report on the event. For herself, she was glad she hadn't known of the invitations before now: she would have been anxious about Charlie's reaction to Will's presence.

'This year, I would have liked him to see your daughter's work, Mrs Dawson,' Mr Powell had continued, making Molly instantly ashamed of her feelings. 'I shall write to him instead and ask his advice about further study for her.'

Molly laid aside her hairbrush and went downstairs to find Agnes and Catherine waiting for her. They drew her out of the house, then each took an arm to walk along the lane.

Molly looked up at the clear blue sky and marvelled that in all the years since the first garden party it had been marred only once by rain.

Today, she felt a happy sense of anticipation. There would be friends and family, as always. Sally would take delight in pointing out the gowns that she had made especially for the day, while Grace and Simon would clamour to sit on Molly or Charlie's lap. True, only one of her daughters was settled but she wasn't the only matron in the area curious to see how many fine young men had been restored to their families. Would today transform Agnes and Catherine's fortunes?

PART TWO

1806

CHAPTER TWENTY-SIX

The mid-November skies were grey and the wind blowing across the marshes beside the river had a vindictive edge. It cut through his layers of clothing and he pulled his jacket tighter around him, trying to shrink inside it to preserve what little body warmth he had. His work today was to cut the alder along the northerly edge of Bysing Wood, exposed to the bite of the wind.

He knew that when he had the axe in his hands and had fallen into the rhythm of chopping, he would work up enough of a sweat to start stripping off the layers he wore: the shapeless woollen jacket, then the waistcoat, until he was down to his grubby work shirt. The charcoal burners at the gunpowder works were greedy for alder so he and his fellow workers could barely keep pace with the demand for the wood they cut. Charcoal was one of the essential ingredients of gunpowder and the French wars had created a high demand for the black powder.

He was sixteen but looked younger, a disadvantage at the works where, unusually, the age limit was strictly enforced because of the dangerous nature of the job. 'Milkmaid', the other men called him, and the name had stuck. He supposed it was down to his still-smooth cheeks and his sandy hair, which tended to curl in the moisture carried by the wind off the creek. He could wish all he liked but there was no sign of a beard yet, so he must tolerate the men's teasing for a while longer. And he must put up with this job cutting wood, rather than one he would have preferred inside the shelter of a building on the site. That would have to wait until he was eighteen.

He'd been working there just a few weeks and no one had questioned his story: that his father had died fighting against Napoleon and his mother had pined until she was carried off by ill health and the last harsh winter. Left alone to fend for himself, with his supposed older brothers also in the Navy, he had told the foreman at the gunpowder works that he was desperate to earn money so that he could eat, which was true enough.

The foreman, looking him up and down, could see how tightly the skin was stretched over his bones. If he thought him too fragile for the only work he had available, he said nothing. He was in desperate need of workers to cut the alder.

'Well, lad, I'll take you at your word that you're a good worker. We'll have to see how you get on. Let's be having your name.'

The foreman glanced up from his desk in the office at the Oare Works, poised to add his new worker to the ledger.

He had hesitated, then said firmly, 'George. George Smith.'

He handed over the last coin in his possession to pay for his lodgings, a share of a room in Widow Booth's cottage in the village of Davington, and from there he walked the path over the fields to the wood each day. It was a far cry from the streets of Rochester that he'd been used to.

The work was hard but it was a great deal better than the life he'd had before. He'd been looking forward to getting away from the Foundling School and starting his apprenticeship; now he wasn't sure why. He'd imagined it to be a step on the road to adulthood, that he would learn a trade. The secretary had made a point of saying how lucky he was to be going into an office.

'This is your new master, Mr Gifford,' he had said. George looked at the grey-haired man, well-dressed and unsmiling, standing by the secretary's desk. 'He'll conduct you to Rochester tonight and you'll start as an apprentice draughtsman in his office tomorrow. At the end of your apprenticeship, seven years from now, you'll have a skill that will serve you throughout your life. You've been given this opportunity on account of the aptitude you've shown for writing and mathematics, so make sure you acquit yourself well and uphold the good name of the school.'

The secretary nodded to Mr Gifford and that was that: the end of George's school career. And the end of his dreams of a trade. Mr Gifford might have given every appearance of being a gentleman but he soon showed himself to be a scoundrel, taking advantage of the free labour offered by the Foundling School. George joined his apprentices from previous years, not at a desk but working underground, digging out chalk to create defences at Fort Amherst. Marched out of Rochester each day, they worked alongside convicts, whose uncouth language and brute strength terrified George. At first he was unsure how he would survive even one day. It turned out that years were to pass in such misery with barely any reprieve.

There had seemed the faintest glimmer of hope of escaping the nightmare when, every twelvemonth, the Foundling School sent a clerk to check on the welfare of their apprentices. Mr Gifford's right-hand man, Noah Taylor, set them at desks and told them to give the appearance of getting on with their work.

'Breathe a word of what you do for the rest of the year and I'll drown the lot of you in the Medway,' he said. None of them doubted he'd be true to his word: they'd learnt to fear him more than the convicts.

Had the clerk thought to question the apprentices' appearance? George wondered. Scrawny, undernourished, hands rough and scarred with cuts, nails filthy, despite Noah's insistence on a thorough scrubbing at the pump before the man arrived. If he had any qualms, it appeared they were soothed by the dinner he was given – a meat pie and a quantity of ale at the local inn – before he was sent on his way back to London, all smiles at a successful inspection.

George knew then that he needed to look for another way out of his predicament but it took four long years, and then escape came only by chance. They were being marched back to Rochester at the end of a day's labour, on a dark and wet November evening. A scuffle broke out between two of the convicts and both guards went to the back of the line to investigate. The convicts' chains made it impossible for them to progress and the procession ground to a halt. George, walking at the head of the line, dutifully stopped too.

'Go on, leg it.'

George, who had been staring at the ground in a kind of stupor, turned to see who had spoken. It was the nearest convict.

'What you waiting for? Leg it,' he hissed again, and rattled his chains. It took a moment or two for George, unchained, to realise his longed-for opportunity had arrived. He glanced back to make sure the guards were too busy to notice, then slipped into the shadows between the two nearest buildings and ran, his boots ringing out on the cobbles. He daren't look round, fearing pursuit. When he collapsed at last in a ditch, on the outskirts of town, his breath was rasping in his chest. He lay there, expecting to hear angry cries and the sounds of a search, but there was nothing. Had the other apprentices made their getaway, too? He wasn't sure – George had been the only one walking so far forward.

If his luck held, they wouldn't realise he was missing until much later. He knew he needed to get on but, half starved as he was, he had little energy. Even so, he made himself walk through the night, to put as much distance as he could between himself and Rochester. There was no food to be had in the fields so he had to steal from barns along the way, apples mainly. As the days went on, he begged at farms for a scrap of bread and a cup of milk. He was under no illusion about the penalty for absconding from an apprenticeship. If he was caught, he'd be sent to prison. No one would listen to his protests about exploitation and the terms of his service; no one would believe his word against that of the respected Henry Gifford of Rochester, benefactor of the Foundling School. The man had no doubt told the school that he'd died or run away.

And so George had found himself in Faversham, with a roof over his head and money to be earned. For the first few weeks, he'd wondered at the wisdom of what he had done. He might have escaped from hard labour, deep underground, but was it any better to be working in all weathers in the woods? Cutting alder and peeling away the bark while his hands bled from contact with the cut branches and the cold wind chapped his skin?

Yet even when the rain poured down and soaked through his clothing so that he shivered in misery, he reminded himself that he was getting a regular wage – enough to pay for his bed and board and a jar or two of ale at the end of the week. And the foreman was reasonable, trusting his men to manage their own workload. Above all, though, he was in charge of himself now. He had his freedom.

CHAPTER TWENTY-SEVEN

At first, George had been ignorant of the process involved in the making of gunpowder. He'd been puzzled by the quantity of wood that the cutters were asked to provide, and had only gradually worked out the early part of the process – the creation of charcoal.

'The charcoal is mixed with other stuff that comes into Faversham by boat,' Thomas told him. George shared his room in Widow Booth's cottage with Thomas, who was a few years older than him and had been at the works a good while longer, working in the cooperage, making barrels to store the gunpowder.

'They use saltpetre from India and sulphur from Sicily, and they mix them with the charcoal from the wood you cut. Then it's packed into the barrels I make, and off it goes to sea again.'

Thomas looked rather pleased with the symmetry of what he'd just described but George's mind had wandered. He thought about the boats he'd seen being unloaded at the wharf, which lay just a mile or two from the works. Faversham, the little market town straggling along the creek, was peopled mainly by those employed in the brewery or at the three powder works in and around the town. A scattering of grand houses in the roads that led away from the town was home to the wealthier residents and the town was thriving. Market days, centred around the ancient arches of the Guildhall, were always busy, with locals and those who came in on the ships to stock up with provisions before making their long return journeys.

The sailors stood out as different in the market but went unremarked, because the locals were so used to the regular passage of ships from foreign lands. Those visitors shopped quickly, buying by pointing at vegetables and other goods, then taking great basket loads back to the wharf. George wondered where their ships went after they'd left Ordnance Wharf. Back along the creek, he supposed, and then to where they had come from, somewhere far across the sea, beyond his imagination.

It wasn't until the day that George was told to take the bundles of cut lengths of alder down to the burners that he discovered more about the process of making the precious 'black powder'. He knew the different paths through the woods a little better by then, and although it was cold and dank under the trees, his route kept him out of the wind, which he considered a blessing.

Abraham, one of the charcoal burners, was harassed. 'Set that lot down over there,' he said, indicating George's burden. 'It needs to be dried out first before I can use it here. I'm on my own today and it seems they expect me to be in two places at once. I've got to get this stack built, keep an eye on the others and now they want me to get the latest batch of charcoal down to the incorporating house.'

Abraham looked round helplessly and George followed his eyes. Three huge stacks of alder poles spaced around the clearing in the woods were alight, trickles of smoke issuing out of the centre of each. Abraham was standing in front of a recently cleared patch of ground, the charcoal from the burnt stack bagged up into sacks.

'I could help,' George said. He looked doubtfully at the patch of clear ground, where Abraham had already piled bundles of alder in preparation for building the latest stack.

Abraham shook his head. It was a skilled job and Abraham didn't trust anyone except himself with the task. He turned instead towards the pile of sacks full of charcoal. Seeing a way of easing the pressure of his workload, he looked hopefully at George. 'Aye, mebbe you could load this lot and take the punt along the Leats, up to the mixing house.' He pointed towards the waterway a short distance from where they were standing, where a boat was moored.

On his journeys across the site to the alder coppice, George had seen men plying flat-bottomed boats along the waterways. They transported materials to the different buildings in the woods and took barrels full of gunpowder to the far end of the site, where horses waited on the roadway to carry them to the barges on Oare Creek.

'Why not?' George said cheerfully. He'd never used a punt, but it didn't look too difficult. And it would give him a break before he went back to the coppicing once more.

'You haven't got any metal about you?' Abraham asked.

'Metal?' George was puzzled.

'Aye, a knife in your pocket? Or metal buttons on your jacket?' Abraham looked him up and down as he spoke.

'No, I don't think so.' George peered down at his buttons – definitely not metal – and patted his pockets, even though he knew there was nothing in them, other than a rag of a handkerchief. 'Why do you ask?'

'No metal allowed anywhere near the mixing house,' Abraham said sternly. 'Or anywhere else on site for that matter. For fear of a spark that might cause an explosion.'

'Oh.' His words startled George. He had a sudden vision of a ball of orange flame tearing through the trees.

'Didn't you know that?' Abraham went on. 'Why do you think they use boats around the site and not horses?'

George was mystified by the question. 'I don't know. I suppose the trees might make it difficult for the horses to get around,' he ventured.

Abraham snorted. 'No. In case the metal of the horseshoes creates a spark against the ground and triggers an explosion. Now get on with you.' He bent to begin work on his latest alder stack.

George moved the sacks of charcoal to the punt, one by one, then began loading them into it, taking care to distribute the load evenly at front and back, with enough room for him to stand in the middle. Then he took a deep breath, seized the wooden pole and stepped cautiously into the boat, causing it to rock furiously until he had the presence of mind to stab the pole into the water. As the craft steadied, he was pleased to discover just how shallow the water was. If it all went wrong, at least he would be in water just over his knees rather than up to his neck.

It was to George's advantage that the waterways of the Leats were not completely straight, but followed gentle curves as they made their way around the site. It meant that Abraham didn't witness his first brush with the bank, which threatened to tip out the dry, bagged charcoal. It happened shortly after he had set off, when a hasty glance over his shoulder reassured him that Abraham was already well out of sight.

Feeling foolish, George jumped out of the punt and used the pole to help him lever it off the bank. He was soon to discover that punting required a lot more skill than he'd thought, and he was grateful not to encounter any experienced watermen as he made erratic progress towards the mixing house. By the time he arrived there, he was proud that the punt was zigzagging far less on the narrow waterway. He'd even begun to think about asking for a transfer to the role of waterman.

His welcome was less than rapturous at the mixing house. A man was on watch for the arrival of the boat. He started to seize the bags of charcoal and unload them before George felt he was safely moored. The shift of weight threatened to destabilise him and he had to make an undignified scramble for the bank, glaring at the over-hasty workman, who was unmoved. 'About time, too. We're down to the last three bags of charcoal.' He paused in his labours to glare back at George. 'Are you going to help me or just stand there, gawping?'

George considered telling him he'd just done Abraham a favour by bringing the charcoal along and it wasn't his job to help him, but thought better of it. He set to and helped unload, then followed the other man's example and dragged the sacks, two at a time, to the door of a long, low building. It was set into the lee of a cliff, away from the water, and George could hear activity from within – voices, as well as the grinding noise of a machine in motion. He peered through the half-open door and would have stepped over the low board placed across the entrance, if the workman's sharp voice hadn't stopped him.

'What do you think you're doing?'

George turned to look at him. 'I was just curious. I've never seen any part of the process.'

'Well, it's forbidden,' the man said. 'You might be carrying grit on the soles of your boots. Anything like that getting into the powder mix is a danger to everyone in that building – and all the others.' He gestured around, and George noticed for the first time that other low buildings were situated nearby, half hidden by screens of trees or piles of earth. 'No one goes in there without changing into special clothing first.'

He looked so fierce as he spoke that George backed away, holding his hands up placatingly, half fearful of causing an explosion just by his presence. He vowed he'd find a way to come back for a proper look if he got the chance, but he supposed he should return the punt to Abraham, then get back to cutting alder.

He was about to step onto the punt, wondering whether it would prove easier or harder to manage unladen, when he heard his name called. He looked up, trying to locate where the voice had come from.

'George! Over here.' Thomas, standing outside one of the low buildings on the opposite side of the track, beckoned to him. 'What are you doing here?' he asked, as George drew closer.

'I've just delivered some charcoal.' George pointed to the building opposite. The sacks had now vanished and the door was closed.

'Come and see where I work,' Thomas said.

George looked down at his clothes and boots. 'Is it safe? I'm not going to cause an explosion, am I?'

Thomas laughed. 'I hope not! No, you're safe here as you are.'

George followed him into a noisy, warm workroom, filled with chatter and banging as the powder barrels took shape.

On the opposite side to the door, windows overlooking a large pond filled the room with light. In one corner, men expertly steamed lengths of wood into the curved shape required to make the barrels and there was a fragrant scent from all of the wood in use. George looked around, taking it all in.

'We've got our own safety rules in here, mind you,' Thomas said. 'No sparks allowed, so we use brass hammers. And leather straps, not metal, to bind the barrels.'

George stood and watched the men at work for a while. Maybe this would be a better place to find a job when he was older, rather than on the waterway. Then he remembered that he must deliver the punt back to Abraham, and get back to cutting alder before he was in so much trouble that he wouldn't have a job at all.

Chapter Twenty-Eight

With the onset of spring, George began to explore. He'd discovered soon after his arrival that there was more than one powder works in Faversham, the main one – known as the Home Works – being situated rather more conveniently on the edge of town. But he'd come to like both his lodgings in Davington and his workmates in Oare and saw no reason to move. As the evenings grew lighter, it was a pleasure to walk with Thomas into Faversham, following the road as it wound down the hill past the cherry orchards coming into flower until they reached Stonebridge Pond. Here George liked to stop awhile, watching the waterfowl busily constructing their nests. The pond was a working one, supplying the waterwheels that drove the mills at the Home Works, but that meant nothing to the birds that made their home there. Boys from the town fished from the water's edge, and George wondered idly what they might catch.

Thomas, however, had no patience with loitering and urged him on to the Fountain Inn, almost within sight on West Street.

'I've got a thirst on from all that sawdust in the workshop,' he complained. 'How much longer are you going to stand here gazing at nothing?'

George could never understand Thomas's lack of interest in his surroundings. Thomas had been brought up in the area but couldn't name a bird, tree or flower, showed no signs of wishing to learn and was, in George's view, simply unobservant.

'Will you come on?' Thomas was growing impatient.

'You go ahead – get me a drink and I'll join you there.'

George supposed he counted as city bred, having been schooled in London from the age of five, but there was something about the countryside that awoke his earliest memories and made him feel at home. He could remember being in a yard that housed chickens, as well as a pig on a bed of straw in a pen behind a barred gate. He remembered more straw in the hen house where he was told to look for eggs. He'd been frightened the hens would peck him.

There was a woman called Nancy, too, dressed in a gown faded by many washes, with a grubby apron worn over it. Her greying hair peeped out from the edges of the cap she wore and she had a round face, which always looked cross. She'd been particularly annoyed when he'd held out the eggs he had found, one in each hand, squeezing them so tightly for fear of dropping them, that he'd spilt the contents all over the dusty cobbles. She'd shouted at him and cuffed his ear, and the black-and-white dog, which was bigger than George, had licked up the broken eggs, crunching the shells.

Although the memories that involved the woman were not happy, he had other, better memories relating to that time. George had realised from an early age that there were places he could hide that Nancy's bulk didn't allow her to reach. Sometimes he climbed into the hay barn and sat looking out of the window slit at one end, wondering what lay in the far distance, beyond the trees. He'd discovered that he could squeeze through the yard gate, past the cows, which gazed at him curiously before going back to their grazing, and make his way to the pond to sit on a fallen log at the edge.

If he stayed still and quiet, he might see water voles plop into the water and swim furiously, keeping close to the bank until they vanished out of sight under the trees. He watched dragonflies dart across the pond, and ducks and moorhens squabble over their nesting territory. Summer brought the swallows, swooping low to pick off the insects dancing just above the surface. In autumn, fallen leaves spread patterns of gold, red and brown across the pond. He even liked to spend time there in winter, his breath hanging in the air as he huddled into his jacket and watched the ducks. They were trying to keep their footing on the patches of solid ice as they waited for the sun to rise high enough to melt a little feeding area for them.

George was reluctant to tear himself away from the tranquil scene at Stonebridge Pond, to exchange it for the noise and bustle of the Fountain Inn. But Thomas would be waiting, so he turned his steps towards West Street, and slipped into the bar to stand with his back to the door while he searched for his friend.

He was deep in conversation with men George recognised from the Oare Works, so he made his way over. Thomas acknowledged him and pointed at a mug of ale, set on the mantelshelf. The fire was not lit, the evenings now warm enough to make it unnecessary. George took an appreciative draught of ale and looked around. It was the usual mix of men, from the three different powder works around the town. But over by the bar there was a cluster he'd never seen before. They were better dressed than the regulars and, he noticed, there was a little space all around them.

George turned away, immediately on the alert. Strangers made him fearful. Now that he was settled and making a life for himself, he had no wish to be apprehended as the absconder he was and returned to his apprenticeship in Rochester.

As soon as he could get Thomas's attention, he asked him, 'Who are those men? Do you know?' He indicated the little group at the bar with a jerk of his head.

'Aye, they're billeted here, in the inn.' Thomas tipped his head back, emptied his tankard and handed it to George.

'And?' George was impatient.

Thomas wiped his mouth. 'They're government men. Sent here to make sure that the Home and Marsh Works are operating flat out to keep the Navy supplied with powder.'

George digested this news. 'And the Oare Works?'

'No.' It was Thomas's turn to be impatient. 'Are you going to fetch me a drink or stand here all night quizzing me? The Oare Works are privately owned, not government run. What we do there is our own business.'

George went off to the bar, relieved. The government men wouldn't be snooping around the Oare Works, asking awkward questions. He looked sideways at them as he waited to be served and decided there and then that, even so, it would be wise to find a new place to drink. It wouldn't be hard. The town had two breweries and you could barely walk ten steps before you passed a painted board, welcoming you to an inn belonging to one or other of them.

CHAPTER TWENTY-NINE

The powder industry employed very few women and girls, which was understandable, George thought, as much of the work was dirty and dangerous. But he felt the lack of female company, although not as keenly as Thomas, who was always on the lookout when they went into Faversham of an evening. George was shy but Thomas was not, and George came to see an advantage in this.

When Thomas fell into conversation with a girl, more often than not she had a friend who would be prepared to smile at George, while giggling at Thomas's teasing. Such encounters were few and far between, though, and most likely to happen on market days when folk came into town from the surrounding villages. Faversham girls were generally kept under the watchful eye of their families. That didn't stop Thomas and George spending many an hour after church on Sunday discussing the merits of the girls glimpsed there and speculating about them when they glanced over their shoulders and giggled behind their hands.

One Sunday after church Thomas and George sat on Ordnance Wharf, throwing pebbles into the water and enjoying the sunshine before walking back to Widow Booth's cottage for the dinner she always cooked for them.

George was staring into the water, frowning. The sermon in church that morning had been about the parable of the lost sheep, and although he hadn't fully understood what he'd heard, the idea of being lost in the wilderness had sent his thoughts skittering. He was now sixteen years old, without a father or mother, and possibly in trouble with the law. His initial thankfulness on finding a place of safety in Faversham had been replaced by restlessness: he had had some schooling but he'd settled into a line of work that offered few prospects.

Thomas jabbed an elbow into George's ribs, eliciting an 'Ow' of protest.

'Why did you do that?' George asked.

'Ssh. Look.' Thomas jerked his head over his shoulder and George turned to see the back view of two girls, who must have strolled past him. Their hair was visible, peeping out beneath their caps, one blonde and the other such a deep shade of brown as to be almost black.

'Did you see their faces?' George asked, his recent gloom now dispelled. 'What were they like?'

'Very pretty.' Thomas said that about any girl they saw. For once, though, his expression was quite different from any George had seen before: he looked almost stunned.

'Did you recognise them?' George asked.

'No,' Thomas said, and frowned. 'I wonder whether they're from out of town.'

At that moment, as if conscious of the two pairs of eyes focused on their backs, both girls turned their heads, giggled, and continued on their way.

George had just enough time to take in the impression of a pale, heart-shaped face framed by dark hair before he scrambled to his feet. 'Let's follow them.'

The girls paid them no more heed, following the bank of the creek before crossing into West Street and almost at once stepping across the road into Tanners Street.

George and Thomas stood with Stonebridge Pond behind them and watched the two girls disappear round the back of the Three Tuns inn.

'I think we should try the Three Tuns in the week,' George said, as they turned their steps towards Davington, Widow Booth's cottage and their dinner. They'd been visiting different inns in Faversham ever since George had become uneasy about the Fountain, but hadn't found one to make their regular haunt as yet.

Thomas nodded, turning back more than once as they climbed the hill, hoping to catch another glimpse of the girls.

'It's too hot,' George complained, stopping to loosen his neckerchief, then taking it off to mop his brow.

'Are you sure it wasn't the sight of those two girls warming you up?' Thomas asked.

'No,' George protested. 'It's just hot.'

'What do you expect? It's summer,' Thomas replied, but George noticed that he was red in the face, too. As they reached the brow of the hill his friend surreptitiously loosened his neckerchief and shook out the hem of his shirt.

Widow Booth was clearly feeling the heat: she grumbled about the sweltering kitchen as she put two thick china plates, piled with meat, potatoes and gravy, on the table in front of them. Both George and Thomas, usually quick to eat and happy to mop their plates clean afterwards with pieces of bread, struggled to finish what was before them.

That night, sleep didn't come easily. The bedroom under the eaves of the cottage had heated during the day, and even throwing the windows wide let in barely a breath of air.

George had tossed and turned for a while before falling into an uneasy sleep.

A blinding flash and an accompanying bang woke him and propelled him from his bed, heart thumping. He felt as though a vivid white pinprick of light was seared on his eyeballs but when he turned to Thomas's bed he lay fast asleep on his back, snoring.

Still sleep-dazed, George stood for a moment, confused. Had it been a dream that woke him? He'd thought it was an explosion at one of the powder works or, almost as bad, a thunderstorm. But now, in the silence of the night, he wondered.

Then another flash lit the room brilliantly for a second, and George began to count. The bang that followed wasn't immediate this time. The storm wasn't overhead, but it was certainly nearby.

He shook Thomas, who had slept on unflinching through the latest episode. 'Wake up, Thomas! There's a storm. We should go.'

Thomas's eyes flicked open and he stared at George.

'What's the matter? Is it morning?' He sounded confused.

'There's a storm,' George said. 'Thunder and lightning. We should go to the works, to offer help.'

Thomas frowned. 'Whatever for? There's nothing we can do.'

Lightning flashed and lit the room once more. After several heartbeats of silence, thunder roared. George began to pull clothes off the chair at the end of his bed.

'What are you doing?' Thomas asked. He'd raised himself up on one elbow and was watching George with a puzzled expression.

'Getting ready to go to the works.' George had his trousers on and was hunting under the bed for his boots.

'George, there's nothing we can do. There's nothing anyone can do except pray. The men on the night shift will have been sent off the site.'

George stopped what he was doing and sat on the edge of the bed. 'They don't need us to go down there, to help?'

'Where did you get that idea from?' Thomas yawned. 'If the whole place goes up then, yes, we'll have to go and help dig out any who are still alive. But the last time something like that happened was over twenty years ago. They learnt a lot from it. That's why all the buildings are spread around the site. If there's an explosion in one it doesn't follow that the others will catch fire.'

They waited as another flash of lightning lit the room. The thunder followed, but the time lapse was longer and the rumble less intense.

Thomas chuckled, as though he was enjoying it. 'There's a few people lying in bed in Faversham with their ears stopped, I'll be bound. But the most dangerous processes have been moved out of town now. There's little risk of roofs being lifted off and windows blown out.'

'So there's nothing we can do?' George asked.

'No,' Thomas said, 'except get some sleep, before it's time to go to work. Those lucky beggars on the night shift have had an hour off.'

George didn't think he'd feel lucky if he was crouched in a ditch on the edge of the site, waiting to see whether the next lightning bolt would send the whole place up.

A drumming against the panes, increasing in intensity, signified the arrival of rain. The accompanying gust of wind sent George hurrying to fasten the window against the storm.

'Go back to bed, George.' Thomas was already plumping up his pillow and making ready to turn on his side. 'The storm's moving out to sea. The rain will damp down every-thing on the site anyway. The only danger now is lack of sleep.'

Feeling foolish, George undressed and got back into bed. He lay and listened to the storm as it moved away, the lightning flashes becoming less frequent and the rumbles fading into the distance.

It seemed barely five minutes later that Thomas was shaking him awake. 'Come on, sleepyhead. Get a move on or you'll have no time for breakfast.'

George lay there for a moment or two, wondering why he felt so tired and groggy, until the memory of last night's storm came back to him. His fear in the night had been very real but now, on a bright summer's morning, it seemed ridiculous.

CHAPTER THIRTY

It was to be another week before Thomas and George could make their planned visit to the Three Tuns. Thomas was put on nights in the cooperage, as the works went on double shifts to meet demand. With the other two gunpowder works in town sending all their supplies to the Navy, it was left to the Oare Works to meet domestic demand, for quarrying and suchlike, and stocks were running low.

George, conscious that he still looked young for his years despite the wisps of a beard that had finally appeared, didn't want to brave the inn on his own so he had to wait patiently for Saturday, when Thomas was due to return to his normal shift. All the while, he wondered whether the girls might just have been visitors, passing through, and nothing to do with the Three Tuns after all. Did disappointment lie ahead?

By the time Saturday finally arrived, George was half inclined not to go into town at all. Thomas was tired and grumpy after working nights and the weather had been unsettled since the storm. A steady drizzle had set in, making the thought of a walk to Faversham less than appealing.

The two were prepared to settle for a drink in their quiet local, which was no more than the front room of a cottage, when Thomas said, 'What are we thinking? Come on, let's make the effort.'

So, collars up and shoulders hunched against the weather, they set off, immersed in their thoughts and speaking little on the walk. The Three Tuns looked inviting, candlelight sparkling in the windows, and George's spirits rose as they crossed the road towards it. Thomas pushed open the door, and they were met by a hum of chatter and the warmth created by a press of bodies. The place was busy and George cast around for a table or a niche where they could prop themselves. He recognised one or two faces from the Oare Works but most of the drinkers were strangers to him.

Two customers moved away from one of the sturdy darkwood uprights supporting the beamed ceiling and George saw an opportunity. 'I'll get the drinks – you take that spot,' he said, pointing at the gap the men had left.

It was unlike George to be first at the bar in a new place but in surveying the room he'd already spotted the dark-haired girl from their Sunday encounter, serving. He made his way over, heart beating fast, wondering whether she would be the one to attend to him.

He didn't have to wait long to find out. 'What can I get you?' she asked. George wondered whether she recognised him. He wasn't sure how much heed the girls had paid him and Thomas.

'I wondered how long it would take before you came in,' the girl said, as she dealt with his order. George, who had been busy looking at the downward sweep of her lashes as she poured the ale, barely noticed what she had said.

She looked at him directly as she placed the brimming tankards on the wooden counter in front of him. 'Now, don't pretend you didn't follow us,' she said, and George, catching on to her words, blushed red to the roots of his hair.

'It's not often you get two good-looking young men together,' the girl continued. 'And I don't think I've seen you in here before. Are you at the Home Works?'

'No,' George said faintly, then added more boldly, 'the Oare Works.'

'Out-of-towners, eh? Like most of the men in here on a market day.' She smiled at him, showing even teeth. 'Are you going to pay me, then? Or just stand there staring?'

George fumbled in his pocket for some coins, then slid them across the counter.

'Thank you kindly. Now, off you go before you have my father after you. He doesn't like it when the young men look at me so.'

She smiled again as she spoke and George picked up the tankards, made to turn around and stopped. 'Your father?' he asked.

'The landlord.' The girl pointed to a notice over the bar. '"Nathaniel Donaldson. Licensee". I'm his daughter, Maggie. And my friend there,' she pointed, and George saw the blonde girl from Sunday, collecting empty tankards, 'that's Judith. Just in case your friend wants to know.'

She winked at George, who made ready to depart with the drinks, before he gathered his wits. 'I'm George. And he's Thomas,' he half called after her, as she moved along the bar to serve someone else.

She smiled over her shoulder at him, then turned back to her customer. He felt as though all eyes must be upon him as he moved across the room, but the only person he could see looking at him was Thomas.

'You took your time,' he said, seizing his drink and taking

a couple of gulps before setting it down on the shelf nailed to the upright. 'That's better.' He let out a sigh.

'Maggie and Judith,' George said.

'What are you talking about?' Thomas looked puzzled.

'From Sunday. That's Judith, there.' George indicated over Thomas's shoulder, where she was still at work collecting tankards. 'And that's Maggie, behind the bar.' He felt strangely reluctant to tell his friend. He already knew that he wanted Maggie all to himself. He also knew what Thomas was like. His natural confidence was nearly always enough to win him the attention of whichever girl he wanted.

Please don't let it be Maggie this time, George thought, wondering whether he should sing the praises of Judith's face and figure. Then he realised that Thomas could barely take his eyes off her and felt a flutter of hope. He turned back towards the bar to catch Maggie looking in their direction. He raised his hand in a half-wave and gave her what he hoped was his best smile. He was gratified to see her smile in return before he noticed a tall, heavy-set man at the back of the bar. He was also looking in George's direction but the scowl on his face was neither friendly nor encouraging.

Even so, George insisted on going up to the bar once their drinks were finished. He didn't want Thomas to have a chance to talk to Maggie, so he seized his friend's tankard as soon as he had drained it. 'I'll fetch us more drinks. You might be able to catch a word with Judith,' George said, already emboldened by the ale he'd taken. Judith was close by, wiping down a table she'd recently cleared. Thomas's eyes lit up, and he was making his way in her direction before George was halfway to the bar, keeping a wary eye on the man he presumed to be Maggie's father. To his relief, he was called through to the other bar and, free of his unnerving presence, he was able to talk to Maggie again.

'Thirsty tonight, are we?' Maggie was already pouring the same again, without being asked. 'And I see your friend hasn't wasted any time.'

She nodded towards Thomas, now deep in conversation with Judith and standing very close to her, his arm up against one of the uprights, effectively blocking her from moving away.

'When can I see you?' George blurted out, then blushed, mortified by his clumsiness.

'You're seeing me now, aren't you?' Maggie said, laughing. Then she relented. 'But if you mean when can you see me outside here, what about tomorrow, after church? Same place as we saw you last week.'

She held out her hand for his money and George could only nod as she moved away to serve the increasing crush. The inn was busier now, and Thomas and George's previous spot was lost to them. George forced his way towards Thomas and Judith, trying to avoid losing any of the precious ale, to arrive flushed and triumphant.

'George, this is Judith,' Thomas said. He already had a proprietorial air, George thought, as he handed over his friend's ale.

Judith smiled at him, then said, 'Well, I'd better be getting on. Mr Donaldson has his eye on me.'

She ducked under Thomas's arm and George turned to see Mr Donaldson once more scowling in their direction. Thomas sulked over Judith's departure until George told him of Maggie's suggestion to meet the next day, on Ordnance Wharf.

'You managed that well,' Thomas said, with a touch of envy. 'I wasn't getting anywhere with Judith.' He appeared bemused that his charm had failed to work its usual magic.

George kept quiet. He wasn't going to confess to his clumsy request, or to the fact that it was Maggie, not him, who was clearly in charge of the proceedings.

CHAPTER THIRTY-ONE

The next day Maggie was as good as her word and she and Judith appeared on Ordnance Wharf after church, to find George and Thomas already waiting. George had been apprehensive all morning. He couldn't quite believe that Maggie would turn up and, when she did, he was once again worried in case she found Thomas more appealing. But, to his astonishment, she drew her arm through his and they walked side by side along the wharf, Maggie doing most of the talking.

'Are you new here? I don't think I've seen you around before. Mind you, I haven't seen your friend, either.' George cast a glance back, to see Thomas walking at Judith's side but, to his surprise, not arm in arm.

'We used to drink at the Fountain. Then we began to try other places,' George said. 'And we found the Three Tuns.'

'Ah, not before you followed us there.' Maggie squeezed his arm playfully and tossed her head, so that her dark curls bobbed beneath her bonnet. She was in her Sunday best, George noticed – a plain green dress with a spencer over it. The spencer, buttoned to the neck, gave her a demure appearance, quite at odds with how she had appeared the previous evening. Then, her low neckline had attracted more eyes than George's as she'd worked behind the bar.

Lost in that memory, he had to pull himself back to the present to concentrate on her words.

'My father keeps a strict eye on me at the inn, but I hope you'll carry on visiting us of a Saturday,' she said. 'And in the week, too, if you're minded. It's nice to see fresh faces in town.'

'And can I see you other than at the inn?' George knew he was expressing himself clumsily again, but they had almost reached the Three Tuns and he was conscious of how soon she would be lost to him.

'Like I said, my father keeps a close eye on me. And he keeps me busy. But now I've a fancy to see the ducks on Stonebridge Pond,' Maggie said.

She glanced across the road to the inn, then drew George onto the path that circled the pond. He looked back to see Thomas standing uncertainly at Judith's side and felt a momentary pang for him, before nervous excitement took over.

Maggie had broken free of him and was now almost dancing along the path ahead, turning back to make sure he was following her. When she reached a clump of willows at the water's edge she stopped and held out her hand. George's heart was racing as she drew him under the overhanging branches and turned to him.

She tilted her face up towards him and he gazed down at her, at a loss for what to do but unable to take his eyes off her lips. She laughed and shook her head, so that her curls bounced around her face, then reached up and put one hand around his neck, drawing his face down. He felt the strangest and most delightful sensation as his lips met hers. They were soft and yielding, and he was lost in the experience, trying his best to respond as, startled, he felt the tip of her tongue before her teeth grazed his lip.

Then she pushed him gently away. 'I'd better be getting back. Don't want Father making trouble when we've only just met.'

She was out on the path before he could gather his thoughts and he stood for a moment or two in wonder at what had just happened, before pushing through the willow boughs in pursuit of her. She'd almost reached Thomas and Judith, still standing at the top of the path, before he caught up with her.

Maggie seized Judith's arm and turned towards the road. 'We'll see you both on Saturday evening. And Sunday, too.' The last words were directed at George, then she and Judith were crossing the road to leave him standing beside a silent Thomas.

Thomas began to stride up the hill. George found himself having to hurry to catch up. He cast sideways glances at his friend but no words were spoken and George lapsed into his own thoughts. His first kiss! As he relived it, trying to memorise every sensation, his stomach gave a little backflip of excitement. He couldn't suppress a shiver, then felt a rush of shame. Kissing a girl on a Sunday surely went against everything he had been taught at the Foundling School. His excitement at what had just happened began to ebb away. Was Thomas disgusted with him? What had happened between him and Judith? He cast another sidelong glance at his friend, but his expression wasn't encouraging. Thomas's brows were drawn together in a frown and his lips were set in a thin line. George thought it better to stay silent so they arrived at Widow Booth's with not a word spoken during the whole journey.

Widow Booth served them their Sunday dinner, looking from one to the other of her lodgers in bemusement. She opened her mouth as if to say something, then thought better of it, defeated by the atmosphere in the room.

George's excitement had turned to misery, which in turn threatened to become anger. He was desperate to discuss what had happened with Thomas but didn't know where to begin now that his friend was behaving so oddly. His anxiety destroyed his appetite and he left half the food on his plate untouched. Widow Booth hovered in the doorway, wondering whether or not to clear the table, until George burst out, 'For Heaven's sake, will you not speak to me? What have I done?' which sent her scuttling back into the kitchen.

'Done?' Thomas glared at him. 'Why, you've . . .' He paused, at a loss, then gathered himself. 'You've stolen a march on me, that's what you've done.' He laughed, although there was little humour in his face. 'I suppose I'm not used to it.'

'Judith?' George said tentatively, not quite sure what question to ask. 'Is she . . . does she . . .?'

'Does she like me?' Thomas said. 'I wish I knew. It would seem not. She's pleasant enough to me, but if I tried to take her hand I reckon she'd slap me.'

George pondered on this. Thomas now had a little spot of colour high on each cheek and he pushed away his plate with some vigour, so that his knife and fork clattered to the floor.

'Maybe she just needs a bit of time,' George ventured. 'After all, we've only just met them.'

Thomas snorted. 'Well, you've only just met Maggie yet anyone would think you were *very* good friends.'

George flushed scarlet. 'I don't know what to make of it,' he confessed.

They sat on in silence, absorbed in their thoughts, then Thomas said, 'I suppose we must go back to the Three Tuns on Saturday.' He brightened a little at the prospect. 'Perhaps you're right and Judith just needs more time to get to know me.'

George nodded vigorously. It was the first time he'd seen his friend so downcast. Thomas, at nineteen years of age, had a wealth of experience in George's view. He was surprised to see him so disconsolate, and so willing to listen to what he had to say.

This pattern was to be repeated over the coming weeks. Saturday evenings in the Three Tuns were invariably followed by a walk home during which Thomas raked over any words Judith had uttered in passing as she moved around the inn, and any supposed glances in his direction.

Sundays, George found, were a repeat of his first encounter with Maggie. A walk from Ordnance Wharf back to the Three Tuns culminated in a swift detour to 'their' clump of willows. Here Maggie was very happy to be kissed – sometimes twice, if he was lucky – before departing to the inn, leaving George to walk home with a ruffled Thomas. His relationship with Judith had, at least, progressed to the extent that she permitted him to take her arm during the journey.

Sunday dinner invariably involved a dissection of what had just occurred, followed by a lift in Thomas's spirits at the prospect of a breakthrough the following weekend. George, meanwhile, was formulating a plan to make Maggie his betrothed. He reasoned that if he could find better employment at the works – in the office perhaps, for surely all his studies at the Foundling School must stand him in good stead – then Maggie's father might look upon him more favourably. If he worked and saved hard, maybe he would be in a position to offer Maggie a home when they married. It would have to be a room in a shared lodging house at first but in time ... George's daydream faltered there. He didn't think Maggie, or her father, would look kindly on a room in a lodging house as a good start to married life. Perhaps he could take up residence in the inn, he thought, then discounted the idea. He didn't like to think of her continuing to work behind the bar – prey to the over-familiar eyes of all the customers – once she was his. A memory of her ready smile, exposing those small, even teeth, and her hazel eyes looking up at him from beneath her luxuriant dark curls swept away all doubts. She had chosen him and somehow they would work things out so that they could be together, even if it took a bit longer than he hoped.

CHAPTER THIRTY-TWO

George had noticed the group of men at the bar: strangers in the area, which was nothing unusual on a market day. On a summer's evening, those who had sold well often stayed on longer than they should, drinking away their profits. That evening, his attention was caught by one particular man, burly and bearded, whom he had seen more than once glancing in his direction.

At one point, their eyes locked briefly then slid apart, before George returned to his conversation with Thomas. He'd had no shock of recognition when their eyes met so he concluded the man was a stranger. But he felt an abrupt return of the unease he had suffered when he first came to the area, fearing he was sought as an absconder from his apprenticeship.

During the winter months after his arrival, the cloak of darkness that covered his movements before and after working hours had given him a fragile sense of safety. But with the arrival of spring and the longer, lighter evenings, he'd found himself looking over his shoulder to see whether he was being followed, or whether the person he had just passed had turned to look back at him. As time had passed and no one had accosted him, he'd lost his anxiety . . . until now.

'I don't feel much like staying here this evening,' he said to Thomas, before draining his tankard.

'But we've only just come in,' Thomas protested, startled by his words.

George sighed. Thomas continued to hope that Judith would favour him, reasoning that she surely would after witnessing his dogged devotion. He no doubt wanted to stay on at the inn, hoping that tonight would be the night when he might steal a kiss.

'I'll see you later, then,' George said, and made his way over to the bar. He waited patiently while Maggie finished serving a customer, nodding politely to her father, who was working in the other bar. He'd only just begun grudgingly to acknowledge George, but they were a long way from him considering George as a potential son-in-law.

The inn was noisy, the candlelight flickering and dancing off the shelved glasses and the beaten pewter tankards hanging from the beam over the bar. George would normally have preferred to spend his evening there, rather than in the room he shared with Thomas in old Widow Booth's cottage. There were plenty of men from the powder works in the same situation as him, without a wife or family to go home to and preferring the company of the inn to a solitary evening spent waiting to go to bed. He rather thought that a few had chosen the inn over their own homes.

Maggie disturbed his reverie by appearing before him.

'I'm leaving now,' he said. 'I thought to say good night.'

'A bit early for you, isn't it? Are you unwell?' Maggie was teasing but George could see the question in her hazel eyes.

He smiled. 'I'm fine. A bit tired, mebbe.'

'Well, it's busy tonight. I'd not be able to spare you much time anyway,' Maggie said. 'I'll see you tomorrow, as usual.'

She flashed him a smile, and as she turned away to serve another customer, George noticed her dark curls escaping from the back of her cap onto her shoulders.

He looked around. There was no sign of the stranger at the bar. He shook his head at his own folly. The man was likely on his way home, market-day celebration over and his wife waiting to give him a scolding over wasting his profits at the inn. His horse would know the way without needing any guidance, allowing his owner to nod off.

George pushed through the crowd and gained the door, pulling it open onto the dark street. It fell instantly quiet once the door shut behind him. He stood for a moment, buttoning his jacket against the cool evening air, then walked down Tanners Street and onto Dark Hill, crossing to take a look at the still waters of Stonebridge Pond. A faint trail of moonlight laid a path across the middle and all was silent, the waterfowl sleeping, heads tucked under their wings. There was a burst of noise from the inn as the door opened to let another drinker in or out, then all was peaceful once more. As George turned to begin the walk up Dark Hill, he heard a horse's hoofs and the rumble of wheels on the town's cobbles.

He was just beginning to feel the pull of the hill in his calves as the cart drew level. He glanced to the side to see whether he recognised the driver. He'd barely registered that it wasn't the stranger from the inn, as he'd half expected, before he heard a dull thud. Someone had jumped down, and in the next instant George found himself seized, his arms pinned to his sides.

'What are you doing?' he protested, twisting to see who had grabbed him.

'I might ask you the same thing.' The voice was low and rasping. 'A fit young lad like you should be fighting for King and country.' The half-light of the moon revealed the features of the stranger from the bar.

'I am,' George protested, heart beating fast. 'I'm at the powder works. Making sure that the King's Navy and the country's quarries are kept well supplied with gunpowder and blasting powder.'

This wasn't about him running away from Rochester, he realised. This was a press gang, looking to furnish the Navy with sailors as the war with France dragged on.

'Aye, well, there's plenty of others can do that sort of work. You're young and healthy, just what the Navy's looking for. The regulating officer's going to be mighty pleased with you.'

His captor's expression suggested he was happy with his prize, George thought, just as a punch to his stomach took him by surprise. Winded, he doubled over and found his legs seized by another pair of hands. Before he could draw breath, he was bundled into the back of the cart, which was already on the move again up the hill.

As the breath returned to his body, George opened his mouth and yelled at the top of his voice, 'Tell Maggie they've taken me. The press men have taken me.'

He hoped that if someone had left the inn and was walking home, they would hear him, but the only sound was the muttered cursing of his captors. They were binding his wrists and ankles with rope, and when he tried to protest one grabbed his hair and yanked his head back, while the other gagged his mouth with a piece of foul-smelling cloth. George coughed and retched as they flung him down. It was only then he discovered he had travelling companions. Two other men lay in the bottom of the cart, bound and gagged as he was, bouncing helplessly around as the horse trotted on into the night, leaving Faversham far behind.

The others were huddled and silent, clearly resigned to their fate. From what George could see, they were a lot older than he was. His heart sank yet further as he understood what a prize he must be for his captors. He'd heard they got ten shillings for every man they took, unless you had the means to bribe them to give you your freedom. George had less than a shilling in his pocket.

CHAPTER THIRTY-THREE

George passed a cold and uncomfortable night after his capture. He spent long hours being jolted through the countryside, finally falling into a fitful doze despite his discomfort, only to find the cart at a standstill when he was shaken roughly awake. His captors were urging him and their other victims to 'Get down now,' as they loosened the bindings on their legs.

George was manhandled off the cart and stumbled to stay upright, his arms still bound, his legs chilled and stiff from the journey. He thought he caught a faint whiff of the sea on the cold breeze, but it was too dark for him to make out anything of his surroundings. He shuffled along as best he could across a cobbled courtyard, captors in front and behind their small group, until he was pushed into a cell, already more than half full with men in as sorry a state as he was. The reek in the air made him gag and he feared he would choke until the leader of the press gang, the stranger from the bar, untied the rank cloth binding his mouth.

'Keep it shut,' he warned George. 'You'll have your say later this morning.'

Then the man left, banging the heavy oak door behind him and shooting the bolts, disturbing some of the occupants of the room who were sleeping on the stone floor. There were muttered groans and curses before they settled down again.

George waited a few moments to allow his eyes to accustom themselves to the gloom, lifted only by dim light filtering through a small barred window set high in the wall. He began to make out the shapes of his fellow prisoners and picked his way among them, in search of a spot to sit for what few hours remained of the night. The edges of the room were fully occupied so he had to content himself with squatting close to where he'd entered. He clasped his hands around his knees, closed his eyes and tried to stop his ears with his jacket collar to block out the snoring and coughing from all around him.

He was startled out of a doze when the door was flung open, letting in a shaft of pale sunlight, and a voice bellowed, 'On your feet, the lot of you!'

His stomach growled with hunger as they were pushed out into the hazy morning light. He'd have been eating his breakfast now at Widow Booth's table if he hadn't been taken. Thomas would have been surprised not to find him asleep when he returned from the Three Tuns, unless ale had addled his brain, and even more surprised at his absence this morning. Would he do anything about it? Or would he think that George had slipped back to the inn, to spend time with Maggie?

George's heart turned over at the thought of Maggie, as oblivious as Thomas to his plight. Would anyone raise the alarm? He thought not. He suspected it would be midday before Thomas and Maggie realised he was missing. And that depended on Thomas choosing to attend church on his own and walk back to Ordnance Wharf as usual, in the hope of spending time in Judith's company. Only then would it become apparent that George wasn't with Maggie, but how would anyone know where to look for him? As far as they were concerned, he had left the inn and simply vanished. Unless anyone had heard his cry for help.

These thoughts occupied George throughout the time the men were kept standing in line, shuffling forward as, one by one, they were pushed through the open door of a building on the far side of the yard. He had just registered that men went in, but didn't come out, when it was his turn to be shoved roughly through the entrance.

'Name?' barked the man sitting behind a desk in the centre of the small and otherwise bare room, a ledger open before him. He didn't look up, his quill poised to scratch the next entry onto the page.

'George Smith,' George said.

'Age?'

'Seventeen.'

'Seventeen, sir,' the man corrected him, looking up from his ledger. As he did so, his eyes narrowed.

George felt a shock of recognition. He was face to face with Noah Taylor, right-hand man of Henry Gifford in Rochester, to whom George had been apprenticed.

'You're not George Smith,' Noah said. He'd been about to dip his quill into the ink, ready to score through the name he had just written, then a smile touched his lips. 'Mr Gifford will be very interested to hear about you. Finally, he'll get justice and you, my lad, will go to prison for breaking the terms of your apprenticeship.'

In the long pause that followed, George could feel his heart beating so hard he thought the sound must fill the whole room. He glanced behind him towards the door, wondering whether he could make a run for it, but two men stood on guard just inside the entrance, impassive.

Noah spoke again. 'Unless, of course, George Smith would like to volunteer for the Navy and offer to serve our great country. No questions asked.'

Noah's quill was poised over the page.

George took a great, shuddering sigh. A vision of Maggie as he'd seen her last, laughing as she served a customer, flitted across his mind. The streets of Faversham, the creek, his room at Widow Booth's, the woods and ponds of the Oare Works flashed before him. Then Noah came into focus again.

Slowly, George nodded. A smile spread across Noah's face as he scratched a few words into the ledger.

'A wise choice, I think you'll find. Welcome to His Majesty's Navy.'

He gestured to George to pass through into the room beyond. As he stepped through the door, he heard the chink of coins behind him. Payment was being made for his capture.

George found himself sitting on the floor once more in the company of the men he recognised from his overnight imprisonment. As each man entered he was handed a tin bowl of watery porridge, a hunk of bread and a cup of small ale. The bread was dry but George's hunger meant he wasn't proud. He soaked it in the ale and ate it gratefully while the porridge cooled, all the while wondering what would come next. He didn't have to wait long to find out.

A wagon drew up outside and the men were ordered to their feet. George barely had time to cram the last of the bread into his mouth before he was roughly hustled out of the door.

'Admiralty Wharf?' the wagon driver asked, receiving a nod from one of the guards in answer. He shook the reins and they were on their way – a short journey over cobbled streets, passing alongside a great waterway lined with vessels, before the cart turned into a grand stone gate, guarded by a sentry, and rumbled into another courtyard. They hadn't travelled far and George wondered why they weren't made to walk, then reflected that some might have made a run for it. He rather thought he would have been among them.

CHAPTER THIRTY-FOUR

George spent a few days in a quayside room not dissimilar to the one where he'd been imprisoned overnight, but less crowded. It was long enough for him to be given a cursory medical examination and issued with his kit – a coarse-wool short navy jacket and two pairs of wide-legged trousers. These were creamy white and George couldn't help thinking them impractical for any sort of work. He was to discover that they were expected to keep them clean and smart at all times on board ship, which would involve a great deal more laundering than he was used to doing. A couple of rough linen shirts and bright cotton neckerchiefs completed his kit, all to be carried in a drawstring canvas bag.

There was much coming and going of ships at the quay. George knew crews were being picked and even though he had no wish to be there, he didn't want to be left behind, either, due to his landsman status. He'd learnt from some of the men he'd got talking to that landsmen, with no skill at sea, were not much desired aboard ship. The same men gave him the impression he'd be lucky to find a captain prepared to take him.

George had imagined he would be trained before he was sent to sea, but most of the men there were seasoned sailors, waiting to join their ships. One man pressed at the same time as George turned out to have past experience, on merchantmen, while another was also a landsman. Walter was an escaped prisoner who had been recaptured, thrown into the same cart as George and given the choice of returning to prison or 'taking the King's shilling'. It was from him that George learnt why he had been chosen for impressment.

'They were watching all the younger ones in the inn, since they couldn't go back to the regulating officer with less than they'd been told to find that night,' Walter confided. 'I heard them discussing it when they came back to the cart after they'd been drinking. They couldn't risk taking anyone while they were inside in case it caused a riot. You was just unlucky – you left the inn on your own.'

George cursed his behaviour that night. His fear that he had been recognised was unfounded, although he had been watched for a purpose – just not the one he had thought. If he hadn't let it drive him from the inn, his life would be proceeding along the path he had mapped out for himself. Now, all was unknown.

His friendship with Walter didn't have time to prosper. George was called to the office that afternoon, asked to sign his name in the ledger and told he would receive a salary of twelve pounds a year.

He couldn't stop himself blurting out, 'But I earned more than that at the powder works.'

The clerk looked up at him. 'And you paid for your board, lodging and all your other needs out of that, did you not?'

George coloured. 'Yes, but—'

Any further protests were cut off as the clerk instructed him, coldly, to report to HMS *Valour* that night. He was bound for the West Indies.

George asked around until he found others preparing to make their departure that evening. They seemed assured and busy, wisecracking with each other, and he felt shy and bewildered once more. But he discovered where he was to board the vessel and even learnt its type – a brig-sloop – which meant nothing to him. From eavesdropping on the conversations around him, though, he gathered that his fellow sailors were happy with their ship and glad not to be deployed on one of the huge men-of-war, one of which was being worked on there.

George had wandered along the quayside and watched the men at work – dwarfed by the great ship with three decks, all lined with the gun-ports that he knew were the cannon placements. He had found its size astonishing and could barely believe it was seaworthy. Once he had discovered that a ship such as that might carry near enough a thousand men, he had heard enough. No wonder his fellow sailors were relieved not to be signed on to its crew. How could it be that a ship might take to the seas carrying near enough the population of Faversham within its timber hulk?

When the men lined up that evening beside HMS *Valour*, he had reason to feel relieved. She was neat and trim, with two masts and barely any gun-ports – he could count only nine on the side next to the quay. And the number waiting to board was barely above a hundred, in his estimate. If he had to go to sea – and every fibre of him still wished himself back in Faversham with Maggie and Thomas – he was glad that it was under these circumstances.

The snaking line of men was boarding, first bypassing a man wearing a blue frock coat with brass buttons who ticked off their name and rank as they went. When George said, 'George Smith, landsman,' the man raised his eyebrows.

'I hope you're open to hard work and learning fast, my boy. The captain must have struggled to fill his crew to have agreed to take you on. There's no room for passengers on a small ship such as this. Every man pulls his weight.'

His expression was fierce and George hastened to assure him that he had every intention of working hard, even as his heart sank. He feared starting at a disadvantage and being picked on – it brought back bad memories of the Foundling School where the older, more experienced pupils had been merciless bullies of the younger children.

The man gave him a curt nod, then jerked his head to indicate he should board. George shouldered his kitbag and took his first steps on board ship, aware at once of the movement of the water as he crossed the gangplank and stepped onto the deck. He wanted to take a moment to look back at the land, wondering when he would next see it, but he was urged on by a voice from behind.

'What are you waiting for? We need to get below and stow our kit before all the best spaces are gone.' George stepped aside to allow his impatient fellow sailor to go below, before he, too, followed suit. He took with him an impression of the docks in the gathering dusk – the grand houses looking down on them, the smaller houses straggling up the hillside behind, open fields in the distance and, in the water all around, vessels at anchor, awaiting stores, repair or crew. Somewhere in the distant darkness was the fort where he had laboured underground, building the defences around this dockyard before he had escaped and fled to Faversham, but he recognised none of it.

Chapter Thirty-Five

George tried to tell himself that life aboard ship was little different from what he had been used to at the Foundling School. Indeed, he was no stranger to routine, to discipline and to regimentation, even though he had been parted from it for five years now. But in truth, he found it hard to bear. He woke and slept – or tried to – when he was told to. His first nights were spent sleepless in a cloth hammock, slung on the lower deck, bodies packed so close around him that he could touch his neighbours by putting out a hand. Exhaustion eventually got the better of him and he learnt to sleep with a stranger's face so close to his that it was if they shared a bed.

He did as he was told, hauling in ropes and swabbing decks, polishing brass and sweeping, all the while keeping his eyes and ears open so that he could understand as much as possible about the nature of his new world. He learnt to look forward to mealtimes for portions were generous even if what was served varied little – salt beef or pork, ship's biscuits, a porridge-like soup and a bit of cheese with a quantity of small beer. George was denied the grog that many of the other seamen preferred to the beer.

'You'll have to wait until you're twenty,' the petty officer said, when George had requested it. 'You need to be a man to handle this stuff.' The seamen waiting in line burst into laughter and George blushed, inwardly cursing his fair skin for letting him down so badly.

He thought often of Maggie and Thomas in those first few weeks, most especially when he was made miserable by the pitching and yawing of the ship. It was explained to him by his shipmates, with a roll of their eyes, that he could expect much worse since they were still in calm waters where such discomforts were caused by a change in the prevailing wind direction or the course of the vessel. He hoped he would become used to it, even as he wondered whether there was a way he might get out of his predicament and return to the life he knew – the Oare Works, Faversham, the Three Tuns, Maggie, Thomas.

Then, as the journey continued and there was nothing but sea all around – sea, a fierce sun and a brisk wind by day, a clear starlit sky by night – his life in England began to recede from his mind.

They were on course for the West Indies, or so he was told. It meant nothing to George. He knew rivers led out to the sea: the Thames, the Medway, the Swale, Faversham Creek – they had all played a part in his life. But he couldn't place himself in this new world, in which the water stretched as far as the eye could see.

George knew that as a landsman he was the lowliest of the low aboard ship, with only the captain's boys below him and they were but twelve years old. He'd started to recognise the hierarchy and the rigid differences between the ranks. He doubted he'd ever get to grips with reading the clues presented by the frogging, gold buttons and epaulettes of the different officer ranks but then, he thought, he'd never need to worry about them, other than to obey their orders.

The lower ranks, though, had their own clear delineations. Ralph, the impatient young seaman George had met on first stepping aboard, informed him that the ones most demanding of respect were the 'toppers', those who shinned up the rigging and dealt with all matters above the deck, including keeping lookout from on high. Their prowess and head for heights made them the elite of the crew. George was most confused by the 'young gentlemen' who, by nature of their position in society as the sons of politicians or the gentry, were in charge of men old enough to be their fathers who had many more years' experience at sea.

'They're in training to be officers,' Ralph explained. 'Their fathers will be friends of the captain and he has them under his protection. You'd do well to keep an eye open around them. Although the bunch we have with us seems a nice enough lot. Not like on my last ship.'

He described how he had been singled out as a trouble-maker by one of the young gentlemen on his last voyage, who had done everything possible to make his life a misery until Ralph and his friends had discovered his weak spot.

'He didn't like mice,' Ralph said, chuckling at the memory. 'And if there's one thing there's plenty of aboard ship, it's mice. So one night, before he was due to turn in, we filled his hammock with ship's biscuit crumbs and added a few of the little blighters we'd caught. You know how hard those biscuits are – the critters were still sitting there munching them when he arrived and made ready to turn in. You've never heard screams like it once he'd swung into his hammock and found it already occupied.'

George dissolved into laughter.

'He left you alone after that?'

'He did,' Ralph said. 'Asked for a transfer to another ship for the homeward journey.'

So, it would be wise to keep on the right side of his ship-mates, George concluded, then went on to quiz Ralph some more. In the next half-hour, huddled below decks and talking quietly to avoid disturbing those sleeping before going on watch, George learnt just how long it would take him to make progress from his lowly state.

'I reckon you can be an ordinary seaman after a year,' Ralph said. 'You seem bright enough and you're quick to learn. Then it'll be another three years before you're an able seaman. After that—'

George cut him off. 'That's all right. Able seaman will do.'

He couldn't imagine still being at sea after four years. Four years! What would have happened to Maggie after four years had passed with no word from him? He could write, he remembered, and resolved to do so as soon as they reached the West Indies. But the letter would take weeks, if not months, to reach her.

Ralph misunderstood. 'Aye, not many men get beyond able seaman anyway. They're happy to stay like that for years, until they leave the Navy.'

It didn't take George long to grasp that life aboard ship was like being part of a family, albeit a family of men, all under the care of the captain. Then again, it was more than a family – a street, maybe – an ensemble of characters who had their own defined roles but could turn their hand to whatever needed doing.

Ralph relished telling George tales of the damage caused by terrible storms and by one particularly ferocious battle they had come through.

'There were holes in the side and the sea were pouring in. We had to get down below and stuff the gaps with whatever we could lay our hands on – blankets mostly – until the carpenter and the cooper could stop them up with planks. The men weren't right pleased that their bedding was soaked

213

through. Then the sails were torn off the rigging by the wind and we had to set to and stitch the rips – made my hands bleed, it did. We ain't got no one except ourselves to rely on,' Ralph added. 'We like it that way.'

George didn't really know what he meant but nodded sagely as though he did.

In the same way that the men had to be prepared to turn their hand to anything, the fabric of the ship was also pressed into multiple uses. It seemed to George that there wasn't an inch of space below deck that was left unused. Every cubbyhole or corner stored a coil of rope, a bag of grain or a stoppered pot of provisions. The galley kitchen gave the cook just enough room to stand, surrounded by the tools of his trade, mostly hanging above his head. Hooks also filled the ceiling of the lower deck where they were used to store the men's belongings as well as their hammocks. Negotiating a passage below decks meant constantly ducking and stooping to avoid being smacked in the face by something unexpected.

George came to love being above decks in the fresh air, in all weathers, with nothing but the open sea all around and the occasional sighting of schools of porpoises and great ungainly birds that rested on the rigging. He became scornful of the George who had first come aboard, nervous of the uncertain shifting of the boards beneath his feet, convinced that the whole structure must be doomed to capsize, made anxious by every creak of the wood as it eased and settled – so much more obvious in the still of the night when all around him snored peacefully. Now George snored peacefully, too, and his days passed in the regular rhythm of shipboard life, so that he almost dreaded arriving at their destination.

He had thought being in the Navy meant sailing from one battle to another. He had learnt from Ralph that their role was far more likely to involve guarding Britain's trading interests in the West Indies from incursions by the Dutch, French or Spanish.

When George had ventured to ask what trading interests he referred to, Ralph had rolled his eyes yet again. 'Where do you think our sugar back home comes from? Our rum, our tobacco, our cotton? The merchant ships pick it up here and take it home, or trade it along the way for something else we need.'

'Something else?' George asked, wondering at how he had managed to remain in ignorance of such things for so long.

But Ralph wouldn't be drawn any further on what he meant.

CHAPTER THIRTY-SIX

One thing George had neglected to discover from Ralph was the nature of the land they were sailing towards. He'd concerned himself far more with understanding the workings of HMS *Valour* and its crew. Now, as land hove into sight, he loitered on the deck and strained his eyes for his first glimpse of Jamaica. He'd learnt that this was to be their destination only that morning, when excitement spread through the ship that land had been sighted. Up on deck, the air was balmy, the wind light, and George could have sworn he could smell the fresh green scent of vegetation and the sharp tang of woodsmoke borne on the breeze. He kept quiet, not wanting to make himself the butt of his fellow sailors' humour, but as the ship gained slowly on the shore, he thought he could add the smell of cooking to the mix.

The lack of wind meant that the pace was frustratingly slow for those now eager to set foot on solid ground after weeks at sea, but by mid-afternoon they had sailed into the mouth of a great bay. As they made ready to anchor, George couldn't help glancing repeatedly towards the shore, even as he concentrated on the tasks he had been allotted. He was not alone – there was a clear sense of excitement among the crew but they were well-disciplined and got on with their duties. Some had been to this place before: Port Royal, as

George learnt it was called. He could make out a row or two of neat buildings spanning the shoreline, one adorned with a clock, while a church tower was the only thing to break the roofline. The land beyond the town was lush and green, and hills rose in the far distance, with an almost blue haze upon them. HMS *Valour* had joined a great many ships of different sizes, either berthed or at anchor a little way offshore.

'We'll take on stores here,' Ralph told George, 'and we'll be allowed a little time ashore so best make the most of it. Who knows when we'll get another chance?'

And so began the next stage of George's education. The crew were granted shore leave, as Ralph had said, and rowed over the water in small boats to partake of rum and whatever pleasures their wages would buy. Once George had got used to the unsettling stability of land, and could walk without lurching, he was delighted to discover that he could buy rum, with no questions asked about his age. He settled on a wooden bench in the shack that served as the nearest bar to port, sipped his rum and looked about. The sailors sitting around him had come from far and wide – Holland, Spain, Portugal, France and Africa, Ralph told him.

'But aren't we are at war with some of them?' George was puzzled.

'Our navies are at war. But these are sailors from merchant ships, getting ready to take goods home after dropping off cargo.'

'But . . .' George gave up on that train of thought and settled, instead, into the new pleasure of drinking rum. He refused to join a party in search of women to entertain them, insisting he wanted to remain true to his sweetheart back home, and was discovered some time later – fast asleep, his head on the table – by Ralph.

217

'We've got to get back to the ship or there'll be trouble,' Ralph said, hauling him to his feet. George could remember little about being half dragged, half carried to the rowing boat, or how he had found his way into his hammock, but he woke the next morning with a pain in his head such as he'd never felt before.

Ralph laughed at his croaked insistence that he needed to see the ship's doctor at once.

'The only sickness you have is too much rum,' he said. 'You'd do well to take some water with it next time.'

'There won't be a next time,' George muttered. It took a bucket of sea water tipped over his head before he could get up and stagger out into the daylight, which hurt his brain so much that he had to go about his duties with his eyes screwed up.

On his next shore leave, he confined himself to walking around the town, admiring the buildings and the tree-lined roads, and gazing with some surprise at the smartly dressed ladies and gentlemen. They walked the streets as though they were in an English town that had been lifted up and trans-planted far overseas. They appeared determined to carry on living the only life they knew, despite the heat that made them pink in the face and damp of brow all day long.

He turned to the source of all knowledge, Ralph, to check that his assumptions were correct.

'Oh, yes, they live just as they do at home,' Ralph said. 'Ask the young gentlemen. They get asked to dine out with the captain while they're here. They'll tell you about the pianos and crystal glasses, the wine at dinner and the dancing afterwards.'

The sailors were more familiar with the seamier side of Port Royal, the drinking and the women, which George supposed made it no different from any seafaring town in England. One big difference between an English town and Port Royal was the weather, of course. His jacket had become a sweaty hindrance that he cast off at the first opportunity.

Their final days at anchor were spent in giving the ship a thorough overhaul, with the decks above and below scrubbed, hammocks and bedding washed and aired, brass polished and personal laundry done – all on the orders of the captain.

Then, inspection of the work complete, they lifted the anchor and were away again but not very far this time – just across the bay into the much larger and busier Kingston harbour. Looking back across the water to Port Royal, George could now see that their first destination took up just the tip of a narrow spit of land jutting into the bay.

He was to discover even more about the ways of the world in Kingston. He became aware of a group of miserable wretches huddled on the quayside after he and many of the crew had disembarked from HMS *Valour*. The captain had warned them that their stay in the town was to be brief, and any purchases of comforts for the next leg of the journey should be made in short order.

Seeing the size of the huddled group, who must have numbered in excess of fifty souls sitting in the dust under the scorching sun, George came to an abrupt halt.

'Slaves,' Ralph said briefly, in response to the puzzled face George turned towards him. 'Just off one of the boats and bound for the plantations. I dare say there'll be a wagon to collect 'em before too long.'

George had never seen such defeated expressions on the faces of humans before. Neither had he ever seen such a quantity of black faces together. Their clothes were pitiful rags, they looked half-starved and, as he stared, he noticed one or two babies clutched to their mother's breasts, all silent.

'Don't stare like that,' Ralph said impatiently. 'It's something you'll get used to round here.'

'But where are they from?' George asked. 'And what are they doing here?'

'Africa,' Ralph replied. 'They're bound for the sugar plantations, like I said. To work there, cutting the cane.'

'They don't look fit to work.' George, looking back as Ralph dragged him away, saw a wagon roll up and a man jump out, cracking a bull whip as he shouted at the group to get on their feet. The last he saw of them as he and Ralph rounded the corner was their attempts, on unsteady legs, to scramble aboard the wagon, the successful ones reaching down to pull up the weaker members of the group.

The sight haunted George and he couldn't rest easy in Ralph's chosen bar. He sighed and shook his head, staring into his drink until Ralph said, 'For Heaven's sake, there's nothing you can do about it. They're just another bit of cargo, traded like the sugar they produce. Half of 'em probably died on the way over. The slave ships' captains don't give a fig. They chuck 'em overboard if they hit a storm and the ship's in peril.'

George, far from being made easy by Ralph's words, was so enraged that he was ready to leap up and set off back to fight the wagoner he'd just seen but Ralph held him back, laughing. 'It'll do no good. It's all about money, like all trade. And we're here to protect trade routes, not to get into fights over the type of cargo being carried.'

George might have been cheered if he had known that his naval career was due to undergo a change in the near future. An act abolishing the slave trade had already been passed in Britain that year, and HMS *Valour* was to become one of the vessels charged with seeking out ships carrying illegal cargoes of slaves into the colonies. But their new orders had yet to reach their captain so Ralph gave George a thorough telling-off as they returned to the boat.

'You spoilt my evening, and everyone else's, too, with that long face of yours. You need to grow up, George, and get acquainted with the ways of the world.'

CHAPTER THIRTY-SEVEN

O ver the years that followed, George was to become more familiar with the islands and harbours of the West Indies than he ever had been with any area of England. At times he felt as though his feet rarely touched dry land for longer than a few days at a time, as HMS *Valour* and her crew undertook their new role, seeking out slave ships involved in the now-illegal trade.

Despite the new law, plantations still needed labour, since their poor working practices led to regular losses among their workforce. The masters of slave ships were happy to run the risk of capture and punishment in return for the huge sums they were paid.

George's captain found that his new role meant he was no longer welcome to dine at the tables of plantation owners, so their stopovers in Kingston were less frequent and of a shorter duration. George found an advantage to this in the discovery of the necklace of much smaller islands from St Martin to Tobago, where they sailed in pursuit of the slave traders who could slip in and out of those harbours unremarked. Here, the captain was still welcome at the table of a clergyman or a merchant starved of contact with the outside world.

As Ralph had predicted, George had progressed from landsman to ordinary seaman and then to able seaman within four years. After the first few months, he'd become accustomed to his lot and, although the loss of Maggie and Thomas still occasioned him pain, the edge of it was dulled.

Tasked with trying to track and stop the smuggling of slaves, for which the relatively small size of HMS *Valour* made it eminently suitable, they were remote from much of the naval warfare at the time. George wondered whether he would one day regret not having experienced it, but the regular skirmishes – and false alarms – as they pursued slave traders through the blue waters of the Caribbean Sea went some way to making up for what he imagined he was missing.

On one of their infrequent returns to England, they were laid up for a month in Portsmouth while HMS *Valour* underwent repairs. George wondered about paying a visit to Faversham, then delayed making the decision. Instead, he was persuaded to accompany Ralph to Cornwall, where he met his friend's family. They spent a happy fortnight being fêted as naval heroes on leave by the inhabitants of his village, and neither Ralph nor George said anything to disabuse them of this notion. The locals were farmers and workers on the land, with no connection to the sea, and George wondered at Ralph's choice of profession until he blushed and muttered something about 'a bit of difficulty over a stolen pig, or mebbe two'. From this, George deduced that, faced with a choice between imprisonment and the Navy, Ralph had chosen the latter. Much like George, in fact.

On their return to Portsmouth, George had been upset to discover that his shipmate and best friend of the last four years wouldn't be accompanying him on the return voyage to the West Indies. Instead, Ralph had been promoted to midshipman aboard a different vessel, which had been struggling to find enough experienced crew. Within hours of their return to Portsmouth he was gone, leaving George disconsolate and unsettled. Embittered by the loss of yet another person who had been dear to him, he began to question his future in the Navy until he was saved from further introspection by the announcement of HMS *Valour*'s imminent departure.

As the crew settled back into their usual routine, George began to fret that he had reached the great age of twenty-one years without amounting to much. His education at the Foundling School was wasted, for what had he done since then except labour in one way or another? First in the underground confines of the Amherst Fort – when he should have been deskbound as Mr Gifford's apprentice – then at the Oare gunpowder works and now at sea. He at least recognised the advantages of the seafaring life. He'd seen places and experienced things that few of his fellows in Faversham could have dreamt of. His insistence that he was saving himself for his sweetheart there had long ago been worn down by Ralph and he'd experienced the delights of the ladies in more than one of the ports across the Antilles and Windward Isles.

Yet it seemed that Fortune was smiling on George, for barely halfway into their voyage, Mr Perks, the captain's clerk, fell sick and was confined to his bunk by the doctor, who feared contagion spreading through the ship if not contained.

The captain, Mr Ramsay, appointed one of the young gentlemen to step into Mr Perks's shoes for the duration of his illness. It was to be an unhappy decision. The captain found fault with the entries in the log – which were blotted so heavily as to be illegible – mistakes in the accounts and a variety of other misdemeanours. Within the week the young gentleman was returned to normal duties.

George was dozing in his hammock after a night on watch when Edward Powell, one of the lieutenants, came in search of him. 'Mr Ramsay wants to see you,' he said, shaking him into wakefulness.

George, who had had very few direct dealings with the captain despite all his years on board, all but fell out of his hammock in his haste. He was still pulling on his jacket as he followed the lieutenant to the captain's quarters, an area of the ship he had never before visited.

Mr Ramsay was seated at the table, eating his breakfast. 'I'm told that you can write, Smith.'

'Yes, sir.' George wondered how the captain knew. He frequently wrote letters for the men on board to send to their wives and sweethearts, whenever they had the opportunity to do so, but this activity took place huddled on the lower deck, in a quiet corner away from their shipmates.

'There's not much that goes on aboard this ship that escapes my notice, Smith.' The captain was busy shovelling egg into his mouth, piled onto a piece of bread, both food-stuffs denied to the inhabitants of the lower decks. George's mouth watered.

'And can you add up?'

'Yes, sir. I studied mathematics at school,' George said.

'At school, you say?'

'Yes, sir. The Foundling School in London.'

'Hmm. But you weren't apprenticed to the Navy from the Foundling School?'

'No, sir.' George shook his head.

The captain wiped his mouth on a cloth napkin while the young boy employed as his servant removed his plate.

'Well, I'm going to give you a trial as my clerk, while Mr Perks remains indisposed. You'll be relieved of your other

225

duties and you can move forward to sleep where the officers sleep.'

George stood as straight as he could and looked directly ahead. 'Thank you, sir.'

'And I dare say you'll find the food more to your liking,' the captain said, with a half-smile, before dismissing him.

And so began a new phase of George's naval career, one that suited him very well. At first, a fear of getting anything wrong made his hand shake – and the resulting script waver – as he filled in the captain's log. But Mr Ramsay appeared disposed to be understanding and George's confidence grew. He'd thought that the clerk must be underemployed, with just the odd letter to write and the daily log to complete, but he was soon disabused of this notion. Every aspect of the ship's day was documented for the purpose of both captain and Admiralty, from the rotas of the watch to the daily diet and the quantities consumed. George frequently found himself hard at work into the evening, until the table was required for dinner.

He had almost forgotten that his was a temporary appointment, until they dropped anchor in Kingston and the doctor declared his intention of getting Mr Perks ashore. George assumed that, with the benefit of medical attention from the hospital there, Mr Perks would be ready to rejoin them by the time they set sail for the next port.

Instead, he found himself faced with the task of writing to Mrs Perks to tell her of the sad demise of her husband. Mr Perks's bedding was washed, his bunk scrubbed, and George was informed that this bunk, along with the post of captain's clerk, was now officially his.

CHAPTER THIRTY-EIGHT

HMS *Valour* continued to patrol the waters between the West Indies and Africa, on the lookout for ships loaded with illicit cargo. They had some successes and the cannons were fired on more than one occasion, but more as a warning than an act of aggression.

They were also drawn into the campaign that saw the Danish, French and Dutch colonies in the West Indies occupied by the British. They got off lightly – the presence of increasing numbers of British naval vessels had the desired effect and the occupations were, in the main, peaceful. The biggest change lay in the greater naval presence in the harbours of the islands, and nights out were rather more riotous, due to the numbers of sailors intent on having a good time. George learnt to hold his rum and developed an affection for the Creole people, who tolerated the behaviour of all these rowdy sailors. Although he could hear Ralph's verdict on the situation, as clearly as though he stood beside him: 'It's a business, George. They love you because of your money.'

If asked, George would have described it as a pleasant life. Their shore leave took place on whichever island they happened to be closest to when they found themselves in need of supplies. More often than not, George dined at the captain's table, and the officers and crew developed a tight-knit camaraderie as months turned into years. At times, George thought longingly of Maggie, as he'd last seen her in the Three Tuns, but in truth his surroundings were so dissimilar from Faversham, whether on land or sea, that it became a struggle to recall the memory.

It was halfway through George's twenty-fourth year that he had an inkling of change ahead. The captain had been in Kingston, dining with the governor, and appeared troubled on his return. He summoned George, holding out a packet of letters, which he said must be logged and answered over the coming days.

'Napoleon has abdicated and the end of the war is in sight,' he said. 'We're to return to England. They're standing down as many crews as possible and I think we will be one of them. The ship's too old now to see much more active service.' He poured himself a brandy and sat at the table, turning the glass between his hands. 'I have a mind to retire. My family has a farm they've been managing for me in my absence and now's the time to take it on myself.'

George was shocked. He supposed he should have considered the prospect that the war wouldn't go on for ever, that his time in the Navy would come to an end, but he'd never thought about what might come next. The following evening, he discussed it with Edward Powell as they climbed into their bunks after dinner at the captain's table. Only the senior officers had been present and Mr Ramsay had shared the news of their order to return to Portsmouth, along with his suspicion that they would be stood down. He'd asked them to keep the news from the men until they were back in England, unsure of the effect on morale.

'They'll be keen enough to get home, but I'm not so sure how the prospect of finding new employment will strike them. Some have been at sea all their working life.'

'What will you do if we are stood down?' George asked Edward, in a low voice, hoping to gain some insight as to what he himself might do.

'Why, I'll return home. I dare say Father will find a place for me although it's my brother, Robert, who's set to inherit.'

'Inherit?' George asked. He had a vague idea that Edward came from a wealthy background but it wasn't something they had discussed. Edward had a natural authority and an easy manner with the men – he had never needed to pull rank or suggest status to get things done.

'Yes, Woodchurch Manor estate, in Kent. Near Margate. We have a few acres of mainly farmland to manage,' Edward said.

'Near Margate, you say?' George's attention was diverted. 'The captain had me visit a man out here who said he was from Margate. A real eccentric, he was. It was in Martinique. He'd abandoned his ship in Kingston some years earlier and apparently fled to the island, hoping the Navy would leave him alone. From what I heard, the Navy were glad to see the back of him. He was described to me as having "gone native". He'd taken a Creole wife, but when I met him he was very sick. He'd suffered from yellow fever and barely survived.'

'What was his name?' Edward asked.

'Nicholas Goodchild,' George replied. 'He looked ancient, having been so ill, but he'd come out in 1790 when he was twenty or so. He can only have been in his late thirties.' George shook his head. 'I wonder whether he's still alive. The captain had me take some money to him. He'd visited him previously, apparently, on the instructions of his family. Do you know them?'

'I can't say that I do,' Edward said, yawning. 'Although I expect my father would know the name. He makes it his business to know everyone in the area.'

'Martinique fell to the French,' George mused. 'I wonder how he fared.'

Edward had lost interest. 'Where will you go?' he asked George. The pair were now conversing in low tones as they lay in adjacent bunks.

'I'm not sure,' George said. 'I was last in Faversham when I was working, but I stayed in Cornwall with a friend a few years back and rather liked it there. Maybe I'll seek him out.'

'Faversham is no great distance from Woodchurch Manor,' Edward said. 'Fifteen miles or so. If you do find yourself there, you must be sure to visit.'

'I will,' George said, wondering privately how likely that was. Once back in England, he had a feeling that he and Edward would find themselves in very different circumstances.

As they settled down for the night, George found that sleep had fled. He had felt completely at ease with his life since he had become captain's clerk and now, listening to the familiar creak of the ship's timbers as HMS *Valour* continued her journey towards what he supposed he must now consider home, he began to feel a little apprehensive about what lay ahead.

CHAPTER THIRTY-NINE

Several weeks later, in the summer of 1814, Napoleon was imprisoned on the island of Elba and the wars with the French that had consumed the better part of twelve years were apparently over. HMS *Valour* was retired from active service in Portsmouth and her crew stood down. Mr Ramsay was true to his word and took over the family farm. George didn't try to sign up for another voyage. It would have been on a merchant ship and, with his seafaring family broken up, he lacked the heart to attempt to fit into another. He knew, too, that he would be lucky to get another post such as the one he'd had. A captain's clerk was normally a short-lived role, a stepping stone to becoming a purser. That, in turn, was a prestigious role and required payment to secure it, for the purser could make money out of buying and selling supplies for the ship. George didn't have the sort of money, or come from the right background, to set himself up in that way.

He began to wonder whether his years on HMS *Valour* had been unusual. Their part in enforcing the ban on slave trading had kept them out of the action that so many of their fellows had experienced. At first George was unsure whether to be envious or relieved when he heard the tales told over quantities of ale in the inns of Portsmouth, but he had a growing conviction that he had been lucky. Was it time to recognise this and move on to something new?

He had written to Ralph, care of his family, intending to visit him in Cornwall, but had received the sad news by return that Ralph had perished, having fallen ill at sea. George had stared at the letter in disbelief. He had never thought such a thing might happen. He had never considered that Ralph might not have made it safely back to England; he had been looking forward to telling him of his own adventures and hearing about his.

George fell to wondering what he should do. On a whim, with no other place to claim his attention, he decided to return to Faversham. He had a fancy to see Thomas again and, now that he thought of it, to see Maggie. The tedious journey from Portsmouth involved twelve hours by stage coach to the outskirts of London, a night spent in an inn, tossing and turning in an uncomfortable bed, followed by another lengthy coach journey. He passed some of the journey daydreaming over his memories of Maggie. There she was, behind the bar at the Three Tuns, her eyes sparkling in the candlelight. And there she was again, down by Stonebridge Pond, clutched so tightly to him he could have sworn he felt her heart beating.

Once his fellow passengers discovered he was newly discharged from the Navy, they wanted to hear of the part he had played in the French wars and he was forced to abandon his daydreaming.

Over the course of many rounds of questions, as passengers alighted and new ones took their place, George managed to construct a history for himself that was a little more exciting than the actuality. And during the course of retelling it, he started to believe it had indeed happened. By the time he arrived in Faversham he had vividly described several close shaves with vessels from Portugal, France and Denmark – all hell-bent on destroying them until the superior power and training of the Royal Navy had put paid to that idea. The George that was let down in the cobbled courtyard of the staging inn on the outskirts of Faversham was a rather more heroic character than the George who had set out from Portsmouth.

Although the journey had been arduous and uncomfortable, it had allowed him to become accustomed to the great change in his surroundings. The colours of the English countryside, albeit under sunny skies, were subdued in comparison to the vibrancy he was used to. In Portsmouth, it had been a shock to find the townspeople soberly dressed in restrained colours, rather than wearing the vivid hues that Creole women favoured. The English trees and vegetation lacked the exuberance of the tropics, and George had to stop himself looking for the distinctive silhouettes of palm trees as the stage coach rattled through the countryside. Even the birds, now singing their evening song as George prepared to set out from the inn, were producing polite, melodic phrases, not the strident tones he had heard from their exotic cousins.

George thought he had absorbed some of this exoticism. He was noticeably more tanned than his pale-skinned fellow passengers and he had caught several admiring glances cast his way by young women who had journeyed on the coach for a little while. It was with a jaunty spring in his step that he made his way towards the Three Tuns through the once familiar streets of the town.

When he pushed open the door, the inn was as busy as he had remembered it. A few faces turned towards him then, after a moment's scrutiny, turned away again. It looked very much the same as it always had inside, yet somehow different. He didn't recognise anyone, and although his eyes sought out Maggie behind the bar, he was disappointed. There were two girls serving customers, neither of whom was she. He approached the wooden counter and waited, ordering his ale before he asked the girl serving him, 'Do you know Maggie? Maggie Donaldson? She used to work here, a while ago now.'

The girl shook her head. 'No, can't say as I do. I've only been here a week, though.' She frowned. 'Wait – Donaldson, you say? That's the name of the landlord here.' She turned and called through to the other bar. 'Mr Donaldson – gentleman here asking for a Maggie Donaldson.'

She took George's money and moved away to serve the next customer while George waited, suddenly struck with apprehension. Half a minute passed before a man shuffled into the doorway between the two bars. George would have been hard-pressed to recognise him as Mr Donaldson if he hadn't been expecting him. He'd aged considerably, having lost much of his hair and, more noticeably, shed weight, Also, he had developed a stoop. He certainly wasn't the formidable figure that George remembered from the past.

'Who's asking after my daughter?' Mr Donaldson was looking up and down the bar. His eyes flicked over George with no sign of recognition.

'Gentleman there.' The girl jerked her head in George's direction and carried on with her work.

Mr Donaldson moved along the bar until he stood facing George, the counter between them. 'What would you be wanting with my daughter?' Mr Donaldson asked.

'I knew her in the past. Near enough ten years ago now. I was in the area and . . .' George was suddenly cautious about how much to reveal '. . . and wanted to say hello,' he finished lamely.

'And what would your name be?' George thought he saw dawning recognition on the landlord's face.

'George. George Smith.'

'Ah.' Mr Donaldson nodded slowly. 'The one taken by the press gang. Is that right?'

'Yes, that's right. I've been overseas, with the Navy.' George felt the need to excuse his absence.

'Well, you won't find her here. She's been gone a long while.'

George's heart sank at his words and the smile that accompanied them, which revealed the loss of several of Mr Donaldson's teeth.

'Do you know where I might find her?'

'Aye, that I do.' Mr Donaldson, surprisingly affable, gave George an address on the outskirts of town, nodded and moved back to the other bar.

George, filled with impatient excitement and eager to be on his way, downed his ale quickly and went back out onto the street.

Chapter Forty

Georges's pace quickened as the house, long glimpsed in the distance, now became clearly visible behind its screen of trees. The address Mr Donaldson had given him had been vaguely familiar – he thought that one of the owners of the Oare gunpowder works had lived there in the past.

As he hurried along, he was going over every detail of Maggie's face, her voice and her hair. He had only to close his eyes and she was before him, behind the bar in the Three Tuns, exactly where he'd last seen her. Before he'd been snatched, before his life had taken a turn that he'd never imagined for himself or planned. Now was his chance to pick up the reins of that life again.

The house sat neatly and squarely on its plot, imposing in its own way but not ostentatious. To George's mind, it signified the address of someone comfortably wealthy and he wondered whether to approach the front door, or the servants' quarters at the back. Then his feet carried him eagerly forwards to the front door, where he had to stop himself hammering on it in his impatience. Instead he rapped twice, boldly but respectfully, then stood back. The door swung open and a man of about his own age stood there, neatly dressed and with something of an air about him, almost as though he were the owner of the house and not just one of the servants.

The man looked at George and waited.

'I'm looking for Maggie Donaldson,' George said. 'I was told by her father that I'd find her here.'

The man looked momentarily startled, before recovering himself.

'She works here,' he said. 'But she's Maggie Matcham now.'

It was George's turn to be surprised. He looked with fresh eyes at the man before him, trying to peel away the years, remembering the time when he'd shared a room with Thomas Matcham and they'd been employed at the powder works in Oare.

'Thomas?' he asked, uncertain.

The man stared at him, hard. 'Who's asking?'

The figure of a woman appeared behind Thomas in the doorway. 'Thomas, the master wants a fire lit in the library after dinner and the girl's gone home. Can you do it?'

George registered her dark hair and something familiar about her stance before it struck him. It was Maggie, but not the woman he remembered, fresh-faced and blooming, trapped in time as he'd last seen her behind the bar in her father's inn. Ten years had wrought changes, and not only in her father.

Maggie was impatient for Thomas's response, while Thomas blocked the doorway, waiting for George to speak. George opened his mouth but words would not come. Instead, there was the dawning realisation that he had misled himself. He had foolishly imagined that time had stood still since he had been stolen from Faversham and that his life would be there, waiting for him to step back into it. Now it struck him forcefully that this wasn't the case.

He finally managed to say, 'Thomas, it's George. We shared a room in Widow Booth's cottage.'

As he spoke, his eyes sought out the figure of Maggie, partly obscured behind Thomas. He had misunderstood, surely. They couldn't be married.

Thomas stepped forward and seized his shoulders. 'Good God, George, I didn't recognise you. Wherever have you been?' Then, registering that George had sagged and grown pale, he said, 'Are you unwell? Maggie, take him through to the kitchen. I'll go and see to this fire.'

George stepped inside, into a spacious black-and-white-tiled hallway, stairs sweeping up before him and candles already lit on a table beside the door. Thomas walked – or, rather, limped – towards a door to the left of the stairs. Maggie took George's arm and drew him to another door tucked away to the right of the staircase, which led through to the servants' area. Her haste told George it had been improper to come to the front of the property. His years in the Navy and in the West Indies had made him forget the ways of his old world but her action served as a reminder.

By the time he was seated at the kitchen table, conscious of curious glances from the cook, he was thoroughly bewildered at the turn of events. Maggie appeared ill-at-ease and no words passed between them as she poured ale and set out cold meats, pickles and bread.

George should have been hungry after his travels that day but he found all appetite had fled. He picked up the ale, glad to have something to occupy his hands. Maggie kept glancing towards the door and he had a feeling she was waiting for Thomas to appear before she spoke. The cook, taking umbrage at the goings-on in her kitchen, retreated into the scullery and began clattering pans.

George was glad of the noise, for the silence was growing uncomfortable. He was even more relieved when at last the door burst open and Thomas entered the room. He appeared to take in the situation at a glance as he seated himself opposite George, wincing as he did so. A sigh escaped his lips and George noticed how his face had filled out and his youthfulness was lost.

'So, George, where have you been? What happened to you? Rumour had it that you were taken by a press gang. Is that true?'

George was far more interested in hearing about what had happened to Thomas and Maggie in the time he'd been away but he dutifully filled them in on the history of his years in the Navy. As he spoke, he glanced between the pair of them, managing to build on his first impressions of Maggie.

She was much changed. It would have been polite to say that she had filled out: she had been buxom when George was walking out with her but ten years had added to her curves and now she was rotund, an effect only enhanced by her petite stature. Thomas, by contrast, had lost weight from a frame that had never been burdened with extra pounds.

George was made impatient by the questions they wanted to ask him and brushed them aside.

'I want to know about you now,' he insisted. 'How have you both come to be working here? When did you ... marry?' His voice faltered.

Thomas adopted the role of narrator and George learnt that within six months of his disappearance, an explosion at the Oare Works had blown apart the cooper's workshop. Thomas had come round to find one of the roof timbers crushing his leg and had been left with a limp, as well as a ringing in his ears. A more serious consequence had been, as

239

he described it, 'an unreasoning fear of ever setting foot on that site again'. His foreman, sorry to lose one of his best workers, had spoken up for him. Strings had been pulled and a position found for him as a servant in the house belonging to the owner of the works.

Thomas came to a halt at this point and George sensed a reluctance to continue.

'And?' he urged, casting a sideways glance at Maggie.

She had remained silent until then, but now she spoke up. 'Thomas carried on coming to the inn after you vanished. Naturally, I was very upset and we went over and over that evening, trying to work out what might have happened, until word reached us that a press gang had been in the area. Even then, I kept hoping you would come back but you didn't, and then Thomas had his accident. We heard the explosion at the inn and when we got word that it had been in the mixing house, right next to where the barrels were made, I feared the worst.' Maggie stopped, as if recounting the events had exhausted her.

Thomas took up the tale again.

'Maggie was so good to me. She came to see me at Widow Booth's whenever she could to cheer me up. I couldn't get into Faversham because of my leg.' There was almost an appeal in his eyes as he looked up at George.

'Then I got offered the job here and when a housekeeper was needed a short while later, I mentioned it to Maggie. I didn't like to think of her working behind that bar, having to put up with all that attention, those remarks . . .' Thomas tailed off and George remembered when he'd felt much the same about Maggie's occupation.

A question mark hung in the air and Maggie visibly steeled herself to complete the story.

'Thomas asked me to marry him after I'd been here six months. We run the house between us now. I'm the housekeeper and I suppose you could say he's the butler, although I'm not sure either of us deserve such grand titles. And we've got three children. They live with Thomas's mother and we see them whenever we can.'

There was a silence when she finished speaking and George turned his now-empty tankard between his fingers. The broad brushstrokes of her account filled in the last ten years for him, each one closing down another part of his now-impossible dream.

'And Judith?' he asked at length.

'Judith?' Thomas frowned, then his brow cleared. 'Oh, Judith. She left the area not long after you vanished. We did wonder whether you'd gone off together. We haven't heard from her since.'

Chapter Forty-One

Thomas got up, poured himself some ale and, without asking, refilled George's tankard.

'Eat,' he said to George, indicating the food on the table. He turned to his wife, who had remained standing throughout, her back to the range. 'Maggie, why don't you sit down?' he said.

George dutifully cut a slice from the loaf and laid it on a plate along with a piece of ham and some pickles. He knew he should eat something before he drank yet more ale, but still his appetite wouldn't come.

'So, how long are you planning to be in the area?' Thomas asked, breaking the awkward silence that had descended.

George was at a loss as to how to reply. His imagined scenario had seen him finding Maggie – a Maggie preserved exactly as he had last seen her – and stepping back into the life he had planned for himself all those years ago, before he'd been taken. It embarrassed him to think of it now. He made a play of eating some of the bread and ham, even though it tasted like ashes in his mouth, in order to buy himself some time.

The cook had come back from the scullery and was glaring at them.

'Well, since I can't get on with what I need to get on with, I'll bid you good night,' she said.

Thomas was unmoved. He said, 'We can tidy up after ourselves,' and nodded, as though to dismiss her.

Cook's snort, as she left, told them all they needed to know about her opinion of how she would find her kitchen in the morning.

'I'm just passing through, on my way to Margate.' Cook's interruption had given George the time he needed to find inspiration. He'd seek out Edward Powell at Woodchurch Manor, he decided, and follow up on his invitation. Anything to get him away from this house, this area and the situation he found himself in.

'It's a shame you can't stay longer,' Thomas said. The relief on his face suggested quite the opposite.

'Where will you stay tonight?' Maggie asked. George wondered whether he detected a note of concern in her query.

'I'll walk back into Faversham and take a room at an inn there,' he said, all at once overcome with weariness. The two days of travelling and the uncomfortable bed the previous night, the shock of Thomas and Maggie's marriage, and the ale had suddenly caught up with him. He wanted nothing more than to be alone and to blot out the discoveries of the previous hour.

'Stay here,' Maggie said. 'You look done in. We can't offer you a room for the night but you can sleep in the kitchen. We'll wake you before Cook comes in the morning and you can be on your way. It'll save you the walk into town and the cost of a bed,' she added shrewdly.

George was on the point of demurring, then thought better of it. He doubted he'd sleep well, wherever he was. He might as well spend a restless night there, as anywhere. And even though he'd left the Navy feeling almost wealthy for the first time in his life, he'd realised that this also was an illusion. He had neither home nor work and there were too many former naval men hunting for jobs. Rather than enjoying his savings, he needed to conserve them.

He tried to raise a smile. 'Thank you. I'll take you up on your offer.'

Thomas drained his tankard and Maggie put away the food from the table, although not before she had cut George another slice of bread and ham.

George looked around the room. There was a narrow bench up against the far wall and, apart from the table, the only other furniture was the high-backed wooden chairs they were using.

Maggie followed his eyes. 'Will you be all right?' she asked, all at once doubtful at having made the offer.

'Oh, I learnt to sleep on my feet in the Navy,' George said, more cheerfully than he felt. 'I'll manage perfectly well.'

'I'll fetch you a cover,' Maggie said, as Thomas bade him good night. She returned a minute or two later with a folded woollen blanket. George was still sitting at the table, rolling breadcrumbs into pellets between his thumb and forefinger.

Maggie handed him the blanket, turned to leave, then stood awkwardly by the door. 'I'm sorry, George. I did wait for you. It was a shock when you vanished like that. And Thomas was so good to me. After he had his accident, we grew close. Almost a year had passed by then. I never thought I'd see you again.'

George looked at Maggie and smiled – the first genuine smile he'd managed to raise all evening. 'It's all right, Maggie,' he said. 'I understand.'

And he did, really he did. She nodded and left the room, and he sat at the table a little longer, pondering the events of the evening. As long as he could reconcile himself to the fact that the flirtatious Maggie of his memories was lost, not only to him but to time, he could give up on his dream. Trying to lodge that thought firmly in his weary mind, he settled himself into one of the wooden chairs, feet up on another, and prepared for an uneasy night.

He woke, stiff and cold, in a room filling with the thin grey light of dawn. His blanket had slipped to the floor and he stared, puzzled, at his surroundings, before his brain caught up. Groaning, he eased his feet down from the chair and tried to rub life into his joints. His neck and shoulders were painful, and although he was thankful for having slept, most likely a gift of the ale, he didn't feel well rested.

An urgent need to relieve himself sent him stumbling out through the back door and into the garden. Outside, the freshness of the air and the first hint of a beautiful day to come raised his spirits. He looked back at the house, the shuttered windows evidence of a household still asleep, and knew he had no wish to face Cook, Thomas or Maggie before he went on his way.

He went back inside, finding water in a jug in the scullery to splash on his hands and face and chase away the last vestiges of sleep. Then he picked up the bread, now dry, from the plate and stuffed it into his mouth along with the ham, took an apple from the blue-and-white china bowl on the side and picked up his pack.

He let himself back into the garden and followed the path to a side gate, praying there was no dog in the house to bark an alarm. If there was, it slept on, and he soon found himself striding out on the road that he felt sure led to the coast, leaving Faversham behind.

He was not the only one up at that hour. Workers were already in the fields, preparing to harvest the corn made fat and golden by the summer sun. The wagons that rattled along the road were going about local farm business and, with the sun now up and already warm on George's face, he began to think he must walk the full distance to Woodchurch Manor.

After he had gone a few miles, he settled himself in the shade of a spreading chestnut tree at the roadside and ate his apple, tossing the core to a crow that had been eyeing him beadily from the edge of the field. As he stood up and stretched, ready to embark on his journey once more, he heard the rumble of an approaching wagon. It sounded heavier than any that had yet passed him. George stood at the side of the road, shading his eyes, and watched as the two carthorses and their load drew nearer.

The wagon slowed to walking pace as it drew level with him and the driver called, 'Are you in need of a ride? Where are you going?'

'Woodchurch Manor,' George called back. 'Somewhere near Margate, I believe.'

'Aye, it's this side of Margate. I pass it on my way to deliver this lot.' The driver jerked his head back to indicate the load of quarried stone. 'Climb up if you want to be spared the walk.'

George did as he was bade and spent the rest of the morning in pleasant conversation with the driver, who told him he regularly travelled between local quarries and Westbrook, near Margate.

'It's mainly for the rich folks, who have a mind to set walls around their property to keep the poor folks out,' the driver said, chuckling. 'If the poor folks want to build a wall they steal the stone from some old ruin. You look out for that now,

246

when you're out and about. You'll see plenty of walls around here made up of a bit of grey flint here, and a patch of red stone there, then some more flint and a few old ale flagons for luck.' He chuckled again and offered George a dip into the provisions he had for the journey.

George gratefully accepted a pie. 'Fresh-baked by the missus only yesterday,' his companion said. The sun told him it was noon already and the horses still plodded on. He'd barely wiped the last crumb from his lips, though, before the driver drew them to a halt.

'Here you are,' he said, nodding to a tree-lined lane leading off to the right. 'You'll find what you're looking for down there.'

George climbed down, full of thanks for the pie and the journey, and stood for a moment, watching the wagon drive off. He hadn't thought of Maggie or Thomas since he'd been on the road, and he pushed away the memory of the previous night that now resurfaced. He set off down the lane, intrigued as a great house gradually revealed itself behind a stand of trees.

Chapter Forty-Two

George crunched across the sweep of gravelled drive that led up to the imposing front door. He'd learnt his lesson and didn't even consider using that entrance, making his way instead to the side of the house where the activity of people in the courtyard suggested something about to take place.

A petite young woman, her brown hair twisted on top of her head, was standing with her back to him, a painted canvas tucked under each arm, as she watched a small procession of men come out of the building in front of her. Each carried a stack of chairs and it looked as though they had vied with each other to see who could carry the most. As George drew closer, he saw that the woman's shoulders were shaking with laughter.

'Edward,' she called, 'stop showing off. You're going to drop them all.'

George switched his attention to the chair-carriers and, sure enough, the largest stack, obscuring the face of the man carrying it, was teetering. George dropped his pack and leapt forward to steady it, just as the man holding them began to lower them to the ground.

'Thanks,' the muffled voice behind the chairs said. 'I was trying to be too clever, as Agnes kindly pointed out.'

The owner of the voice emerged from behind the stack: red in the face and damp of brow under the heat of the midday sun. It was Edward Powell. He looked amazed to see George, then beamed and clapped him on the back.

'You've made your entrance at just the right time. We could do with an extra pair of hands. It's our annual garden party tomorrow and it's always a mad rush to get ready for it.' He wiped the sweat off his brow with his sleeve. 'Here, if you can take some of the chairs off the pile, I'll show you where to put them.'

George glanced back at his abandoned pack and caught Agnes watching them. She turned away at once, but not before he'd glimpsed wide eyes under strong brows and had the impression he was being appraised.

George followed Edward's bidding and helped to set out the chairs on the lawn at the back of the house, below a grand, sweeping terrace. He tilted the chairs so that their backs rested against the tables, as instructed by Edward, 'in case it rains or there's a heavy dew – there'll be hell to pay if anyone gets a damp posterior.' Then he went back to collect his pack, finding no sign of Agnes in the yard, before return-ing to the house. Here he found himself put to use for the rest of the afternoon. The physical labour and teamwork brought back memories of his time aboard ship, and he was happy and exhausted by the time dusk fell.

'We'll put you on a mattress in my room,' Edward said. He had randomly introduced George to various members of his family whenever their paths had crossed during the exertions of the day. Now they were having dinner, in the setting of a grand dining room but in an informal way, doors open onto the garden. An array of dishes was laid out buffet-style on the sideboard.

'The kitchen is busy preparing for tomorrow,' Edward said. 'Meals are always like this when the garden party is happening.'

249

George was glad of it – the room looked as though it had hosted many a formal dinner party and he had neither the clothes for such a thing nor the appetite for it. He'd stuck his head under the pump once they had finished work, and had made the effort to rake his fingers through his hair, but he feared he must look a sight. He'd been introduced to Edward's brothers, Robert and Francis, but hadn't yet discovered where Agnes fitted in. Was she their sister? There were many people drifting in and helping themselves to food, seeming quite at home but clearly not all family. George deduced, from scraps of overheard conversations, that they were guests who came down each year just for the garden party. There was nothing for it but to ask Edward the question about Agnes.

'And Agnes – is she your sister?'

'Ah, no, although she often feels like it. We practically grew up together, until us boys were sent away to school.'

He and Edward had moved outside now to the terrace, glasses in hand, as they watched Mr Powell walk around the lawns with another man. Mr Powell appeared to be pointing at things in the borders while the man nodded and made notes in a small book.

'That's Agnes's father, over there.' Edward was referring to the man at Mr Powell's side. 'He's the head gardener. Agnes is an artist and she's having an exhibition in the old stable block tomorrow. That's why we were moving the chairs – she needed to get the walls whitewashed and her paintings hung.' Edward made a wry face. 'We always tend to leave things until the last minute.'

The light was fading and George, who had been yawning ever since dinner, wasn't sorry when Edward suggested they turn in. They'd need to be up at dawn to get the last jobs done before the gates opened in the early afternoon for the garden party.

One of the servants must have been in to make up the mattress, for it was already laid out with sheets, a blanket and pillow by the time George took his pack up to Edward's room. He took the precaution of shaking out his one clean shirt, hoping it would look less creased by the time of the party the next day, before climbing into his bed. It was more comfortable than anything he'd slept in for a long while and he barely had time to register the thought that he was hoping to see Agnes tomorrow before he fell into a deep sleep.

CHAPTER FORTY-THREE

Surely a bare five minutes had passed before Edward was shaking him awake. George struggled to keep his eyes open until, registering Edward standing fully dressed before him in a bedroom already filled with sunlight, he was alert in an instant.

'What time is it? Why didn't you wake me?'

Edward laughed. 'You looked as though you could do with the sleep so I didn't have the heart to do it. Don't worry – it's not yet seven o'clock.'

George yawned and threw back the covers. 'And a glorious day, by the look of it.'

'We're nearly always lucky. Even this year, although I'm told most of the summer so far has been on the cool side,' Edward said. 'Come to the dining room when you're dressed. We can have some breakfast and see what jobs need to be done.'

Half an hour later, with coffee, eggs and hot rolls inside them, they were out on the lawns, which still sparkled with dew. George shivered – it was cool before the onset of the day's heat and he was still a little tired.

As the morning raced by, under an increasingly warm sun, George longed for that early freshness. He started the day by helping the Powell brothers to hang lanterns in the woodland walk, then to set up parasols among the tea tables. There was just time to erect an awning over the long table, from which the tea and cakes would be dispensed, before Edward said they must change and make themselves presentable before the guests arrived.

George looked longingly at the pump outside the kitchens – he would have liked nothing better than to strip to the waist and cool off there but, mindful of his surroundings, he had to content himself with the jug and basin in Edward's room. Then, with barely enough time to dress, the gates opened and George found himself without a companion. Edward, as a member of the Powell family, was very much on duty.

George wandered outside and stood for a while on the terrace steps, watching the visitors spread over the lawns. It was apparent that most of them had been before – they were purposeful in either making for a favourite part of the gardens or staking their place at a tea table in the shade. Hardly anyone seemed to be standing still, at a loss, as George was.

He thought back to his arrival, barely twenty-four hours previously, and remembered Agnes in the courtyard with her canvases. Hadn't Edward said she was holding an exhibition? Now he had a legitimate purpose: he strolled away from the terrace, against the flow of people still coming in, to make his way to the stable-yard. There he found an easel set up outside the old stable block, a hand-painted canvas set upon it bearing the words 'Exhibition today by local artist Agnes Dawson'.

George stepped through the open door into the old stable block and into a cool, whitewashed space. The walls were hung with canvases, rather sparsely, he thought, for the works weren't large and required the visitor to step up close to view them. The room was empty and his footsteps rang on the cobbled floor as he moved towards the nearest wall of paintings.

He saw that these were all portraits, the first depicting what appeared to be a family group of a man and a woman and three younger women, presumably the daughters of the family but well grown. The women stood behind the seated older couple and George thought he could recognise Agnes as the middle daughter in the row of three. He was intrigued – he remembered the portraits hanging on the walls of the public corridors at the Foundling Hospital, richly detailed paintings in heavy gilt frames. Here, the formality of the seated people was in contrast to the background, which consisted of soft swirls of colour, with no detail whatsoever, bringing the subjects into sharp focus. And none of the works was framed, which went some way to explaining the impression of sparseness that he had had on first entering the room.

He moved on to look at the rest of the portraits, finding one of the three Powell brothers: Robert seated, Edward and Francis standing, unsmiling, at each shoulder. There was one of Mr and Mrs Powell at the front door of Woodchurch Manor and an unusual one, this time of a man at work in the gardens. He was half turned away from the viewer and all the detail was in the flowerbeds that he was tending.

'What do you think?'

George hadn't heard anyone come in and spun round in surprise. Agnes stood there, her hair more neatly dressed than the day before and wearing a plain dress in a dark colour, at odds with the summer's day yet it somehow gave her a presence greater than her small stature.

'They're very good.' George coloured faintly. 'Well, at least, I think they are. I like them but have to confess to knowing nothing about art. Is this your family?' He moved to stand in front of the first portrait.

'Yes.' Agnes pointed. 'My sister Sally, me, my sister Catherine and my parents.'

She turned to look at George. 'We haven't been introduced, but I assume you are a friend of Edward. I'm Agnes.'

'George,' George said, blushing again as he held out his hand to her. 'George Smith. I was at sea with Edward.'

'Ah, then you'll have some tales to tell, I imagine,' Agnes said. George racked his brains to oblige but she continued, 'Have a good look around. You're my first visitor and I hope you won't be the only one, but I fear everyone else is far more interested in the tea and cakes.' She smiled wryly.

'Oh, I'm sure they will come,' George hastened to reassure her.

Agnes frowned as she looked critically around the room. 'I'm not sure what visitors will make of the some of the paintings. They may not fit with the taste of the day.'

George made the sort of noises that he hoped suggested polite disagreement, then moved on to the rest of the work. There were studies of flowers and feathers, of a robin singing from a bough and cats playing in the sunshine – detailed works that captured their exact likeness. He was conscious of Agnes observing him and dutifully spent a minute or two examining each one. But he found himself drawn back to the family portrait he had first seen.

'You'll be able to see the family in the flesh today,' Agnes remarked. 'They're all here somewhere. Then you can tell me whether I've captured a true likeness.'

George, desperate to keep the conversation going, was about to ask whether the paintings were for sale. He had no interest in buying one, having no wall of his own on which to hang anything, but it was all he could think of.

The arrival of a group of young people, who all seemed to know Agnes, prevented further conversation. He heard her address Catherine by name, and he spotted Francis Powell at her side. They took up position in front of George's favourite portrait so he took the opportunity to slip away, pleased for Agnes that he hadn't been her only visitor.

He strolled through the grounds for a while, taking the chance to appreciate them properly. How lucky Edward was to have been brought up in such surroundings, he thought, looking back at the house, so stately in its setting of lawns and lake. It could hardly be any more different from his own childhood, which, even though the early years were spent in the countryside, could not be described as idyllic. As for the Foundling Hospital, it had been a bed, food, a routine. He had never experienced the kind of family life that Edward and Agnes must have enjoyed.

George's stroll led him to a doorway in a stone wall, tucked away at the end of a path and half hidden by trees. He stepped through it to find himself in another garden; a garden within a garden, he thought, a little bemused. Here there were more flowers, but also fruit trees, rows of vegetables and a glasshouse at the back. He wandered along one of the paths then stopped, uncertain as to whether he should really be there. He detected a movement by the glasshouse and saw a man there, with a wheelbarrow. He had his back to George but he recognised him as the head gardener, Agnes's father, pointed out by Edward the previous evening. He was too far away for George to see whether she had captured his likeness well in the portrait. He half wondered whether to go over and speak to him, then heard a woman's voice, calling from the doorway he had just stepped through.

'Charlie! Come and join us for tea now. Mr Powell will be making his speech very soon. And Sally is here with Luke and the children – they're asking for you.'

George watched as Charlie set down the wheelbarrow and made his way back to the gate, where he took his wife's arm. As the pair left the garden, he caught a glimpse of her red-brown hair, fading to grey, and a simple blue dress. To George's relief, they left the gate open. He gave them a moment or two, then followed at a discreet distance, but they were soon swallowed by the crowd.

George, too, went to the tea tables where he found Edward seated with Francis, Catherine and others he recognised as the visitors who had followed him into Agnes's exhibition.

'There you are,' Edward said. 'Just in time for tea and to hear Father's annual speech.' He leant back in his chair, glanced at the tea table and waved a hand. Shortly afterwards George found himself in possession of a cup of tea and a plate containing an array of delicate pastries, delivered by one of the young servants.

When Mr Powell started to speak, several people drifted away from the tables towards the bandstand but his voice carried in the still air and George could make out most of what he said, even above the murmur of the crowd. He welcomed everyone, thanking those who had helped to make the day such a success, including his family, the staff of Woodchurch Manor and, specifically, his head gardener and team. He urged everyone to pay a visit to something new that year – an art exhibition by the very talented daughter of the head gardener. Then he stepped down from the band-stand and the music recommenced.

'I wonder whether there will be any more of these parties,' Edward said, frowning into his empty cup. 'Robert is taking over the running of the estate now and he says we can't afford it. Not unless Father sells some of his art collection.' He looked up at George. 'Speaking of which, have you been to see Agnes's work yet? I think I'll walk over there now to get out of this sun.'

'I've seen it already but I'll come back with you,' George said, scrambling to his feet. 'Perhaps you can help cast some light on whether or not it's any good. I'm clueless about art.'

If he wanted to get to know Agnes better, he might need to brush up on his knowledge, he reflected, as they made for the old stable block, gathering more of Edward's friends and acquaintances as they went along.

CHAPTER FORTY-FOUR

George came to believe it was a very happy accident that had brought him to Woodchurch Manor. He'd helped to clear up after the garden party, collapsing into a chair at the dining table as dusk fell to make the most of what Edward's mother referred to as a 'cold collation'. He was so hungry after his exertions that he would have eaten anything, and the cold meats, salad and potatoes from the walled garden, followed by syllabub and home-grown raspberries appeared to him as a sumptuous feast.

The garden party had gone well. Mr Powell was clearly very happy, while Mrs Powell declared herself relieved that it was over for another year. The food and drink revived George sufficiently to join the procession of family and guests after dinner, intent on enjoying the woodland walk now lit by lanterns.

'It's the one thing we save for ourselves every year, after we made the mistake of opening it to the public the first year,' Edward said. He laughed and refused to be drawn on what had happened then, other than saying that Robert had disgraced himself with one of the servants. Then he changed the subject. 'We're very grateful for all your help,' he said to George. 'What are your plans? How long will you be with us?'

George's good humour left him abruptly. He'd been caught up in the moment and hadn't stopped to consider what came next. He knew only that when he'd seen Agnes for the second time that afternoon, in company with Edward, he'd felt as though he'd like to stay longer to get to know her better. He was intrigued and also a little in awe of her: a lady artist. Now, he felt unsure of himself. The Powells had been so easy-going and welcoming towards him, but he couldn't impose on their hospitality much longer. He decided honesty was the best policy.

'I don't have any plans. Things didn't work out as I had hoped in Faversham.' As he spoke, George realised he had barely thought of his humiliating encounter with Maggie and Thomas in the last forty-eight hours. He frowned. 'I suppose I must seek out some work.'

'I wondered whether that might be the case,' Edward said. 'The reason I ask is that – while you are, of course, most welcome to stay with us for a while – I had someone approach me about you today.'

'Really? Who?' George immediately thought of Agnes and his heart beat a little faster.

They were deep in the woodland walk now, the lanterns bathing the path with a golden glow, the shadows inky black on either side. As the path looped round a section of the lake, George stopped to look at the reflection of the lanterns dancing and sparkling on the water as the evening breeze blew ripples across the surface.

'Charlie Dawson, the head gardener,' Edward said. 'He liked the way you worked today – saw that you could turn your hand to anything – and thought you might make a good member of his team.'

'Oh,' George said again, trying to keep the disappointment out of his voice. So it hadn't been Agnes after all. And he wasn't sure that he wanted a manual job again, not after the years he'd spent as a captain's clerk. But then it struck him that it would keep him close to Agnes. 'Do you know exactly what he had in mind?'

'Some work in the gardens, I think. But also trips with him to London and around the country. I think he needs records kept, that sort of thing. He knows what you did until recently.'

It sounded a little better than George had first imagined, he had to admit. And he had enjoyed the physical labour of the last day or so. The surroundings here at Woodchurch Manor were also very much to his liking. They had reached the end of the woodland walk now, and as they stood by the lake and looked back up at the house, the ground floor lit by candlelight and a canopy of stars twinkling above the roof, George felt a rush of hope for the future.

'There's a room over the old stable block that goes with the job. Why don't you talk to Charlie tomorrow and find out whether it's to your liking? I think it would be good to have you around, too,' Edward said, and he drew George back towards the house where the family and guests were regrouping for more drinks and to play cards.

A room over the old stable block sounded appealing, George thought. He wasn't sure whether Agnes used the downstairs as her studio, as well as a gallery, but she would certainly be somewhere nearby.

The next day, he wasted no time in seeking out Charlie, whom he found once more in the walled garden. The sleeves of his blue work shirt were rolled back, revealing his tanned skin, and as he straightened George noticed his strong, wiry frame. His hair was thick, although greying at the temples, and his face was lined – from working outside in all weathers, he assumed. Charlie was already smiling in welcome and holding out his hand, and George had to fight off the sudden shyness caused by his proximity to Agnes's father.

'Edward told you I'd been watching you, did he? Well, I could make good use of you about the place if you're willing,' Charlie said, and he outlined what was on offer, which was very much as Edward had said. Charlie took George to see the room over the old stable block, which would have delighted him ordinarily but he was a little downcast to see no sign of Agnes in the downstairs room, where all the paintings had now gone from the walls.

Charlie misunderstood his reaction and said, 'The room's rather bare but I dare say my wife can find you a few odds and ends to make it more homely.'

George didn't want to appear ungrateful so he rallied, expressed his thanks and said that the room and the job would suit him very well. They shook on it and descended to the stable-yard. As they were about to part, George promising to present himself for work the next day, he thought to ask about the success of Agnes's show.

'Did your daughter sell any of her paintings yesterday?' he asked.

'Aye, she did. Mr Powell is a great champion of her work and he took the family portraits. Some of the flower studies found a home, too.' Charlie spoke with pride. 'And the portrait of our family is back where it belongs, hanging over the fireplace,' he added.

George nodded and they parted, but not before he thought he caught a quizzical look on the head gardener's face. He would have to be careful not to make his interest in Agnes too obvious, he thought, at least not for a while.

Chapter Forty-Five

George joined the gardening team at a busy time. As August drew to a close, the final summer fruits and vegetables from the walled garden were being harvested for the Woodchurch Manor kitchens. George enjoyed picking the produce in the sunshine, then helping carry great wicker baskets of pears, raspberries, blackberries and beans to the cool larders of the kitchens, ready to be turned into jams, jellies, chutneys and other preserves. He supposed some might consider his fortunes had taken a turn for the worse now that he was dining in the kitchens along with the gardening staff, rather than upstairs with the Powell family, but he considered himself very lucky.

He enjoyed working outdoors, and although he had no previous experience of gardening, he discovered he had an aptitude for it. He asked questions all the time and found that he retained the information, which was important, given there was so much to learn. Once September arrived, the new focus in the garden was to prepare it for winter: pruning and cutting back plants in a way that seemed almost brutal to George. There was still harvesting to be done, picking sloes, quinces and any remaining apples, but the weather was already changing. The sun might still be hot at midday under skies of the brightest blue but mornings and evenings were noticeably cooler as the days grew shorter.

After a day in the garden, George fell into bed and into a deep sleep every evening, only to wake looking forward to each new day. True, he hadn't seen as much of Agnes as he had hoped, or of Edward, but he'd been so absorbed in everything he needed to learn that it hadn't mattered too much. Then, halfway through September, he found himself invited to eat with the Dawson family on Saturday, once work was over for the day, and to dine with the Powells on Sunday after church.

The invitation to the Dawsons' followed a day George had spent working side by side with Charlie in the walled garden, learning how to prune roses. He had easily mastered what needed to be done to the species in the borders but found it harder to understand how best to deal with the climbers trained along the walls. The thorns were sharp and it wasn't long before George's arms were lacerated, earning him a scolding from Charlie.

'At least roll down your sleeves,' he said, looking with some concern at the blood seeping in trails over George's forearms. 'Did your mother never teach you any common sense?'

George shrugged. 'They'll be fine,' he said. 'And I don't have a mother – or one that I've ever met,' he added, as an afterthought.

Charlie didn't immediately respond but carried on clipping, working his way methodically along the wall. But during the course of the afternoon, he wheedled George's past history out of him, from his earliest memories of Nancy and the black-and-white dog, to the years at the Foundling School and his ill-fated apprenticeship.

'I was luckier than you in that respect,' Charlie said. 'I at least had a master, Mr Fleming, who saw some good in me.

My position here today is all down to him.' He clipped away, then added, 'I was brought up in the poorhouse, you know, in Margate. My mother died a year after we got there, and my father had been lost at sea. Then my little brother died, too. It was a long time ago now.' Charlie looked thoughtful. 'But I can't imagine what it must be like never to have had any family at all – no mother or father, no brothers or sisters.'

They clipped on together, working in silence, each wrapped up in his own thoughts. Then George said, 'I've never known any different. I suppose it just feels normal to me.'

Nothing more was said that day, but the following morning Charlie invited George to eat with them on the Saturday. 'And Molly, my wife, is going to look out some things for that room of yours. The nights are getting colder so you'll need a warmer cover than just a blanket. There's a rug for the floor, and one or two other things, too.'

George accepted gratefully, hugging to himself his excitement at the thought of spending a few hours in Agnes's company, at the same table. That was worth more to him than a warm bedcover, he thought.

The very same day, Edward sought him out to apologise for having seen so little of him. 'Father wanted Robert and me to accompany him to London on business, and very tedious it was too.' Edward made a face. 'I'm thinking of returning to sea if I can. I'm not sure that a life on the land is for me.'

George looked at him in consternation. He wondered whether his own position at Woodchurch Manor would be affected if Edward departed. Edward hadn't noticed his expression, though, and pressed on. 'I came to invite you to join us after church on Sunday. We can catch up on each other's news then.'

George didn't like to say that he had yet to find the local church, having so far been only too happy to lie abed on a Sunday morning, enjoying the luxury of a day off. Instead, he said he'd see him after the service and would be delighted to join the family. Privately, he thought it would be odd to dine in the house once more, rather than the kitchen.

The invitation to the Dawsons' was the most eagerly awaited of the two. George presented himself there at five o'clock, as instructed. After work, he'd had a thorough wash at the stable-yard pump and was wearing a clean shirt and the only pair of his breeches that were fit to be seen. The cottage was one of a little group on the edge of the estate, built for workers at Woodchurch Manor. It looked out over the fields, with a wooded copse at the back, and on that late afternoon in September George thought it a very lovely spot. His heart thumped painfully at the thought of Agnes as he stood on the doorstep and rapped on the door. He wondered, too late, whether he ought to have brought a gift – but what? He could hardly have picked flowers from the gardens: Charlie's eagle eyes would have known at once where they were from.

Agnes opened the door and George was both delighted and nervous all at once. She ushered him in, showing him through to the kitchen where he had an impression of noise and warmth, of polished wood and delicious aromas. Charlie appeared to be teasing his wife, who was flapping her apron at him while Catherine, arranging late-flowering roses from the garden in a vase, rolled her eyes.

Molly turned at George's entrance and said to Agnes, with a frown, 'The parlour, Agnes, not in here.' Then she laughed and said to George, 'I'm sorry, how rude of me. I'm Molly and you must be George. Agnes, take George and your father into the parlour so I can get on in peace, or there won't be any dinner on the table.'

George found himself appraised by Molly's frank brown eyes before Agnes beckoned him along the corridor into the parlour, where all was suddenly calm. It had the air of being a room little used, although the fire was already lit.

'Sit down,' Agnes said. 'So, how is Pa treating you? Not overworking you, I hope?'

George's eye had already been caught by the family portrait over the fire and, rather than sitting as instructed, he went over to take another look at it. 'I'm enjoying the work,' he said truthfully. 'Your father is a very good teacher.' He turned to Agnes. 'Have you done any more painting since your exhibition?' He was painfully conscious that his question sounded stilted and he longed for the conversation to flow more easily. He was relieved when Charlie entered the room.

'Yes, I've been asked to do a portrait of Sally, my older sister, and her husband and children. And I'm hoping that I might be able to study somewhere, if Ma and Pa are in agreement.' She glanced at her father as she spoke.

Charlie frowned. 'We've already talked about this, Agnes. Your mother won't countenance you going to London and I agree with her. I'm sure a place can be found for you closer to home – Margate, perhaps.'

George, whose heart had plummeted at the thought of losing Agnes so soon, was relieved by Charlie's words until he saw the effect they had on his daughter. Her brows knitted and he could have sworn that the temperature in the room, warm on this rapidly cooling September evening, had dropped by a few degrees.

Charlie, also noticing Agnes's expression, added hastily, 'But we have a guest and he doesn't want to witness our family disagreements. He's come here to enjoy our company.'

Agnes continued to sulk until her father sighed and said, 'I've a mind to have a drink to wash away today's toil and I'm sure George feels the same. Would you fetch us a couple of glasses of ale?'

He watched his daughter leave the room, every aspect of her demeanour spelling out her displeasure. 'Perhaps you'll find your manners in the kitchen,' Charlie muttered, half to himself. Then he turned to George with a wry smile. 'A houseful of women is a challenge at times. I longed for a son, but it wasn't to be.'

Such family interactions were a novelty to George. If he'd ever wondered what he might have missed, he supposed he'd imagined a harmonic family idyll. He was beginning to gain a more balanced view, underlined as the evening progressed, but first Charlie wanted to engage him in a discussion about ripping out some of the old planting in one of the garden borders and replacing it with a new scheme entirely.

They were interrupted by Catherine's call to table, Agnes having delivered their ale and disappeared back to the kitchen. Charlie waved George through and he found the wooden table set with plates and cutlery. The vase of late roses stood in the centre, with three steaming serving dishes ranged around it.

'Sit down,' Molly said and then, as George hesitated, unsure of which place to take, she added, 'Here, next to me.' Charlie took the chair at the head of the table while Agnes and Catherine seated themselves opposite Molly and George. Catherine was given the job of ladling out the rabbit stew, Agnes told to add potatoes to each plate, and Molly dished out the greens, serving Charlie and George plates piled high with food. Charlie poured a red wine that surprised George by being as good as anything at Captain Ramsay's table – and the captain had prided himself on being a connoisseur. When he remarked on it, Charlie said, 'A gift from Mr Powell's cellars. He's a generous employer.'

The discussion around the table was fast and furious, with frequent changes of topic, and George was glad to sit back, enjoy his food and just observe. The rich gravy of the stew was flavoured with thyme, the potatoes flecked with chopped parsley and the vegetables with caraway seeds. The dinner was every bit as delicious as the aroma had suggested.

As Agnes and Catherine cleared the plates and dishes from the table and they waited for the apple pie, just removed from the oven, to cool, Molly turned to George.

'Charlie tells me your childhood was spent in London, at the Foundling School, in circumstances not unlike his own here in Margate, and that you were some years at sea. Were you apprenticed to the Navy?'

George, who had drunk rather well of the fine red wine, found his tongue loosened by it. He had never really been asked to tell his story before and now it had happened twice in a matter of days, first by Charlie and now by his wife, whose sympathetic brown eyes were fixed on him, while her daughters also regarded him with some interest from across the table.

He launched into his story, telling of his early memories of the countryside, followed by the structured routine of the Foundling School, such a shock to him at the age of five. Then, aged twelve, his apprenticeship to Mr Gifford, 'that scoundrel', finding himself in Rochester where his employer had flouted the terms of his contract and set him to work as a labourer. He spared them the details of the conditions he had worked under and the convicts he had laboured alongside, and was glad he had done so when he saw Molly dab at her cheeks with a handkerchief. He told of how he had run away and found a job cutting wood at the gunpowder works near Faversham, settling into his life there until he was taken by a press gang. It was his bad luck to find himself in front of a regulating officer who knew him from his days as an apprentice. Faced with a choice between the threat of prison for breaking his apprenticeship or volunteering for the Navy, he had chosen the latter.

'But the man who took you on as an apprentice, this Mr—' Agnes broke off, having forgotten his name.

'Gifford,' George supplied.

'Yes, Mr Gifford, he was in the wrong, employing you as he did. Surely he was the one who should have been sent to prison.'

'It would have been the word of a sixteen-year-old foundling against a man of business.' George said. 'But I was lucky in my captain and my ship. It was my family for the next few years.'

He'd told only the bare bones of his story but, as a guest, he felt it impolite to dominate the conversation. And he was aware of the pie, rapidly cooling in the centre of the table. Agnes and Catherine were both regarding him with a mixture of fascination and, he feared, horror. The latter was partly because, as he now saw, Molly had clearly been moved to tears by his story and was struggling to hold in her sobs.

'Catherine, please serve the pie,' Molly said, her voice muffled by her handkerchief. Charlie looked perturbed and George was mortified.

'I'm so sorry, I didn't mean to cause distress,' he said.

'You mustn't apologise.' Molly had reappeared from behind her now sodden handkerchief, cheeks burning and eyes full of yet more tears. 'That's a very sorry tale indeed.'

'Did you ever wonder about your mother?' Agnes asked.

'Not at first. Only when I got to the Foundling Hospital and the others talked about the tokens their mothers had left for them.'

'Tokens?' Agnes asked.

'Yes,' George said. 'Buttons, fabric scraps, playing cards, things like that. Proof of their intention to return for their babies one day.'

'And did any of the mothers come back?' Agnes asked.

'Not that I know of,' George said.

'How could anyone do such a thing?' Catherine appealed to the table, halfway through serving up slices of pie. 'Abandon their baby like that and never see them again.'

George shrugged. It was a question he had ceased to ask himself, for what good did it do?

Molly spoke, in a voice so low that they had to strain to hear. 'Perhaps they had no choice. Perhaps their families had cast them out and they had nowhere to go and no means of feeding themselves, let alone a child.'

Charlie gave her a sharp look. 'Agnes, would you fetch the cream from the larder, please?' Then he launched into a story about work, while George and Molly lapsed into silence – the former wondering whether it had been wise to recount his history after all.

CHAPTER FORTY-SIX

The dinner at the Dawsons' had ended on a happy note, Charlie successfully diverting attention from George and Molly. Agnes had seemingly forgotten her earlier quarrel with her father and was now perfectly cheerful. George would have liked to spend more time with her, but had to excuse himself shortly after the meal was over for he found he had a headache brewing, perhaps due to consuming too much wine. Or maybe it was a result of the emotions roused within him by recounting his past. He rose, bidding them not to disturb themselves as he would show himself out. But Molly and Charlie both stood up too, Charlie telling him he must come again as George expressed his thanks for the dinner. Molly took a package from the side and pressed it into his hands.

'It's just a few of our old things that you might be able to use in your room. Charlie told me how bare it was and it's a shame not to have a few home comforts.' She bit her lip, perhaps reflecting on how few such things he had experienced in the past.

George hastened to thank her for her kindness, both for the package and for the dinner.

He was glad of the cool air as he walked home in the dark, hoping it would soothe the pounding in his head. He cut through the grounds of Woodchurch Manor, where the ground-floor dining room was lit by candlelight, family and guests still at table. George was already regretting sharing his tale with the Dawson family at dinner – he would never have done such a thing at the Powells'. Was the wine responsible for loosening his tongue? he wondered, as he reached the stable-yard. Horses stamped restlessly in the new stable block, at right angles across the courtyard to the old one. He stood for a moment, looking up at the stars and taking in deep breaths of cool air before he let himself in and climbed the stairs.

Once he'd lit the candle in his room, he undid the string around the package and opened it on his bed. First, he pulled out a quilt, hand-stitched with patches of red and cream. George stared at it, then reached out to touch it. He'd never owned such a thing before. He shook it out and laid it over the bed. It was well-washed and faded in some areas and the backing had worn thin, but it brought a welcome splash of colour to the room and he had to drag his eyes away to see what else was in the parcel. There was a rag rug, as Charlie had promised – in practical drab shades of green and brown, as well as an earthenware plate, a little jug and a jar of preserves.

The kindness brought tears to George's eyes and he felt as though he should go back and thank Molly all over again, but his headache persuaded him that he should take to his bed. He hoped an early night would erase it by morning, along with the unwelcome feeling that he had somehow said the wrong thing during the course of the evening.

He slept well under the warmth of the quilt, and as he walked to church the next morning under the clearest of blue skies, his headache had vanished. He'd asked Charlie for directions to the church the previous evening and found it easily enough, although it was hidden away on a tiny lane that led between the road to Woodchurch Manor and the estate cottages where Charlie lived.

As he passed the manor, its white façade gleaming in the early-morning sun, he noticed that the leaves on the trees were changing colour, the green – a little tired after the summer's heat – turning yellow where an overnight frost had caught the edges.

George shivered. It was still chilly in the shade but the sunshine promised warmth by midday. Spring might be the traditional time of new beginnings – particularly in the garden, when all the new growth flourished, but for him autumn this year felt like a new start. He had a job, which might prove to be a new career if he wished it, somewhere of his own to live for the first time, Edward, a friend, living close by – and the tentative promise of a romance.

He walked through the open door of the tiny church into the stone-flagged interior, the light pouring through the leaded window behind the altar. There was the faint scent of beeswax polish on the air, intermingled with candlewax, and the simple whitewashed walls reflected the sunlight. The congregation was already seated – the Powell family on the right and the estate workers on the left of the central aisle.

George was about to slip into a pew on the left when he saw Edward signalling for him to join him. He felt awkward as he did so, cursing his tendency to flush at the merest hint of embarrassment. The service was about to start, the studded oak door closing with a thud as George took his place in the pew.

He glanced to his left and found himself directly adjacent to Agnes, seated at the end of a pew with her parents behind her. He felt the flush rising again and, glancing back to acknowledge Molly and Charlie with a nod, he hoped that any curious onlookers would put his heightened colour down to a brisk walk in the chill of the morning. Then he looked to the front of the church and did his best to focus on the service – but only a few minutes passed before he found himself sneaking a glance at Agnes.

She was sitting with her hands clasped on the hymn book in her lap, and looking straight ahead. She wore the same dress of dark green serge that she had worn for her exhibition, with a little jacket for warmth, and a bonnet that partly hid her face but revealed her dark hair coiled at the nape of her neck. She appeared oblivious to his gaze.

George tried not to fidget but he struggled to concentrate on the sermon, gazing around the church and letting his eyes alight on Agnes as often as possible. It was only when he caught Edward glancing at him curiously that he forced himself to look forward again. He thought he did a good job of appearing attentive to the service from then on, although he discovered that he could still see Agnes out of the corner of his eye without turning his head. She sat as still as a stone, except when called upon to kneel in prayer or stand and sing.

The Powells left their pews ahead of the rest of the congregation and George smiled again at the Dawson family. He was glad when the Powells lingered in the churchyard to exchange a few words with the vicar, for it gave him a chance to speak to Molly as she left with her family.

'I wanted to say thank you for the parcel. It was very generous of you. The quilt is so warm and . . .' George struggled to find the right words '. . . so lovely. I hope it can be spared?'

'Indeed it can. It was one of the girls' early attempts at quilt-making. The stitching is not very fine.' Molly smiled, as if at a memory. Then, as George lingered, hoping to find an excuse to speak to Agnes, she added, 'I believe you are to dine at the Powells'? They are about to depart.'

George turned and saw that they were indeed leaving by the lych-gate. Edward glanced back at him so he bade a hasty farewell to the Dawsons, thanking Molly again for dinner the previous evening.

He hurried after the Powells, glancing back in search of Agnes as he passed through the lych-gate, only to find Molly watching him with a curious expression on her face. He didn't have long to muse on this for Edward began to regale him with the contents of a letter he had received from one of the other lieutenants on HMS *Valour*, who had returned to find his fiancée not only about to marry another man but also with child by him. He appeared to have got over his disappointment by spending several nights drinking heavily in Truro, Edward said, waking to find himself in gaol, apparently having run up a bar bill he couldn't pay. George did his best to appear engaged with the story, but in truth his naval days had already begun to feel part of a distant past.

A fire was burning in the dining room at Woodchurch Manor and drinks were served around it, although by the time the servants were laying the table the doors had been flung open onto the terrace and the guests had moved outside to enjoy the sunshine.

George was engaged in conversation by Mr Powell, who wanted to know how he liked his new employment. 'Charlie does a splendid job. These gardens are the envy of all my visitors,' Mr Powell said, contemplating the view from the terrace. 'It takes quite a team to manage the upkeep these days. I'm sure you will be a great asset.' Then he was gone, drawn away by his wife to speak to one of the guests.

Edward was involved in a conversation on the other side of the terrace and George, attempting to make his way over to him, was waylaid by a nearby group, who asked how he knew the family. His explanation of his naval link with Edward was met by approving nods, but when they questioned him about what he was doing now and he began to explain about his new role in the gardens he sensed he'd lost their interest. He cut his tale short and stood silently as they discussed a play they had attended in London, with much laughter as they gossiped about members of the audience. George edged backwards, hoping to escape the group without appearing obvious, and casually turned to the gardens. When he turned back, the circle had closed.

Feeling a mixture of relief and irritation he sought out Edward once more but was accosted by another knot of guests. He had the impression it was at the behest of one of the ladies, although it was a gentleman who said, 'I don't believe we've been introduced.' As George obliged, he felt the appraising glance of the lady sweep over him. She was older than him and elegantly dressed; he noticed that she moved closer as he explained about his naval career and subsequent link with the Powells. This was greeted by approving nods once more and questions followed as to his future plans. This time, George was ready for the reaction when he divulged his new role as a gardener.

'How . . . delightful,' the enamoured lady said, enamoured no more as she moved away to talk to someone more worthy of her attentions.

George excused himself and was glad to find Edward standing briefly alone. He was about to tell him what had just happened when they were called to table and he was once more separated from his friend. George dined sitting between a deaf gentleman of a great age and a dowager duchess, neither of whom seemed to require anything from him, being fully engaged with the neighbours on the other side of them. The no-longer enamoured lady was opposite him but the table was wide and the deaf gentleman bellowing too loudly for them to do anything other than exchange wry glances, hers accompanied by an arched eyebrow.

When the diners stood to take their coffee outside, George sought out Edward again and asked to be excused, pleading a headache, which was, in fact, a reality once more. He escaped by way of the garden, making his way to a hidden section behind the stable block, unvisited by guests. Here the less-attractive essentials of the garden were kept: the pile of rotting-down manure from the stables and heaps of clippings waiting to be burnt. George had discovered that if you progressed beyond this there was a little copse with views over the surrounding countryside. It was a good place to sit and think.

As he looked out over the fields beyond the fence, mist was starting to collect in the hollows where the land dipped, low hills lying shadowy in the distance. He thought back to the landscape of the islands in the West Indies, so different under the brilliant blue skies. Yet he could see similarities, too, although the colours were so much softer, more muted. He liked how his life had been over the last few weeks, in particular his work in the gardens, meeting Agnes, Charlie and the rest of the family. He would try to get to know them better in the weeks to come, he decided. By Christmas, he hoped he would be much closer to Agnes, in particular. The thought made him smile and he sat on, gazing out over the fields, lost in thought until the chill in the air forced him to stand, stretch and make his way back to his solitary room in the old stable block.

PART THREE

1814

CHAPTER FORTY-SEVEN

If Molly's family thought she had behaved oddly at dinner with George, no one mentioned it. She felt as though the word 'Guilty' was branded on her forehead, such was her renewed pain over what she had done. She remembered Catherine's words after George's blunt depiction of his upbringing: 'How could anyone do such a thing? Abandon their baby like that and never see them again.' And she remembered her own feeble attempts at justification. She felt sure that Charlie had noticed something odd and, once George had departed and the table was cleared, the washing-up done and everyone in their beds, she was expecting him to question her about it. But he said good night, turned on his side and fell into a deep sleep as quickly as he always did.

She lay there, eyes wide open in the gloom, staring at the ceiling and going over everything George had said about his early years. It was the closest she had ever come to hearing a true account of what life was like for a foundling and she was shocked. She had believed what she had been told by the officials at the Foundling Hospital, that these children had a better chance of a good future there than with their impoverished mothers. And it was true that George had found his own way in life and had had the sort of naval career that she would have wished for her own son. But she couldn't forget what he'd said about his early years in the countryside, how he'd been educated but unloved during his schooldays and how he'd been exploited by the man to whom he was apprenticed. The contrast with the sheltered and happy upbringing of her own daughters could hardly have been greater.

She tried to reassure herself that his experiences didn't mean such things had befallen her own son. Yet there had been a moment when George first stepped into the kitchen when she imagined she glimpsed a resemblance to Nicholas Goodchild. It must have been something about his brown eyes, for his hair was far too light. That his name was George had convinced her she was wrong, although it had been a shock to hear it. George was the name she had given her son. She knew, though, that all foundlings were given new names, to further the complete break with their past and set them on the road to a different future. His name alone was enough to convince her that this young man had no link to her.

Charlie shifted in his sleep and Molly feared her restlessness had disturbed him. She was ashamed at taking comfort in the thought that the ill treatment visited on George had not necessarily been suffered by her son. And she had, at least, given George some things to make his room more comfortable and cheerful. Then she remembered that it was Charlie who had pushed her to do this – she had initially been reluctant, asking how he knew that the lad wouldn't just make off in the night with their second-best spare quilt and the few other odds and ends she had grudgingly put together. Her cheeks burnt at the memory.

Molly fell into a restless sleep, only to be woken again when Charlie rose. It felt as though only a few minutes had passed and it took a great effort to stay awake. It was Sunday, she remembered, and they must go to church.

She could barely suppress her yawns as she went about preparing breakfast but Charlie, Agnes and Catherine seemed unaware that anything was amiss. They were discussing the arrival of Sally, Luke and the children later that day and deciding how they might entertain Grace and Simon.

The walk to church in the fresh air revived Molly a little and, while she waited for the service to start, she thought about what she would prepare for their Sunday dinner on her return home. A late arrival in a nearby pew disturbed her reverie and she looked up to see George, pink-cheeked and flustered. He turned in his pew to acknowledge them and Molly nodded a greeting, then fell to examining the back of his head as she went over his conversation of the previous evening once more.

She noticed that George kept turning to look to his left and, after he'd repeated the action a few times, she realised that he was watching Agnes. Was Agnes aware of his attention? she wondered. She hadn't mentioned anything about George, but that wasn't unusual: her daughter lived in her own little world and had been oblivious to any would-be suitors in the past. Molly had imagined Agnes making a good match, a well-to-do merchant from Margate, perhaps. But she was twenty now and no such man had appeared. Would George make a good husband for her? She regarded him speculatively. Charlie appeared very taken with him, although they'd worked together for little time. And a gardener wasn't quite what she'd had in mind for her daughter. Then she stopped. How could she think such a thing? Charlie was a gardener and she still had reason to remind herself what a happy choice she had made in her husband.

The service was under way now and, with an effort, Molly disciplined her thoughts and concentrated on the words of the sermon. She had some success until weariness threatened to overwhelm her and she was glad when the congregation was called upon to stand and sing a rousing hymn.

The Powells and their guests, George included, left the church first as usual and Molly had returned to thinking about the preparations for their afternoon meal as she made ready to follow. She was surprised to be accosted by George in the churchyard, intent on thanking her for the package she had pressed on him the previous evening. She had reason to be thankful that Charlie's good sense had prevailed, for George really did seem most grateful, forcing her to make light of the gifts. She watched him leave, hastening to catch up with the Powells and, as he did so, a feeling of misgiving crossed her mind. For the second time, she had a sense of familiarity. She vowed she would take the chance to talk to him further when the opportunity arose. Could it be that their paths had crossed somewhere in the past? She couldn't imagine how that might be, or devote any further time to thinking about it, for her family was waiting for her to walk home. She must apportion jobs to the girls and to Charlie, or there would be no dinner on the table by the time Sally's family arrived. Addressing this vague feeling of unease would have to wait for another day.

*　　*　　*

Molly's family might not have paid any attention to what she felt had been her odd behaviour during Saturday's dinner, but they certainly noticed how tired she was on Sunday afternoon.

Once dinner had been cooked, served, eaten and cleared away, Molly announced that she was going to sit in the parlour and suggested that Grace and Simon might like to join her for a story. Sally peeped in half an hour later to discover Molly fast asleep in her chair and Grace and Simon playing on the floor with the best tea service, which was usually shut away in the china cabinet. Caught between horror at the damage two very young children might have inflicted on the china – but luckily hadn't – and a fit of giggles at the sight, Sally scooped up her children and took them into the kitchen to play with their granddad. Then she returned to the parlour and replaced the china as quietly as she could. Molly woke up and caught her red-handed but was only disposed to laugh about it once she knew what had happened.

She yawned, stretched and laughed again. 'It looks as though my story was so dull I sent myself to sleep.'

'I'll make you some tea,' Sally offered. About to leave the room, she stopped, hand on the doorknob. 'It's not like you to fall asleep, Ma. You're not poorly?' She waited for an answer, head on one side and eyebrows raised.

'No, don't be silly. I had a bad night, that's all. And this room is warm – it made me sleepy.'

The fire had been lit again, in honour of their visitors, and it was true that the parlour was stuffy. Molly yawned again, got to her feet and went back into the kitchen where she had to endure some teasing about the need for an afternoon nap now that she was so old. Her protest that she was only in her forties, certainly not old, was ignored and the afternoon played out in the usual noisy family fashion until Sally, Luke and the grandchildren went home.

Charlie insisted that Molly should have an early night and she was happy to agree: not out of tiredness, for the short nap had done her good. Instead, a memory had stirred within her that afternoon and she was impatient to act upon it.

Many years earlier, she had tucked a bundle into the back of the cupboard in her bedroom and hadn't looked at it since.

Now she had a burning desire to see it again. It would be safer to wait until the following day, when Charlie would be at work in the gardens, but the idea had taken hold and would not be denied.

Molly closed the bedroom door behind her and went swiftly to the cupboard. She needed a chair to stand on to reach right to the back of the top shelf but she found what she was looking for at once, lifting out a bundled-up knitted woollen blanket. Stepping down off the chair, she laid the blanket on the bed, noting with some distress that moths had eaten holes in the dusty cream wool. Heart beating fast she unwrapped the now-fragile material, on high alert for the sound of Charlie's footsteps on the stairs.

The blanket contained a piece of fabric, tightly folded and thankfully untouched by moths. Molly shook it out, revealing it as a handkerchief, and a cut playing card tumbled from the folds onto the floor. She picked it up and was standing with the blanket and the handkerchief clutched to her cheek when she heard the door behind her swing open.

'Ma.' Agnes was on the threshold. 'Have you seen Catherine? She's not in her room and. . .' She stopped, looking curiously at Molly. 'What have you got there?'

Molly dashed away the tears that threatened to spill onto her cheeks, gathered the bundle together and hastily thrust it back into the cupboard. Then, her back pressed against its closed door, she turned to face Agnes. 'It's nothing. Just something I hadn't seen for a while. What did you say about Catherine?'

Chapter Forty-Eight

The discoveries of the hours that followed left Molly reeling. It was quickly established that Catherine was nowhere to be found in the cottage and no one could recollect seeing her since they'd waved Sally off at about half past five that afternoon.

Molly told herself it was still only nine o'clock in the evening, and although it was dark, it had been so for only a couple of hours. 'Perhaps she's at Woodchurch Manor,' she suggested, as they all stood in the kitchen, Agnes looking as though she might cry and Charlie with a frown creasing his brow. 'She might have gone to see Francis and lost track of the time.'

'She wouldn't have gone without telling us,' Charlie said but, nevertheless, he began to pull on his work jacket, taking it from its usual place on the back of the kitchen door.

'I'll just go up there and check. I won't be long.' He was already halfway out of the door and Molly felt a rush of fear. It was so unlike Catherine. She was quiet and dependable, not lost in her own world and sometimes temperamental, as Agnes could be.

Molly paced the floor anxiously as they waited for Charlie's return, quizzing Agnes as to whether Catherine had said or done anything unusual over the last few days.

Charlie burst back through the door within the half-hour, grim-faced. 'Francis is missing, too. It looks as though they have gone off together.'

Molly stopped pacing and stood as if turned to stone, her mind racing. Then she spun around and hurried up the stairs to the room that Agnes and Catherine shared. At first sight, all seemed much as usual but she opened the clothes press and ran her eyes over the contents. It was instantly apparent that some of Catherine's clothes were missing. Acting on instinct, she pulled back the covers on Catherine's bed and there, lying on the sheet just below the pillow, was a folded piece of paper, with 'Ma and Pa' inscribed on the front.

Molly snatched it up and flew down the stairs with Agnes – who had followed her up to the bedroom – close behind her.

'They planned something.' Molly handed the note, unopened, to Charlie, who unfolded it and quickly scanned the words.

'They did,' he said, frowning. He handed the note back to Molly who read it, Agnes peering anxiously over her shoulder.

Dear Ma and Pa,

By the time you read this I hope Francis and I will be well on our way. We are going to get married. Francis has given up asking his father for permission; he will never agree. We will have to accept the consequences but we love each other and I hope that you at least will be able to understand and forgive, even if Francis's father can't.

I am sorry to cause you worry and distress but we had to act now or face even more trouble in the future.

Your loving daughter,
Catherine

Charlie had taken up a lantern and was making ready to head back to Woodchurch Manor. 'Has either of you any idea where they might have gone?'

Molly shook her head and turned to Agnes. Catherine's sister was more likely to know if they had let anything slip but Agnes, too, shook her head.

Charlie took up the letter. 'I'll have to show this to Mr Powell,' he said. He didn't look as though he relished the prospect but, before Molly could utter words of encouragement, he had hurried out again, leaving his wife and daughter alone.

Without a word, they sat down at the kitchen table. Molly feared that another long and sleepless night lay ahead. She should make a hot drink, perhaps, but her thoughts rendered her powerless to move. Catherine and Francis had been such good friends from childhood and it had seemed only natural that they had become sweethearts, despite the difference in their circumstances. Francis had hoped that Robert and Edward's return to the estate would soften his father's attitude to their wished-for marriage but it hadn't. Now that he had reached his majority he had clearly decided to take matters into his own hands.

Molly wondered what Catherine had meant by 'even more trouble in the future'. A niggling suspicion began to grow within her. She thought back to Catherine's impassioned words the evening before, when George had spoken about his experiences as a foundling. Catherine had questioned how anyone could abandon their baby in such a way, and Molly remembered her own reply: 'Perhaps the mothers of these children had been cast out by their families.' Is that what Catherine feared? Was she with child? Had this precipitated their rash action? Had she and Francis feared that Mr Powell would force them to give up the baby?

She shivered, causing Agnes to get up to fetch her a shawl.

'Here, Ma. I'll stoke the range again, shall I, unless you'd rather go up to bed?'

Molly shook her head. She wouldn't get a wink of sleep until Charlie came back and told them what was happening. She took up a basket of mending and she and Agnes stitched into the night, with many a sigh passing between them.

Charlie returned after midnight and Molly got to her feet, the mending discarded on the floor.

'Have they been found?'

'No.' Charlie pulled out a chair and sat down, his head in his hands. Then he sighed heavily. 'No,' he repeated. 'Mr Powell has decided there is nothing we can do tonight. We have no idea where they have gone, or how they travelled. No horses are missing from the stable and Francis's brothers can offer no clue as to their whereabouts.'

'But . . .' Molly's mind raced. 'Shouldn't he send riders out on the Canterbury road? To stop at every inn and see if they're there?'

Charlie shrugged. 'They may not have gone in that direction. They could have gone to Margate, to take a boat to London.'

'Then surely someone should go to see whether they're waiting there for the first boat in the morning?' Molly had returned to pacing the floor.

'Molly, Mr Powell has decided to let them get on with it.' Charlie looked drained and tired. 'Francis has his majority and can marry without permission. Mr Powell is angry but inclined to wait until we hear that the deed is done, to avoid a scandal, I would imagine. He talks of cutting Francis off without a penny but that is tonight's anger speaking. I think he may eventually come to see things differently although he may never forgive the disobedience.'

'Then we must look for them,' Molly declared. 'Catherine is nineteen and can't marry without permission.'

'Would you want to prevent the marriage?' Charlie asked. 'I'm inclined to take Mr Powell's view – don't imagine I haven't fully considered the matter,' he added hastily, seeing the look Molly threw his way. 'They care for each other and have done for many years. It was wrong of them to go off in this way, causing upset and distress, but they must have thought they had no other choice. Once they are married, they will write. Or they will return when the money runs out.'

Molly wondered what money he referred to, for Catherine surely had none. Francis had an allowance, she supposed. She could see the sense of what was proposed but she didn't like to think of the dangers to which Catherine might be being exposed, even with Francis at her side. Memories of her own flight from the area all those years before came back to her even as she tried to suppress them.

Charlie broke into her thoughts. 'I'm going to bed. It will be time to get up again for work soon enough.'

Molly watched him leave the room. She should have gone after him, asked him how awkward his conversation with Mr Powell had been, reassured him that all would be well. But she sat on, barely managing to say good night to Agnes when she, too, declared that she must sleep.

Had everyone abandoned Catherine? Molly felt anger towards Mr Powell, for thinking her daughter not good enough for his son, for refusing to search for them. Charlie should have insisted on it. Then, as she sat on in the silent kitchen, she began to wonder whether it wasn't, in fact, the best decision. If they were brought home, Mr Powell would forbid the marriage and, if her suspicions were correct and Catherine was with child, it was far better that the wedding should take place. Perhaps a grandchild would soften Mr Powell's attitude.

Yet she couldn't bear to think of Catherine not at home with a baby on the way. She knew only too well what it was like to manage under such circumstances although, thankfully, Francis was standing by Catherine.

She would ask Charlie again in the morning about searching for their daughter. She couldn't decide whether or not to share with him her suspicions about the baby – would it just make him even angrier? She would think on it while she slept, Molly decided, climbing wearily up the stairs to bed. She wondered if sleep would be any easier to come by than it had been the night before.

CHAPTER FORTY-NINE

Exhaustion guaranteed that Molly did sleep but lightly so she awoke at once when Charlie got up in the morning.

Charlie was sitting on the edge of the bed, rather than tiptoeing around the room as he usually did, collecting up items of clothing and dressing as silently as possible. 'It's early, Molly. I couldn't sleep.'

Molly's eyes felt gritty with tiredness but within a few seconds of waking she was pulled back to the events of a few hours before. 'Charlie, even if Mr Powell doesn't want to look for Francis, there's nothing to stop us searching for Catherine, is there?'

Charlie sighed. 'I've been thinking much the same myself. But where? And how? With no clues, we don't know where to start. And Mr Powell will never release me from my duties if he knows what I plan to do. At least, not until his anger cools.'

Charlie ran his hands through his hair. His back was still turned to Molly but she saw the misery in his hunched form. She debated whether to give voice to her suspicions. Would it make matters worse? Then it all came out in a rush.

'I think Catherine may be having a baby. I fear it was

something that was said the other night, when we were talking about foundlings, that pushed them into this.'

Charlie twisted around to stare at her. Molly couldn't read his face in the gloom but when he spoke his voice was choked with anger. 'The little fool. Whatever were the pair of them thinking?'

Molly spoke up in defence of her daughter. 'Charlie, they've been close for years, since they were children. Francis tried to persuade his father to let them marry but you know he wouldn't have it, not while Robert and Edward were in the Navy. He feared the loss of them, meaning Francis would be heir. When his brothers came home, Francis must have thought he would have his father's blessing at last.'

'I know all this and it doesn't excuse their behaviour.' Charlie began to dress, his irritation obvious in his movements.

'No, it doesn't. And they're both old enough to know it. I blame myself for letting Catherine run up to Woodchurch Manor whenever she wanted. She's been such friends with Francis for so long that I thought nothing of it. We should have tried to separate them, made her see that it wasn't to be.' Molly frowned. 'Anyway, they've taken matters into their own hands and, when all is said and done, do we really object to Catherine marrying Francis? If there *is* a baby then it's no bad thing. Mr Powell's first grandchild – perhaps it will change his mind about everything.' Molly was not entirely convinced by her own argument.

'Mr Powell likes things done his way,' Charlie said. 'Catherine has placed me in an awkward position. I'm not sure he believes I was ignorant of their plans.' He sighed. 'I'm going to the gardens. Let's see what the day brings. Perhaps Mr Powell will have changed his mind overnight and will send someone after them, although if what you suspect is true, that may not be the best plan after all.'

The day brought no further news of the pair and no clues as to how they had managed their disappearance. Mr Powell remained furious and stubborn in his insistence that he would cut Francis out of his will, according to Charlie who reported back that evening. He had had a frosty encounter with his employer in the garden, which Charlie confessed he hadn't helped by pointing out that Mr Powell had given the pair hope by saying he couldn't countenance their marriage while Robert and Edward were still at sea.

'I told him he'd implied to Francis that, once his brothers returned, he would be at liberty to marry as he wished,' Charlie said. 'It didn't go down well. His reply was, "Marry, yes. As he wished, no." Then he stamped off without another word. I took that to mean Catherine isn't good enough for Francis.'

Molly grimaced. 'We all knew that was the case. Mr Powell should have put a stop to the friendship and so should we. It was easier to let it drift on, I suppose.'

She and Agnes had spent much of the day discussing that very thing, as well as racking their brains as to where the truants might have gone. Agnes had sensibly pointed out that Francis – or, at least, the Powell family – had far more connections around the country than they had. The solution to the puzzle most likely lay with him.

Although Catherine was underage, she and Francis could marry in church provided banns were read on three successive Sundays and her parents didn't appear with an objection. Since Molly and Charlie didn't object to the marriage as such, there was little point in trying to trace the fugitives.

297

Agnes was sure they wouldn't stay away from home for too long – surely a month at the most.

'I think we must try to be patient,' Molly said, although she certainly didn't feel it. 'They are together. Francis cares for Catherine and he won't let any harm come to her.' She clung to this fact. Catherine's situation was unlike her own, alone and unmarried with a child at the age of eighteen. Her child's father had had no interest in his son – he'd already married another without ever acknowledging the situation in which he had placed Molly.

Molly's brave words were, at least, borne out by letters received after four long weeks had passed. Francis and Catherine wrote separately to say they had been married at a church in Holborn, in London, and that no one should worry about them. They apologised for the distress they must have caused, assuring their respective parents of their happiness but giving no clues as to where they were staying or any indication as to when, or if, they would return.

Molly, overjoyed to receive the news, was quickly disconcerted by the lack of information. 'If only they'd supplied an address,' she lamented. 'We could go and fetch them home. They are married now so surely all can be forgiven.'

'Perhaps they don't want to be found, or at least for the moment,' Charlie said. 'I imagine they have stayed in London and perhaps are enjoying the experience.'

Molly remembered only too well her own experiences of the city. They had not all been happy ones. But Catherine was a married woman now, with a husband to protect her. No doubt Charlie was right and they were making the most of their time there, with trips to the theatre and going out to dine. Even so, if Catherine was expecting a baby, Molly would have preferred her to be at home. Her relief and delight in hearing from them was quickly replaced by frustration. Would they write again and, if so, how long would it be before they could expect another letter?

CHAPTER FIFTY

Since Catherine's abrupt departure, Charlie had said little on the subject. Molly knew that it made life difficult for him with Mr Powell. He worked as hard as ever in the gardens but she saw it irked him that his employer believed Catherine to be an unsuitable wife for his son. He was angry with his daughter, too, and after the first week of their absence Molly stopped trying to discuss it with him.

She and Agnes wondered daily what had become of Catherine, how she was and what she might be doing at that very moment, but at dinner with Charlie, they talked of other things. Molly did her best to remain cheerful: the letter had at least reassured her that the marriage had taken place but now she was more restless than she had been before.

Charlie departed on one of his trips to London, taking George with him as a first introduction to the type of business to be done in the gardens. They had a list of plants to be procured for late-autumn planting, and another of those to be reserved for the following spring, Mr Powell having unbent enough towards his head gardener to authorise the trip.

'When you return, we must ask George to dine with us again. I'd intended to ask him before now but . . .' Molly sighed.

'We won't be gone long. Four days at most. Let's plan to invite him on the Saturday after we return.'

Charlie left in good spirits on a crisp late-October morning, under clear blue skies. He always enjoyed his trips to London – not for the city itself but for the chance to share news and tips with fellow head gardeners and to discuss the successes and failures over the year.

Molly and Agnes paid a visit to Sally and her family, for the house felt empty with just the two of them at home and they were in need of a diversion. They decided to prolong their trip by an extra night to stay with Aunt Jane and spend time with Lizzie and Mary. There was no hiding the fact that Francis and Catherine had run off – in any case, the news had already spread to Margate. Molly was relieved that she was at least able to say they were wed, but if she had hoped that would be an end to it, she was disappointed. Her relatives wanted to talk of little else and it was dispiriting to have no further news to offer.

Aunt Jane was disposed to blame Molly, who felt the weight of her disapproval for having apparently allowed Catherine to run wild. She could only be thankful that no one else was aware of her suspicions about a baby and she was careful to let nothing slip. Aunt Jane moved on to chastise her for allowing Agnes to indulge in art, perfectly suitable as an idle pastime for a young woman but not to be considered as a full-time occupation. It was clear that she believed Agnes would follow the same route as her sister, if she was not made to see the error of her ways.

So it was that mother and daughter were pleased to return home on the Thursday, having failed to amuse themselves as they had hoped. They had been back barely an hour and Molly, having unpacked, was standing in the kitchen

301

considering what to prepare for dinner, when she heard voices outside and footsteps on the path. There was a hesitant knock at the door. Then, before she could move or call out, it swung open. It took Molly a moment to register who was standing on the threshold, before she stepped forward, arms outstretched.

'Oh, Catherine.' Her tears began to flow at once, causing Catherine, who was clinging to her, to sob too.

'Oh, Ma, I'm so sorry.'

After a minute or two, Molly held her away to look at her, then turned her head to call up the stairs, 'Agnes, your sister's here. She's home.'

Then Molly registered Francis standing awkwardly on the step. 'Francis! Come in, come in. Sit down, the pair of you. We must congratulate you both.' Molly, pink-cheeked and flustered, was full of questions. 'Shall I make tea? Have you come far? Are you staying?'

She bit her lip. Were her last words too close for comfort to the question she was avoiding? Did Mr Powell know they were back?

'If only your father was here, Catherine. He'd be so happy.'

No sooner had she spoken than the back door opened once more and Charlie stepped through it, a broad grin on his face. Molly uttered a cry of surprise and looked from Charlie to Catherine and back again.

'Did you . . .? How . . .?' She could barely formulate her questions.

Agnes took charge. 'Sit down. I'll fetch everyone a drink.'

Molly sat down in a kind of wonderment, unable to take her eyes off Catherine. Her daughter was a little fuller in the face, she thought, and she tried not to glance too obviously at her figure, which was now hidden as she was sitting at the table.

'So, how has this come about?' she asked.

Catherine spoke first. 'Pa found us in London. He convinced us that the best thing to do would be to come home.' Tears began to roll down her cheeks and Molly noted, approvingly, that Francis reached out and took her hand.

'But how . . .?' She turned to Charlie for an answer to her question.

'Well, we knew they had married in Holborn. I mentioned this to George and he said it was an area that he knew a little, since it wasn't so far from where he'd been at school. He's got a good head on his shoulders – while I was taking care of business in the gardens he did a little tour of the churches in Holborn. It wasn't hard to find the one where the marriage had been registered and he worked his charm to discover the address that Mr Francis Powell had used to call the banns. As luck would have it, the new Mr and Mrs Powell were still staying there. And here we are.'

Charlie was beaming – Molly hadn't seen him look so happy in over a month.

She turned back to Catherine. 'Well, the tale of how you managed your escape to London can wait but, Francis, an interview with your father can't be put off. If he discovers that you have come here, without a word to him—'

Molly stopped, but Francis spoke up: 'You are right and I know it. I wanted to see you first, Mrs Dawson, to apologise for our actions, having already done so to your husband.' He looked at Charlie, a serious expression on his face. 'We truly felt there was nothing else we could do. If my father won't be mollified by my apology then I will take the consequences.'

'You must prepare for the worst but it's best got out of the way. Then we'll all know where we stand.' Charlie had lost his smile and grimness had returned to his features. 'Mr

Powell may not be best pleased at the part I played in finding you.'

'Surely not,' Molly protested, then subsided. Charlie knew his employer well. He might choose to be displeased that his head gardener had gone about personal business while working for him in London, even though it had resulted in Francis's safe return.

Francis got to his feet. 'Then let us go and see him now.'

'Should I come with you?' Catherine looked up at him and Molly could see the fear in her face.

Francis considered. 'No, it's best if I see him alone first.'

He bent to kiss his wife's cheek, then left by the kitchen door, Charlie at his side. Molly watched them through the window as they walked up the path, heads together, perhaps discussing how best to handle Mr Powell. She turned back to her youngest daughter.

'Well, Catherine, you'd better tell all.'

The recounting of Catherine's tale filled the next half-hour. She confessed that she'd prepared a bag and hidden it in the garden, slipping away shortly after Sally and her family had left. She had met Francis along the road to the highway, where they joined a coach belonging to a friend of his, who was sworn to secrecy about the whole affair. They had travelled through the night and taken lodgings in Holborn, which Francis's friend had also arranged.

Catherine admitted that the excitement of their adventure had soon worn off and she had been terrified that Mr Powell would somehow discover their whereabouts and come after them. Each week, after the banns were read in the local church, she'd waited for the knock on the door, but it didn't come. They had been wed in a small private ceremony with Francis's friend and one other as witnesses.

At this point, Catherine couldn't hold back her tears. 'I so wished that you and Pa and Agnes – and Sally and her family – could have been with us that day. I missed you all so much the whole time we were away. We almost gave up several times but we had gone through such a lot to get that far.' She sighed. 'And then we stayed on in our lodgings while Francis decided what to do next. He went to see various connections of his friend to try to get work. He knew a lot of other people in London he could have asked but he didn't want word to get back to his father.'

Catherine stopped, and Molly was relieved to see that her face brightened. 'Francis has been so good to me throughout everything. There was a time when I felt that we'd done the wrong thing, that I'd ruined his life, but he refused to let me think so.'

There was another question that Molly needed to ask but she was at a loss as to how to go about it. She thought for a moment, then said, 'Agnes, just go to the end of the lane and see whether your father is coming back.'

Agnes set off to do as she was asked, without appearing to realise she had been got out of the way.

Molly turned to Catherine. 'I have to ask – are you expecting a baby?'

Catherine's lip wobbled and she looked perplexed. 'I . . . well, yes – but how did you know?'

Molly pressed on. 'And is this why you ran away?'

Catherine nodded, unable to speak as more tears flowed. Her handkerchief was a sodden rag and Molly passed her own to her, all the while listening out for Agnes's return.

'Why didn't you tell me?' she asked.

Catherine stuttered out her answer between sobs: 'I feared that if anyone knew, they would make me give up the baby, our baby. Like the foundling babies. Mr Powell wouldn't agree to us marrying and a baby would have made things worse. He'd have given it away,' she finished dramatically.

Molly shook her head but before she could say anything further, Agnes came back into the kitchen, Charlie and Francis following close behind her. Francis was a little pale, Molly thought, and, finding his wife in tears, he glanced sharply between her and her mother.

'What did he say?' Molly asked.

'Well,' Charlie was cautious, 'he was angry with Francis and, as I suspected, with me. But I do believe he may come round. I told him that his son and his wife would be staying with us for a while and that he was, of course, welcome to visit. He muttered about that but he didn't ban them being here. I'm hopeful he will think it through and work out how to make the best of it.'

'Mother will put in a good word,' Francis said. Molly thought he looked despondent.

She tried not to let her rising irritation at Mr Powell's attitude be apparent. If he came looking for his son at her house – a house that, of course, belonged to him – she was going to have to watch her tongue or she would be tempted to give him a piece of her mind.

Instead she said, 'You are both welcome to stay here for as long as you need.' As she spoke, she could hardly contain her delight at having Catherine home again. 'This Saturday, we will have a dinner to welcome you back – I'll invite Sally, too. And George,' she added, to a nod of approval from Charlie, 'to say thank you for the part he has played in all of this.'

CHAPTER FIFTY-ONE

By the time Saturday arrived, Francis and Catherine had recovered from their journey and settled into the little front bedroom that had once belonged to Sally. Francis was clearly ill-at-ease, unused to living in such a confined space with others, Molly suspected. There had been no sign of Mr Powell, who was evidently determined to take his time in deciding what should happen next.

For dinner, Molly had roasted a joint of beef, a gift from the Woodchurch Manor kitchens. It had been sent over when they had heard of Mr Francis's return – and his exile. Agnes had collected whatever she could find in the way of autumn foliage to brighten a vase for the table – branches of leaves turned red and golden by the frosty nights, along with hips and haws. Lit by candlelight the kitchen looked very welcoming, Molly thought.

Sally arrived alone, having left Luke and the children behind, and lost no time in drawing Catherine into the parlour, where Molly found them, heads together in sisterly confidences, their hair – brown and chestnut – almost intertwined. From the look cast in her direction as she entered, Molly suspected that Sally now knew Catherine's news about the baby. They had contained it within the immediate family so far – there was time enough for the news to spread once Mr Powell had, she hoped, come round to the marriage.

'George has just arrived,' Molly said. 'And the food is ready. Come and join us.'

It was a tight squeeze around the table, with George and Francis added to the five Dawsons, but it pleased Molly. She liked to see the house full and her family all around her again. After Charlie had said grace, Molly decided to speak up.

'I just wanted to say thank you to George for the part he played in returning Catherine to us. I can't tell you how delighted I am to have her back, and to welcome her new husband, Francis, to our family.'

Charlie raised his glass. 'To the bride and groom. And to George, without whom this family dinner wouldn't be happening.'

Everyone raised their glasses, then a buzz of chatter broke out as Sally and Agnes dished out the vegetables while Charlie carved. As they settled to their meal, Catherine turned to Francis, looked him in the eye and smiled, and George leant across the table to ask Charlie a question. Molly quietly observed everyone with a great feeling of contentment. It was a scene of family harmony that made her heart swell with pride. If the rift between Francis and his father could be healed, all would be well with the world indeed. She reflected that they would attend church as a family the following morning. Would this be a good time to make the first overtures to Mr Powell?

Molly ceased her musing to discover that the conversation around the table had turned to talk of Francis and Catherine's forthcoming baby. Sally had broached the subject, without thinking that George, as an outsider, might not know.

'You're expecting a baby?' he asked, looking from Francis to Catherine. 'Congratulations! That's very good news. And so soon – it's even better that you're home now, to be with your family.' He turned to smile at Molly and missed seeing Catherine turn red.

'I was expecting before we left,' she blurted out. 'That's why we ran away.'

There was a sudden silence around the table. Even though everyone except George knew, it was a shock to hear it spelt out so bluntly. Then, as Catherine burst into tears, everyone spoke at once and Molly got up in a hurry to go and comfort her.

George had now flushed scarlet. 'I'm sorry if I spoke out of turn. Please excuse me. I'm not fit for polite society – I've spent too much time aboard ship in the company of men. I didn't mean to cause you distress. But— ' He held back for a moment, then it all came out in a rush.

'I think you have behaved very well. You've done exactly the right thing. Your baby will have both a mother and a father. It won't end up as I did, sent to live with a stranger, then brought up in the Foundling Hospital with no parents to care for me.'

Agnes broke in: 'I've thought often about what you said before. About how mothers left tokens with their babies in the hope that one day they could reclaim them. Forgive me for asking, but do you know what tokens were left for you?'

Molly noticed the eager way that George turned to Agnes, glad of her attention, although she feared that her daughter was oblivious to his emotions.

'I do know,' he said. 'I was shown them when I left the Foundling Hospital. There was half a playing card – the king of hearts – cut in a rather jagged way, so that there could be no mistaking the correct match of the other half, I suppose.'

Molly's heart missed a beat, then began to pound. A cut playing card was a common token at the Foundling Hospital, she knew. Even so, to hear George describe it in this way was unearthing long-suppressed emotions.

'And there was something else,' he said. 'It was a fragment of embroidered cloth that had been cut from the corner of a larger piece. A handkerchief, at a guess.'

He looked around the table where everyone was now listening.

'And was there anything special about the embroidery?' Sally, the seamstress of the family, wanted to know.

'Yes, there was the initial M and some blue flowers stitched around it, which I was told were forget-me-nots.'

The collective murmur that ran around the table masked Molly's gasp. She heard a roaring in her ears as her heartrate increased to an uncomfortable level.

'Have you the tokens?' Agnes asked. She was looking at him as though he might produce them from his pocket.

'They had to be left behind, locked away with all the others.'

'And what happened next? Did they tell you the name of the person who had left you?' This from Francis, who had heard nothing of George's story before.

'No. You would only learn that if you were reclaimed – which hardly ever happened.' George paused, reflective, then continued, 'After that I was handed over to a Mr Gifford, to be apprenticed to him as a draughtsman in Rochester.'

'How old were you?' Francis interrupted.

'I was twelve, and I would be nineteen before the apprenticeship was supposed to end. But Mr Gifford had lied to the Foundling School about the nature of the work and I found myself forced to labour alongside convicts, digging out the chalk caves of the Fort Amherst defences.'

Another gasp, this time from Agnes and Catherine, for George had left this out of his story on the previous occasion.

'Once a year, a clerk from the Foundling School visited the apprentices. Mr Gifford brought us back into the office and his henchman threatened us with drowning if we revealed what we did for the rest of the year. But one day the supervision was lax as we were marched back into Rochester after our day's work. I took my chance and made a run for it. I carried on running, on and off, for several days until, half starved, I found myself in Faversham. When I discovered a job at the powder works there, I began the next phase of my life, this time under my own management.'

Molly was only half listening as he spoke. This couldn't be a coincidence. There couldn't be an identical set of tokens: at least, not another letter M embroidered on the cut corner of a handkerchief. Her mind raced. Agnes had come into the room when she was holding the tokens. Had she seen them? Or had she gone back later to look at them? Had she somehow passed this information to George?

She knew she was being ridiculous. That had been the evening when Catherine had disappeared. Agnes would have had no opportunity, or reason, to go in search of the tokens. In any case, strange as it seemed, it had to be a coincidence. George's name was proof of that. His name would have been changed by the Foundling Hospital. Her George could not be this George.

At the end of his tale, she asked, 'George, did they tell you what your name was when you were brought into the Foundling Hospital?' Her voice sounded hoarse to her ears.

George looked mildly surprised at the question. 'No. I was known as John Tempest there. I changed my name when I found work in Faversham. I chose George from the coin of

311

the realm that I used to pay for my lodgings in advance and I picked the most common surname I could think of.'

He looked around the table. 'I didn't want anyone thinking me John Tempest, who'd absconded from his apprenticeship, did I?'

Molly registered that he was pleased with his quick thinking before she slid to the floor in a faint.

*   *   *

When she came to, she was surrounded by concerned faces and Agnes was flapping a napkin in front of her face, saying, 'She needs air.' Charlie was holding a glass of water and looking worried.

It took Molly a moment or two to realise what had happened until, seeing George's face surrounded by all the members of her family, it came flooding back to her. For a moment, she thought about passing off her fainting fit as due to fatigue or the heat of the kitchen – which was clearly what her family thought. Then she realised that would be wrong.

She struggled out of the chair in the parlour, where she had been carried unawares, wincing as she did so for she must have banged her head as she passed out.

'I've got something to show you all,' she said.

CHAPTER FIFTY-TWO

Molly carried the bundled woollen blanket down the stairs from her bedroom in a kind of stupor. She was trembling as she knelt on the parlour floor, fumbling to unwrap it. It was as though her hands belonged to someone else.

She heard an intake of breath from Agnes, who must have recognised the blanket, having seen Molly with it on the night that Catherine disappeared. Then there was total silence in the room as she laid out the tokens on the moth-eaten wool: the half of the king of hearts and a threadbare handkerchief, the corner cut off, traces of embroidery around its edge.

Molly, on her knees with the others in a semi-circle around her, gazed up at their faces. Charlie was frowning, uncomprehending. George had gone white. Agnes's hand covered her mouth, Catherine was on the verge of tears and Sally, like Charlie, looked blank. Francis had stepped behind his wife and his head was down so Molly couldn't read his expression.

'George, from what you have told us this evening, you must be the baby I had to leave behind all those years ago, before I was married. I've kept these tokens all that time in the hope that one day . . .' Molly tailed off.

'In the hope that one day – what?' George demanded. 'That one day, nigh on twenty-five years later, I'd stumble upon you and your happy family?' He almost spat out the last few words, then turned on his heel and left the room. A few seconds later they heard the kitchen door slam with some force.

Molly stayed on her knees and a terrible silence filled the room. She wanted to bow her head in shame and horror but instead she stared straight ahead as tears rolled down her cheeks. She tried to marshal her thoughts. Should she go after George, or stay in the room to face the consequences of her words?

It was Sally, not Charlie, who stepped forward to help her to her feet.

'Come on, Ma. Let's sit you down. You've had a shock. We all have.'

Molly glanced at Charlie and saw that his brows were drawn together in a frown. He wouldn't meet her eyes.

'Someone should go after George,' she said faintly. Then, a little louder, 'I should go after George.'

No one made a move or spoke – it was as if Molly's words had turned them to stone. Finally, Francis said, 'I'll go after him. You've a lot to discuss.' He took his wife's hand and kissed it, then went swiftly from the room. In the silence he left behind they heard the kitchen door close, more quietly this time.

'Oh, Ma, how could you?' Catherine's words lifted the spell, for suddenly the girls spoke over each other.

'Why did you keep this secret for so long?' This from Agnes.

'How much older is George than me?' from Sally.

It was Charlie whom Molly really wanted to hear from, but he kept silent. This troubled her more than his anger would have done.

314

She tried her best to answer her daughters' questions, explaining that George had been born at a difficult time in her life when she was on her own in London and she had given him up because she believed it was best for him, although it had nearly broken her heart. Then, when Charlie had found her in a bad way and saved her, bringing her back to Woodchurch Manor to get well, they had married and she hadn't told him about the baby. Molly glanced at Charlie, who remained stony-faced. She pressed on, her voice trembling. 'Then you were born, Sally, and I thought my son must be settled somewhere by now and I worried over whether or not it would be wrong to try to find him. I thought your father would support me but I never did.' Molly swallowed hard, holding back her tears as painful memories resurfaced. 'And then Agnes came along, and Catherine, and by then it was all too late. Not a day went by when I didn't think of him, though, and wonder where he was. Your first teeth, first steps – everything reminded me that I had missed those moments.'

Molly's eyes flicked towards the door. She was torn between going after George and explaining to him, too, or staying with her family, who were now looking at her as though she was some sort of stranger. She hung her head and twisted her wedding band around her finger.

'I have to go home now,' Sally said, with a sigh. 'Luke will have sent the carriage.'

'I'll walk you to the end of the lane,' Charlie said. Molly started at the sound of his voice and looked up, but he was already halfway out of the room.

Sally was agonised. 'Ma, I don't know what to say. I'll need to think about it. All these years, the family I thought I had—' She stopped, then squeezed her mother's shoulder before following her father out of the room.

Agnes and Catherine looked at each other, then said, in unison, 'We'll come too,' and hurried from the room without a backward glance.

Molly succumbed to a storm of weeping after they'd gone. Then, after a few minutes, she tried to pull herself together. She should go after George, even though her heart failed her at the thought. She sat on a little longer, then stood up, walking through to the kitchen where the table remained uncleared after their dinner. She'd been so happy to have everyone there. Now it felt as though it had taken place in some distant past.

She was frightened of facing George's anger but it had to be done. He didn't deserve to be left without an explanation for a moment longer. She took her shawl from the back of the door and stepped out into the darkness, flinching slightly at the chill in the air.

She struck out across the lawns of Woodchurch Manor, hearing the night noises all around her. The sky was clear and filled with stars, and the crisp air carried a hint of woodsmoke, from the fireplaces within the house, she supposed. She could see people moving around within the lit ground-floor rooms.

Molly passed like a ghost around the building and walked across the cobblestones to the stable-yard. A dim light came from one of the rooms in the old stable block and she paused a moment, watching the indistinct outline of a figure passing back and forth across the window. She remembered when Charlie had proudly shown her his room in the stable block all those years before, when she'd disappointed him and followed her heart. Her foolish heart, as it turned out. Molly sighed deeply, then mounted the stairs to the first floor.

She knocked at the door and Francis called, 'Come in.'

He was seated and it was George who was pacing but, seeing Molly, Francis got to his feet too, stood in front of George and gripped his shoulders momentarily, then nodded to Molly and left the room.

George stood looking at Molly, although she supposed glaring might have been a better description.

'George, I can't begin to tell you how sorry I am,' she began, feeling the inadequacy of her words as she spoke.

'Not half as sorry as I am,' George interrupted. 'Abandoned by my mother, wondering all these years why and where she might be, only to discover that she's married and has brought up three daughters while I've – I've …' The enormity of what he was describing prevented him speaking.

Molly summoned every ounce of courage she had, sat down and began again. 'I don't expect you to understand or forgive my actions but I hope you will at least hear what I have to say. I have judged myself many times over and can only expect you to do the same, but I want you to know that I loved you dearly and would never have given you up unless forced to do so. I was heartbroken when I felt I had no other choice.'

Then Molly launched into her tale, the tale she had told Charlie and her daughters but this time filling in more of the background for George. She told him about the house in Covent Garden where she had been living when he was born and the manner of work that the landlady there had insisted she must undertake to pay off her debt. She told him how she'd fled, taking him to the Foundling Hospital as she had no money to support them. At least he would stand the chance of a better life there, or so she had believed. She told him how devastated she had been afterwards, how she'd worked in a riverside tavern, saving all her money towards reclaiming him, and how she'd almost been tricked into marriage on the understanding that she would be able to get him back. She told him how, when she had realised the deception, she had fled once more, every farthing of her savings lost, and Charlie had found her, quite by chance, when she was in a very bad way.

They talked on into the night, while Molly tried to explain her actions in not reclaiming him once she was married, although her reasoning sounded more and more flimsy to her each time she repeated it.

He'd asked the question she'd dreaded, 'Who was my father?' and she had hesitated, mind racing, before she'd stuck with the story she had planned on the walk over from the cottage.

'I barely knew him. I was young, it was a fleeting infatuation and I never saw him again.' She made it as truthful as possible and she sounded as ashamed as she felt. She hoped he would assume it was someone in London but he didn't ask any further questions. Perhaps he had enough to take in for the moment, she thought.

When she made her weary way home long after midnight, George appeared a little mollified by her tale. He submitted to a brief hug and nodded to her as she wished him good night. As she walked back through the darkness she couldn't stop her teeth chattering and her whole body shook as she shivered. The grass was crisp beneath her feet and she supposed a frost must have formed under the clear skies, but the shivering didn't stop even when she reached home. She'd half wondered whether the door would be locked against her but it swung open as usual and she stepped into the dark kitchen. There was enough moonlight through the window to see that the table had been cleared and the washing-up done.

The house was silent as Molly crept up the stairs but it felt to her as though everyone within it was lying awake behind closed doors, listening for her return. She held her breath as she turned the doorknob and stepped into her bedroom. Charlie was a dim shape beneath the blankets, face turned away from her. She hoped he was asleep but the air felt charged with tension and, sure enough, he turned towards her as she slipped into bed beside him. She longed for him to reach out and hold her close, but instead he said, 'So, do you want to tell me why you kept this a secret?'

CHAPTER FIFTY-THREE

Once more, with great weariness, Molly recounted her tale, edited again to suit her audience. Charlie had never asked her to explain how she had come to be in a state of near nervous collapse when he had found her in the Apothecaries' Garden. He had simply focused on making her well again, bringing her back to the Woodchurch estate with him and caring for her without putting any pressure on her. She knew he was, in many ways, just happy to have her back in his life after she had once rejected him. For her part, she had never ceased to be grateful for his loving care of her.

Now, she had to justify once more why she had let George remain a foundling. No matter how many times she repeated it, it never made any more sense. She supposed that as time went on, it had just seemed easier to let her secret child remain a secret.

They were talking in low tones, with long silences between Molly's answers and Charlie's next question. Her eyelids had begun to droop and she was finally slipping into sleep when he asked her, 'And who is the father? Is it that artist friend of yours?'

She was wide awake again immediately. 'No!' she protested, as vehemently as she could while keeping her voice down. 'He's only ever been just that – a friend.'

Then she gave him the same answer she had given George: a fleeting infatuation, someone she had barely known and hadn't seen since. She held her breath and waited for him to question her further but he didn't say a word. Instead, he turned on his side and left her staring, unseeing, into darkness that was rapidly giving way to dawn.

Was she doing the wrong thing by keeping this final piece of the puzzle to herself? She knew it would be hard enough to share the facts about George with her sisters, Aunt Jane and Uncle William. It felt easier to pretend that George's father was a passing fancy, now lost in the mists of time, than to confess he was her cousin Nicholas. He was, in any case, the black sheep of the family now. And Molly, having got George back, had no wish to share him with anyone else.

She couldn't repress a shudder, though, at the thought that keeping this one last secret might have repercussions in the future, then lay rigid, hoping Charlie wasn't aware of her anguish. His regular breathing told Molly he had fallen asleep so she sighed, turned on her side away from him and willed sleep to come.

When she woke it was daylight and Charlie was no longer in their bed. She could hear voices from downstairs and she lay for a few minutes, gathering her thoughts. She was on the verge of a headache and she had had little sleep. Molly didn't relish facing her family but it had to be done: it was Sunday and they must show themselves at church.

By the time she had washed, dressed and made her way downstairs she found Charlie, Agnes, Catherine and Francis waiting in the kitchen. The pot of breakfast porridge had grown cold and unappealing and Molly barely had time to take a mouthful of buttered bread and a sip of tea before they were all out of the door. Charlie walked by her side, as usual, but he did not take her arm and they made a solemn procession as they walked along the lane to the church.

Molly was convinced that the Powells were casting glances her way throughout the service and she wondered whether Francis had called in on them after he had left George. Had he been eager to share the news of the upset in the Dawson household, and the reasons for it? More distressing, though, was George's absence. He had made a point of regular attendance over the last few weeks, although Molly suspected that had had more to do with a wish to see Agnes than religious fervour. Even as the thought crossed her mind, her blood ran cold. Agnes – George had conceived a passion for Agnes. If he had followed it through, if they had never uncovered his identity . . . As the full import of this struck home, Molly could barely suppress a moan. Her daughters glanced sharply at her and Charlie stiffened at her side. She let her head hang and focused all her attention on her hands, clasped tightly in her lap.

Agnes had shown no signs of being aware of George's attention and she wasn't sure whether anyone else had noticed. Had she mentioned her thoughts to Charlie? She wasn't sure – lack of sleep was clouding her mind.

They made their way home from church in the same quiet manner as they had arrived, although Molly was aware of Catherine and Francis conversing in low tones behind her as they walked. As they entered the kitchen and Molly thought of the food that must be prepared, she made a sudden decision.

'I'm going to lie down,' she said, and without looking at any of them, she left the room and climbed the stairs, closing the bedroom door behind her. She lay fully clothed on the bed. A seed of resentment was starting to grow. She felt as though she had done everything right by her family: she had loved her husband and daughters as if there was no one else in the world with any claim on her. She had suffered her guilt and her memories in silence and she had convinced herself that she had done the right thing.

Now it seemed she had made a mistake: George's appearance had cast a whole new light on her actions. Yet did she deserve such disapproval? Did she deserve to be an outcast in her own family? The pounding in her head threatened to keep her from sleep but finally she slipped from consciousness into a tangle of wild dreams, from which she woke to find Sally standing beside her bed.

Molly stared at her eldest daughter, puzzled. She hadn't been in the house earlier, surely.

'I came over with Luke, Ma,' Sally said, as if reading her mind. 'I couldn't stop thinking about what was said last night, and about George.'

Molly closed her eyes briefly at the mention of her son's name. For a few short moments on waking she had forgotten about the trouble in the family. Now it all came flooding back.

'Come downstairs,' Sally said. Her voice was gentle. 'You must be hungry.'

Molly eased herself off the bed, feeling suddenly shivery in the chill of the bedroom, and splashed her face with water before following Sally down the stairs. Everyone was sitting around the table and a scratch dinner had been eaten, put together by Agnes and Catherine from whatever they had found in the larder.

There was an awkward silence when Molly appeared but Grace and Simon were delighted to see their grandmother and both climbed into her lap, vying for space. Molly was content to sit back, burying her nose in their hair and listening to the conversation around her.

She had little appetite and picked at the plate of food pressed on her by Sally, ending up feeding most of it to Grace and Simon when she hoped no one was watching. George was never mentioned but the feeling grew in Molly as the hours passed that she should pay him another visit. Was he sitting alone in his room, brooding on last night's discovery? Did he suspect a family gathering was under way, and would he be resentful at not being invited? Molly daren't suggest that she should visit him, however. It had begun to feel as though her family had unbent a little towards her and she feared shattering the fragile truce that had developed.

George would have to be gradually introduced into the family a little at a time, she decided, until everyone had grown used to him and he was comfortable with them. It wasn't going to be easy but, for the first time that day, she felt a faint stirring of delight. She was looking forward to getting to know the son she'd thought she had lost for ever.

CHAPTER FIFTY-FOUR

It felt to Molly that Monday, the start of the new week, was a day of tentative new beginnings. Charlie had left early for the gardens, as usual, and she thought she had detected a slight thaw in his attitude towards her the previous evening. At any rate, he hadn't questioned her further, and their afternoon as a family had felt almost normal, although Molly's ache in her heart over George – alone and yet nearby – hadn't faded.

She had devoted her attention to Agnes and Catherine in the morning, conscious that Catherine and Francis's homecoming dinner had been blighted by the revelations about George. There was a new baby to prepare for and she resolutely kept her thoughts focused on this rather than her lost son, even though he was now working somewhere close by in the gardens. Francis had taken himself off. Molly rather hoped he had gone to repair his relationship with his father and not to discuss private Dawson family business with the Powells.

The morning passed swiftly in making plans, and by the afternoon Molly, Agnes and Catherine were sitting at the kitchen table, cutting the patches to make a quilt for the baby crib. They looked up in surprise when the door opened. Molly half expected to see Francis and was already wondering whether he had dined at Woodchurch Manor when she registered that it was Charlie standing there. He usually ate in the kitchens at Woodchurch Manor along with the other gardeners and, on the rare occasions that he didn't, he always told her in advance.

Charlie's expression was unreadable but Molly had the instant conviction that something was wrong. She stood up and gestured to her chair.

'Sit down and I'll get you something to eat,' she said, moving towards the larder to bring out the remains of a side of ham.

'George has gone,' Charlie said abruptly.

'Gone?' Molly turned to him, still standing by the door. 'Gone where?' Her voice faltered.

Charlie shrugged. 'I don't know. He didn't come to work in the garden this morning. It's not like him to sleep in, so I sent one of the boys to his room. He came back to say George wasn't there and it looked as though he had left. I went to take a look myself and the room is empty.' He stopped, then added, 'He left the things you gave him – the quilt folded on the bed, although I'm not sure he even slept in it last night.'

'Did he leave a note?' Molly was conscious of her daughters' eyes on her, while Charlie was staring at the floor.

'No, he didn't. I'm sorry, Molly.' Charlie was facing her now and Molly saw, all at once, that the old Charlie was back, the one she recognised. He held out his arms to her and she went to him, bursting into sobs as he held her to his chest.

If only she had gone to see George the previous day. If only she had listened to her heart, she might have prevented him leaving. She had spent barely any time with him or found out anything beyond the bare bones of what he had told them all. He must despise her for how she had behaved, Molly thought, as she sobbed. She had dared to believe that George would come round to the idea of having a family. She had hoped that she would be able to spend the rest of her life making it up to him. Now he had left their lives as quickly as he had arrived.

Molly was conscious of the silence in the room but she didn't care. A part of her knew that George's departure would make it easier for them all. The family would knit together as it had been before he appeared. All would look the same on the surface but it would never be the same for Molly. She reached a decision: he couldn't be the one to leave this time. They must go after him. She would go to his room to search for clues.

She pulled free of Charlie's arms. Barely conscious of how she must look with her tear-stained and flushed face, she took her shawl from the back of the door and left the kitchen without a word.

Molly didn't encounter anyone in her hurry to reach the stable-yard and all was quiet within the old stable block. The door to George's room stood open and, within, it was just as Charlie had said. Specks of dust swirled in the shafts of light through the window and all was silent, as if the occupant had long gone. The quilt that Molly had given George was neatly folded on top of the blanket, the rag rug still set on the floor beside the bed. Molly lifted the bedding and the mattress but there was no sign of a note. Clearly George had no intention of being found.

Molly sat down on the bed as thoughts jostled for space in her mind. Did George have money? Had he been paid at the end of last week? Where would he go? He'd mentioned living in Faversham but did he have any links there still? How long ago had he left Woodchurch Manor? If it was that morning, might they find someone who had seen him go?

With that last thought in mind she hurried home, hoping that Charlie would still be there. Thankfully, Agnes or Catherine had thought to provide their father with some food and he was just finishing as she arrived back in the kitchen.

'If he left this morning, someone might have seen him go,' Molly began.

Charlie pushed back his chair and stood up. 'I've already asked. The gardeners and household staff were up and about very early, but none saw him. It looks as though he left yesterday, or maybe under cover of darkness. There's no clue as to the direction he took.'

Molly was vividly reminded of the helplessness she had felt when Catherine and Francis had vanished. Was she destined to relive it? Would George write once he was settled somewhere else? This last thought brought her some relief and, with a heavy sigh, she sat down at the table.

If Molly had known then that days were to turn into weeks, weeks into months and still no word, she might have insisted that enquiries were made at once in Margate or at the inns along the road to Canterbury. As it was, the month turned, October became a dark and chilly November and Molly's worries about George only grew. She hoped he'd found work and somewhere safe, warm and dry to sleep.

She passed the time as best she could with needlework: garments for the expected baby, and a sampler, one that this time would include the names of all her children. Perhaps they would hear from George by Christmas; she held hope in her heart that he might return in time to celebrate with them. But the day came and went, and although the girls decorated the house with green boughs from the garden, and they cooked a goose provided by the Woodchurch Manor kitchens, Molly knew that the smile she tried to keep pinned to her face wasn't fooling her family. They had come to accept her sadness and even take part in it: Agnes was heard to say rather wistfully that she would have liked to know what it was to have a brother.

'He could have been godfather to our baby,' Catherine said, looking across the table to Francis, who nodded in agreement.

December marked the end of Catherine and Francis's stay with Molly and Charlie. Mr Powell had thawed sufficiently to allocate them a cottage, so that they would have a home when the baby came. They were due to take possession of it on New Year's Day and Francis had been given a post on the estate: something far less prestigious than either Robert or Edward, but he professed not to care.

'I don't mind,' he said stoutly. 'As long as we have a roof over our heads and I can put food on the table, that's all that matters.'

Molly had a suspicion that, Mr Powell having made his point, in six months' time they would be invited to live at Woodchurch Manor with the rest of Francis's family. She wondered whether they would decline. Francis had, she thought, adapted remarkably well to the much-simpler life he had been leading over the past few months. Catherine would be happy as long as she was with Francis, but Molly rather thought she would resist being absorbed into the Powells' household.

However, whatever she felt about the treatment of Catherine and Francis, she had to acknowledge that Mr Powell had been very generous towards Agnes. He proposed paying for her to study with a tutor in Margate, deeming London out of the question following consultation with Will Turner. The few successful female artists of the time had gained rather a reputation in the city, not solely based on their skills with the paintbrush, and Molly had been grateful when Mr Powell said that even Will Turner agreed this would not suit Agnes. Instead, he had recommended his Margate tutor so everyone was happy: Molly still had her daughter close by, Agnes was fulfilling a long-held dream, and Mr Powell could congratulate himself on his forward thinking.

CHAPTER FIFTY-FIVE

Molly found her spirits still low in January – the gloom and chill of the weather seemed but a reflection of her own mood. She was glad to have her needlework to occupy her, both by day and in the evening. She would look up from it to find Agnes or Charlie watching her, her husband's brow creased with worry, but Molly couldn't raise the energy to pretend that all was well. Perhaps once spring came, life would feel better again.

In fact, she didn't have to wait until spring, for Catherine's baby was born in the middle of February and Molly was delighted with her new granddaughter. She showed every sign of having inherited Catherine's colouring, for her dark hair had reddish highlights and was luxuriant enough already to show signs of a curl. Having her granddaughter so close by – their cottage was just a few doors away – was both a novelty and a pleasure and Molly spent more time in Catherine and Francis's house than she did in her own.

Mr Powell was an early visitor to his son's cottage, along with his wife. Molly and Catherine exchanged surreptitious glances during the visit for he couldn't hide his delight. He appeared quite enchanted and barely able to take his eyes off the baby, insisting on continuing to hold her long after she'd fallen asleep in his arms.

'Well,' Mrs Powell said, 'I don't recall you being so enamoured of the boys when they were babies.' She smiled and turned to Molly and Catherine. 'He was very good with them once they were running around but he had no interest in them when they were tiny.'

'I don't believe they were quite as charming as this little one,' Mr Powell said, reluctantly handing his granddaughter back to her mother.

'I fear you are right,' Mrs Powell said wryly. 'Bald, or so blond as to appear bald, with rather round faces. Of course, they grew up to be very handsome,' she said hastily, looking apologetically at Francis, who was maintaining a discreet distance from his father.

'You must bring her up to the house very soon,' Mr Powell said, getting to his feet with every appearance of being unwilling to depart. 'Her uncles will want to meet her and the staff are full of impatience. Have you chosen a name for her?'

'We thought Eleanor,' Catherine said, trying to sound firm although she was a little nervous of Mr Powell.

'Very good.' Mr Powell nodded approvingly. 'My mother's name, you know.' Molly saw Catherine and Francis exchange glances and half-smiles. 'We must make plans for the christening. Come along, my dear,' this to his wife, 'we must impart the news.'

A few days later, a silver rattle and a beautifully embroidered baby gown were sent over from Woodchurch Manor, along with an invitation to the proud parents and the Dawson family to take tea on Saturday afternoon.

Molly kept her satisfaction to herself at the way things were working out. It was early days and Mr Powell might easily revert to his previous irritation with his son. She was taken aback, though, to discover what Mr Powell was planning when they presented themselves for tea, as requested. They were served by a maid she hadn't seen before at Woodchurch Manor, which was not unusual in itself until Mr Powell, once everyone had been accommodated, introduced her to them all.

'This is Judith, whom we have engaged for her skills in nursery care as well as on the domestic front. Of course we realise that Catherine and Eleanor are very well looked after by Mrs Dawson,' Mr Powell had, it seemed, noticed Molly stiffen at his words, 'but we hope that Catherine and Francis will be agreeable to Eleanor spending a day or so here each week, with us. Her mother, too, of course,' Mr Powell added, seeing Catherine's expression. 'We would be so happy to spend time with our first grandchild. Judith will be on hand to help and, as Eleanor grows, if Catherine would like to make use of those few hours, she would be more than welcome to do so.'

Judith was dismissed from the room and the conversation turned to more general matters. Robert was keen to discuss the news that had just begun to circulate about Napoleon's escape from the island of Elba. The men in the room, gathering together around the fireplace, were of the opinion that he would try to return to France and, if successful, that war was inevitable once more.

Molly moved to sit at Catherine's side and, when asked in low tones by her daughter whether she thought Mr Powell's idea was a good one, she nodded. Privately, she suspected it was the start of a great deal more Powell family involvement in the lives of Catherine and Francis but this could be no bad thing for their future, and that of Eleanor. Her gaze roamed around the room and alighted on Charlie, deep in conversation with Edward Powell. Edward's back was towards her but she could see that Charlie was frowning. She supposed they were talking about the possibility of war once more and she glanced down at Eleanor with a little jolt of fear. She hoped nothing lay ahead that might bring harm to any of her children or grandchildren. After so many years of war over-seas, they had become used to the idea of the country being at peace once more.

When Eleanor started to fuss, the visitors made their excuses and returned home, Agnes remaining behind to report to Mr Powell on her first weeks of tuition. Molly walked at Charlie's side, behind Catherine, Francis and the baby.

'What do you make of this talk of war?' she asked.

Charlie was dismissive. 'It will be over before it starts,' he said. 'I doubt there's an appetite for it, even in France.' They walked on in silence for a while, then he said, 'I'll be taking a trip next week. Mr Powell has asked me to check an order we are due to receive in spring. He has reason to believe all is not as it should be. I'll be gone a few days.'

Molly was surprised: his trips, these days, were predicta-ble, usually taking place at the same time each year, with the first towards the end of March. 'I will have plenty to keep me busy here, but I hope the weather is kind to you. Remember how cold it was last year at the end of February? We've seen little snow yet and I will pray it stays so until your return.'

At church the following day, Catherine, Francis and Eleanor were invited to join the Powells in their pew. Catherine glanced apologetically at her mother as she followed her husband but Molly smiled back. She didn't begrudge her daughter this sudden acceptance: it was only what she had wished for, after all.

After the service Catherine was waiting for them outside the church, the Powells having left first as usual. Molly linked arms with her daughter and they walked slowly on as Eleanor slept peacefully, wrapped in a blanket in the crook of her mother's free arm. Molly glanced back to see whether Francis and Charlie were following, and noticed her husband once more in conversation with Edward Powell. A sudden shower, blown in on a chill wind, sent her scurrying for home with Catherine, eager to protect Eleanor from the elements, so she forgot to ask Charlie what he'd been talking about when he arrived a little later.

He went on his way early the next morning, promising to return by Friday. Molly sleepily advised him to wrap up well before she snuggled back into the warm bed, grateful for another hour's sleep before she got up to start the day.

CHAPTER FIFTY-SIX

While Charlie was away, Molly found that she missed him far more than she had expected. She was busy with Catherine and Eleanor, of course, but once she returned home the house felt very empty and quiet. Agnes now stayed in Margate with Aunt Jane and Uncle William during the week so that she could pursue her studies and so, for the first time, there was no one to keep Molly company in the evenings.

By the time Friday came, Molly was listening out for the sounds of Charlie's return. She went to bed late, feeling uneasy: it was most unlike him to be away longer than he had said and without sending word to her. She awoke every hour, convinced she had heard footsteps on the path or the rumble of a cart on the lane but, no matter how she strained her ears, no such sound disturbed the night.

The next morning, she visited Catherine as usual but found it hard to settle and asked apologetically whether her daughter would mind if she returned home. 'I don't want to miss your pa's return,' she said. 'It's unlike him to stay away and not send word. And look at the weather.' She glanced outside where the rain was falling in sheets, so that the fields appeared to be filled with a grey mist.

'You get on hóme, Ma,' Catherine said. 'Francis and I have promised to take Eleanor to Woodchurch Manor this afternoon in any case. Although how we will manage it in this rain, I don't know.'

Molly would normally have worried about her grand-daughter getting soaked and taking a chill but her agitation over Charlie's absence overshadowed everything. She had a growing conviction that something must have gone badly wrong on his trip but she hurried home, half expecting him to be waiting in the kitchen for her.

It was growing dark, rather earlier than usual due to the heavy clouds that were still dispensing rain, when Molly finally heard sounds that filled her with hope. The gate creaked open and there were footsteps and voices outside the kitchen door, accompanied by much stamping of feet. She rushed to open the door, then stopped on the threshold, not knowing what to make of what she saw.

Two men stood outside, one a little in front of the other and both of them so wet that it was impossible to identify them by the colour of their hair, which was plastered flat to their heads. Their clothes were a uniform shade of drab, all colour removed by their excessive wetness.

'Well, are you going to stand there gawping or are we to be allowed in?'

The voice, from the man at the front, was clearly Charlie's, although she was hard pushed to recognise him in the gloom. Flustered, Molly stood aside. Who was Charlie's compan-ion? Why had he been away so long? Relief at his safe return threatened to turn to anger at his tardiness.

Now both men were standing dripping in her kitchen and Molly hurried to fetch towels, which she feared would barely mop up the worst of it. It was only as the second man thanked her and began to rub his hair vigorously that Molly recog-nised him for who he was.

'George!' she gasped.

She turned to Charlie and opened her mouth but nothing came out beyond 'How . . .'

'If you can find us something to eat after all our travelling, I'll tell you,' Charlie said.

Molly, startled by their appearance, realised she'd neglected the most basic hospitality.

As she turned towards the larder to bring out whatever she could find, Charlie said to George, 'We need to be rid of these wet things. Follow me.'

He dripped his way upstairs, George behind him, and Molly could hear them moving around in the bedroom. She set soup to heat on the range and put a pork pie on the table along with pickles and bread. When they came back down the stairs, Molly had to suppress a smile. George was wearing some of Charlie's clothes, which were too long for him so he had had to roll up the trouser legs and the sleeves of the shirt. He was broader than Charlie, though, so the fit was a little snug and slightly comical. She took care not to show her amusement, because she didn't know how George felt about her. She couldn't risk him taking offence.

The two men fell on the food as though they hadn't eaten in a long while and Molly watched, trying to curb her impatience. She longed to know how George's return had been brought about.

Finally, Charlie sat back and wiped his mouth. 'So, I imagine you're wondering how I went off to attend to garden business and came back with your son.'

Molly winced at his last words. It felt like a sensitive subject and she wasn't sure how George would react. Yet he appeared relaxed and was helping himself to another slice of pie.

'In fact, I didn't tell you the whole truth. Well, none of it was the truth,' Charlie admitted. 'Edward Powell told me at tea last Saturday that he'd had a letter from George, who was in Portsmouth. With talk of Napoleon being on his way back to France and war on the horizon, he was set to rejoin the Navy and wanted Edward to come and serve alongside him.'

George still appeared unconcerned and was cutting into a piece of cheese, which Molly had added to the table as an afterthought.

'So, with Mr Powell's permission and with Edward coming along as a guide, I went to Portsmouth. It was easy enough to find George – Edward had a fair idea where he'd be staying. But it was less easy to convince him to come back with us.'

Charlie took a deep draught of the ale that Molly had served them both.

'Do you want to tell the rest?' Charlie asked, turning to George.

'No, you carry on,' George said, with a grin that was another surprise to Molly. She was intrigued: he and Charlie seemed to have developed an easy relationship.

'George had been working on merchant ships, travelling up and down the coast, since he left us,' Charlie continued. 'He was determined to go back into the Navy, feeling that was where he had had the best experiences of his life. Edward and I told him we thought Napoleon would be vanquished again and that he'd find himself stood down in a matter of months, or even weeks.' Charlie picked up an apple, one of the precious few left from their summer store, and sliced into it thoughtfully. Molly glanced at George and saw him shake his head. Was he unconvinced by Charlie's reasoning? She bit her lip to stop herself asking her husband to get on with the story.

'Anyway,' Charlie continued, 'Edward and I told him he had a secure position at the garden and, more importantly, his family was here. I explained to him that the discovery of who he was had come as a shock to all of us at first, alongside the realisation that you,' he glanced at Molly, 'had kept his existence a secret all these years.'

'I also told him we wanted him back. That it went without saying that you, his mother, had been devastated at losing him again so soon, and that Sally, Agnes and Catherine had, with time, got used to the idea that they had a half-brother and missed him. Also, there was a new baby in the family for him to be introduced to, his half-niece, I suppose.

'I, too, have got over the shock of the news. I always wanted a son to follow in my footsteps and I recognised, rather late, that I had one. There was a problem, though.'

George was refusing to meet Molly's eyes.

'As I think we both know, George was rather taken with Agnes. He was horrified when the realisation dawned on him that she was his half-sister. After that first evening and your talk with him, Molly, he was beginning to come around to the idea of his long-lost family, but by the following morning he was filled with embarrassment. He couldn't bear to think about his attraction to Agnes, what it meant and what could have happened. He thought the best thing to do was to leave at once, with no word of farewell.'

Charlie turned to George. 'Have I got it right so far? Do you want to take over?'

George nodded and shook his head in answer to Charlie's queries, but still didn't speak.

'I've tried to convince him that no one, apart from the two of us, and now Edward, had any inkling of his feelings for Agnes. And I've pointed out that perhaps it was natural to feel an affinity for her, because they are blood relations.' Charlie didn't look entirely convinced by his own reasoning, but he pressed on.

'In any case, Agnes has no idea of any of this. She thinks of nothing much beyond her art.' Charlie sighed. 'So here we are, after the devil of a journey from Portsmouth on roads half flooded. We had to walk the last few miles from an inn beyond Canterbury, otherwise we would have been stuck there for the night. No one was prepared to take us further in such miserable weather.'

'Well, you made it safely home and that's what matters,' Molly said. 'And I'm so pleased to see you both.' She turned to George. 'You can stay here from now on. Catherine and Francis have left so the bedroom opposite Agnes is free . . .'

She saw George's expression and cursed her clumsiness. 'Agnes is hardly here now. She's studying in Margate in the week and I dare say the weather has prevented her from travelling home today.' She ploughed on, trying to ensnare George with a web of words, all the time wanting to hug him but terrified to touch him in case she frightened him away.

'George isn't necessarily here to stay,' Charlie warned. 'We persuaded him to return with us for a visit. He's still set on going back to join the Navy but he's agreed to spend a few days here first, getting to know us better.'

Was she to have only a few brief hours with her son before he was lost to her once more? Molly wondered. All at once her tentative happiness threatened to turn to despair.

CHAPTER FIFTY-SEVEN

Once he had been reassured that Agnes wouldn't return that night, George was persuaded to stay in the house. Molly was overjoyed but did her best to hide it, not wanting to overwhelm him with attention. She offered to light the parlour fire so that they could be more comfortable, but both George and Charlie said they were happy to stay by the range in the kitchen. Shortly afterwards, George rather apologetically took himself off to bed, citing the long journey and lack of sleep since leaving Portsmouth as the reason. Judging by Charlie's yawns, Molly thought he wouldn't be far behind him but he stayed behind to talk a little more to Molly.

He could offer her little more information than he had already given her, warning her again that George might not stay but saying that they could, at least, try to build better relationships with him while he was with them.

'I owe you an apology, Molly,' Charlie said, as he stood up and stretched, preparing to go upstairs to bed. 'I shouldn't have behaved as I did when you told us about George. It wasn't a total shock to me. When you were very ill in London, at the inn on Paradise Row, the doctor told me he thought you might have had a baby.'

Molly hardly knew what to say. So Charlie had known all this time?

'I chose to ignore it,' Charlie went on. 'I didn't want to know about it and I never asked you. Then I suppose as the years passed I forgot about it. I never considered how it must have felt for you.'

He thought for a moment, then continued, 'If we could turn the clock back, maybe we'd both choose to do things differently. But we've been offered another chance and we're very lucky. George is a fine young man.'

Charlie was now grey with exhaustion and he had begun to shiver. Molly sent him up to bed, with a promise to follow as soon as she'd put the kitchen to rights. By the time she climbed into bed beside Charlie he was breathing deeply and evenly. She lay awake for a while, feeling happier than she had done in a long time. Whatever happened, George was back in their lives and she hoped he was here to stay but, even if he left again, she thought this time they would retain their connection.

Sunday morning brought sunshine and Molly woke early, determined that they would all go to church for they had much to be thankful for. Despite their exhaustion of the previous day, George and Charlie were not far behind her in coming downstairs. She made porridge for breakfast, with the promise of a proper meal to follow after church.

The lane was muddy after the rain but the air was fresh, and there was a hint of warmth in the sun as they walked along together. Molly could hardly suppress her smiles at the novelty of it all. News had, of course, reached the Powells, with the return of Edward the previous day, and they turned towards the Dawsons as they entered their pew, smiling and nodding to each of them in turn.

Molly was particularly fervent in her prayers and singing that day. At the end of the service Catherine, who had been sitting with the Powells, was waiting outside to greet them. She wasted no time in addressing George directly: 'I'm so pleased to see you back, George. And I'd like to introduce you to Eleanor.' She gently tucked the blanket under Eleanor's chin so that George could see the face of her sleeping infant. 'Francis and I wondered if you would do us the honour of being her godfather.'

Molly drew Charlie away so that the pair could converse and they walked slowly on.

'If he agrees to Catherine's request, he will have to stay rather longer than he planned,' Molly said, trying to keep her joy in check. 'The christening won't take place immediately.'

They walked on a little way, then stopped in a patch of sunlight to wait for George to catch up.

'Who is he talking to?' Molly asked, shading her eyes as she looked back. Catherine and Francis were now walking up the lane behind them but George had got no further than the lych-gate, where they could see him talking to a woman.

'I think it's the new servant at Woodchurch Manor,' Charlie said. 'The one engaged to help with Eleanor. Judith, isn't it? Shall we walk on? He'll join us when he's ready.'

Molly was curious, but agreed. George must be allowed to do as he pleased while he was with them.

She was at the kitchen sink, peeling potatoes, when George came in. She was taken with the way he looked: somehow different from when they'd left for church that morning.

'I've met someone I used to know when I lived near Faversham.' George's voice was full of enthusiasm. 'She's been taken on to help with your granddaughter.' He was addressing Molly – quite easily, she was delighted to see. 'My friend at the time, Thomas, was sweet on her.' George's face clouded, then brightened again. 'I've said that I'll walk over to the house later so that we can catch up on what we've both been doing over the years.' He surveyed the preparations that Molly was making, suddenly doubtful. 'Will that be all right?'

'Of course,' Molly said. 'The fire's lit in the parlour and Catherine and Francis are in there with Charlie. They eat with us on a Sunday. Why don't you join them?'

She smiled as she continued to prepare the vegetables. The more George could be drawn into the family, the better. His acquaintance with Judith was unexpected but could prove very useful. It was another thread that might just bind him to Woodchurch Manor and the estate.

Dinner was a relaxed affair and Molly was delighted to see that George was happy to take a turn in cuddling Eleanor as they passed her around between them during one of her wakeful spells. Sally and Luke arrived with their children, once dinner had been eaten, bringing Agnes with them. There was much exclaiming over George's return and the tale of how Charlie had found him had to be told and retold several times.

Molly noticed that George seemed a little uneasy in Agnes's presence but, after a decent interval, he asked to be excused so he could keep his appointment with Judith.

After he had left, Molly asked Catherine about his response to being asked to be godfather to Eleanor.

'He said he would be delighted, provided he was still here,' Catherine said. Molly felt her hopes slide once more but she concentrated on her family for the rest of the afternoon and tried not to keep anxious watch for George's return. Sally and her family had departed by carriage, taking Agnes back with them, and Catherine and Francis had also gone home before George returned, when it was quite dark.

He appeared very cheerful and said he had spent an interesting afternoon, catching up with Judith's news. She had settled in well at Woodchurch Manor and apparently enjoyed looking after Eleanor, whom she declared to be a very easy baby.

Molly smiled as though the compliment was directed at her. She and Charlie were seated by the fire in the parlour, and she had taken up her sampler once more, now that the quilt for baby Eleanor was finished.

George pulled up a chair and stared into the fire for some time before asking Molly what she was stitching. She held it out for him to see and, at first, he stared at it in puzzlement.

'What is it?' he asked eventually.

'A sampler,' Molly replied. 'It will hang on the wall, above the ones that the girls stitched when they were younger.' She pointed to where the girls' samplers were hanging, one above the other, at the side of the fireplace. George stood up and went over to inspect them.

'I think I can tell which one Agnes made,' he said. 'You can see a touch of artistry there.'

Molly smiled. 'Indeed. She was creative, even then. But they are all incomplete.'

'Are they?' George looked again, then looked back at Molly. 'But they seem finished to me.'

'This one,' Molly said, 'will have your name on it, at last.'

George sat down again, without saying a word. The crackle of the fire was the only sound to disturb the silence in the room. Molly hoped she hadn't overstepped the mark but she pressed on, regardless. 'I was sad when the girls stitched their samplers and I couldn't say a word about you. I never dared to hope that one day I'd be able to stitch a sampler of my own, showing a family of six, but that day has come.

346

Sally has been displaced as the eldest. I'm not sure how she'll take it.'

Molly, having tried to make light of it, bent her head over the sampler once more, hardly daring to look at George.

'I'll have to have a word with her about it,' he said. Molly ventured a glance at him and saw that he was smiling. She thought she caught the sparkle of tears in his eyes, which threatened to overwhelm her, so she bent to her work again. They sat on in silence for a bit longer, then George spoke again.

'You know, I think I will stay for a while. I'll move back into my old room in the stable block, though. I'd like to be godfather to Eleanor, and to get to know you all properly. And to work back in the gardens, if you'll have me?'

His last words were directed at Charlie, who did a good job of feigning to wake from a doze, yawning and stretching.

'Don't worry, lad, I hoped you'd say yes. I've already got jobs lined up for you tomorrow morning.'

CHAPTER FIFTY-EIGHT

Eleanor's christening took place on a Sunday in late June. The little church on the estate was packed with relatives and guests, invited by both the Powells and the Dawsons. George looked nervous, Molly thought, but very handsome in the new shirt and jacket he had bought for the occasion. The godmother was from the Powell side, a friend of Robert – a close friend, according to rumour, who might well become part of the family in the not-too-distant future.

Eleanor had been peacefully asleep during the first part of the service and didn't take kindly to being rudely awakened, holy water or not. She proved she had a good pair of lungs, drowning out a good deal of the rest of the service and leaving Catherine scarlet with embarrassment.

The christening celebration took place at Woodchurch Manor and the weather was good enough for the doors to be thrown open onto the terrace so that the guests might enjoy the grounds. It was George's first encounter with Molly's sisters as well as with Aunt Jane and Uncle William. Molly had made a trip to Margate to visit her family there, to break the news of the son whom she had kept secret for such a long time. Lizzie and Mary thought at first that she was teasing them. When she persuaded them that she wasn't and she did, indeed, have a son even older than Sally, they were bewildered.

'But why did you never tell us before? How did you manage to keep this a secret for so long?'

Patiently, Molly explained that it had happened in London, that she'd given George up to the Foundling Hospital and never expected to see him again, that she had lost contact with his father before their son was born. She left her sisters still confounded by what she had told them and went next door to recount the same tale to Aunt Jane. Here she met with a rather different reception. Aunt Jane, once she had absorbed the news, gave Molly a thorough scolding for her behaviour so that Molly was transported back in time to her seventeen-year-old self, living in her aunt and uncle's house.

'How could you have done such a thing, Molly? I suppose that's London for you. I can only think it must have been the company you kept there that made you behave in such a way. If only you'd stayed here in Margate where you had my guidance, and your uncle's, to keep you on the right path. The shame of it ...'

Aunt Jane shook her head as she contemplated the news. It wasn't the giving up of George to the Foundling Hospital that was causing her aunt such distress, Molly felt sure. It was that Molly had borne a baby out of wedlock. She reminded herself that she was a grown woman with children, and grandchildren, of her own and that she didn't need to listen to her aunt's censure.

'We'll look forward to seeing you and Uncle William at Eleanor's christening, Aunt Jane, and to introducing you to George.' Then Molly had made her excuses and departed swiftly, thankful that she had finally shared her secret with her family, if somewhat shaken after having done so.

With the christening ceremony over and the guests now back at Woodchurch Manor, it was time to start introducing

George to her Margate family. Everyone had already thoroughly scrutinised him, of course, since he had been standing at the front of the church throughout the service. Molly began to feel nervous; she hoped Aunt Jane wouldn't speak out of turn. She had become more outspoken with age, taking delight in using the excuse of deafness to share her thoughts less than discreetly.

Manners dictated that her aunt must be introduced first, so Molly gently pushed George in front of her and said, 'George, I'd like to introduce you to Mr and Mrs William Goodchild, my uncle and aunt.'

George shook her uncle by the hand and turned to her aunt, saying 'I'm delighted to meet you. I wonder whether I may have made the acquaintance of a relative of yours when I was with the Navy in the West Indies. I met a Nicholas Goodchild in Martinique, who said he was from Margate originally. It's an unusual name, so it stuck in my mind.'

Uncle William looked disconcerted while Aunt Jane went white, then bright red. Molly inhaled sharply. Nicholas Goodchild – she'd thought him dead and apparently her aunt had thought the same. In the few moments it took to comprehend fully what George had said, it dawned on her that he'd met his own father, without either of them having the faintest idea that they were in any way related.

Why hadn't George made the connection with the name Goodchild before? She supposed that she was Molly Dawson to him and he had never asked her maiden name. He himself had become used to being called John Tempest at the Foundling School – she doubted whether the name Goodchild had ever cropped up.

The conversation had moved on without her and Molly struggled to follow it. George had a grave expression on his

350

face and he was saying, 'It would have been three or four years ago now. I'm afraid he wasn't in good health then. I'm so sorry, it was thoughtless of me to speak so lightly of him and to have given you such a shock.'

George looked pleadingly at Molly as if to ask for some help, but she was still reeling from the news. Aunt Jane recovered enough to grasp George's arm, unwilling to let him go before he had searched his memory for every single detail of his visit to her son.

Molly lost the thread of the conversation once more as she fought for composure. She would have to question George again later – now it was important that she got her feelings under control. She'd believed that being sparing with the truth about the identity of George's father had been the right thing to do, never dreaming their paths could cross. Nicholas had known she was with child, but nothing of the baby's birth or its name. It was an unhappy coincidence that couldn't lead to anything further, she was sure, but she had to try hard to slow her heartbeat to a more normal rate. She was grateful when Charlie came over to say that George's presence was required as Mr Powell was about to propose a toast and he wanted the godparents at his side, along with Catherine and Francis.

Molly found she was trembling as she followed George back across the room, Charlie at her side. He glanced curiously at her but she shook her head to signify that she couldn't talk now, as the speeches had begun. She wouldn't be able to share the true reason for her state of mind with him, but the fact that George had met Aunt Jane's son on a small island so far from home should be enough to satisfy his curiosity.

It was still a struggle to rein in her thoughts as Mr Powell spoke, but she raised her glass automatically at the same time as everyone else, and focused on how happy Catherine and Francis were. As Molly had suspected, Mr Powell was so pleased to have a grandchild, his first, that the rift with Francis was all but forgotten, at least by him.

She rather thought she had been wrong that the new Mr and Mrs Powell would resolve to stay in the cottage just a few doors from her own. Mr Powell would have a suite of rooms prepared for them at Woodchurch Manor if they said the word and Molly thought they might, but Charlie was of the opinion that Francis would press for a house of his own to be built elsewhere on the estate: something modest but a definite step up from their current cottage.

'That might all work out rather well,' Charlie said mysteriously. They had moved outside now, enjoying the fresh air and the sun on their faces. Molly had told Charlie about the strange coincidence of George's meeting with Nicholas Goodchild and of Aunt Jane's shock at the news. Then she'd moved swiftly on to draw his attention to all their relatives who were now gathered together on the lawns below the terrace, talking to Francis and Catherine. Judith, the nursemaid, was showing Simon and Grace their new cousin and Molly at last felt the anxiety of the last hour begin to lift.

'Look how lovely Simon and Grace are with Eleanor. So gentle.'

Charlie followed her gaze. 'A whole new generation growing up. How lucky we are, Molly.' He took her hand and kissed it and she leant in to his shoulder, filled with happiness.

Then she sighed as she caught sight of one of her daughters. Agnes had drifted away from the family group on the lawn and was gazing intently into a flower border.

'I fear Agnes will never marry,' Molly said.

Charlie followed her gaze and chuckled. 'She's found a new subject for a painting, I expect. Give her time. Let her explore her talent. In any case, I rather think we may well have another wedding to celebrate within the year.'

Molly looked up at him, puzzled. 'Who do you mean? Robert Powell? Or Edward?'

Charlie shook his head. 'I can't say. I've been sworn to secrecy.'

Molly was busy telling him he had no right to tease her like that when George appeared at their side. 'What a glorious day,' he said, looking down on the guests on the lawn. 'How happy everyone is.'

He stood and contemplated the scene in silence for a few moments, then turned to Molly and Charlie. 'I've been wanting to tell you how glad I am that I came back.'

'We half dragged you, as I remember,' Charlie said, giving him a playful tap on his shoulder. 'And it's as well we talked you out of your plans to join the Navy again. Here we are, four months later, and it's looking as though it's all over for Napoleon. They didn't need you, after all.'

Molly feared George would be offended by Charlie's words, but he just laughed.

'In any case, we want you here,' Charlie continued. 'In the gardens. And in our lives.'

He put his arm around George's shoulders and Molly relaxed. She should have known better than to be alarmed: they spent a lot of time together at work and they had grown close.

'Anyway,' George said, looking directly at Molly, 'I wanted to say that I feel blessed to be a part of your family—'

'It's your family, too,' Molly interrupted, taking George and Charlie's hands in hers.

George smiled. 'I stand corrected. Part of our family. And I have some news.' His smile grew broader.

Molly glanced at Charlie. Was this what he had been referring to earlier? He was unable to meet her eye, but he was smiling too.

'I've not only found my family,' George went on, 'but I've also found someone I never realised I'd lost, someone who has been hoping for a very long time that one day we might meet again.'

Molly began to think that this was a day when everyone was going to talk to her in riddles. She tried her best to look as though she followed what George was saying, but she could feel a frown creasing her brow.

'It turns out that Judith was never interested in my friend Thomas in Faversham – she was interested in me!' George sounded as if he could scarcely believe what he was saying.

'When I vanished, taken by the press gang, she always held out the hope that one day our paths would cross again. They have, and thankfully I'm older and wiser now.' George's smile had grown even broader, if that was possible.

'I'm going to ask her to marry me and I hope – I'm sure – she'll agree. But I wanted to tell both of you first. I'm too old to need your permission but it's important to me that you approve.'

George's smile was replaced by an anxious expression.

Charlie opened his mouth to speak but Molly, fearing he was about to say something flippant, hastily spoke first. Tears were already rolling down her cheeks as she squeezed her son's hand and said, 'George, I couldn't be happier.'

'My thoughts exactly,' Charlie said. Even though she now knew he had expected George's announcement, Molly could see that he was finding it hard to keep his emotions in check.

'And may we be the first to wish you every happiness for the future. If Judith makes you as happy as Molly has made me, you will be a very lucky man indeed.'

George spent just a few more moments at their side, then made his way down onto the lawn. Molly watched through a haze of tears as he sought out Judith, leaning over her to kiss Eleanor, who was still cradled in her arms. Then George drew Judith to one side and even at a distance, Molly could see a worried look had come over her face. George spoke a few words into her ear, and Judith's face instantly wreathed in smiles. She nodded, wordlessly, then George kissed her cheek and said something else to her. They both turned towards the terrace, George with Judith's hand now clasped in his. They were met with answering smiles from Charlie and Molly, although Molly's was a little tremulous as she tried to hold in her tears. Charlie drew his arm through hers and together they went down the steps of the terrace.

He stopped at the bottom to pluck two roses from the borders, presenting one to Molly. 'Let's go and give our good wishes to Judith, too,' he said.

Molly buried her nose deep in the petals and inhaled the scent as they walked across the lawn towards her family. She shook her head in wonder. 'A new chapter,' she said. 'A whole new chapter in all our lives.'

ACKNOWLEDGEMENTS

Thank you to my agent Kiran, at Kean Kataria, and my editor, Eleanor Russell, at Piatkus for their unfailing words of wisdom and support. Thanks also to Hazel Orme for bringing clarity to *The Secret Child* with her skilful copy-editing.

Special thanks to the Tuesday Writers – Alison, Helen, Jane, Jess, Keith, Sarah, Simon and Sindy. Our weekly writing sessions are a joy; their enthusiasm unflagging.

Thank you to Jamie, Jack, Julia, Lauren and Kate for their encouragement and flowers, and to all my friends for cheering me up and cheering me on. Lastly, credit and thanks to Martin Goodsmith for introducing me to the area around Faversham, Oare and Conyer, which provided the background and inspiration for George's story.

Historical Note

This novel is a fictionalisation of a period in history and although every effort has been made to retain historical accuracy, some liberties have been taken with the setting and historical events of the time.

Jane Austen and J. M. W. Turner were born in the same year (1775) and both had associations with east Kent. Jane Austen's brothers, Francis and Charles, both served in the Navy. In around 1804, Francis Austen was appointed to organise a corps of Sea Fencibles based around Margate, Ramsgate and Deal to defend the Kentish coast from the French.

The remains of the gunpowder works at Oare, near Faversham, can be visited today – it is now a country park with a heritage and nature trail around the site.

The location of Woodchurch Manor and its estate is loosely based on that of Quex House, with the garden descriptions influenced both by the gardens there and at Goodnestone (where Jane Austen visited and walked).

HISTORICAL NOTE